# THE TEXAN'S WEDDING ESCAPE

## CHARLENE SANDS

# THE LOVE CHILD

## CATHERINE MANN

**MILLS & BOON**

First Published in Great Britain 2018
by Mills & Boon, an imprint of HarperCollinsPublishers,
1 London Bridge Street, London, SE1 9GF

*The Texan's Wedding Escape* © 2018 Charlene Swink
*The Love Child* © 2018 Catherine Mann

ISBN: 978-0-263-93599-8

51-0418

This book is produced from independently certified FSC paper to ensure responsible forest management.

For more information visit: www.harpercollins.co.uk/green

**Charlene Sands** is a *USA TODAY* bestselling author of more than forty romance novels. She writes sensual contemporary romances and stories of the Old West. When not writing, Charlene enjoys sunny Pacific beaches, great coffee, reading books from her favorite authors and spending time with her family. You can find her on Facebook and Twitter, write to her at PO Box 4883, West Hills, CA 91308 USA, or sign up for her newsletter for fun blogs and ongoing contests at www.charlenesands.com.

*USA TODAY* bestselling author **Catherine Mann** has won numerous awards for her novels, including both a prestigious RITA® Award and an RT Book Reviews Reviewers' Choice Award. After years of moving around the country bringing up four children, Catherine has settled in her home state of South Carolina, where she's active in animal rescue. For more information, visit her website, www.catherinemann.com.

# THE TEXAN'S
# WEDDING ESCAPE

**CHARLENE SANDS**

This book is dedicated to my friends and terrific
authors Leanne Banks, Lynne Marshall
and Robin Bielman, who all had a hand in
helping me plot the delicate balance of this story.

I love you all to pieces!

# One

He hit Delete on his laptop, wiping out names and phone numbers of the women he'd dated, wanted to date or just plain thought were freaking gorgeous. Instantly, Cooper Stone's fun-loving, party-till-you-drop days were over, ended by a finger stroke on the keyboard. It was equivalent to burning his little black book, only nobody carried a little black book anymore. Things had gotten too damn sophisticated, but the end result was the same. Cooper Stone was out of the running. It was a long time coming, six months to be exact.

He wouldn't miss those names.

Not like he missed his buddy, Tony Abbott.

One minute he was laughing alongside him in the car, their heads thrown back, enjoying life to the fullest, and the next, he was silenced by the stony sound of death. The quiet in that moment still rang in Cooper's head, still tormented him. Everything had stopped, everything had gone numbingly cold. Tony had died instantly and the drunken driver behind the wheel of the car that had plowed into them had escaped without injury. So had Cooper. And he'd never forgiven himself for that.

Deleting those names was only a formality. He hadn't been a party animal since that night. And he never would be again. Some things just left a mark and the imprint of that horrible crash brought him full circle. He now lived quietly on his ranch at Stone Ridge and poured himself into his entrepreneurial businesses.

"Hey, Coop, you need some company today? I'm willing to drive out with you."

"Thanks, bro. But you don't have to do that. I've got this."

Cooper rose from his desk in the study and put on a lightweight tan jacket. It was late spring, the sunshine giving way to gray clouds that were moving in fast. Texas weather could never be counted on and it was fitting, he supposed, that this day was as glum as his mood. These bad-weather days made it easy for him to stay inside and work, giving him an excuse not to visit friends or to go to parties. Ole Coop wasn't fun anymore. And that was fine with him.

"I'll be back in a few hours."

His brother, Jared, slapped him on the back but had a look of concern on his face. "Take care and I'll see you later, okay?" That was code for "Drive safely and I love you." Jared was his baby brother who, at twenty-eight, wasn't such a baby anymore. But he worried. Just about everyone worried about him. "Okay."

It took Cooper five minutes to drive off Stone land on the outskirts of Dallas and another twenty to get to the suburb of Providence. He made a stop at the bakery and as soon as the woman behind the counter spotted him, she said, "A dozen raspberry-jelly doughnuts coming right up."

He gave her a nod. "Thank you kindly."

And within a few minutes Cooper was back on the road,

the bakery box on the passenger seat beside him. He drove down the highway, leaving Providence in the dust, and eventually arrived at the Eternal Peace cemetery. When he turned into the driveway, passing a new grave covered by a hill of fresh flowers, a punch of pain attacked his stomach. A fresh grave meant loss. People were hurting: fathers, mothers, sisters, brothers, wives and children. He'd never given mortality much thought until Tony died in the prime of his life.

Cooper drove on until he reached the gravesite nestled under a tall oak. He parked the car, took a deep breath and got out. With box in hand and head down, he made his way over to Tony's resting place. The wind kicked up, the air chilly as he began speaking.

"Hi, Tone. It's me again. Been a month. Got you your favorite doughnuts." He sat on perfectly mowed grass. "You remember, the ones we never did get to eat t-that night."

He opened the box and took out one of the powdery confections. "They're your favorite, pal." He bit into it and chewed. One bite was all he could ever muster before putting the doughnut back in the box. "Wow. That was good."

At the sound of leaves crunching behind him, he turned around. It was Loretta Abbott, Tony's mother. Cooper rose immediately. "Hello, Loretta."

"Am I interrupting?"

"Gosh, no. Just having a little chat with Tony." He didn't know what else to say.

She gave him a sad smile. "You're a wonderful friend."

He wasn't. He was alive and Tony was gone. Cooper should've seen that car coming. He should've been more alert. Instead of relaxing at the wheel, joking with his friend, getting him killed.

He strode over to her and put out his arms. She walked into them and they embraced. "I'm glad to see you," she whispered.

He nodded. "Same here."

"I knew you'd be here. That's why I've come."

He backed away enough to really look at her. "Did you want to talk to me?"

She nodded, tears filling her eyes. "Yes. I'm sorry for interrupting, but I knew you'd be here on the anniversary of my Tony's accident."

He took a big swallow. "You could've called me or come to the house. You know you're welcome anytime."

The wind howled, blowing her soft brown hair out of the knot at the top of her head. "I'm afraid, I wouldn't have had the nerve to come. But something drew me here today. Somehow this way, it wouldn't be too hard to ask you what I'm about to ask you. I'm sorry to say, I'm a bit desperate and I need a favor."

"Of course. Anything. I told you if you ever needed anything to come to me."

Another sad smile graced Loretta's face. "I'm counting on that. It's about Lauren."

Tony's younger sister? She'd been working in Dallas, following in the footsteps of her mother as a nurse. Cooper hadn't seen much of her until the funeral.

Back in the day, when he and Tony were kids, they'd played travel football together for the Texas Tridents. Their friendship had only grown over the years. Often they'd spend time at each other's houses for days on end and throughout the summer months. As they got older whenever Loretta'd had to take a double shift at the hospital, he and Tony would watch Lauren until Mrs. Abbott got home. Seemed like eons ago. "What about Lauren?"

"She just got engaged to Roger Kelsey on a whim and it's all so terribly wrong. Now, she's planning to get married in less than a month. All because Roger's putting pressure on her." Loretta wiped at her tears with a tissue. "What's wrong with my girl waiting a little longer, to make sure of her feelings? We've all had a terrible shock when we lost Tony, and Lauren getting engaged—to Tony's business partner, no less—makes no sense. Roger never paid any attention to her while Tony was alive, but as soon as my son dies, he turns on the charm and proposes marriage?

"Lauren thinks she knows best, and she won't listen to me on this. She says I'm being overprotective. It doesn't add up, Cooper. Not at all."

Cooper didn't like what he was hearing. Normally he'd chalk Lauren's engagement up to falling hard when you're at your most vulnerable. After all, this happened immediately after Tony's death. Granted, some people married after only knowing each other a few weeks and found marital bliss that way but not that often.

But Lauren marrying Roger Kelsey?

Roger was a charmer and a playboy who went through women with the stealth of a panther. Tony would have seen red and never approved.

A deep sigh rose from Cooper's chest. One of the last conversations he'd had with Tony pounded in his head.

"I think Kelsey's siphoning money from my profits. Things aren't adding up," Tony had said. "I don't have solid proof yet, but I'm working on it. If my suspicions are correct, he's breaking the law and cheating me blind." Tony had vowed to get to the bottom of it.

Cooper faced Loretta, certain now he had to intervene. Not only for Loretta and Lauren, but because Tony would've wanted him to. "I'm sorry, but what can I do? Just name it."

"Oh, Cooper, I was hoping you would say that," she said, relieved. Her face relaxed and she looked at him with the tiniest hint of a smile. He was glad he could comfort her. There wasn't anything he wouldn't do to help Tony's mother.

"I need you to stop the wedding."

* * *

As soon as her mama opened the front door and Cooper walked in, something warm and fuzzy ran through Lauren's veins. At twenty-six, she thought she'd be over her fascination. But that rugged face, that sharp profile, the amazing sky blue in his eyes—all spoke of happy times during her childhood when the boys, Tony and Cooper, would include her in their antics. She'd loved being with them, even if they were both six years older and dreadfully overprotective of her.

When she'd turned twelve, barely old enough to understand crazy, out-of-whack hormones, she'd developed the worst crush on Cooper Stone. It had lasted two long and lean years until she'd graduated middle school. Then, in high school, she'd fallen hopelessly in love with Brendan Marsh. Her crush on Brendan ended after five weeks when she'd discovered Toby Strickland, Providence High's premiere quarterback. Shortly after, there was Gregory Bell, pitcher for the Providence High Pirates.

Her list of crushes was long. She was forever falling in and out of love. Katy, her bestie, and the rest of her friends would tease her, saying she wasn't a flake, just a hopeless romantic. But she'd matured while in college. She'd only fallen for one boy at UCLA. Unfortunately he wasn't the One and as soon as they'd come to that mutual conclusion, they'd parted ways.

This time, her love for Roger was the real deal. He'd been there for her during that trying, heartbreaking time right after Tony passed away. He'd been her rock. Her support. Lord knows she'd needed that so much during that time. Roger had made her laugh and given her hope. And they'd cried together, comforted each other.

She knew it deep down in her heart. He was Tony's partner, friend and a wonderful man. How could she not love him?

Yet tonight, seeing Cooper in her mother's house brought a measure of familiarity and comfort. She had a favor to ask him and she hoped it wasn't asking too much. "I'm so glad you came for dinner," she said, walking over to him.

He put out his arms and she flowed into them. Being in his strong embrace cushioned her heart and made her feel closer to the brother she'd lost. Cooper had blamed himself for the accident, but everyone knew it hadn't been his fault. He hadn't been the one drinking and driving. He couldn't possibly have known the other driver was going to careen off his side of the road and slam into them. So hugging Cooper was a way for her to comfort him, too. A way to tell him she didn't hold him responsible for her brother's death.

"I'm glad, too, Laurie Loo."

She chuckled. "You haven't called me that for at least a decade."

"Yeah, I know. You used to hate it."

"I'll let you in on my secret. I only pretended to hate it." She'd actually thought his nickname for her was kind of sweet. It was the way he'd say it, with deep affection rather than mockery, that kept her crush for him alive.

"Come in, Cooper," her mother said. "Dinner's almost ready. Why don't you and Lauren have a seat in the family room while I go check on things?"

"You need a hand, Loretta?" Cooper asked.

"No, no, no. You two go on and catch up. I'll be fine," she said, stepping out of the room.

"Mama likes doing it all herself. That's never going to change. Even though she retired from nursing, she can't seem to keep still. I suppose it's a good thing." Except when she was meddling in her life.

Her mother meant well, but her irrational arguments against her marrying Roger weren't fair. Yes, her mama married her father after dating only two months and, yes, their marriage had gotten off to a rocky start. But Mama hadn't really known him, not the way Lauren knew Roger. David Abbott'd had a wandering eye and her mother had been too blinded by love not to see it. Until her father had picked up and left his family.

Before he'd died, he'd been married and divorced three other times. So, of course, her mother would think that Lauren wasn't thinking this through. Sadly, her mother had scars that hadn't healed and she didn't want her only daughter to end up that way too. And that was part of the reason Lauren needed to see Cooper. For backup. Her mama trusted Cooper. If he could give her the approval she needed, she was sure her mama would back off.

Cooper nodded. "No doubt. Keeping busy is healthy for the soul."

"Well, then, Mama's soul is in ridiculously good shape."

Lauren led him to the brushed-suede sofa in the family room and gestured for him to sit. The cushions sank a bit as they both took a seat. Lauren crossing her legs and garnering an appreciative look from Cooper. She'd dressed up for the occasion, a soft, cocoa, lacy dress and heels, a far cry from the scrubs she usually wore. Suddenly her nerves started bouncing like a Ping-Pong ball. This was an important night. She needed an ally.

Cooper gave her a megawatt smile. "You look great. How've you been?"

"I am great," she said. "I have news and I wanted to share it with you right away."

"Okay," he said, leaning back against the sofa, giving her his full attention. "Sounds important."

She put out her left hand and her square-cut, two-carat diamond ring sparkled under his nose. "I'm engaged to Roger Kelsey. Isn't it wonderful?"

Cooper held her hand to peer at the ring on her finger. A little zing flittered through her system. She may not have completely gotten over her little crush on him from ages ago, but that wasn't love or anything close. Nope, Cooper was a dear family friend and…well, he was like a big brother to her.

"What it is," he said, his eyes softening to hers, "is a little sudden, isn't it, Lauren?"

"I know, Cooper. Mama said the same thing, but she doesn't know how glorious Roger makes me feel. So what if we haven't been dating long. They say, when it's right, it's right."

"Who's 'they'?" he asked.

She gave her head a tilt. Not Cooper, too. Her mama hadn't been overjoyed about her quick engagement and now Cooper, Tony's brother from another mother, was giving her a hard time. "You're big-brothering me again."

"Tony's not here to do it."

"I know." She put her head down. It hurt terribly to think Tony wasn't going to be at her wedding. They'd been close all their lives, until that fateful accident. "It's not that I don't appreciate it, Cooper. I know you're just looking out for my welfare, but this time, I've got it."

"Got what?"

"*It.* You know, love, marriage, everything that goes with it. It's under control and time for me to settle down. I'm twenty-six years old and I want more out of life. The one thing Tony's death taught me is to not take life for granted. I'm ready, Cooper."

His gaze roamed over her face as she waited breathlessly for his approval. More than anything, she wanted his blessing. Finally his lips parted in a small, encouraging smile. "Okay. Well, then, I'm happy for you."

"Oh, Cooper. Thank you!" She lunged for him and squeezed his neck, hugging him tight. Whiffs of his manly cologne surrounded her, but she was too happy to dwell on how much that appealed to her. "This means so much to me…you'll never know." Tears welled in her eyes. She had his blessing. It would be easier for her mama to accept her marriage to Roger now. "There's one thing, though…a favor I need to ask you. You're not like family to us, you *are* family, and…well, since my dad is gone, and now Tony, too, I was hoping that on my wedding day, you'd do me the honor of walking me down the aisle."

Cooper paced inside Loretta's kitchen. He'd come in here the second Lauren had excused herself to take a phone call and now he was realizing how hard this mission would be. If he spoke negatively about Kelsey without any proof of his bad intentions, Lauren would shut him down. He'd seen it happen before. Lauren was strong-willed, stubborn and independent. Through the years, Tony had learned how to rein her in. He'd gained her trust and had actually gotten her to listen to him at times. But he wasn't Tony. Cooper only had a brother and was the first to admit he had no skills understanding the female mind. Not when it came to stopping a young woman from possibly making a big mistake.

A little voice in his head told him to back off and let Lauren find out about Kelsey on her own. A leopard always revealed his spots…or some such notion. But Lauren had been hurt enough and so had Loretta, for that matter. He'd given Tony's mother his word.

Loretta was busy putting hot rolls into a lined basket. He pulled the aroma into his nostrils, but the garlicky cheese scent did nothing to whet his appetite.

"Say what's on your mind," the older woman said quietly.

Cooper ran a hand down his face. "Loretta, she's asked me to walk her down the aisle. Man, that puts me in a difficult spot. Lauren is so damn happy."

"What did you say to her?"

"What could I say? I couldn't hurt her. I told her it would be my honor to take Tony's place by her side."

The hand Loretta put on his shoulder was warm and comforting. "She doesn't know her own heart, Cooper. Trust me on this. She's thought herself in love half a dozen times in her lifetime. Kelsey is not the man for her. You won't hurt her, but he will."

He hadn't told a soul about Tony's suspicions about his partner cheating him, but maybe now was the time to broach the subject. "Loretta, what's going on at Kelsey-Abbott? How often do you go into the office?"

"Me? I've been a nurse for thirty-five years. What do I know about real-estate development? I told my Tony years ago not to include me in his will. I'm comfortable and have everything I need."

"So, you're saying that Tony's half of the company—"

"Goes to Lauren. Yes, that's the way we'd agreed."

Cooper stared at her. Soon, Loretta's eyes began blinking almost as fast as his mind was spinning. "Oh, dear. You don't think that he's marrying her to gain control of the entire company, do you?"

It wasn't unheard of and, in fact, the more he thought about it, the more it made sense. If Roger Kelsey was married to Lauren, there would be no need for anyone to check over the books, to reframe the partnership, to find out he'd been cheating Tony. It was likely that Lauren wouldn't want to get involved in the company at all, not if her new husband had everything under control. She was as dedicated to nursing as her mother had been. "Could be, Loretta," he murmured.

"Hey!" Lauren came bounding into the room, a big smile on her face. "There you are. I was wondering what happened to you, Cooper. And my ears are burning. Were you both talking about me?"

"Yep, as a matter of fact we were," Cooper said, giving

Loretta a glance. "You told me you haven't picked a venue for the wedding yet."

"Yes, that's right. We're going to do something simple."

"But, honey, you've always dreamed of a big wedding," Loretta interjected, disapproval clouding her soft brown eyes. "That's the least Roger can do for you."

"I know, Mama. But there isn't time for that and I'm fine…with it." The disappointment on her face told a different story.

"You shouldn't be fine with anything. You should be ecstatic. We're talking about your wedding day, honey."

"Problem solved," Cooper announced and two curious female gazes landed on him.

He hoped like hell he wasn't making a whopper of a mistake, but the idea taking shape in his mind wasn't anything short of brilliant. What he needed was time with Lauren to make sure she wasn't getting in over her head and marrying this guy impulsively. Which seemed likely. Tony hadn't trusted him, Loretta thought she was being rash and now Cooper was smack-dab in the middle of it all. Keeping Lauren close—and away from Roger—was key. There was only one way he figured he could pull that off.

"You're getting married at my ranch at Stone Ridge. I insist. You'll speak your vows at my home. I'll open the place up to you and you can come and stay with me while you make your plans. Heck, both you and your mama are welcome to stay on the ranch. The two of you can work together and, Lauren, you'll have the wedding you've always dreamed about. I promise not to get in your way."

A promise he would probably have to break because he planned on protecting Lauren from being hurt no matter what.

Lauren's pretty, pale green eyes brightened. She opened her mouth to say something but after a split second, she clamped her lips shut again, her shoulders falling. "I can't let you do that. It's too much."

He wasn't above playing the guilt card to get her to agree. After all, he was an expert at self-imposed guilt trips. Ultimately what he needed was time to convince Lauren not to marry Kelsey and this was his plan A, B and C. He had no other options.

"Tony often spoke to me about giving you a beautiful wedding when the time came. And, yes, I may have some reservations about how quickly this is all happening, but in my heart I know your brother would've wanted it this way."

Tears sprang to her eyes and she trembled. "Oh, Cooper."

And then she was in his arms, her supple, firm body plastered against him, her gratitude brimming. When she turned her head slightly, his nose was in her hair, her subtle, fresh, flowery scent teasing him.

"I take that as a yes," he whispered.

Her head bobbed up and down. "Yes," she said, raw emotion in her voice.

He glanced over at Loretta hopelessly.

A full-out approving smile graced her face and she gave him a big nod.

Which sort of worried him a bit, he wasn't gonna lie.

"I have the best news, Roger," Lauren said, coming to sit next to him on the den sofa in his penthouse apartment overlooking the Dallas skyline. The view here was amazing, just as amazing as the tall, dark-haired man she was to marry. She admired Roger's always-groomed look, his sense of style and his abundant confidence. Up until Tony died, she'd only seen Roger as a casual friend. But he'd been magnificent to her ever since the funeral and they'd had a whirlwind love affair. "My brother's best friend has offered us the use of his ranch to hold our wedding. Stone

Ridge is magnificent. There's no need to have a simple courthouse wedding, after all. And Mama is pretty sure we can get it all together in a month."

Roger pursed his lips, deep in thought. "A ranch wedding?"

"Not just any ranch, honey. It's Tony's best friend Cooper Stone's ranch. You may have met him at the funeral." She hated bringing up that sad day. The memory still seared a hole in her heart.

"Sounds like a lot of work," Roger said. "Can't we just get married without all the fuss?"

Lauren shrugged, feeling deflated. "Yes, I suppose. But finally Mama is on board and even seems excited about planning the wedding with me. And, well, I've always dreamed about having a beautiful wedding."

Roger stared at her and then leaned forward and kissed her cheek. "Can we keep it small, at least?"

"Yes, of course. No more than one hundred people. I promise."

"A hundred?" His voice hit a high note. "That many?"

"That's not very many when we consider your employees and our mutual friends, plus my dear friends at the hospital. I'm so excited about this. Please, please, say it's okay with you."

He scratched his head. Roger didn't like to mingle and didn't like crowds. But a woman only got married once and she was sure he'd come around and be just as happy about the wedding plans as she was.

"Yeah, it's okay with me."

She bounded out of her seat, wrapped her arms around his neck and hugged him for all she was worth. "Thanks, Roger. You've made me very happy!"

"That's the plan, isn't it? Happy wife, happy life."

"Oh, we'll sure have that," she said, smiling. "I'm taking a good chunk of the vacation I've stored up to plan the wedding. Oh, Roger, it's gonna be so much fun."

"If you say so. But remember, I've got that big, new deal coming up this month. I'm going to be extremely busy."

"But not too busy to help with the wedding plans. I've always wanted a June wedding. I can't wait to start planning."

She got up from the sofa and grabbed her purse. "I'm off now. Mama and I have a date to start the plans."

Roger stood and walked her to the door. "Just don't break the bank on this," he said.

"Never. If I'm one thing, it's frugal. Had to be, with my dad leaving us and my mama a nurse. We didn't have much, but we always managed." With Tony's financial help, she'd made it through nursing school without having to take out a huge college loan.

Roger kissed her briefly. As she waved goodbye to him from the elevator, she took one last look at his apartment. With its sleek furniture and state-of-the-art kitchen, everything about the place screamed edgy. It was sure a far cry from the humble home she lived in with her mother on Masefield Avenue.

After Tony died, Lauren had given up an apartment she'd shared with a fellow nurse. Her mama needed her, but in truth, Lauren had probably gotten just as much comfort as her mother had from staying in her childhood home on the outskirts of town.

Pretty soon, though, once she married, she'd be living in the heart of Dallas with Roger.

The drive home at this time of evening wasn't easy. Dallas traffic bottled up and she found herself on the road rocking out to Carrie Underwood singing about bad boys and payback.

It was a good twenty minutes later when she pulled onto

Masefield Avenue. A man holding a ledger under his arm was just leaving the house. He nodded to her.

"Evening, miss," he said.

"Hello." Puzzled, she slowed her steps and watched him get into a car and drive off.

She entered the house. "Mama?"

"In the kitchen, honey," Loretta said.

Her mama glanced at her as she stepped into the room. The table was littered with papers and paint samples. "Well, I finally got that estimate to paint the entire house, inside and out. And looks like if I agree to have them start tomorrow and pay them cash, he's gonna give me a nice discount."

"Mama? What are you talking about? We have a wedding to plan. We can't have painters in here."

"Honey, actually it's the perfect time to have the house painted. I've delayed it for so long because it's a nuisance to have workmen here and everything all covered up. You know what the smell of paint does to my sinuses. But, if we take Cooper up on his offer, we can move into his place until the wedding. That'll give the workmen more than enough time to get the house done."

"Mama, it was awfully sweet of Cooper to invite us to stay at his ranch, but he wasn't serious."

"Oh, yes, he was. He called up today asking when we were coming."

"He did not."

"He did. That Cooper is as fine as they come."

"He's still feeling guilty about Tony, Mama. That's all it is. He doesn't really want us underfoot."

"Well, it's too late for that now. I told him yes."

"Mama, you didn't." It wasn't like her mother to be this impetuous.

"Honey, this house hasn't been painted since your father left. You know how many years that's been? More than fifteen. The paint's peeling in every room! I've got the money saved up for this, and it's the perfect time."

"But how…what am I supposed to… Mama, I can't believe you did this without checking with me first."

"It'll be fine, darling. You're taking time off to plan the wedding starting Monday so you won't have to commute to the hospital. It'll be like a little staycation, isn't that what they call it?"

"Yes, that's what it's called, but that means staying at your own house."

"Oh. Well, no matter. I've given Turner Painting a cash deposit. So pack a bag or two, sweetheart, and don't forget your wedding binder. We're moving to Stone Ridge tomorrow."

# Two

On the drive out to Stone Ridge, Lauren couldn't stop wondering if she'd been bamboozled into moving into Cooper's house by her wily mother. Boy, when her mama put her mind to something, she was like a wrecking ball. That was one of the traits she loved most about her. And her mama wasn't about to let an opportunity like this one slip between her fingers. She wanted her house painted inside and out, and they didn't have the funds to move into a motel for the weeks it would take to finish the project. So what if her mother saw living at Stone Ridge as a perfect solution to a problem? Even Lauren saw the merits. It was just that…she didn't want to take advantage of Cooper.

Sure, he was wealthy and could afford having guests in his home, especially if those guests were like family. Maybe he was lonely and wanted company.

She scoffed out loud at the thought.

"You say something, honey?"

She cleared her throat. "No, Mama. Just a little froggy."

Her mother smiled.

Cooper couldn't be lonely…not for female companion-ship, anyway. That man was hot with a capital H. Lauren had noticed. Any red-blooded woman would. And she wasn't going to beat herself up about how hard her heart pounded when he walked into a room. She'd crushed on him as a girl, and you never really get over first crushes. Especially if the crush had deep, sea-blue eyes, a square jawline and long, thick, dark blond hair. Especially if the man filled out his shirt with broad shoulders and gran-ite arms.

Cooper Stone was all man, all Texan, all the time. She giggled.

"What's funny?" her mother asked.

"Nothing. Oh, look, Mama." She distracted her mama by pointing to the gates of Stone Ridge. "Gosh, I haven't been here in ages. I've forgotten how beautiful it is."

Acres upon acres of rich green pastures surrounded the property. This time of year, the dogwood trees that lined the road to the house were in full bloom, flourishing in pinks and whites. She recalled Cooper telling her years ago those trees were his mother's favorite thing about the ranch.

For Lauren, catching her first glimpse of the house as they drove up was the ultimate experience. The design had a modern-day, country-home feel, with slate stone and cedar wood and a beautiful wood-framed, glass double-door entry. It was hardly a traditional ranch house from the past, but more a contemporary marvel.

The barns and stables were quite a distance off, so the scent of fresh blooms didn't have to battle with cattle smells and packed earth. It was something, this ranch, and suddenly inspiration hit, giving Lauren a million ideas for her wedding. She particularly noted the well-groomed garden leading up to the steps to the mosaic stone-front entrance.

She parked her Honda and took a breath. "Ready for this?"

Her mother only smiled. "You have no idea how much."

It did her heart good to see her mother finally coming around, finally warming to the idea of her marrying Roger. Once the initial shock had worn off, her mother seemed to be all-in.

Lauren was jumping over one hurdle at a time, heading toward the finish line.

It was awesome to feel this way. To know her life had direction. The shock of Tony's death had stymied her and she hadn't known where to turn. Then she'd starting dating Roger, and found him compassionate. They'd shared their grief over losing such a wonderful man and things just sort of rolled along from there. Up until that point, she hadn't had much luck in love.

Her friends said she was a dreamer, a passionate soul who got restless too easily with the opposite sex. As grounded as she was in nursing, her private life hadn't been all too…stable.

Cooper drove up in his four-wheel-drive Jeep and pulled in front of her car, grabbing her attention. He parked, then gripped the roll bar in one hand and hopped out.

"Oh, look, there's Cooper," her mother said.

How could she miss him? He was slapping dust off his chaps and blue chambray shirt as he began his approach, his stride confident, his smile welcoming. All golden tanned and muscled, he sauntered over.

"Hey," he said.

The rich, deep tone of his voice made her gulp air. She'd grown up in Texas and rugged cowboys were a dime a dozen.

But Cooper Stone was in a class by himself. And the feminist in her said she could react this way about a handsome guy without tripping over guilt about Roger. Her fiancé.

Plus, Coop was doing her a big favor.

"Hi, Cooper. We made it," she said lamely. Of course, they'd made it. It wasn't as if she'd traveled across state lines to get there. Stone Ridge was a mere twenty miles from the Dallas city limits.

"I can see that." He ducked his head into the turned-down window, which brought his face within inches of hers. "Morning, Loretta."

"Cooper, it's good to see you. Looks like you're working already."

"I like to get my hands dirty every so often, reminds me of my heritage." He winked. "I was helping my crew tear down an old shack we had on the property. Glad I made it back in time to greet you."

He pulled off his tan leather gloves and stuffed them into his back pocket. "Let me help you carry your luggage into the house," he said. "I'll show you to your rooms."

"Are you sure we're not putting you and Jared out? We don't want to get in your way," Lauren said. She'd never even considered the fact that this might inconvenience his brother, too.

"You're not putting me out," Cooper said automatically, which made her feel a ton better. "And my brother has his own place. He lives up the road at the other end of the pasture, and he's on board with having the wedding here."

"Good to know," she said. She didn't know Jared very well. He was younger than Cooper and Tony by a few years. She was happy that Jared didn't mind. "But if we ever get in your way, you just say the word and we'll make other arrangements."

"Lauren."

Okay, so maybe she was overdoing it, but Lauren wasn't too good at accepting big favors like this. Or was it something else, something that had to do with her breath catching as soon as Cooper smiled at her?

"We appreciate your hospitality, Cooper," her mother said.

"Anything I can do to help." He walked around the car and gave her mother a hand as she got out of her seat.

Lauren climbed out, as well, and popped her trunk. Her life for the next month was crammed into her luggage, four bags in all. Her mom had brought two bags.

Cooper walked to the trunk. He didn't blink an eye as he hoisted four of the bags like they weighed nothing. "I'll get the rest on my next trip out."

"I can get them," Lauren said, pulling two pieces of rolling luggage out and setting them on their wheels.

"Cooper, for heaven's sake, I'm not ancient," her mother said. "Give me one of those bags."

Copper grinned. "Sure thing." He handed her the smallest one. "Here you go."

In that one move, he'd saved her mother's pride, telling Lauren he had enough confidence in his own manhood to allow her mom to help. Lauren made a mental note. Add that to the growing list of things she found appealing about Cooper Stone.

Once inside, Cooper stood in the foyer and pointed to a wide, winding staircase. "I've given you both the rooms facing west. You'll see some amazing sunsets."

"Thanks, Cooper," she said. "Gosh, it's been so many years since I've been to your ranch. This place is completely transformed."

The living room was huge, with a floor-to-ceiling fireplace made with sleek slate and light wood. A sitting area faced the fireplace and another faced a set of windows overlooking the gardens and green pastures beyond. Overhead, thick beams lent a slightly rustic tone to the contemporary décor.

"I'll show you around a little later, after you get settled in." He began climbing the stairs and the two of them followed until they reached the first guest room.

"Oh, this is lovely," her mother said immediately.

"Then I chose correctly," he said. "I figured you'd like this room, Loretta."

It was bright and cheerful with white-shuttered windows and ivory furniture upholstered in a floral motif. The room almost looked too girly for a bachelor's ranch home.

Cooper dropped off her mother's bags and then led Lauren to the next guest room, done in light blues with pale gray walls and stained mango wood furniture that instantly made her feel at peace. "This is nice."

"Glad you like it." He set her luggage down on the bed. "Here you go. I'll see you later after a quick shower and change of clothes."

Her eyes dipped to his body, an involuntary movement that brought a flush to her cheeks. If he noticed, he didn't react.

"Okay, thanks again. See ya."

"Lauren," he said, a serious tone in his voice.

"What?"

"Stop thanking me. Please."

She scrunched up her face. She couldn't help it if her mother had drilled manners into her, could she?

"I'll try."

He gave her a nod. "Good enough."

And then he was out the door, heading for a shower.

This time, she forced an image of Roger into her head. Yes, that was a nice, safe place to be.

Cooper pulled out a pitcher of lemonade just as Loretta walked into the kitchen. "My goodness, what a pretty kitchen you have."

Cooper only smiled. He'd had this house built seven

years ago on the same spot as the old ranch house. His mother hadn't minded tearing the old place down. She was quite progressive and didn't like to dwell in the past. She and his dad had had a good life, but after he'd died, she'd spent all her energy on helping Cooper plan out a new modern-day version of the house. And his mother was a perfectionist, down to the last detail.

The enormous room had white cupboards, dark granite countertops and stainless-steel appliances. There was everything imaginable, from a brick oven to a six-burner stovetop with a covered grill to a table that seated eight. "My mom's doing."

"How is Veronica these days?"

"Mom's good. She's remarried, as you know, living down in Houston. Her husband keeps her pretty busy traveling."

"Well, you tell her I said hello next time you talk to her."

"Will do. Lemonade?"

"Sure, thanks."

He poured them both a glass and handed one to Loretta. "I'm glad you're here."

"Me, too," she said as she glanced out the kitchen doorway. "Cooper, I had to do some scheming to get my daughter here," she whispered. "But I know it's the right move. Otherwise, I'd never be so underhanded."

"What did you do?"

She smiled. "Hired a crew to paint my house inside and out."

He grinned. "Did you now?"

"Had to, and even paid them extra to get the crew to start today. I needed a reason to get Lauren to move out of the house. She's a little uncomfortable about it."

He knew the feeling. Hell, he hadn't had a woman here since he'd given up dating six months ago. Now he had two females under his roof. "She'll be fine. I'll try to ease her mind a bit."

Loretta's eyes softened. "You're a blessing, Cooper."

"I'm nothing of the sort, Loretta."

"You've got a good heart for doing this."

He scratched his chin. "About that, Loretta. I hope you know you're both welcome here, but I'm not exactly sure how this is all going to work. I mean, Lauren's set on marrying this guy and I can only do so much. I came up with this plan pretty quick and all." He hadn't really thought it through, but Loretta seemed set on breaking up Lauren's engagement, or at the very least, making sure Kelsey was an upstanding man, deserving of her daughter's hand.

The only real plan in his head was to keep watch over Lauren while he tried to find out Kelsey's true intentions. His gut was telling him her fiancé was no good, and he trusted his gut. If the guy had been cheating Tony, then he should be exposed for the creep that he was. Protecting Lauren was Cooper's job now…at all costs. If his secret plan went awry, he could lose Lauren's friendship, but it was a risk he was willing to take. He owed Tony that much. Hell, he owed the entire Abbott family.

Period.

"It's a start. We can keep an eye on Lauren better at your ranch, without too much interference from Roger," Loretta said, breaking into his thoughts. "We'll figure it out as we go."

That was an understatement.

"How's your brother?"

"Jared's good."

"Will we be seeing him while we're here?"

"From time to time. He's got an office up at his house and we have dinner a few times a week."

"You two boys have certainly made a success of this ranch," she said.

"We just picked up where Dad left off. He started the place and taught us the business. Luckily, we both love ranching. Jared's the brains and I'm the brawn in the duo." Cooper smiled and sipped lemonade.

Lauren walked in, her eyes taking in the entire kitchen. "Wow. A girl could go into crazy cooking mode in this place."

"Feel free. I'm sure Marie wouldn't mind a bit."

"Marie? Is she…?"

"She is. She's the same housekeeper we've had since I was a boy," he said, handing Lauren a glass of lemonade. "She's getting on in age, so we keep her duties light. She splits her time between here and Jared's place, but we've also got a cleaning crew that comes in to help her out," he explained. "Have a seat, ladies."

While they took their seats at the table, he scrounged around for the oatmeal chocolate-chip cookies Marie had made yesterday. "Ah, here they are." He set the plate on the table. "Snacks. Have some."

"They look delicious," Loretta said, taking one.

"They are," Cooper said, gesturing for Lauren to take one, as well.

"If I do, then I'll have to jog another mile or two to work it off."

"You jog?"

She nodded. "Yes."

"And she does yoga, too," Loretta added.

"Well, I know nothing about yoga, but anytime you want a jogging partner, I'm your guy."

"Really?"

She seemed surprised and that surprised him. "Yep. What, you didn't think cowboys jogged?"

Lauren laughed. "Well, no. I guess I can't picture it."

"See me in the morning and I'll paint you that picture."

"You're on," Lauren said. She delicately picked up a

cookie and took a small bite. "Oh, these are delicious." She began nodding her head. "I can see I'm going to need to step up my game if this is how Marie cooks."

"It is a challenge," Cooper admitted. "So, where would you like to start? I can show you around the house and then we can take a tour of the grounds. Were you thinking of a church wedding or having it here?"

"I'm...not sure. I'll have to speak to Roger about that. Up until a few days ago, we were going to the courthouse to get married."

Loretta frowned slightly. The idea of her daughter marrying this guy unsettled her, but she was hiding it well.

"I'm sure you have to get to work, Cooper," Lauren said.

"I have a few hours. Let me give you a tour of the house first."

After cookies and lemonade in the grand kitchen, Cooper began showing them the finer points of the room including how to work all the digital electronic appliances and how to turn on the television set in the refrigerator door, which also told the time and local temperature. By the time he was through, Lauren's head was spinning. But her mama took it all in stride as if she was tickled pink to be here.

Lauren still felt awkward about the entire situation.

"The kitchen is always available to you," he said. "If Marie's here, she's usually really good about having meals ready. If there's something you want, just ask her, and if she's not here, have at it. Feel free to cook something yourself."

"I think Lauren might take you up on that, Cooper," her mama said.

"Fine with me." Cooper's gaze connected with Lauren's and all that blue coming her way made her dizzy.

It was a mother thing, putting words in Lauren's mouth.

She didn't like it, but her best friend Katy said her mother did the same thing to her quite a bit. And she had made that crack about *crazy cooking mode* earlier. Still, she wasn't at ease here yet. She hoped that would change.

Next, they followed Cooper through the living room and formal dining area, as well as a great room that housed a bar, a reading nook and a giant flat-screen television. The room was the coziest in the house, done in warm colors, with lived-in leather sofas and a rustic red-brick fireplace. He showed them how to turn on music from an in-wall stereo system with enough lights and buttons to rival an airplane dashboard.

*Warning to self. Do not even think about it.* She'd be sure to foul up the music system.

Then Cooper led them down the hall to his study, which he used as an office. Across the hall was a full state-of-the-art gym. "Wow," she said under her breath. Of all the things he'd showed her thus far, this was the only thing she really envied. "I'm impressed. Do you...?"

"Yep, I get my cowboy ass—uh, excuse me, Loretta—in here a few times a week."

"That's obvious," Lauren said without thinking. She resisted slapping her hand over her mouth. Goodness, she had to keep her lips buttoned more around him or he'd think she was flirting or something.

Cooper blinked once and then let the comment pass.

The gym had a shower area with a complete set of sundries, a sauna and an indoor Jacuzzi. Everything was framed in travertine and marble. The shower alone was bigger than a walk-in closet.

"Again," he said, "feel free to use anything here you'd like."

A sliding-glass door in the gym led them outside to the back of the house. The gardens were colorful, day lilies, peonies and primrose erupting into full bloom everywhere.

A snow-white lattice gazebo sat smack in the middle of the grounds and off to the side crystal-blue waters flowed down a rock waterfall into a pool. A long stone-and-glass fire pit was surrounded by lounge chairs. It was perfection.

"It's like a resort," Loretta said.

Cooper laughed. "I used to throw some great parties here."

"Tony told me. He loved those parties."

Cooper's face fell. "I know. God, I miss him."

Lauren saw his pain and reached for his hand. "We all do." He stared into her eyes a moment and nodded. Her mama took both of their hands and squeezed. And they stood there for a while, hands entwined.

After a time, her mama spoke up. "Tony wouldn't want us to be sad. He'd want us to celebrate his life."

It was hard for Mama to be the cheerleader in this, but she had a point. Tony would hate their grieving. He would want them to get on with their lives. "You're right, Mama."

Cooper sighed with what seemed to be remorse.

"Well," Lauren said, contemplating their surroundings, "this place will make for a beautiful wedding. There's plenty of room to speak vows by the pool. Maybe under the gazebo."

"But Cooper has some other spots to show you, honey," her mother said. "Don't you, Cooper? You know, those places you told me about out by the lake."

"Yeah, I sure do," he said, coming out of his slump. "I was planning on taking you there today. That's if you're up to it."

"I'd love to see the lake," Lauren said.

"Actually, you two go on." Loretta briefly closed her eyes. "I'm a bit tired. I'd like go up to my room and take a rest."

"We can wait for you, Mama. Do it another time," Lauren said.

"Nonsense, Lauren. You need to work this out as soon as possible and Cooper has the time today."

"That's right. I sure do."

"Can I help you up the stairs?" she asked her mother as they went back inside and sat down.

"Lauren, I said I was tired, honey, not decrepit."

Out of the corner of her eye she saw Cooper try to hide a smile by twisting his mouth in an unbecoming way. Which was saying something, because Cooper was pretty much handsome no matter what kind of face he made. Then he faked a cough to contain a laugh, but her mother didn't seem to notice.

"Of course you're not decrepit, Mama." A nurturer by nature, the last thing Loretta wanted was to be deemed incapable of taking care of herself. Lauren should've known not to put it that way, but being here was a bit daunting, no matter how welcoming Cooper was at the moment. With planning her quickie wedding and all the changes in her life lately, Lauren was a little bit at loose ends.

She turned to Cooper, the tilt of her head telling him she knew he'd been laughing at her. "Am I good to go like this?" she asked, gesturing to her attire.

"Let's see. Boots, jeans, check. The hat I'll take care of. Spring weather can be iffy. Do you want to bring along a light sweater?"

"Nah, I'll rough it. Besides, the sun is out and it doesn't look like it's going anywhere today."

"Okay, then I'll see you two later." Mama popped out of her chair like a piece of well-done bread from a toaster. "I'll just go up to my room now."

"Have a good rest, Loretta," Cooper said.

After her mother walked out of the room, Cooper turned to Lauren, a smirk emerging on his face again. She rolled her eyes.

"What?" he said, innocent as a baby.

"You're a brat, you know that, Cooper Stone."

"At least you aren't inferring I was decrepit."

She punched him in the arm. It felt good, to give back his teasing in a playful way.

"Ow." He put his hand over the arm she'd just whacked. No way had she hurt him. Those muscles were like granite. A silly smile appeared on his face. "Now that's the Lauren Abbott I remember."

She smiled back. "Be careful or you just might see more of her than you want."

"That could only be a good thing," he said softly, placing his hand on the small of her back, grabbing his hat and leading her out the door.

The kind words and special touch brought familiarity. And a mass of tingles she hadn't expected.

Cooper stood by the Jeep. "Drive or ride?" he asked Lauren.

Her pretty green eyes narrowed, as if she thought he was messing with her again. "Isn't it the same thing?"

"Well, I can drive us in the Jeep to see the grounds or we can mount up." He pointed to the stables just within eyeshot. "On a horse."

"Oh." She shook her head. "I haven't been riding in eons. I think the Jeep is the safest bet today."

"Okay. Another time," he said. He hadn't quite figured Lauren out. At times she seemed impetuous, a girl who liked to take a risk. That was the girl who'd punched him in the arm just a few minutes ago. That punch had surprised him in a good way.

She was back to being the girl he remembered, never taking any guff from anyone. Whenever Tony had teased her, she'd always shot back at him, giving as good as she got. Marrying Kelsey on a whim after six months of dating was another impulsive move on her part. That's why he was puzzled. Lauren seemed hesitant in coming here. Was she uncomfortable around him? Was she feeling manipulated into living at Stone Ridge for the month? Or was she having second doubts about the sudden marriage?

He hoped it was the latter. He hoped she'd put a halt to the wedding on her own terms so he could end this ruse. But at least having her here lent him the time he needed to find out what Kelsey was really up to. He could keep an eye on Lauren, as well.

"Hop in," he said, opening the door for her. She climbed in and buckled her seat belt as he took his place behind the wheel. "Ready?"

"Ready."

He grabbed a tan suede hat from the backseat and plopped it on her head. It sank onto her forehead and pushed her blond locks down past her shoulders, making her look damn cute.

"This yours?" she asked.

"Uh-huh," he said. "Hang on to it when we take off."

Then he revved the engine and pulled away from the house.

After a minute she asked. "Where is the lake?"

"Back there." He gestured behind him. "We passed it a ways back."

"But aren't we going there?"

"Yep, but there's someplace else I thought you'd like to see."

"You're full of surprises, Coop."

He liked the sound of his nickname falling off her lips. That and the way she looked in his hat was messing with his head a little. "Not really. Pretty much what you see is what you get with me."

At least it always had been. Now he wasn't quite so sure. He'd surprised himself when he'd invited Lauren to have her wedding here. And he'd surprised himself even more by asking her to move into his house. He had underlying motives for having her here, true, and saving her from heartache would be something Tony would've wanted from him.

That one fact made all of this seem more palatable.

"Here we are," he said, stopping the Jeep in front of a stand of shade-bearing oak trees. "We have to walk from here."

He came around the end of the Jeep and helped Lauren gain her footing as she got out. He held her steady and she gazed at him, gratitude glowing in her eyes. "I know where you're taking me."

His brows lifted. "You do?"

"Of course. Tony would talk about this place incessantly and I would be green with envy."

"Yeah, this was a special place to us," he said, taking hold of her hand. "Be careful, the land's uneven here. Lots of roots breaking through the soil."

They walked a bit, her hand gripped in his, reminding him just how long it'd been since he'd held a soft woman. And Lauren was that and more. He didn't like noticing her that way, or feeling even remotely attracted to her. She was cute and funny and nice. Emphasis on *nice*. Any other thoughts about her weren't going to happen. He had a job to do. Protect Lauren. Stop her wedding if need be. Make sure she didn't get hurt and pray she didn't hate him for the rest of her life.

"Just a little bit longer now."

And then he came upon his childhood fort, a mismatched set of planks built between the lower branches of a thick oak. The place looked the same as he remembered, though a bit more weathered, but the roof was intact and the wood beams were holding strong. A rope ladder, made of thick hemp, scraped against the dark tree bark.

"You're smiling so wide right now," Lauren said.

"Am I?" This place always made him happy.

"There's a twinkle in your eyes, too."

"Careful, Laurie Loo. I've never taken a girl here before. Don't make me regret it."

"Never. I'm glad to be here. I guess this is where you and Tony conspired."

"It is. Mostly we pretended to be looting pirates or badass cowboys. My dad gave us the wood and told us to have at it. I think we were ten at the time."

"So you built this all by yourselves?"

"Hell, no. After three attempts, my dad intervened. He said he didn't want us breaking our necks when the whole thing collapsed. But he taught us one important lesson."

"What was that?"

"That things aren't always as simple and easy as they initially seem. Your brother and I were so damn eager to do this on our own, certain we could figure it out. But after failing a few times pretty darn badly, we finally realized the project was too big for us. Our pride was bruised and we were embarrassed to ask for help after insisting we could do it all on our own. And Dad was great about it, without rubbing our noses in I-told-you-sos. He was proud of us for not giving up and for finding a way to make it happen."

"Wow. Your dad was pretty wonderful."

"He was a good man."

A sudden chilly breeze blew by and Cooper gazed upward. Clouds were moving in fast, turning the sky gray, and he caught Lauren trembling. "We should go. The weather's about to change and it can put you in a world of goose bumps. If we're lucky, we can make it to the lake before the wind gets out of hand."

"Sounds good," she said. "And thanks for bringing me here, Cooper."

"Welcome." He took her hand again. As they began to

forge their way back to the Jeep, the air grew chillier, the clouds completely obscuring any sunlight.

"Damn," he said. "I think we're in for it."

"In for what?"

Suddenly, off in the distance, lightning ignited the sky. Clouds crashed against each other and rain poured down as if a giant water balloon had burst. Caught in a flash storm, they were getting soaked.

"Wow! That came on fast," Lauren said.

"Sure did." He gauged his options. "C'mon, let's make a run for it."

"Where?"

But he had already changed their direction. The Jeep would provide no protection. There was only one place to go. Still holding her hand, he guided Lauren along the muddied path leading them back to the fort.

Once they arrived, Lauren took a look at the ladder rope. "You're kidding, right?"

He shrugged. "Either that or get soaked to the bone." Which she already was. "C'mon. I'll help you up."

"Okay," she said tentatively.

And then she was climbing the rungs as he held the ladder firm, her butt in his line of vision. It was a beautiful sight, one he shouldn't be noticing. But he had to keep his eyes sharp, just in case she lost her footing. At least, that's what he told himself as she ascended the ladder.

She threw herself inside the fort and he followed her. They nestled together against the back wall, out of the spray of raindrops. Lauren shivered, her blouse soaked and plastered to the beautiful swells of her breasts. The transparency was hard to miss and, for a moment, Coop couldn't tear his gaze away. Then sanity rushed in. He began unbuttoning his shirt. "Here you go. Put this on."

Her face flushed cherry-red. She was aware of the sight

she made. She accepted his shirt without argument and he helped her put her arms into the sleeves. "Thanks."

She hugged her knees to her chest and sighed. "Well, guess I was wrong."

"About?" He sat next to her, in his undershirt, his legs straight out, his boots just inside the confines of the fort.

"The weather."

It was too much to hope she'd admit she was wrong about marrying Kelsey. Wishful thinking never got him anywhere. He'd have to tell Loretta his suspicions and start scouring Tony's computer for hints that Kelsey had been cheating the business. And he'd have to start as soon as possible.

"It's actually pretty cool to be here, storm and all," she said. "Tell me more about you and Tony. What did you do when you came here?"

"I already told you," he said. "Pirates and cowboys."

She nodded, seeming suddenly sentimental. "Isn't there more?"

"We'd bring our lunches and eat, and then sometimes just lie back, sort of like we're doing now, and dream."

"What did you dream about?"

"Growing up. Racing cars. Dating girls. Boy stuff. I remember one of the last times we ever came here. I think we were fifteen. Samantha Purdue had broken up with Tony. He was crushed. We came up here with a six-pack of beer I'd swiped from home and chugged while he cried his eyes out."

"Wow. Over Samantha Purdue?"

"Yeah, it was stupid. The very next week, Tony was crushing on another girl." The memory made Cooper smile. "Your brother was girl-crazy."

"Maybe that's why he never married. What about you?"

"Me?" He shook his head. "I wasn't girl-crazy. More like, girls made me crazy."

She chuckled and a drop of rain fell from her hair and drizzled down her cheek. He braced her face in his hand and wiped away the rain with the pad of his thumb. Her skin was the softest silk. She smiled sweetly at him then, and something shifted in his chest.

"I meant why didn't you ever marry," she said quietly, gazing at him with those pale green eyes.

The impact of her question shook him to the core. He had no right touching her this way. He dropped his hand from her face and looked out at the driving rain. "I had some serious relationships in the past. They didn't work out. There's time for me."

"So you do want to marry eventually?"

"Yeah. One day. In the very, very distant future." Right now, women were off the table for him. He'd purged his "little black book." He was officially taking a break.

"And you? Did you ever imagine yourself getting married so young?"

"Young? I'm twenty-six. In the olden days, I'd be considered a spinster."

"Yeah, but it's not the olden days."

"I know, Coop. It's just that I've been kinda boy-crazy all my life. No one ever stuck. Maybe it runs in our DNA. Maybe Tony and I weren't very different from my father," she said quietly. "I've always worried about that. My father never seemed satisfied with what he had. You know his history, four marriages and divorces."

"Nah, you're not like him."

"I'd crush on one boy and then another, and I never wanted to settle."

"You shouldn't settle. Ever. You should be dead sure."

"My friends tease me about it, but Mama says it's just that my heart is big and it takes a whole lot to fill it."

"And Roger does that for you?"

Lauren bit her lip, hesitating for a fraction of a second too long. "Yeah, he does."

He wasn't convinced and, when she trembled, he wrapped his arm around her shoulders and pulled her in tight, warming them both up.

He hoped like hell Kelsey was true blue.

Otherwise he'd have to punch the guy's lights out and send him packing.

# Three

After dinner that night Cooper sat facing Loretta in the dining room while Lauren was in the kitchen, cleaning up. "That was about the best darn chicken soup I've ever had," he said. "But don't tell Marie I said so."

"I won't," Loretta answered, beaming. Apparently after her rest, Lauren's mom had decided soup and homemade biscuits would be perfect on a rainy day. And she'd been right.

"Thanks for cooking tonight."

"Of course. It's my pleasure and the least I can do. What do you do when Marie isn't here to cook for you?"

"I scrounge around for leftovers. Marie's pretty good about making extra for the nights she's not here. Or I order in or scramble an egg or something."

"An egg? I can't imagine that would fill you up at all, Cooper."

"Well, I don't do that often. I've been known to meet up with a friend for dinner."

"A female friend?" Loretta asked coyly.

He grinned. "Don't have too many females in my life right now. Aside from you and Lauren."

"I think we're probably all you can handle right now. Don't you?"

He grinned. "Absolutely. Listen, while I have you alone, I need to tell you something. Come into the study with me. I don't want Lauren to overhear."

"Fine. I'll follow you."

He led Loretta down the hall and into his study and promptly closed the door. He didn't have much time, and he'd rehearsed how he was going to put this to cause her the least amount of grief.

"Loretta, I have a confession to make. Please sit down."

She stared at him curiously for a moment and then settled on the sofa. He took a seat on the opposite end.

"What is it?"

"It's just that when you approached me about Lauren and her decision to marry so quickly, it made me think of something Tony had told me just prior to the accident. I didn't want to bring it up at the time because it could be painful, but now that we're in this full speed, I need to tell you the truth."

"And that is?"

"Tony told me that he didn't trust Roger Kelsey. He thought his partner was cheating him and up to no good with the company. Tony was trying to get proof and confront him."

"You mean Roger was stealing from my son?"

"Yeah, that's what Tony seemed to think when he confided in me. Of course, he would've never approved of Lauren marrying the guy. It was the deciding factor in me helping to break up this wedding. Tony had good instincts and I trust that he was going to get that proof, but then the accident happened."

"Well, now…that makes it all the more important that Lauren break up with him."

"Yeah, that's how I see it."

"What if we told Lauren about Tony's suspicions?" Loretta asked. "Surely she'd take Tony's word over his."

"We have no proof. If we tell Lauren now about Tony's suspicions and she confronted Kelsey, it would give him time to cover his tracks and then we may never find out the truth. If the guy is that cagey, he'll win Lauren over and prove that he's straight as an arrow. Then she'll…"

"Blame us for interfering."

"Exactly. I'm sorry, Loretta."

She took his hand and squeezed. "No, I'm glad you told me. I only wish Tony would've shared this with me."

"I'm sure he didn't want to burden you and, of course, at the time, Lauren wasn't involved with Kelsey."

"That's true. And I was always saying that I didn't know a thing about real estate." Tears dripped from her eyes. "I never showed much interest in my Tony's business."

"He loved you, Loretta. And was so proud of you. He'd tell everyone you were the best nurse in the Lone Star State."

"Thanks, Cooper. I appreciate that, and I know that's how Tony felt. He would tell me that often." She straightened in her seat, no longer sorrowful. Instead a protective glint filled her eyes. "Now this sudden engagement makes all the more sense to me."

"Yeah."

"My Lauren is going to get hurt."

"I hope not. I'll do my best to make sure of it."

"Thank you, Cooper."

"So, that said, I'm going to need to get into Tony's laptop. Do you have it?"

She thought a moment. "Yes. I think I do. Most of his personal things are in boxes in my garage."

"Great. I'll need to get into that, if it's okay with you."

"Of course, it's okay. I'll make some excuse to go home tomorrow and get it for you. Cooper, should we alert the authorities about any of this?"

"Not now. We have nothing but Tony's suspicions. And on the slim chance that this guy wasn't cheating Tony, Lauren would probably never forgive either of us for going behind her back and causing her fiancé grief."

"Good point," she said with a nod, although her shoulders slumped in defeat.

Yeah, this was going to cause the Abbotts pain.

No matter what Cooper found.

Lauren had been jogging ever since college, but keeping pace with Cooper this morning was proving harder than she thought. He took it seriously and, given that he was six-foot-two, his strides were much longer than hers. Ten minutes into the run, she broke out into a sweat trying to keep up. After another ten minutes she was lagging, but as soon as he noticed, he slowed his pace. "You want to head back?" he asked.

"Not on your life," she answered. "And don't slow down for me. You can go on ahead."

He wasn't hard to watch from behind. He wore a Rangers baseball cap flipped backward on his head, a black tank exposing thick, tanned, muscular arms and a pair of gray sweatpants. Stripped down like this, the cowboy could pass for a city dude.

"Nah, I like the company."

"Don't ruin your workout for me."

"You're only making it better, Laurie Loo."

She laughed at his attempt at charm, but did appreciate him slowing down a bit. At this point, he'd taken her past his stables and corrals and then down a service road. The dawn air was cool but the sunshine overhead promised to dry out all the places the storm had muddied the day before.

She was able to take in more of the Stone Ridge scenery at this much slower pace than during yesterday's drive in the Jeep. They passed green pastures, lush from spring rain, with cattle grazing in groups. Every so often Cooper would lead her through a patch of shade from an oak or mesquite tree, providing temporary shelter from the dawn sunshine.

As they were rounding a bend, the lake came into view, a picturesque vision of tall trees reflecting off the waters lit by a stream of sunshine. Glossy and smooth as glass, the small lake was postcard ready and a perfect place to speak vows.

Lauren stopped running. "Oh, Coop."

He turned around, but kept running in place.

"This is amazing. What's it called?"

"The lake."

"The lake? You mean you don't have a name for it?"

"No. We've always just thought of it as the lake."

"Oh, man. That's a shame. Something this beautiful should have a name."

He shrugged. "C'mon. Let's see it closer up."

They jogged together until they reached the bank. Lauren sipped from her water bottle and gazed at the snow-white ducks flying in, taking a dip, splashing water everywhere and then taking off again. On the opposite bank, a mama duck waddled out of the water, her six little ducklings following behind, disappearing into the dark shade of an oak tree.

"I can picture my wedding here," Lauren said. A sense of wonder and awe filled her inside. She could see it all in her mind: chairs decorated with big bows set out in rows on the thick grass, a canopy of woodsy flowers over the archway where they would speak their vows. This was more her style, making a commitment outdoors, the natural surroundings seeming to convey a sense of truth and honesty. "I think this is the place."

She turned to Cooper, expecting to see him nod in agreement, or at least smile, but he was deep in thought. Heavy thought, it appeared, as his mouth was pulled down into a frown. Was he thinking about Tony?

"Coop?"

"Yep," he said, masking whatever emotion he was feeling by plastering on a smile. "I heard you. This is the place."

"Yes, thanks for bringing me here. I can't think of a better spot to be married."

"Okay, then," he said sharply. "Settled."

"Yeah," she said. He was struggling hard to maintain a smile. "Unless, you'd rather we do it somewhere else. Maybe you'd like to save this place for when you get married?"

"Hell, no. That's not happening anytime soon, Lauren. I brought you here, remember? If you want a lakeside wedding, that's what you'll have."

Still, his tone left her wondering. "Are you thinking about my brother?"

"I won't lie. Tony's been on my mind a lot lately."

"If it's too much for you to walk me down the aisle, Coop, please let me know."

"It's not that, Lauren. I'm honored to walk you down the aisle. But something keeps niggling at me. I don't see what the rush is all about."

"That's because you don't get me."

"I don't?"

"No, and neither does Mama. I've been impetuous in the past so I understand your skepticism, but I'm sure this time. I know what I want."

"Okay, if you're sure."

But even as he said it, the words rang...not false, but off somehow.

"I'm sure. Thanks again, for everything you're doing."

"Happy to do it," he said and then took hold of her hand. "C'mon. Let's walk back to the house now."

"Okay, sure." She turned around to give the lake one last glimpse. "I can't wait to tell Roger. Would you mind terribly if he came out to see the lake sometime?"

"Don't mind at all."

"I'm so excited."

"I'm...glad."

A short time later she entered the house alone and dashed up the stairs, eager to share the news with her mama. Cooper had excused himself, stopping at the stables to speak with his foreman.

She knocked on the bedroom door. "Mama, it's me."

"Come in, honey."

Lauren walked into the room as her mother was combing her hair. She wore it up most the time in a stylish twist with stray chocolate brown tendrils streaming down. "I was just getting ready to head out."

"Where are you going?"

"I have to speak with the painting contractor today," she said, giving her hair one final glance in the mirror. "He had some questions and wanted my approval on some things."

"Would you like me to go with you?"

"No, it's not necessary, honey. I thought I'd stop by Sadie's while I'm there. She's not been feeling well."

"Sorry to hear about Sadie. What's wrong with her?"

"She's feeling very tired lately. And that's unlike her. Usually she can run circles around me. She seemed out of breath when we spoke on the phone. So, what's got your eyes twinkling this morning? I know when something makes my girl happy."

"I am happy. Actually, I'm thrilled. I found the place

where Roger and I are going to say our vows. Cooper and I jogged over to the lake earlier. It's perfect, Mama. Just like a dream."

"A dream, huh? That's saying something."

"Yes, I can't wait for you to see it."

"I'm sure I will. In due time."

"Mama?"

Her mother grabbed her hands and squeezed. "I'm just as thrilled as you are, sweetheart. But I've got this appointment today and I'm a bit worried about Sadie, so I've got to run."

"Sure, Mama. I'll show you the lake another time. You'll think it's perfect, too."

Her mother kissed her on the cheek. "'Bye, sweetheart."

"See you later, Mama."

Her mother picked up her purse and dashed out the door.

Lauren blinked. Their conversation sure seemed strange, as if she'd caught her mother red-handed today. She seemed guilty about something. Out at the lake, she'd gotten a similar "off" vibe from Cooper. Was there something in the coffee this morning?

She shoved her misgivings aside. Now that she knew exactly where the wedding was to be held, she could concentrate on the next order of business in planning her perfect day.

Later that morning, after a shower and making some phone calls, Cooper drove up the road to speak with Jared. They had contracts to discuss but, more importantly, he needed to explain what was going on with Lauren and Loretta. Four years younger in age, Jared had a sensible head on his shoulders. He was the money man in the family. While Cooper ran the everyday workings of Stone Ridge along with Jim Bartlett, his foreman, Jared made sure all the numbers added up. They were two halves of a whole when it came to the ranch.

Now, sitting in his brother's kitchen, Cooper explained about his part in stopping Lauren's wedding.

"Are you nuts?" His brother's forehead wrinkled in four parallel lines.

"I probably am," he said. "But what choice do I have? Loretta is concerned about Lauren. And so am I. If she's being used and taken advantage of, I can't allow it."

"*You* can't allow it?"

"Yes, bro. Tony would never want his little sis to marry this guy if he's only trying to get control of the entire company."

"And now that's your problem?"

"Yeah, I suppose it is. Loretta came to me for help and I couldn't refuse her. I just couldn't."

"Lauren knows nothing about this?"

"Not a thing. She thinks… I'm some sort of saint for offering to have her wedding at the ranch. And, bro, she asked me to walk her down the aisle." He gulped air, his gut churning at the notion.

Jared ran his hand down his face. "Man. Are you sure you know what you're doing?"

"No. But I have to help Loretta and try to keep Lauren from getting hurt. And there's something else. I'm swearing you to secrecy here."

"You can trust me."

"Hell, if I can't trust you…never mind. The deal is, Tony confided in me that he thought Kelsey was manipulating the numbers and cheating him. Tony didn't trust his partner and was in the process of investigating it on his own. And I thought, if I could find some proof, that would be enough to convince Lauren to break it off with him. If we go to her without proof, she probably wouldn't listen. She'd think it was her mother's way of interfering, since Loretta has already tried to convince Lauren it's too soon and she shouldn't rush into marriage. But the fact is, Kelsey only showed interest in her after Tony died."

"Sounds suspicious to me."

"Yeah, I know." Cooper sighed. "Loretta's getting Tony's laptop out of storage today and I'll scour the thing and see what I can find."

"If you need help with that…"

"I was hoping you'd say that. You're the numbers man in the family. I just might take you up on the offer."

"Sure, I'll help. But, Coop," he said, "tread lightly. This could all blow up in your face. If Lauren gets wind of what you're doing, she'd never forgive you. And if you and Loretta are wrong, again, you stand to lose family friendships over this."

"I'm hoping it doesn't. All I can do is try."

"And in the meantime, you've got Loretta and Lauren living at the ranch for the next few weeks?"

"Yeah."

Jared's head tilted a bit. "I saw Lauren at the funeral. She's all grown up now. Very pretty."

He'd noticed. "Your point?"

Jared began shaking his head. "She's living under your roof."

"So is Loretta. Again, your point?"

"Just be careful, Coop. That's what I'm saying."

Careful? If he was careful, his best friend wouldn't be dead. If he was careful, two women wouldn't be living with him at the ranch. If he was careful, he wouldn't have concocted this crazy scheme. "I'm afraid it's too late for careful."

Jared's chuckle grated in his ears. "All right then, just be…smart."

Smart had nothing to do with it. What he needed was luck.

An hour later, Cooper drove away from Jared's home,

slightly relieved his brother now knew the situation and had his back. He parked the Jeep in the garage and entered his house to the sound of giggles coming from the kitchen. Heading toward the laughter he found Marie serving Lauren and her friend Katy homemade ice cream. Chocolate mint with brownie chunks. The women were lapping up the cones and smiling like little girls.

"Hi, Cooper," Lauren said. "You remember my best friend, Katy Millhouse, right?"

Katy, a brunette with big brown eyes and an engaging smile, waved. "Hi, Cooper. It's nice to see you again."

"Same here, Katy. Welcome to Stone Ridge. How've you been?"

"I'm doing well. Marie just made my day. This ice cream is delish."

"Want one?" Marie asked him, her kind, light blue eyes twinkling. She held a cone in her hand and was scooping away.

His longtime housekeeper knew him so well. He had trouble resisting delicious things, but he really shouldn't stick around. He should let Katy and Lauren get on with their business. With the laptop on the table and papers strewed all over, it looked like they were heavy into wedding planning.

*Crap.* His gut clenched. She was really going to do this thing. And he was really going to try to stop her.

He couldn't very well refuse a cone already scooped and ready to go. "Sure thing. Thanks, Marie."

He took a seat at the table and she handed him his cone. "Here you go."

He plunged in, taking a big lick, and glanced at Lauren, who was doing the same. Her tongue darting out to circle the top of her cone, her eyes closing at the taste and the luscious throaty sounds coming from her mouth were more than mildly erotic. The cone nearly dropped from his hand. What the hell? He had to stop noticing things like that about Lauren.

He averted his gaze, making eye contact with Katy instead, and the ridiculous fast beats of his heart slowed to normal.

"Katy's going to be my maid of honor," Lauren said to him.

"A good choice. Congrats, Katy."

"I'm super excited, Cooper," Katy said. "We've been talking about weddings and marriage since junior high school and…well, everyone always thought I'd marry first, since Lauren is so—"

Lauren shot her a look.

"Picky," Katy said slowly, garnering a nod from her friend. Cooper wondered what she'd really meant to say. "But she finally found the right guy."

"Picky?" he asked.

"You know, she could never make up her mind. She always had crushes on guys and dated a lot in high school and then in college—"

"There was only one guy in college, Katy. Remember?" Lauren said a little defensively.

"Oh, right, right. But all that's changed now. She's marrying Roger. It's going to be perfect."

Cooper gave Katy a smile. What else could he do but keep quiet, finish his cone and get out of there, pronto. He took one last big bite of the ice cream. "Delicious as always, Marie. I'll be in my office if you need me." He rose from the table.

"Oh, um…" Lauren began. "We were wondering if you could help us out. I promise it won't take long, but we're stuck on two different invitations and Marie likes them both equally. We need another opinion."

Cooper glanced at Marie, standing at the sink, shrugging her shoulders. She was so darn diplomatic she wouldn't want to influence the decision. He was trapped. He'd promised he'd help Lauren with any of the planning, if she needed it.

"Okay, sure. I've got a few minutes."

Lauren gestured for him to take a seat next to her. He did so hesitantly, and Lauren scooted her chair closer, pulling the laptop in front of both of them. Katy sat next to him on the other side, but it was only Lauren's sweet strawberry scent that filled his nostrils, only Lauren's arm accidently brushing his, that brought him up short. It didn't help that his brain was revisiting the image of Lauren licking at her ice-cream cone just a few minutes ago.

"So, it's between these two," she said, pulling up the invitations on the screen. "We're limited in choices because of such short notice. This company promises to overnight them to us, so we can get the invitations out immediately."

"I've already sent out email Save the Dates," Katy offered.

This was all above his pay grade. What did he know about Save the Dates and wedding invitations?

But Lauren was asking his advice and he kept telling himself it was what she would've asked of Tony, if he were still here.

"What do you think?" she asked.

He gazed at the two images side-by-side on the screen. One was bold, with modern lines and block print on pure white paper. The other had soft, flowing script on ivory paper. It wasn't hard for him to choose. "This one," he said, pointing to the latter. "It reminds me of you."

"It does? Why?" Lauren asked, blinking her eyes.

"Because it's sort of gentle and understated and easy."

"Easy?" She laughed. *Shoot…* That wasn't what he meant at all.

Beside him, Katy chuckled.

"I mean, it's not as chaotic as the first one. It's easy to

read, everything seems to flow. Hell, I don't know, Lauren. What does Kel—uh, Roger say?"

"Roger's not into planning the wedding. He's very busy right now. He says, whatever I want. As long as I don't break the bank."

"He put her on a budget," Katy added.

Cooper turned to face her. "Did he now?"

"Considering, he thought we were going to get married by the justice of the peace or something," she said, her voice dropping to a whisper, "he's being very generous."

And was probably using the money he'd cheated Tony out of to finance the wedding. "Generous? I thought the groom was supposed to grant the bride's every wish," he said as kindly as possible.

Lauren glanced at him thoughtfully. "I suppose. But Roger's not into all this wedding stuff."

"Maybe he should be," Cooper said. "You deserve the wedding of your dreams."

Lauren's face fell, and he kicked himself for putting it so bluntly. But every doubt he could plant in her mind, helped his cause.

He could also point out that she now owned half of the real-estate development firm of Kelsey-Abbott. She could spend some of that cash on her wedding if she wanted to. But he didn't want her losing any money if the wedding didn't happen, so he kept that thought to himself.

Let Kelsey take the hit when the wedding didn't happen. It would serve the guy right.

As soon as Cooper left the room, Katy grabbed Lauren's attention. "Oh, my goodness. Cooper is such a hunk."

"A hunk?" Lauren tried her best to sound nonchalant. It wasn't as if she hadn't noticed. Cooper Stone wasn't a man a girl could ignore. He had rugged features, dark blond hair and mesmerizing eyes. Not to mention a solid muscled-packed body. But Cooper had always turned her head and he'd been one of her big crushes when she was younger. She'd just gotten used to the fact that he was deliciously manly. "I suppose he is."

"You suppose? Is he dating anyone?"

"Not that I know. But he doesn't exactly confide in me about his love life."

"If he did have a girlfriend, I'd imagine she wouldn't take too kindly to having you living here with him."

"For heaven's sake, Katy. Mama's living here, too, and… well, he's not that irresistible that I can't keep my hands off. He's like family. And you're forgetting that Roger is the man I'm marrying."

"I know all that." Katy got dreamy-eyed, her expression going mushy soft. "But a girl can fantasize, can't she?"

"*You* certainly can, but keep me out of those fantasies." Yet having Katy think of Cooper in those terms didn't set right. She didn't want Cooper to star in any woman's fantasies. How bizarre was that?

"You went jogging with him this morning. How does he look in his running gear?"

"Katy!"

Her friend grinned wickedly and then they both burst out laughing.

After their chuckling died down, Katy got serious. "Now that Cooper helped you pick out the invitations, we have to find you a dress. We can get something off the rack. They have some really good buys this time of year. And a fitting shouldn't—"

"I have a dress."

"You do?"

"Yes, I've decided to wear Mama's dress. She's kept it in pristine condition all these years and it'll be a nice touch."

"I've seen your mom and dad's wedding picture. It's a lovely dress but, honey, it's a little outdated, isn't it?"

"It is. But I'd pay a fortune in a bridal salon for a vintage dress like this one. I've discussed it with Mama and she's thrilled to have me wear her dress."

"Thrilled?"

"Well, as happy as she can be. She's still not totally convinced I should get married after dating Roger less than six months."

"But you are sure, right?"

"Of…course. I'm sure," she said. "He's a good guy."

"And you love him?"

"Yes." She didn't hesitate. She only wished Roger would be more interested in their wedding. She needed his input, but he was a busy man and some guys just weren't into all the fuss involved with planning a wedding. At least, that's what she'd read in several bridal magazines. She shouldn't feel bad, but instead just look at it as an advantage. The bride got her choice on everything. She'd adopted that line of thinking, to keep from being disappointed.

"Okay, we're checking off boxes and accomplishing a lot. Next, we need to pick out the menu for the wedding dinner. You have an idea of what you want, right?"

"I sure do." Lauren opened her bridal journal and turned to the pages that dealt with food options. Through the years, she'd managed to collect pictures and recipes of only the most elaborate meals to serve at the wedding.

"This looks delicious," Katy said, pointing to a French dish that only a chef of the highest caliber could create.

"I bet it is." Lauren sighed.

She glanced through the rest of the meals, shaking her head as she flipped from one page to another. All the dishes she'd picked were way out of her league. While she'd had a blast choosing items to go inside the book, she hadn't been practical. Not at all.

"I can't use any of this," she said to Katy, slamming the book closed. "It's time for a reality check. Let's compile a list of local caterers and see what they have to offer."

"Sounds like you're thinking practically now. Okay, let me work on that. I'll make some calls and get a few referrals. You can work on the music."

"Music?"

"Yeah, you'll need a band to play at the reception, right?"

"A band? I hadn't thought of that. Can't I hire a DJ?"

"Well, sure. You could. But I'm thinking there's so many starving musicians in Dallas who would love to play at your wedding. And remember, Jodie's brother is in a country band. She told me he's playing in a roadhouse not too far from here. You could scope the band out with Roger and see if it works."

Jodie Canton was Katy's coworker at the *Dallas Post*, the local newspaper. They were both associate editors. "You think so?"

"Live music is really a nice touch and I bet you could get them for what you'd pay a DJ."

"Really? A live band could be fun. I'll run it by Roger and see what he thinks."

"Okay, great. Now onto the flowers…"

Two hours later after Katy left, Lauren speed-dialed Roger's number. He didn't pick up right away and then, after five rings, answered abruptly. "What?"

"Hi, honey. Did I catch you at a bad time?"

He sighed and his exasperation came through loud and clear. "No. It's fine. I'm a little busy. What's up, Lauren?"

"Uh, well. I just wanted to go over some of the plans I'm making with Katy, to make sure I'm on the right track."

"Can we do it another time?"

"Sure…if you're too busy. But, Roger, you haven't seen the ranch yet. I really wish you could spare some time to see it." *And me.* She hadn't seen him in several days. "It's where we'll say our vows," she said, unable to hide her disappointment.

"Okay, sweetheart," he said, softening his tone, as if he'd read her mind. "I promise to come by tomorrow afternoon. You can tell me everything then, all right?"

"Yes. Oh, I can't wait to see you."

"Me, too," he said. "Love ya, Lauren."

"Love you, too."

She hung up the phone and the nagging teensy doubt in her head vanished. She did love Roger. And he loved her. They were going to have a wonderful life together.

"Mama's gonna be a little late tonight," Lauren said to Cooper as he walked into the kitchen. She was still sitting at the kitchen table in front of her computer, where he'd left her and Katy hours ago. "She said not to wait on dinner."

"Anything wrong?" Cooper leaned against the granite counter, admiring Lauren's shoulder-length hair, the sunshine pouring in and highlighting the blond strands.

"I hope not. She's visiting our neighbor Sadie tonight. Mama's got a big heart. And Sadie lives alone. If she's not feeling well, my mother wouldn't leave her. She's got a nurturing nature."

"Probably why she became a nurse."

"You know, I couldn't imagine her doing anything else with her life," Lauren said.

"And what about you?"

"I love nursing, too. It feels sort of weird, you know. Taking this vacation and not being at the hospital. I've never taken a month-long break."

"You making progress with the wedding plans?"

"Yes. Katy's been a big help. Otherwise, I think I'd go crazy with all the details."

"Something tells me you can handle it, Lauren."

She gazed at him with those killer meadow-green eyes. "Thank you," she said softly.

He pushed away from the counter and opened the fridge. "So, are you getting hungry?"

"I could eat."

"That's good, because I'm starving. Let's see what Marie left for us."

Behind him, he heard Lauren closing down the laptop and rising from her chair. A flowery scent invaded his nostrils as she sidled up next to him.

"Looks like roasted chicken and potatoes. And there's salad, too."

"Let me take care of this," she said, bumping hips to move him away. The contact of her body surprised him. In a very good way that was all wrong. "It's the least I can do." He stood aside, watching her pull the pan out of the fridge, backing out butt-first, her blond locks falling onto her face.

*She's Tony's sister. She's Tony's sister.* Yet his heart pumped a little faster anyway and he didn't like where his mind was going.

"You've been inside all day. Wanna have our meal out on the patio?" He needed air. And a way to distance himself from her. As big as his house was, it seemed awfully small in the kitchen with Lauren bustling around like she belonged there.

"Right, slaving away at my computer is tough work," she joked. "But eating outside does sound pretty nice. Let me heat up the food and set the table."

"I'll help," he said to be mannerly. He took the pan of roasted chicken out of her hands and they worked like a team reheating the meal in the oven and getting dishes down from the cupboard.

"You're pretty handy to have around." She walked out the wide doors leading to the patio, holding plates, forks and knives. He followed behind with two stemmed glasses, a corkscrew and a bottle of wine.

She set out the dishes and utensils and turned, giving the bottle in his hand a glance before lifting her pretty eyes to him.

"Would you rather have soda or tea?" he asked. What was he thinking? Wine was a bad idea.

"I love wine."

"Pinot okay?"

"I love Pinot." She chuckled and shook her head.

"What?"

"Nothing really. It's just you don't strike me as the Pinot type."

"I don't? What do I strike you as?"

"Beer. And not that light kind, but ale. Yeah, I can picture you gulping from a tall mug of ale."

"Like a pirate or something?"

Lauren tilted her head and studied him.

His facial scruff was in need of a good trim and his hair was probably sticking out in all four directions. But it wasn't disapproval on her face, and her smile radiated toward him, warm and inviting. The green in her eyes deepened to sage as she thought about it.

"Yeah, like a pirate, Cooper."

He studied her. She was dressed casually in a pair of jeans and a blue tank, her skin looking creamy-smooth under the fading sunlight. "But the cowboy in me prefers whiskey, straight up."

"Do you now?"

He nodded, gazing into her smiling eyes. "Yep."

It felt too much like flirting, something he had mastered before he'd given up women. A shudder ran the length of him. He was in uncharted territory. Lauren was a friend. She was also someone else's fiancée. He had to remember that. "I'll...go get the food." And before she could protest, he ordered, "Have a seat, Lauren."

A few minutes later he returned and sat still as an oak

as Lauren served him his meal. She'd insisted on dishing up the food. The sky was burnt orange now, the sun low on the horizon, and the air was just the right side of cool. Once he got Lauren talking about being a nurse, all he had to do was feed his face and listen. But even the listening wasn't easy. Her voice, so animated, so suddenly, sweetly passionate, touched him deep down. He finished his meal and leaned way back in his seat, sipping wine. Every so often he had to look away, pretending interest in the sunset, fighting a war going on inside his head.

"Coop?"

"Hmm." He turned to face her.

"Am I boring you? I've been rattling on."

He smiled. "I don't mind. Sorta nice hearing how much you enjoy your work."

Her brows rose in skepticism and she sipped the last of her wine. Her glass landed in a soft clink on the table. "That was delish."

"Want more?"

"No," she said, shaking her head. "I'm a lightweight. Two's more than enough. In fact, I'm feeling a bit buzzed. After I do the dishes, I think I'll take a walk to clear my head."

"You don't have to do dishes."

"In my head, I do. So, no arguing."

"Fine. The dishes will keep. Take your walk now while there's still some light."

"Okay, I will. But those dishes better be here when I get back."

"Yes, boss."

"It was really nice having dinner on the patio."

He gave her a look.

"I know, I know. I'm burning sunlight."

He laughed and waited until she was out the front door and down the path, to step onto the veranda. As long as

Lauren was walking straight, which she was, he could put aside his doubts about letting her go alone. Her buzz couldn't be that bad, could it?

Once she was out of sight, he turned to enter the house but the sound of a car grabbed his attention. Loretta was pulling into the portico. Perfect timing. She killed the engine and he met her in time to open the car door for her.

"Evenin', Loretta. How's your friend?"

"She's struggling, but I think I cheered her up a bit. Thanks for asking, Cooper. Where's Lauren?"

"She just went for a walk. Did you get it?"

"I did. It's in the trunk." Loretta pushed a button and her trunk opened.

He helped Loretta out of the car and then walked around to pick up Tony's laptop. "Got it. I hope he doesn't have a secret pass code or anything."

"He does."

Cooper's shoulders slumped.

"But I know it." Loretta grinned. "My son trusted me with his passwords."

"That makes life a lot simpler."

"Yes. I hope you find something."

"Me, too."

Cooper sighed. A lot was riding on this. As soon as he got the goods on Kelsey, all of the deceit would be over. Lauren was a good woman. As good as they come. And she deserved a better man than Roger Kelsey.

# Four

"Holy crap." Cooper glanced at the clock in his study. He'd been listening for Lauren while sitting at his desk searching her brother's laptop for clues and had lost track of time. She'd been on her walk for over an hour.

He picked up his phone and texted her just in case he'd missed hearing her come in. When she didn't answer, he locked the laptop in a drawer and made his way down the hall. Taking the stairs two at a time, he moved as quietly as his boots would allow, hoping to find Lauren safe and sound in her bedroom.

Her door was open and he popped his head inside. The room was empty.

Not good.

He debated half a second to tell Loretta, but he didn't want to alarm her.

Instead he made a beeline down the stairs and out the door that led to the garage. Lauren probably didn't have her phone with her. Not in those tight pants anyway, or he would've noticed.

She'd been getting under his skin lately. He'd been noticing *all* the appealing things about her.

Like her honeyed hair catching the morning sunlight.

And her smile, sometimes sweet, sometimes mischievous, yet always bright.

The cute way she nibbled her lip while pondering something.

Luckily, he'd also noticed the direction she'd begun walking in earlier.

Damn. He should've never let her go on that walk alone. Stupidly, he'd let his effort to distance himself from her get in the way of good sense.

Hopping in his Jeep, he took off toward the stables and corrals but found no sign of her. All of his crew had gone home, except for Buddy, a security guard who watched the premises.

"No, sir. I haven't seen her, Mr. Stone," he said.

"Okay, why don't you head out in the opposite direction? Call me immediately if you find her."

"Yes, sir."

Cooper continued at a slow pace, scouring the land with a flashlight as he drove deeper and deeper onto the property. His pulse racing, his gut churning, he sent up prayers for her safety. Somehow Lauren had become more important to him than he'd realized. The thought of her out there, possibly harmed and lost, made him a little frantic.

And he *never* got frantic.

He was just about ready to call Jared to enlist his help, when he spotted something quite a distance from the road. "Lauren, Lauren!"

"I'm here, Cooper," she called out.

Thank God. He bounded out of the Jeep, shone the light in her direction and ran for all he was worth. He found her sitting on the ground, holding her bloodied leg, and he immediately bent to his knees and grabbed her tight around the shoulders. She felt small and delicate in his arms.

"Oh, man, Laurie Loo."

He brushed his lips to her hair, a soft little peck that said he was damn grateful he'd found her. He hugged her longer than he probably should have, unable to let go of her so easily. She was soft and so sweet, looking up at him like he was a savior. His chest swelled. Was he feeling more for her than friendship? He pulled back carefully to look into her eyes. "What happened?"

"I got lost about half an hour ago. I thought I knew the way back, but it's so dark and everything looked so different. And then I practically face-planted on a big rock. I caught myself but not before putting a good gash on my leg."

That's when he noticed that her pants were ripped below the knee. The gash appeared long and angry. She'd stripped away the bottom half of her cotton tank top to wrap around the wound.

"There's a lot of blood," he said. "Does it hurt?"

"It stings. But it's not fractured and I stopped the bleeding, so I consider myself lucky."

There were no tears on her face, no panic. She knew how to handle herself in a crisis. "Lucky?" He shook his head. "I guarantee you won't feel lucky in the morning."

"And here I had this secret plan to beat your butt at jogging tomorrow."

He smiled. How could he not? Lauren was something else. "I'll take a rain check, honey. But for now, let me get you back home. Can you stand?"

"I think so," she said.

He offered his hand and she stood, hopping up on her good leg, while keeping the pressure off her injured one. He slid his other hand around the creamy-smooth band of exposed skin around her waist. It startled him how delicate and soft she felt. She leaned against him and wrapped her arm around his waist. They moved slowly, Cooper taking on most of her weight, his fingers splaying wide, reaching to just under the swell of her breasts.

*Oh, man.* An instant insane reaction zeroed in down past his navel. He imagined touching her breasts but that crazy thought fled his mind the second she began to tremble. He had to remind himself Lauren was engaged and could never be his.

He stopped walking. She'd lost a lot of blood tonight and her face was pale. She gazed at him helplessly.

"Forget this." On impulse, he scooped her up gently, one arm at her shoulders, the other beneath her knees. "Rope your arms around my neck," he told her.

She tugged at his neck and he repositioned her. "Better?" he asked.

She squeezed her eyes shut. "Much."

He handed her the flashlight. "Point us back to the Jeep."

"That I can do," she said, sounding apologetic.

Hell, he should be apologizing to her. "I should've never let you go out by yourself tonight. You told me you were buzzed."

"I was fine," she whispered breathlessly. "It was a stupid accident."

He started moving again, taking long, careful strides. "You're not familiar enough with the ranch to go traipsing around in the dark without a phone or a flashlight."

"I guess I wasn't thinking straight."

"I should've known that, too."

Her fingertips grazed his right cheek and he turned to her. They were inches apart, her face so close he could feel her breaths. "Cooper, it wasn't your fault," she said softly.

He wasn't going to argue the point anymore. He simply nodded and kept walking. When they reached the Jeep, he was very deliberate in his movements getting her into the passenger seat. "You all right?"

"I'm fine."

He reached inside to pull the seat belt strap for her, his forearm grazing her breasts. "Uh, sorry."

"No problem."

Glad *she* thought so. He made quick work of securing her belt and then took off his shirt and handed it to her. "Here, put this around you," he said. "It might get chilly on the ride back." Already the night air had cooled some.

"Thanks," she said, eyeing him in his ribbed T-shirt. "You're always taking care of me."

He was always undressing for her, but he didn't point that out. "You're like…my sister. It's my job."

She pursed her lips and, if he didn't know better, he'd think she was pouting.

"Does Roger take care of you?"

"Roger? Um, he knows I'm capable. He's—"

"Let me guess…always so busy."

"He is. But he's coming by tomorrow afternoon to help with the arrangements. I hope that's okay with you, Cooper."

"Sure." He gunned the engine and took off. There was no further talk of Roger.

Minutes later he pulled up to the house and opened the Jeep door for her.

"I can try to walk," Lauren said.

"Don't think so. You'll never make it up the stairs."

Her mouth opened and then closed. Whatever protest she had on her lips was left unsaid. He wasn't budging. He bent to lift her and adjusted her in his arms. He was getting used to the feel of her, the softness of her skin, her flowery scent. He carried her inside the house and up the stairs.

Loretta's bedroom door was shut, the light was off. She was probably asleep and there was no sense waking her. He moved down the hallway to Lauren's room and entered.

A sliver of moonlight filtered in, casting enough light for him to see where he was going. Cooper walked over to her bed. "I'm going to put you down now."

"Okay," she whispered.

He carefully released her and she slid down his body until her feet hit the floor. His groin tightened and he gritted his teeth. It was torture keeping his intentions pure around her. Suddenly, his best friend's little sis was testing his willpower. He couldn't give in to temptation.

But as she tried to apply pressure to her leg she wobbled and he was there to catch her. "Whoa."

She was in his arms again, leaning against his chest. "Are you in pain? Should I call a doctor?"

"No, Coop," she said, her head resting against his shoulder. "I'll take care of it. I'll redress the wound and clean it up a bit and then take some aspirin."

"What can I do?" he asked quietly.

"Help me into the bathroom. I'll…need some privacy to dress the wound."

"I can wake up your mom. She can help you."

"No, don't be silly. I'm an ER nurse, I've done this a thousand times."

"Fine. I'll hold on to you."

He helped her hobble into the bathroom and sit on a vanity chair. "I'll be right back. I have a first-aid kit in my room. Okay?"

"Okay."

He was back in thirty seconds and set the blue-and-white box on the counter. "Here you go. What else can I do?"

"I'm going to soak my leg a bit and then dress the wound. I have to get out of these pants."

She stared at him.

"I'm going. I'm going. But I'll be right outside the door if you need me."

She nodded and he left just as she started stripping out of her blood-soaked jeans.

He sat on her bed and waited what seemed like eons. He heard her moving around, the water in the tub being turned on and off. That was exactly how *he* felt, being constantly turned on by Lauren, and then trying like hell to turn it off. The problem was, it all felt so natural being around her. But she only saw him as a big brother figure and he couldn't very well disappoint her. Could he?

"Cooper? Are you still there?"

"I'm here."

"Please bring me my jammies. They're in the top right drawer in the dresser. They're blue."

Cooper found them right away, a silky blue top and a pair of pants to match. "Got them."

She opened the door and one hand came out to grab at them and haul them away. Then the door shut again. "Thanks."

A few minutes later she was standing against the open door in her sleek pajamas that fell over the contours of her body, the silk hiding very little of her form. She looked beautiful, so much better than when he'd found her bruised and disheveled earlier. Her face was beet-red, though. "This is embarrassing."

"It's not the first time I've seen you in pajamas," he said, trying to hold on to her image as a kid and not think about the woman standing right in front of him.

She sighed. "That's true. But that had to be fifteen years ago or something."

"You dressed the wound?"

"Yes, and I took some meds. I think I'm going to live."

She hobbled over to him and he thought to back away. To keep his distance. But there was determination in her eyes and, man, he couldn't resist planting his boots and seeing what she had in mind.

"Thank you, Cooper," she whispered. "You've been wonderful."

She reached up on tiptoes to plant a sweet kiss on his cheek. But when she put weight on her bad leg, she stumbled. He caught her, holding her tight, his hands gripping her upper arms. Her eyes flashed, all that meadow green working magic on him. Holding her like this felt right—and that was all wrong. But when she dipped her gaze to his mouth, the longing in her eyes did him in.

"Cooper."

He put his hands in her hair and tilted her head up. Their eyes locked, wrecking his resistance, wrecking any semblance of rational thought. He brought his mouth down and touched his lips to hers.

It was Fourth of July fireworks and sweet cake on Sunday morning all rolled into one. She was soft and delicate and amazingly sexy. But one brush of the lips wasn't enough; he needed more, demanded more. She made little noises in the back of her throat and the sounds were like music and laughter and brightness. His body grew tight and hard and Lauren seemed just as lost, just as needy. She hugged his neck, ran her fingers through his hair and he deepened the kiss even more.

"Lauren?"

It was Loretta calling out from her room. He froze and stared at Lauren. She stared back, wide-eyed. She waited a beat and then said, "Y-yes, Mama?"

"Okay, just making sure you got home from your walk."

"I did, Mama. I'm in bed."

"Good night, sweetheart."

"'Night, Mama."

Cooper released her and ran a hand down his face.

*Oh, man.*

Lauren seemed equally stunned.

"Cooper, what was that?" she asked so softly he could barely hear her.

"That was me, not being brotherly. Not being smart. God, I'm so sorry, Lauren. I was worried about you tonight and that was my relief coming out. That's all it was. I promise you."

"But, Cooper. That kiss was—"

"All wrong, Lauren. It was a mistake and I take all the blame."

"Blame? You're constantly blaming yourself for everything. I had something to do with that kiss, in case you didn't notice." She was whispering but her words rang loudly in his ears. He wasn't buying them. He couldn't.

"I noticed. But, no." He began shaking his head. "No. I got caught up in the moment is all. I'm sorry and I hope you can forgive me."

With that, he strode quietly out of her room.

Heading straight for the bar and a double shot of whiskey.

The good stuff.

Lauren sat up in bed and rubbed her temples. She hadn't gotten much sleep last night. The ache in her leg and the memory of kissing Cooper—just the way she'd fantasized as a young girl—made her fuzzy-brained. It was an awesome kiss, filled with passion, filled with heat. He was a take-charge kind of guy and he'd certainly taken charge of the situation last night. Being in Cooper's arms had been heavenly. And that kiss, though way too brief, had blown her mind. Cooper's reaction told her it was good for him, too.

What had provoked it? He'd said it was over his concern for her. That, she believed. But could it be more? No one had ever kissed her like that before. Not even Roger.

She chewed on her bottom lip. She shouldn't be comparing the two men. Roger was her fiancé. She was planning their wedding. And last night with Cooper was just a fluke. Something he said wouldn't happen again. She had to believe him. Didn't she?

Strong midmorning sunlight poured in through the shutters and warmed her skin. The day had begun without her. Maybe it was a good thing she'd missed breakfast. How would she react when she saw Cooper today? It would be weird, that was for sure.

She swung her legs over the edge of the bed and her feet hit the floor. Putting slight pressure on her injured leg to test it, she rose. There was no pain that made her wince, thank goodness, just a dull ache that would fade with time and pain meds. The gash wasn't deep enough for stitches, but it was long and ugly. Still, not as bad as it could've been.

Thirty minutes later, after washing up and dressing, she was ready to face the day. She limped to the window and looked out on the ranch, which was already bustling with activity. There was a soft rapping at her door. Her mama was probably wondering why she had overslept and missed breakfast.

"Mama, I'll be right there."

She limped to the door and opened it.

"Not your mama," Cooper said, briefly smiling. Surprised, all she could do was stare into his blue, blue eyes. Dressed in jeans and a crisp, tan shirt, he stood tall in the doorway, concern on his face.

"No, I can see that." She gulped air.

"I came to check on you. How's the leg?"

"Better. The pain is manageable and I'm walking...well, limping. I'll be fine, Cooper."

"Good to hear." He sighed and rubbed the back of his neck. "Listen, about last night."

She froze. He wanted to talk about the kiss? In the light of day? She braced herself against the doorjamb.

"I don't want things to be awkward between us, Lauren. What happened was about me being worried."

"So you said last night."

"It's the truth. I hope you and I can put this past us. We're friends. I don't want to ruin that."

"No, I don't, either, Coop."

He smiled and a shot of heat warmed her up inside. Apparently he liked it when she used his nickname. She had to remember not to do that again. "Okay, then. We're good?"

She nodded. It was in both of their best interests to lock that kiss up and toss the key away. "Yeah, we're good. Of course."

"I'm really glad you're feeling better."

"Thanks."

"Oh, and when your mother came down to breakfast, I explained what happened…about you getting hurt. She was concerned but wanted you to rest. She's downstairs now, cooking up your favorite breakfast. If you don't go down, she'll probably come up and check on you."

"Sure, I'll go down."

"Need help with the stairs?"

Thinking about him touching her again after that kiss put fear in her heart. The good kind of fear, that thrilled and excited and immediately an image of Roger nestled into her brain. Goodness, she'd almost forgotten about him. What a terrible fiancée she was. "No, thanks. I can manage."

He stared at her a moment, the handsome planes of his face immovable. It was hard not to get caught up in that stare. "Okay, then," he rasped. "Have a good day, Lauren."

She took a big swallow. "Thanks. Same to you."

He walked away and after she closed the door she pressed her back up against it.

Boy, that conversation was weird and *awkward*. Maybe it was just her. She'd have to get over it. She had enough on her plate right now. And her dear Roger was coming out to the ranch this afternoon.

She smiled. Once she saw him, she'd get her head on straight.

Cooper locked himself up in the study and concentrated on the files on Tony's laptop. He wasn't a numbers man and all the accounts looked in order. But then, he wouldn't know it if a big fat discrepancy jumped up to bite him in the ass. He had no clue what he was looking for. The files were massive, with contracts and conditions and specs for new building projects as well as the ones they'd already completed. Real-estate development was more complicated than the running of a ranch. Maybe he hadn't given his buddy enough credit for his smarts.

After two hours of digging, Cooper found a folder named Family. Clicking on it, he leaned back in his chair and smiled as pictures came up of the Abbotts. Of course, Tony would keep photos of his family on his personal computer. They'd meant a lot to him. He eyed a photo of the whole Abbott family: a young Loretta with her husband David, Tony and a pip-squeak Lauren, smiling into the camera on their front doorstep. He was guessing Tony was probably twelve and little Lauren was about six when the photo was taken.

He clicked on the next batch of photos and watched the family evolve before his eyes. Lauren in grade school. Tony playing football, graduating middle school. Christmas. Easter. Fourth of July.

His own scrawny face popped up in some of those photos. He shook his head, laughing at himself. "You were one skinny dude, Cooper," he muttered.

He'd forgotten some of those moments, but their documentation brought everything racing back to his mind and he found himself smiling and missing his best friend.

Some days it was so bad he'd absently reach for his phone to call his buddy and then it'd hit him all over again. Tony was gone.

"I'm trying," he said to a photo of the two of them sitting inside their fort. "Trying to find the truth. Trying to help Lauren."

He clicked on another photo in the folder labeled Lauren's Nursing School Graduation. And there she was in her pristine nursing uniform, a little cap on her head, looking serious with a proud gleam in her eyes.

"Beautiful," he murmured.

Kissing her had been crazy, but he'd never expected to react to her with so much heat. Hot need had poured through his veins once he'd tasted her and, heaven help him, where that kiss would've taken them if Loretta, calling from the other room, hadn't interrupted them. He shivered at the notion.

Lauren had participated fully, too. She'd been giving and generous, soft in his arms and… No, he didn't want to think about it. She was forbidden to him. And, damn, if that didn't test his strength. He'd given up women after Tony's death and he wasn't about to break his own vow with the one person he was trying damn hard to protect.

One thing was certain: he wasn't going to seduce her away from Roger. That notion had never crossed his mind when he'd come up with this plan. Especially now, after kissing her—a kiss he couldn't take back—he was even more determined to get the goods on Kelsey as quickly as possible.

He was ready to click out of the pictures folder when another subdirectory caught his eye. Uncle Bucky. As far as he knew there was no Uncle Bucky in the Abbott family. It was a code word he and Tony used as kids. When their roughhousing got out of hand, one of them would call "Uncle" and the other would say "Uncle who?"

Uncle Bucky meant stop at all costs.

Cooper clicked on the folder and another subfolder popped up.

Winding Hills Resort.

The name rang a bell. Tony had mentioned it before he'd died.

This might be exactly what Cooper was looking for.

Lauren sat at the kitchen table writing out her wedding invitations. She had pretty handwriting; at least that's what she'd been told by her friends who often asked her to do the invitations for special occasions. She'd helped with invites for Katy's brother's swearing-in party when he became an officer with the Dallas police department, as well as a few other friends who were getting married. She didn't mind doing it. It sort of felt like therapy, and just knowing she was helping her friends made it all worthwhile.

She concentrated on each envelope, keeping her lines straight, her letters even. Halfway through the stack, her mother came into the room, her shoulders slumped, worry lines around her eyes making her look ten years older.

Lauren stood from the table, her heart in her throat. "Mama, what's wrong?"

"It's Sadie, honey. She's had a stroke." Her mom began shaking her head. "I knew something wasn't right with her. She wasn't herself. She was all alone in that big house when it happened. Good thing the mailman was delivering a package to her door and heard her calling out."

Tears dripped down her mother's face. "I just got off the phone with her doctor's office. I was on her emergency contact list. Honey, I know the timing is bad, but I have to go see her."

"Of course, Mama. Of course. Do you want me to drive you?"

"No, sweetheart. Don't stop what you're doing. You've

got a hundred details to get to and I'm only sorry I can't be here today to help with your invitations like I promised."

"It's okay, Mama. I've got everything under control. And Roger's coming out today. So, I'll have his help. You go on." She hugged her mother, giving her a big squeeze. "I love you, Mama."

"I love you, too, honey."

That's when she noticed the luggage sitting in the kitchen doorway. "Are you staying overnight?"

"Oh, I think I'll have to. I don't know how long I'll be, honey. It depends. Sadie's only son is stationed overseas. With him being a career soldier, who knows when he can get back to see his mother. She doesn't have anyone else but me."

"I know, Mama. She needs you. And I've got Katy and Roger to help me."

"All right." Her mother sighed. "I'll be on my way now. If you're sure."

"I'm sure."

"And your leg? How's it feeling this afternoon?"

"Better. It's just ugly, but the pain's almost gone. Don't worry about me. You just be careful." She kissed her mother's smooth cheek. At sixty-two, her mother still had soft and supple skin. Hopefully those good genes would be passed down to her.

Being a nurse all those years had kept her mother fit and toned, too. They said you never got over being a nurse. The nurturer inside always came through. For her mother, that was certainly the case.

"Here, let me see you out," she said.

She picked up the suitcase and walked her mother to the car. Her sore leg was healing; she was barely limping now and that was a good thing. She stowed the luggage in the trunk and kissed her mother one last time before sending her off. After watching her pull away, Lauren lifted her face to the sun. The rays beat down, soaking into her skin, announcing the coming of June.

Images of her wedding day by the lake poured into her mind. She hoped for a beautiful day like today to speak her vows. She hoped for everything to go smoothly.

"Your mama going somewhere?"

Startled, she jumped and spun around to face Cooper. She pushed at his chest. "You scared the dickens out of me."

His chest was granite and he remained immobile, except for the wide grin spreading across his smug mug. "Sorry."

He didn't sound sorry. "Where did you come from?"

"I've been locked away in my study. Working. You didn't answer my question. Where's your mama going?"

"Our neighbor Sadie had a stroke this morning. Mama went to sit with her at the hospital."

"That's rough."

"Yeah, it is."

"I noticed you putting her luggage in the trunk."

"She doesn't think she'll make it back tonight." And then it dawned on her: she would be alone with Cooper in his big, beautiful house. "But Roger's coming," she blurted. Yes, things were definitely weird between her and Cooper since that kiss. "He should be here in an hour or two."

Cooper nodded. "Okay. Well, then, I guess I'll see you later. I'm heading over to my brother's right now."

"Okay. Tell Jared I said hello."

"Will do."

With that, she entered the house and headed straight for the kitchen to finish addressing her invitations. Tomorrow morning they'd go out in the mail and that would be one more thing she could cross off her list. She was making progress.

By three o'clock, she was done. Her cell phone rang and she picked up right away. "Hi, Katy."

"Hey. How's it going? This is the maid of honor daily call."

"It's going good. Got the invitations all done. But I, uh, got a little hurt last night."

"What does that mean? How hurt?"

"It's not too bad and it should heal in time for the wedding."

"It's gonna take three more weeks to heal? What on earth did you do?"

Lauren took a minute to give Katy the details about her stumble in the dark.

"So, hunky Cooper came to your rescue? Did he carry you up the stairs and into your bedroom?" Katy joked and when Lauren paused overly long to answer, a loud gasp resounded through the phone line. "He did. He pulled a Rhett Butler?"

"I couldn't walk and, yes, he carried me up the stairs."

"Oh, man, to be a fly on that wall."

"Nothing…happened. Uh, much."

"What does 'uh, much' mean?"

"You know how much I love Roger, right?"

"Yeah, I do. He makes you happy and that's all I care about. So…what aren't you telling me?"

"It's just that…well, Cooper kissed me last night. But he claimed it was only a nervous reaction because I scared him when he couldn't find me and…well, he was worried sick about me."

"And what did you do?" Katy asked.

She sighed, recalling the mind-numbing kiss that had ended way too early. "I kissed him back."

Katy's "wow" was less than a whisper.

"It's just that…you know I've had an on-and-off crush on Cooper since forever. So, I indulged. Out of curiosity. That's all it was."

"Because the kiss was lousy, right? Tell me it wasn't any good."

"Okay, yes, it was a...lousy kiss." She might go straight to hell with that lie.

"Liar."

There was no fooling her bestie.

"Because just on general principles alone, a guy as hot as Cooper Stone would definitely be a good kisser," Katy persisted.

She didn't want to think about it.

"Lauren?"

"Hmm?"

"What are you doing?"

She had no clue. She wasn't even sure why she'd told Katy about kissing Cooper. It wasn't as if anything was going to happen. Cooper had said it himself. It was a mistake. And she had to agree with him.

"What I'm doing is waiting for Roger. He's due here any minute."

"Okay, good." Her friend sighed in relief. And Lauren felt better about everything, too. Roger would make things right.

"I almost forgot the reason I called. That country band I told you about has a weekend gig starting this Friday night in a little honky-tonk in town. Maybe you and Roger could check it out."

"That's a great idea. Thanks, Katy. The best maid of honor ever."

"Yeah, I'm getting the hang of this. It's fun. And I'm emailing you a list of caterers I found. I think you'll find someone on there you can use for the wedding dinner."

"Perfect."

The doorbell chimed and Lauren instantly rose. "Someone's at the door. I think Roger's here. I'd better go."

"Tell him I said hello. 'Bye, Lauren."

"'Bye, Katy."

Lauren straightened out her clothes. She'd meant to change from her slacks into a dress, but her wound wasn't a pretty sight. And Roger had complimented her once on this pale sage blouse. Taking a look at herself in the foyer mirror, she finger-combed her hair and then went to the door. Taking a deep breath, she opened it. "Roger, I'm so glad you're here."

"I made it." He removed his sunglasses, looking very *GQ* standing there in a slate suit and charcoal tie. He bent to give her a peck on the cheek. "This place is quite a drive from civilization."

"It's just twenty miles from town. And it's beautiful here. Come inside." She took his hand and led him into the parlor. "I can't wait to show you everything."

"Yeah, about that. We have to make it quick. I've got an early flight out tomorrow morning."

"Tomorrow?"

"Yes, at 8:00 a.m. I'm right in the middle of this big project, Lauren. And I've got meetings in Houston and San Antonio."

"But I have a lot to talk to you about."

He gave her hand a squeeze. "I know, but we were supposed to have a small wedding, babe. Remember? I told you, if you wanted to do this, you'd be pretty much on your own. And I'm here now, so show me what you want to show me. I can stay a couple of hours."

"Just a couple?"

Her disappointment didn't seem to unsettle him. He smiled, showing off pearly white teeth and distracting twin dimples. Cradling her in his arms, he murmured, "Yes, and I can think of better things to do with you than go over wedding plans."

She pursed her lips. Going to bed was Roger's answer to settling their disputes. Not that this was a dispute or anything, but right now, his charm wasn't working on her. Their wedding plans were important and even though he'd told her he couldn't get involved in the details, she'd thought he'd be around more to give his opinion on things.

"Roger, it's just that I thought we could have dinner and spend some time together."

"We will, Lauren. Once I get back from this trip next week."

"You're leaving town *for a week*?"

He sighed and shook his head. "Lauren, after we're married, we'll have a ton of time together. You know this project is important. It's something Tony and I worked on together. And now the brunt of the work has fallen on me."

"Sorry my brother's death gave you a heavier work-load."

She squeezed her eyes shut. *Oh, man.* Had she really said that? Was she resentful of Roger because he put his work ahead of their wedding plans or was she still hurting because her brother wasn't there to build his company as he'd always dreamed?

"You don't mean that," Roger said. "You know Tony wasn't just my partner, he was a friend. I'm only trying to hang on to the company we built. For Tony as much as for us."

A knot formed in the pit of her stomach. She felt small and ridiculous for suggesting such a thing. Of course, Roger was working super hard doing the work of two men, trying to hold on to the deals that were made while Tony was alive. She was a partner in the company now and had no knowledge of what went on there. She had her own career. Roger was taking it on all by himself. For both of them.

"I'm sorry," she said. "I really didn't mean it. I shouldn't have said that."

She didn't understand why she'd blurted it out, but

Roger smiled after her apology. He didn't hold a grudge and he understood she was still grieving for her brother.

"Are you going to show me that lake now?"

"Yes, of course. It's just a ways down the road. And this is the perfect time of day to see it."

Exactly two hours passed. After showing Roger the lake, and being given a lukewarm okay to hold the wedding there, she also discussed the possibilities of caterers and bands with him and showed him his own wedding invitation. She'd texted him a picture of it, but at least now he'd seen it firsthand. Not too much else had been decided from their talk and now her allotted time with him was up. She stood next to Roger by his midnight-blue Cadillac.

"You're doing a great job, Lauren. I've got faith in you," he said.

She didn't want to be a Debbie Downer, so she gave him a smile. "Thanks. I'm doing my best. I hope it's good enough."

"It'll be fine." He sounded dismissive. As if, as if… he really didn't care. They could have just as easily been talking about what movie they would see next, for all his enthusiasm. But she wanted more than fine. She wanted to start her married life off with fireworks, not a caution sign. And Roger was definitely sucking the joy out of her wedding plans.

"Hey," he said, tilting his head and eyeing her. "Don't pout. Although, on you it's kind of cute." He glanced at his watch. "Oh, damn. I've gotta run. I have to pack and put together my agenda for the next week. Sorry, babe."

"It's okay. I get it. Have a good trip, Roger."

"Will do." Then he pulled her into his arms and kissed her solidly on the lips. His hand slid through her hair and she was momentarily lost. But his kiss didn't have the usual impact. She was miffed at him, but when Roger finally broke it off, he didn't pick up on her mood.

Or if he did, he was in too much of a rush to deal with it. Or her. "I'll call you," he said. "I promise."

"Okay. Talk to you soon."

After he pulled away, she stood there on the walkway a few moments until his car was out of sight. Then she turned toward the house and found Cooper standing on the veranda, his arms folded across his chest, his blue gaze pinned on her, as if he'd been there a long while. He looked rugged and solid, the scruff on his face more attractive than he could ever know. The contrast between Roger and Cooper wasn't hard to notice. *GQ* versus *Modern Cowboy*. City versus country.

An unexpected queasiness settled in her belly. And the reason pounded in her skull. Roger had ticked her off and now Cooper was there. Making her heart do little tiny flips.

Wow. She couldn't go there. Ever again. She'd *flipped* over too many guys in her past and that phase of her life was dead and buried. She wasn't a boy-crazy young girl anymore. She had a reputation of being fickle and indecisive to live down. Not just for her family and friends, but for herself, too. She'd outgrown her silly crushes and fantasies. She wasn't going to allow herself any notions about Cooper Stone.

Not when she had a good, stable fiancé to love.

She put up her hand and waved to Cooper. "Sorry you missed Roger."

He nodded and pivoted around, walking into the house. The door shut behind him. Kind of hard.

Had he just slammed the door on her?

# Five

Locked in his study again, Cooper was pissed and anxious and frustrated. Seeing Roger kissing Lauren goodbye ticked him off on too many levels. It'd been hard to watch. He ground his teeth together; at this rate, he'd have those back teeth worn down to a nub in no time.

The look on Lauren's face after Kelsey had left the ranch was stamped in his mind. The guy couldn't spare her more than a few hours? He was a jerk and wasn't fit to touch Lauren, much less marry her. One glance at her sad face when she'd turned to Cooper tugged at something deep inside. His anger boiled over to an emotion far more dangerous…jealousy. It was a sharp knife twisting in his heart. She deserved much better.

After an hour of going over inventory, Cooper shoved away from his desk and stared out the window. It was dark now. The sun had set a short time ago and there wasn't much to see. He sighed and picked up his cell, pushing his brother's number on speed dial.

"Hey, didn't I just see you a couple hours ago?" Jared said.

"Did you get a chance to look over those files?"

His brother laughed. "Are you serious? You dropped off the laptop—what?—three hours ago. I haven't looked at anything yet."

"Okay. Gotcha. I was hoping something glaring would stick out, is all. Something I overlooked."

"Maybe, but doubtful. Things don't work like that. It could take days, bro, if I find anything at all, so don't get your panties in a knot. You need patience, Coop."

Cooper ground his teeth again. "Yeah, that's not so easy. I don't have a lot of time. Lauren is…making a mistake."

"Yeah, I know. But unfortunately it's hers to make. I don't suppose you're getting in too deep?"

"What the hell does that mean?"

"It means, are you doing this for Lauren and Tony or for yourself?"

"Myself?"

"I've never seen you so invested in a…woman. You're chomping at the bit on this one."

"Fact is, I stuck my nose in and now I have to follow through, Jared. What was I supposed to do when Loretta came to me? I couldn't refuse her. And now that I know, or think I know, what this guy is up to, I can't drop it."

"So you don't have feelings for Lauren?"

"No."

"Okay, just checking. Because remember what happened between me and Helene. I don't want that to happen to you."

"It won't. Helene was lying to you the whole time."

"Just like you're lying through your teeth with Lauren."

"That's different."

"The fact is, I thought it was a casual thing until it wasn't. I was in over my head with her," Jared said, a bit of longing in his voice.

"She broke your heart."

"She used me and, yeah, broke my heart. I've been over Helene for a while now. I'm more cautious and I don't get involved with women much anymore. But you're the one I'm worried about. You're deceiving Lauren and when she finds out, this won't end well."

"Hopefully, it won't come to that. Hopefully, you'll find something on the computer."

"No pressure or anything, bro."

"Hey, what am I supposed to do?"

"Butt out."

"It's too late for that. I'm worried about Lauren and Loretta. I couldn't stand it if these women get taken by Kelsey. Even if Lauren winds up hating me, she'll eventually come to realize I was only trying to save her and her company. She's got almost blind trust in Kelsey and I don't trust the guy. I know this is a big favor…"

"I'm on it," Jared said.

Cooper ended the conversation and strode out of the study. What he needed was to blow off steam. Let the weights and incline treadmill kick his ass and rid him of restless energy. He entered the gym with that in mind.

An hour later and totally wiped out, Cooper felt better. Nothing like a hard workout to clear the head. He entered the shower and hot steam immediately soaked into his abused muscles. He finished up with a shocking spray of cool water and then dried off.

Refreshed, he exited the shower area and came face-to-face with Lauren.

Her eyes widened and her lips parted. Her surprised expression probably mirrored his own. "Oh, I'm so sorry."

Her gaze dipped down to the towel wrapped around his waist. The only thing he had on. She swallowed hard, blinked and looked back up at his bare chest. A warm gleam entered her eyes.

*Dang it.* Why'd he have to go and notice things like that? He forced a smile. But he was noticing more than her eyes. Her neon-pink bikini, for one, caught his attention, as well as the luscious swells of her breasts, her flat, toned stomach and all that creamy, exposed skin. Before he could get more than a glimpse, she hoisted her towel up like a shield of protection.

"Don't be sorry," he managed to say, the sound more like a croak.

"I didn't mean to disturb you. I was going to soak in the indoor spa for a few minutes. For…my leg."

It was too late not to be disturbed. She was hot. And sexy. And sweet.

He secured the twist of towel at his waist and tried to think about cow dung to keep his body from reacting to her. With no real barrier but his towel, she might easily figure out where his thoughts were heading if he wasn't careful. "Be my guest."

"But, uh, are you sure? You're done in here?"

*So done.* "Yeah."

He gave her leg a glance. It looked better; the color was coming back. She should heal just fine. "I think it's a good idea."

"Thanks. I'll just go…" she said, backing away from him. As if…as if she was thinking the same thoughts he was. Any awkwardness they felt couldn't compete with the edgy desire floating in the air. It was scary.

"What happened with Roger?" he blurted. It wasn't as if he wanted to prolong their conversation, but he had to know what was going on between the two of them.

"He likes the lake for the ceremony."

"Good. He didn't stay too long."

"No, he had business. He's going to be gone a week."

The son of a bitch. Cooper kept still, holding back a reaction.

"It's just inconvenient," she continued. "I was hoping we could…never mind. You don't want to hear all this. I'll manage."

Her meek tone of disappointment singed his nerves.

"Hey, have you had dinner yet?"

"No, I wasn't too hungry before."

"Marie left us tamale pie. I was going to have some out on the pool deck. Want to join me later?"

She hugged the towel tighter, so it covered up all her lush parts. He was partially insane for inviting her to dinner so late at night, but the sane part of him wanted to put a smile back on her face.

"Sure," she said. "I'll meet you outside…say, at nine?"

"Yeah, nine is good. You go on and enjoy the spa."

"Okay, thanks again." She turned, still tightly clutching the towel to her front.

But he got a sweet view of her ass and the soft folds of skin that didn't quite make it into her bikini bottoms as she walked away.

The dim overhead light, clink of utensils and laughter and shouts of noisy patrons gave the honky-tonk the ambience it needed to draw a small crowd for open mic weekend. The band Lauren came here to see was about to play. Her partner in crime, Katy, had come down with a stomach bug suddenly, leaving Lauren in the lurch tonight.

Her eyes touched upon Cooper, her stand-in fiancé, who looked every bit the part of a swoon-worthy cowboy in a black felt hat, snap-down, blue-plaid shirt and crisp new jeans. He'd been a good sport about taking her tonight. Not that she'd asked. He'd insisted. A woman alone in the Dallas Palace meant one thing—getting hit upon over and over—and he'd offered to spare her that complication. So here they were.

"Want another beer?" he asked from across their café-size table.

"Sure," she said. Why not be adventurous?

Cooper caught the attention of their very blonde, very buxom waitress and lifted two fingers her way. She gave him a nod and if that coy wink was accidental, Lauren would eat his hat. She'd noticed the attention Cooper drew from female eyes the second they'd walked into the place. She had no right or reason to be jealous.

Heavens no.

Yet a sharp pang kept jabbing at her belly every time a woman eyed her...friend.

She certainly hadn't had friendly thoughts about him last night in the gym. Not when she'd practically stripped him bare with her eyes. It hadn't been too hard, considering he'd been nearly naked at that point. The image of his powerful shoulders and chest ripped with muscles would haunt her for a long time.

But everything had gotten back to normal during their tamale pie dinner. Dressed casually and in a more subdued frame of mind, they'd simply relaxed on the patio deck and had quiet conversation over a delicious meal.

"I'm surprised you're not drinking whiskey," she said over the din of conversation surrounding them.

"Love to. But I need to keep my wits about me."

"I can drive home, Coop. If that's what you're getting at."

His gaze dipped to her mouth before he met her eyes.

Goose bumps erupted on her arms and a wave of heat filled her stomach. Maybe that's not what he meant at all.

"Yeah. Designated driver and all that."

Pulse racing, she nibbled on her lower lip, not quite sure if he was telling the truth. But just then Westward Movement took the stage and she sighed, relieved.

"There they are. Katy says they can play any kind of music and the vocalist is pretty good."

"We'll find out soon enough."

"Yes, we will. Before they go on, I think I'll use the ladies' room."

Cooper stood and pulled her chair out.

"Thanks."

She bumped a few shoulders on her way to the restroom at the back of the club. When she was done, she hesitated by the back wall.

It was Saturday night and she hadn't heard from Roger all day. On impulse, she dialed his cell phone number. She thought it odd when he didn't answer. Next, she called the hotel and asked to be connected to his room. After the first ring, a female voice answered. "I hope you're calling about our dinner. We ordered over an hour ago and we're starving."

"Uh, hello?"

"Is this room service?"

"No, this is Lauren Abbott. Who are you?"

There was a pause. Her pulse pounded as a few more seconds ticked by. "Oh, Lauren. Hi. I'm sorry. This is Roger's secretary, Pam. How are you?"

"Pam?"

Auburn-haired divorcée Pam Hutton was on the trip with her fiancé? This she did not know.

There was noise in the background and then Roger's voice boomed in her ear. "Lauren, hello, sweetheart."

"Roger? What's going on?"

"Nothing, why?"

"Because you…well, you didn't tell me Pam was going on the trip with you."

"You make it sound like a vacation. We're working."

"Working? It's almost ten o'clock on Saturday night."

"We're busy, honey. We've been working so hard, we

almost forgot to eat dinner. Don't tell me you're jealous? You know you don't have anything to be worried about. I'm doing this for us. For you and me."

"Still, Roger. I was surprised to hear her pick up the phone."

"Hey, I know. But…trust me. As soon as we eat, we're calling it quits. I have an early morning meeting tomorrow."

"On Sunday?"

"Yes, I'm meeting with the mayor of Houston for breakfast. If all goes well, the project will be approved. Tony would be pleased. Winding Hills Resort was originally his idea."

That was odd. She remembered it the other way around. Tony didn't think Winding Hills Resort was a good idea. He'd said they weren't ready for such a massive project. There was way too much risk involved and it could bankrupt the company if anything went wrong. But Roger had been pressuring him about it.

"It was? I thought Tony was against it?"

"No, you've got that wrong, sweetheart. Listen, I'm beat. How about we discuss it when I get back?"

"Okay." But by then it could be too late. She sighed. What did she know about real-estate development, anyway? Roger was the expert.

"Good night, sweetheart. Love ya."

"I love you…too."

He hung up first and she stood there with the cell phone to her ear, her stomach queasy. Rapid thoughts fired through her head and she shook them off. She trusted Roger. He'd given her no reason not to and, besides, if he'd asked, she would've told him she was out having drinks with Cooper Stone at a honky-tonk. Innocent as it was, her fiancé might have gotten the wrong idea, too.

That settled, she returned to her table and to Cooper.

The band began playing a cover of a Lady Antebellum song, about needing and wanting in the middle of the night. The vocalist brought the message home with grinding clarity, the tune touching deep into Lauren's soul. When she glanced at Cooper, his attention wasn't on the music. It was on her.

"Everything okay?" His blue gaze caressed her face, calming her.

"Everything's good." Looking at him made it so.

Rising from the table, Cooper offered her his hand. "Dance with me, Lauren."

This was a mistake. A horrible mistake. But an image of Roger and Pam having a late-night dinner in a hotel room surged into her head and she grasped Cooper's hand, eagerly following him onto the dance floor.

It was awkward at first, with Cooper holding her at arm's length, but surprisingly his footsteps and fluid moves on the parquet floor eased the tension as he led her into twirl after twirl. They circled the space, laughing and grinning.

The vocalist's beautiful tone resonated in her ears and the band solidly hit every note. Patrons bumped into her, their bodies crowding her on the floor, and soon she was pushed closer and closer into Cooper's arms. He took it all in stride, never missing a beat, and the room seemed to wind out of control as she spun around and around.

When the song ended, beads of sweat drizzled down her forehead. She wiped at them with the back of her arm, completely disregarding feminine etiquette. Cooper's forehead was moist, too. Up close, his musky scent bombarded her senses.

He leaned over and spoke into her ear. "Want to sit down?"

She shook her head. She hadn't had this much fun in a

long time. "Not unless you're plum tired out," she drawled, mocking his stamina.

He raised an eyebrow, meeting her challenge. "Not on your life."

To her dismay, Westward Movement chose that time to play a sentimental ballad. But both of them refused to back down. Texans didn't shy away from a gauntlet thrown.

Again, Cooper kept her at a safe distance and they moved fluidly around the dance floor. The song was much slower than the one before. She shuffled her feet, matching Cooper's pace, and their bodies edged closer and closer as if magnetically drawn to each other.

Cooper's raspy voice reached her ears. "How does it feel being Roger's business partner now?" he asked out of the blue.

She blinked her eyes. "I don't know. It doesn't feel like anything really."

"So, you haven't gotten involved in Kelsey-Abbott?"

"No, not really. I leave all that up to Roger. Why do you ask?"

"Just wondering if the ER nurse is ever going to make it as a real-estate mogul."

She laughed. "Hardly. I can't read a contract for beans, but I sure as hell can read a medical chart."

Cooper nodded, and she got lost in the music again. As the soulful song continued, their legs brushed, her arms wound around his neck and her head rested on his chest. Her ears filled not with the music but with the steady and rapid beats of his heart. Wrapped up in Cooper, she lost sight of everything else. That couldn't be a good thing, but each breath they shared, each step they took, each innocent touch of their bodies, called to her and made her think stray thoughts.

*Dear Lord.*

She didn't dare look into his eyes.

She heard him swallow.

Scolding herself, she begged for mercy. She had to find a way out of this growing fascination she had for Cooper. She was done allowing her fickle mind to rule her destiny. She wasn't falling for Cooper Stone.

She couldn't.

She wouldn't.

She lifted her head from his rock-solid chest to tell him that very thing. To break away from his hold and to get a grip on her silly emotions. But one look into the blue blaze of his eyes and she was lost. Totally and unbelievably lost. The image of Roger she tried pulling up faded away like a speck of sand carried in the wind, and all she could see right now was this fine, magnificent man.

"Lauren," he rasped as he halted his steps. Taking her chin and lifting her face closer to his, his mouth came down slowly, giving her an out, giving her time to back away. But she was locked in, connecting to him as she had no other man. Feeling his desire underneath the belt buckle of his jeans wasn't helping.

His rough, rugged intensity captivated her. He was a man's man. A man any woman would want. And he was ready to kiss her again. And she…she didn't have the will-power to stop him.

He must have seen the turmoil in her eyes and then the final acceptance. He wasted not a moment. The man of action claimed her mouth, brushing his lips over hers, igniting a spark in her that flamed from the initial touch.

She hugged his neck harder, tighter, and he groaned deep in his throat. The kiss intensified and the first stroke of his tongue against hers sent her spiraling. Little moans erupted from her mouth as she kissed him back and settled into the luscious scent and taste of him.

Luckily, they didn't stand out in the smoky, crowded room. They weren't making a spectacle of themselves. But she could feel his arousal against her belly. She could hardly believe that Cooper Stone wanted her this way. He was, and had always been…unreachable.

But in the moment, she was his.

And it scared the life out of her.

The song ended and so did the kiss. They parted and stood facing each other on the dance floor, staring into each other's eyes. Cooper didn't try to explain it away. He didn't say it was a mistake. He just stood there, eyes gleaming, touching her even though there was no longer a physical connection.

"Miss Abbott?" a young-sounding man called out behind her. She swiveled around.

The guitarist with long brown hair from the band was smiling at her and she had to blink several times to rejoin reality. "Yes, I'm Lauren Abbott."

"Nice to meet you." He put out his hand and she took it. "I'm Jodie's cousin, Stevie Johnston. Jodie told me you might be interested in our band playing at your wedding." He turned to Cooper. "And you must be the lucky groom?" He put out his hand. "Stevie Johnston."

"Oh, no. He's not the groom," she blurted. "He's a… friend. Cooper Stone."

Cooper shook the guy's hand. "Nice meeting you."

Stevie eyed the two of them and blinked, passing off any confusion he might've had. "Same here. No pressure or anything, but if there's a song you'd like to hear us play during our next set, we'd be happy to accommodate you."

"Oh…um. No, that's not necessary," she said. "I think… you're a good fit. Your band is really good."

"Thanks. We try."

"Just curious. How did you know who I was?"

He grinned. "You probably don't remember me, but I was a patient of yours a few years ago. You treated me in the emergency room and I never forgot you. You were like an angel from Heaven, holding my hand while I cried my eyes out, thinking I might be dying. I was eighteen at the time and had crashed my motorcycle."

Lauren didn't remember. She'd treated too many accident victims to recall them all, but she wouldn't tell Stevie that. "I was just doing my job and I'm glad I could help you."

"You told me to give up motorcycles and follow my true path."

"Music?"

"Yeah, and as you can see, I took your advice."

She smiled.

"Jodie tells me you're still a nurse. That's a good thing."

"Thanks for saying that. It means a lot to me."

"Well, here's how you can reach me, if you're interested." He took a card out of his jean jacket pocket and handed it to her.

"Stevie, I'm glad you're doing well and, yes, I will definitely be giving you a call."

"Cool. Nice meeting you both," he said and then turned and walked back toward the stage.

Lauren headed for their table. The business card in her hand reminded her she was getting married in less than three weeks and had come there to hire a band for the wedding, yet all she could think about was Cooper and that hot kiss they'd just shared.

"I think we should go," she said to Cooper, fidgeting with her purse, refusing to look at him.

"Yeah," he said quietly. "Let's get out of here."

He didn't take her hand or offer his arm.

She had no clue what was going on inside his head.

Or, for that matter, what was going on in hers.

But she was about to find out.

# Six

The dark moonless night made the drive from Dallas with Cooper intense. A grating silence sliced the air. Cooper drove down the highway, his foot heavy on the pedal, the wheels of his SUV quickly eating up the asphalt.

Lauren's phone rang, the sudden sound nearly making her jump out of her seat. A photo of her mama's smiling face stared at her from the screen. She assembled her wayward thoughts and answered her cell. "Mama? Is everything all right?"

"No, dear. I'm sorry to say Sadie had another stroke. It's a mild one, but the doctors are concerned and I can't leave her side. She's going in and out, and it puts her mind at ease when she wakes up and sees me here. I wanted you to know I won't be coming back to the ranch tonight. Maybe not for a few more nights."

"Oh, I'm so sorry to hear that. But I'm worried about you. Where are you sleeping?"

"I've been showering and catching naps at Sadie's house. And I know my way around this hospital, honey.

Everyone's been very accommodating. Don't forget, I've worked here for years."

"I know. But, Mama, I'm not far from Dallas right now, I can come. Give you some relief."

"No. Don't do that, honey. I'll be fine. You have enough going on. And, honestly, I'm just sitting here with her." Then almost as an afterthought, she asked, "What do you mean you're not far from Dallas?"

"I went to see a band play tonight. We might use them for our wedding. Katy recommended them and they're just outside the city limits."

"It's late, honey. Is Roger with you?"

"No, Mama. He's not with me."

"Then Katy?"

"No, she's sick. Poor thing caught a flu bug. I'm with… Cooper."

"Oh, good." The relief in her mama's voice grated on Lauren's nerves. Blind faith, that's what it was. In Cooper's ability to keep her safe. The moon and the stars were lining up in his favor and she fought the notion, waging a war inside her head.

"Maybe I should move into Roger's apartment in town," she said. "To be closer to you."

Cooper's head jerked in her direction and she turned away from his intense stare. "I mean, he's out of town for several more days and I'm sure… I don't think he'd mind."

"Don't you dare leave Stone Ridge. Not on my account." Her mother's voice had a stern tone she didn't often hear. "You have appointments at the ranch. I know you've got tables to rent and caterers coming to give you quotes and florists coming out to see the lake."

"Yeah, that's all true, Mama." She thought about it a few moments. It would be inconvenient to move into town, even temporarily. She'd told Roger, since their engagement was short, she wanted to spend the remainder of that time with her mother. And he'd seemed perfectly fine with that. "Okay, I guess you're right. It's just… I feel bad for Sadie and for you."

"I'll be fine. You just concentrate on what you have to do."

"Thanks, Mama."

"Tell her hello," Cooper urged.

"Cooper says hello to you, Mama."

"Give that man a hug for me, will you?"

"I, uh, sure Mama."

"Good night, sweetie."

She hung up the phone, dropped it into her purse and stared out the window. Now what? She had Cooper on the brain. His scent traveled over to her, subtle and arousing, and the memory of that kiss was never far from her mind. They were going to be alone. For days. Together.

And that was only if she made it through tonight.

Thankfully, Cooper didn't say a word on the rest of the drive home.

Once he pulled into the garage and shut down the lights, she gripped the door handle and got out of the SUV, her high-heeled boots rapidly tapping against the garage floor. The door to the house was locked and Cooper brushed by her to open it.

As she entered, everything inside was quiet but for the tick-tocking of a clock in the parlor. Timed lights were on there and in the dining room, covering the high ceilings in beautifully sculpted shadows. She bypassed those rooms and headed to the staircase, Cooper just steps behind her. She was so mixed up inside, she wanted to lash out, to break something. Nothing was right anymore. Nothing seemed logical. Nothing made any sense.

She took one step up and then faltered. She couldn't go on this way. She couldn't go to sleep and wake up in the morning pretending nothing had happened between them tonight. Or last night in the gym. Or the first time he'd kissed her, either.

So she turned to face him. The shadows made him look dangerous and rugged and breathlessly appealing. But she couldn't let that sway her.

"Why'd you do it, Cooper? Why'd you kiss me?"

He ran his hand down his jaw and looked her straight in the eyes.

"You want the truth?"

"Yes," she said, taking a big gulp of air. "I want honesty."

"I couldn't...*not*."

Her brain didn't process that because she was shocked. "That's not a reason."

His eyes widened in horror that she didn't believe him. "It's the only one I've got."

"What, that you find me so darn irresistible that you can't keep from kissing me?"

Cooper took a step forward, gazing deep into her eyes, searching her face for a moment. "Apparently."

"Well, stop it."

"Is this where you slap my face and tell me to snap out of it?"

His *Moonstruck* reference didn't make her smile. This was serious. Cooper was messing with her mind. "Don't joke about this."

"I'm... I'm just as confused as you are, Lauren."

"And why is that?"

"Because there're a dozen reasons that I shouldn't be having this conversation with you. Mostly because you're here under my protection and I—"

"Your protection?" She scrunched her face up. Wow, was he off base. "It isn't the 1800s, Cooper. I don't need protecting."

The way his gaze latched onto hers frightened her a bit.

He wasn't kidding. Nor had he misspoken, if she read his expression correctly. What in hell was going on?

"Okay," he finally relented. "But why did you kiss me back? Have you asked yourself that question?"

"That's all I've been doing."

"And?"

She could only give him the truth, as she knew it. "It's because…well, I've had a crush on you."

There, she'd said it. She'd gotten her big secret off her chest. And now may the big blue ocean drag her out to sea, swallow her up and rid her of mortification.

"I know that."

She blinked. Her heart raced even faster than when he'd kissed her. "You do? How?"

"A guy just knows. And, of course, Tony had a big mouth."

"My brother told you! I didn't think he knew, either."

"Doesn't matter now. What does a teen crush have to do with tonight?"

*Oh, no.* She squeezed her eyes closed briefly. "Don't make me say it."

He shook his head, appearing entirely clueless. "Say what?"

Where was that big, blue ocean when she needed it? "That my crush lasted a bit longer than that, Cooper. And when you kiss me, it's just an indulgence of mine, because…because I've imagined it for so long."

Cooper stood there, immobilized. There was a stark expression on his face. His mouth was tight, his eyes blinking rapidly. Finally he scratched his head so hard a lock of hair fell onto his forehead. "So you're saying you kissed me back because of some fantasy notion in your head?"

*Gosh, kill me now.* "I wouldn't exactly put it that way. But, yeah, let's just say I was curious."

"Maybe the first time could be chalked up to curiosity.

But the way you kissed me tonight wasn't like a woman in love, about to be married to another man."

Tears rushed to her eyes. He was right, but it was all wrong and she wasn't going down that fickle road again. She couldn't be like her father. She couldn't leave one man for another time after time. She'd spent her entire teen years doing that very thing and it was time to stop. *Damn it.*

She summoned strength and lifted her chin. "It was curiosity, Cooper. It killed the cat, remember? Don't you see? It can't be anything else." She backed up onto the next step of the staircase and whispered, "It just can't be."

"Horseshit," he muttered. "We've been circling around this thing between us for days now."

"There's no *thing*, Cooper." There couldn't be, and she'd lectured herself a dozen times about this. She couldn't fall for the next best wonderful thing, even if Cooper Stone was that and so much more. She'd made a commitment to Roger and it had to stand. It had to be honored.

Nearly missing the next step in her retreat, she reached for the staircase railing behind her. At that moment, Cooper lurched forward, ready to catch her fall, but she backed far away from him.

"You're afraid of me," he said. It wasn't a question. "That tells me all I need to know."

Her heart pounded hard, a little voice singing sweetly in her ear, telling her not to listen to her brain, telling her to go with her heart. She didn't trust that voice. "You're wrong, Cooper. I'm not afraid of you. I'm afraid...of myself."

His dark blond brows rose, his face softening as his gaze locked onto hers.

She wanted to scream at the unfairness in all of this. "Please don't mess this up for me," she said softly.

Cooper's sigh echoed in the room. "I just want you to be honest with yourself."

"Why does it matter to you?"

"I care about you, Laurie Loo. If you love Roger, I won't stand in your way. Did you get a chance to talk to him today?"

It was none of his business. Really, it wasn't. "Yes."

"He called you?"

She nodded, and then because her mama hadn't raised a liar, she shook her head. "I called him." And found a woman in his hotel room. And Lauren was pretty certain he'd lied to her about that resort project.

But Cooper didn't need to know that. Cooper didn't need to know anything more than that she was engaged to be married very soon. And that's all there was to it. "I'm going up now."

"Go. I'll be down here, having a drink or three." He sent her a crooked smile. One that always charmed. And then he was gone.

"I don't know what I would have done without your help, Katy. All this wedding planning is overwhelming," Lauren said on a deep sigh. She appreciated her bestie spending her Sunday off here at the ranch, helping her decide on the caterer, ordering the chairs and tables, picking out the theme colors of sage green and pale pink. Tomorrow she had a florist and a photographer coming to see the wedding location.

How strange this all felt. It was as if she was living in two separate worlds right now. One where she was the devoted fiancée planning and anticipating her dream wedding, and the other where Cooper Stone was the star of her fantasies. She couldn't have it both ways.

She had to put what happened between her and Cooper aside and move forward with her wedding plans. Things were in motion and now it was too late to back out. Not that she wanted to. She wanted to marry Roger. She couldn't let a few kisses from Cooper tilt her world upside down. She felt guilty enough about those kisses. And her mind was set on getting married.

"Hey, no problem," Katy said, breaking into her thoughts. "It's fun. As long as I'm spending someone else's money, that is." Katy had a silly smile on her face. Thankfully her flu had only lasted one full day. Now she was as upbeat as ever. She sipped iced tea and glanced at all the papers strewed about the kitchen table. "Aren't you having fun, Lauren?"

"Uh…well, I suppose." Her hesitation was showing, and darn it, she didn't want Katy or anyone else to know she'd been having doubts. Her wedding day would be here before she knew it. "There's so much to do in such a short span of time."

"You know…you don't have to rush into this. If it's too much for you, you can always push the wedding date up."

"The invitations have already been sent." And there simply wasn't time for getting cold feet. She nibbled on her lower lip, her mind wandering to Cooper World. He was always halfway on her brain, invading her thoughts, troubling her, reminding her she was about to make a lifelong commitment. Shouldn't she be thinking of Roger during this time? Shouldn't she be anxious to become his wife?

She'd texted him twice today, asking him to call her. She needed to hear his voice. To be reassured and comforted by him. Up until now, he hadn't returned her texts or called.

Her fiancé was MIA.

Katy's arm came around her shoulder, warming her in a hug, something she really needed right now. "Hey, I can see something's bothering you. What's up? Wedding day jitters?"

A ridiculous tear emerged and slid down her face. She wiped it away with the back of her hand. "I'm not sure. This is silly. I'm an emotional wreck today. Sorry, Katy."

"Don't be sorry. I've heard lots of brides get like this before the wedding. And your wedding is on fast forward. I can see how all of this is making you a little emotional."

"Go figure, me being a bridezilla."

"You're not even close. Look how much you've already accomplished without much fuss at all."

"I guess so."

"Hey, you know what? We've been head deep in all this wedding stuff all day long. I think you need to let your creative juices flow on something else. Why not take advantage of this amazing kitchen and put your skills to use? You promised me you'd make me dinner here one night. Why not tonight?"

She wasn't in a creative mood at all. In fact, her mood was becoming glummer by the second. She hadn't seen Cooper since last night and her head was spinning. Where was he? How awkward would it be when they saw each other again? Why couldn't she put him and that kiss out of her mind?

Yet she didn't have the heart to refuse Katy's request. Her friend had helped her so much today. Plus, they'd skipped lunch. Making dinner in this to-die-for kitchen might just perk her up. "What should I make?"

Katy put her elbows on the table and rested her chin on her fists. "Surprise me."

It appeared she had an audience of one. "Okay. I'll do my best."

An hour and a half later, the skirt steak marinated in oils and garlic sizzled on the countertop grill, and bacon-wrapped asparagus steamed in a quick-fry pan. Lauren's corn soufflé was just about ready to come out of the oven. After she put together the quinoa salad drizzled with balsamic vinegar, Lauren's masterpiece meal was almost done.

"My mouth is watering," Katy said as she set out the dinner plates.

"I hope my cooking doesn't disappoint," Lauren said.

"Something sure does smell good in here." The sound of Cooper's voice brought butterflies to her belly. She turned, finding him leaning up against the kitchen doorway, arms folded, one boot crossed over the other, nonchalant. How could he be so calm? So incredibly at ease, when she'd been confused, frustrated and full of self-doubt.

"Oh, hey, Cooper," Katy said. "Are you joining us for dinner?" She took out an extra plate from the cupboard. "Chef Lauren has been working magic in your kitchen."

Lauren remained quiet as Cooper's gaze focused on her. "Chef Lauren? That's a new one."

"She's been dying to get her hands on your, uh…appliances." Katy's gaze darted from Cooper to Lauren and she immediately clamped her mouth shut.

*Oh, man.* This was weird. "Of course you're welcome to join us, unless you have other plans tonight?"

"No other plans," he said, his eyes meeting hers solidly. "But are you sure?"

She blinked and nodded. She couldn't very well ace Cooper out of his own kitchen. "I'm sure."

"Thanks. I'd love to try one of your creations."

"Great," Katy said. "Lauren's going to have to share these recipes with me. My brother's birthday is coming up and Pete's the ultimate bachelor, a cop who solves crimes but doesn't know a spatula from a potato peeler."

Lauren chuckled. "I wouldn't go that far. Pete's a pretty smart guy."

"Still, I think he'd love a home-cooked meal for his birthday."

"Go for it." Lauren turned back to her cooking and Cooper came up behind her.

"Need some help?"

Her heart sped wildly. She needed to get a grip. She spun around and crammed two pot holders into his hands. "Please take the soufflé out of the oven."

"Soufflé? Yeah, sure." He grinned at her and she made fast work of tending to the quinoa salad as he pulled out the dish and brought it to the island countertop.

A few minutes later they were all seated at the table, Katy chattering on and on about Cooper's cool kitchen and the wedding and anything else that popped into her head. Dear sweet Katy was the buffer Lauren needed between her and Cooper. And because of it, her nerves settled down as she glanced at Cooper, so strong, so incredibly sexy... yes, sexy. The guy couldn't help it. He was hunk material and she prayed that was all there was to her crazy infatuation.

Cooper made approving noises in his throat as he tasted the meal. "This is really good," he said.

"Thanks." She hadn't really said much to him at all tonight. "I love experimenting."

"So, did you always like cooking?" he asked as he forked up a piece of steak.

She nodded. It was a safe enough subject. "I was sort of forced into it. My mom worked long shifts at the hospital. So I'd play around with food, started following some cooking shows, and then got pretty decent at it. It was important for my mom to come home to a home-cooked meal already prepared for her. And it meant Tony didn't eat pizza and frozen dinners every night, too."

"You're amazing," Katy said. "Such a nurturer."

Cooper stared into Lauren's eyes and nodded. "The food's delicious. Katy's right. You are amazing."

Katy's eyes widened; Lauren's bestie clearly noticed there was something going on between them.

They finished the rest of the meal in silence and as soon as Katy scooped up her last bite, she rose. "Let me help with the dishes and then I'm out of here. I have to be at work early tomorrow."

"Don't be silly. You're not doing the dishes," Lauren said. "You've already done enough for me today."

Katy glanced at Cooper, who rose from his seat and began clearing off the table. "We've got this," he said. "But it was nice having dinner with you, Katy."

"Same here, Cooper. I'd better get going." She glanced at Lauren. "Walk me out?"

"Uh, sure."

Katy grabbed her hand and tugged her to the front door. "What on earth is going on between you two?" she whispered.

Lauren opened her mouth to deny any charges but then slammed her lips shut.

"There is something, isn't there?" Katy asked in a tone that required an answer.

Lauren nodded. "But I don't know where it's headed. And what to do about Roger."

"Are you saying you might be falling in love with Cooper?"

"I don't know. I don't know. What should I do?"

After Katy picked her jaw up off the floor, a look of sincere concern entered her eyes. "This isn't you being fickle, is it, honey?"

"I hate that word."

"I know, but this is serious. If you don't love Roger, or have any doubts, you need to break it off with him. You can't marry a man you're not sure about."

Lauren's shoulders slumped. "Oh, God. I know that. But what if it's just me being me. I mean, look at my father's history. Married and divorced four times. He couldn't choose. He was fickle."

"Your dad was a cheater. I'm sorry to say it so bluntly, but he was, and that's so not you. You're not like your father. You're a woman with a big, loving heart, and right now, if that heart isn't pointing you toward Roger, you need to recognize that. Soon."

"How soon?"

"As soon as you know."

Lauren let out a long-suffering sigh. "You're right. I have to figure all this out."

"You do that. And let me know if I can help in any way." Katy kissed her cheek. "I have faith in you. You'll work it out."

They hugged tight and then Katy was off.

Lauren took a steadying breath and walked back into the kitchen. Cooper stood by the sink with a dish towel on his shoulder, rinsing a dish. "Let me clean up," she said rather harshly and then softened her tone. "I mean, I made the mess. You must have something more important to do."

"Actually, I'm pretty free tonight." His eyes flickered over her body and a blast of heat rose up her neck. She was a mess, with flour smudges on her shirt and a grease stain on her jeans, her hair falling out of her tiny ponytail. "You go on. I can handle this."

Her sense of duty and her manners kicked in. She wasn't going to have Cooper clean the kitchen by himself. "No. You go on. I'll take care of this."

He didn't budge.

She walked over to the sink and nudged him away. Or tried to. Living up to his name, the man was made of stone. "Cooper." Exasperated, she reached for the soapy dish he held and the darn thing slipped, broke in two and sliced into Cooper's right hand. Blood spurted from his palm. Soon the entire sink was covered in it.

"Oh, no. I'm so sorry."

"It's okay," he said through clenched teeth.

It was so not okay. The pain must've been something fierce. She gripped his hand, quickly wrapped the dish towel around the cut and applied pressure. The towel soaked through and turned crimson immediately. She grabbed for another. "We've got to move. I need to stop this bleeding."

She held his arm upright and they strode out of the kitchen and up the stairs. She knew where the first-aid kit was stored: in his master bathroom.

She was such a fool for arguing with him. Such a fool for being stubborn. When would she learn? When would she see that fighting whatever this was between them was fruitless? It only caused more problems.

They made it into his bathroom quickly. "Lean against the counter." She pulled his arm over the sink and ran warm water over the cut. She cleansed it the best she could as blood continued to ooze out, but thankfully, not as profusely as before. "One second. Keep your hand still."

She grabbed the first-aid kit from the cabinet and took hold of his hand carefully. The wound was about half an inch long, not as bad as she'd initially thought. She applied antibiotic cream to his palm, gently working it in, and then wrapped a gauze bandage between his thumb and index finger, winding it around and around to immobilize his palm. Tying it off, she studied her work. "There," she said. "How's that?"

"The patient will live," he said.

"I'll have to rewrap it again soon. But hopefully most of the bleeding has stopped."

He nodded, glancing at his bandaged hand.

"I'm so sorry, Cooper," she said. "I'm such a jerk for arguing with you."

"You're not a jerk," he said quietly.

"I am."

"If you insist."

She snapped her head up and found his eyes twinkling. During the crisis, she'd been working next to him by the sink, but now, as he turned toward her, she found herself sandwiched between his legs. Her heart sped and her mind raced. The most worrisome thing was that nothing about this situation felt wrong.

"You're teasing me?" she asked.

"You know what they say about payback…it's a bitch."

"I don't tease you…"

"Just every second of every day you're under my roof." There was reluctance in his tone, but sincerity, too, and her bones were beginning a slow, steady meltdown. "You're smart and sweet and pretty and—"

She put two fingers to his lips. "Shush."

It was a mistake to touch his mouth, to witness the blue spark in his eyes. To see him struggle with desire as much as she was. He reached up with his good hand and held her fingers there. Then he kissed them, one at a time, slowly, his gaze touching her as candidly as his kisses.

"Cooper," she breathed, but a refusal died in her throat. It was the only thing dead inside her. Everything else bounced and jumped and marched through her body like a thirty-piece band.

"What?" he said, unfolding her hand and planting tiny, moist kisses there.

*Strike up the band.*

"This isn't—"

"It feels right, Lauren. Like it's meant to be. Tell me you haven't felt it, too."

"Too many times in my lifetime."

"That isn't what this is about," he said. "And you'd be lying to yourself to say it was."

*Oh, God.* It was true. It was different with Cooper. He

wasn't only a crush. He was a friend, a man she admired, someone who would never hurt her. "I don't lie."

"Exactly," he said, taking her shirt into his fist and inching her forward a little bit at a time. When his gorgeous face lined up with hers, his lips came down hard, crushing and claiming and cradling her mouth in one generous kiss after another. Their hips met; her body, fluid and eager, meshed with his. This was no joke: the man was serious and every bit of his hard body was insisting she take notice. How could she not? How could she back away from a man she'd always secretly wanted?

She looped her arms around his neck and managed her engagement ring off her finger. She couldn't even think about Roger now, and what she would say to him. But the ring slipped off easily—it was never a good fit—and she palmed it into her pocket.

Did this make her un-engaged? In her heart, yes.

Cooper groaned and held her even tighter, his arms around her waist, pulling her closer. His arousal pressed against her, exciting her, making her whimper. Everything else around her dropped away. She was where she wanted and needed to be at the moment. With Cooper. It was like a freaking dream, one she'd had as a young girl, one she'd always wanted. But Cooper had always been forbidden, off-limits and, yeah, sort of an impossibility. Until now.

Their tongues touched, setting off an explosion in her body. Heat, passion and incredible want turned her inside out. Grabbing the material of his shirt, she pulled it apart—hallelujah for snap-down buttons—exposing his solid, rock-hard chest. Her fingers inched up his torso to palm the flat planes. His skin was hot, his heart pulsing under her fingertips.

"Coop," she whispered, pressing her lips to his chest. Kissing him, touching him, she was in Heaven.

He lifted her face from his chest, kissed her then moved her slightly away. "Fair play," he murmured. He began working the buttons of her shirt and soon the night air was cooling her flamed skin. In what seemed like one swift move, Cooper managed to get her shirt off and to drop her bra to the floor. Then his hot mouth resumed licking at her flesh.

He cupped one breast in his hand and suckled her, moistening her nipple. A shot of heat arrowed down her belly, traveled below her waist and landed at her core. "Ahhh," she cried, her voice high.

Cooper was merciless as he continued to the other breast. When she didn't think she could stand it anymore, he lifted her into his arms, kissing her as he strode the distance to his massive king-size bed.

They were both bare from the waist up, and after he lowered her onto his bed, he came over her like a giant, gorgeous beast. "You want this?" he asked, desperately searching her eyes.

She gulped and nodded. "I want this," she whispered.

It was a formality. Because in Cooper's arms, she was toast. He had to know it, had to feel it as strongly as she did. She craved him from deep down and it wasn't only lust, but much, much more.

The corner of his mouth twitched up as he nodded. He rose from her and cradled her foot in his hands. One shoe dropped onto the floor then the other. "Lift your hips," he commanded.

She arched her back and he unzipped her jeans and tugged them down and off her legs.

His gaze landed on her teensy-tiny bikini panties and he smiled. The bright hungry gleam in his eyes encouraged her boldness. When she might've covered up, she simply laid there naked and allowed him to look at her.

After removing his boots, he climbed onto the bed,

kissed her a dozen times and then moved down the edge of the mattress. He stroked her thighs, his caresses bold, demanding, and then he parted her legs. The scruffy whiskers on his face abraded the softest, most tender part of her body. And then her panties were gone and his mouth began an amazing torturous journey over her, inside her, kissing, stroking, his tongue gliding home.

She gripped the bedcovers and gritted her teeth. Moans of ecstasy poured out of her mouth. This was beyond heavenly. Beyond anything she'd ever experienced. He grasped her behind, lifting her slightly, and tasted her over and over, making incredibly erotic sounds with his throat. She'd never felt prettier, more desired. His fingers and mouth worked magic, and her cries echoed in the room as strong, hot waves built higher and higher inside her.

"Cooper," she called out as her final bit of restraint shattered in a moment of perfect release.

"I'm right with you, baby," he rasped.

Yes, he was. It was exactly where she wanted him to be as her sated body relaxed in the aftermath of her orgasm.

Cooper came up over her. "You are beautiful like this, but we're not done."

She smiled and curled her fingers into his hair. "I hope not," she said softly.

His deep ocean-blue gaze pierced her again, those rays homing in, killing her with the depth of his emotion and desire. "You've destroyed all my willpower," he said.

She closed her eyes, smiling. "I feel the same way."

He kissed her tenderly, suckling her lower lip and murmuring, "Maybe it's time we gave up the battle."

"I surrender," she said, meaning it from the bottom of her heart.

"Laurie Loo, you have no idea…"

She roped her arms around his neck and brushed her lips against his, over and over. "I think I do."

A guttural groan escaped his throat and he worked like mad pulling his jeans off. His briefs came next and then he was naked, rising above her, his form solid, rock-hard. And, oh, man, was he well-endowed.

She touched him, her fingertips sliding over his shaft, and he jerked back, surprise and pleasure twisting his face. Cooper seemed to inspire audacious behavior and, for her, it was new, exciting and incredibly empowering. She wanted more, to taste him the way he'd tasted her, and as she lifted up to do that very thing Cooper shook his head, pulling away. "I want you that way," he murmured, "but it'll be the death of me right now, baby."

Hunger blazed in his eyes and a desperate plea for understanding. He didn't want to deny her anything, but he was just as blown away as she was. Emotions filled her up inside and she nodded to him, telling him she understood.

He opened his nightstand drawer and came up with a gold packet. A moment later, sheathed in a condom, Cooper covered her mouth with his, his hands moving over the slope of her breasts and lingering there, caressing her to the point of unbelievable craving. Below her waist, her nerves pulsed, swamped with heat.

"Relax, Laurie Loo," he whispered, easing himself inside her.

Her body accommodated him, expanding to the length and width of him. Their joining brought tears to her eyes. But she wouldn't cry. Cooper couldn't get the wrong idea, that she was somehow sorry about any of this. Because, she was so *not* sorry. Being cradled in his arms, joined with him, his body slowly driving inside her, stroking her as he covered her in kiss after kiss, only brought joy to her heart.

This time, she hadn't made the wrong choice.

This time, she was in it for keeps.

All other men in her life faded away and only Cooper

was there, filling her. Granting her freedom from her otherwise bad mistakes.

She moved with him now, her body a physical and emotional mate to his. She touched him everywhere, caressing his back and shoulders, gripped the firm slope of his ass, and, oh, man, he was strong, powerful. She tugged on his hair, kissed the scruff on his face and licked at his skin.

It was better than any dream she might've had of him.

He was real. And glorious.

And as his thrusts grew harder, she rose with him, higher and higher, until she couldn't hold on any longer. Her second release came fast and hard, and her cries rang out, sounding blissfully tortured.

"Lauren, baby," Cooper rasped in awe as he, too, reached his uttermost climax.

He ground out her name as he thrust into her one last fulfilling time.

And then silence surrounded them.

He fell on top of her, spent and heavy, his skin still deliciously steamy. She held him tight and they lay together that way for beautiful seconds. Those moments of realization becoming precious to her. Was it that way for him, too?

Finally, Cooper rolled off her and gathered her into his arms. His eyes sparkling, a charming smile on his face, he spoke quietly. "Wow. That was something."

She laughed, joy crowding her heart. "I'll say."

"Are you all right?" he asked.

"I'm wonderful."

He nodded, and gripped her tighter, drawing her even closer. The subtle musk of his aftershave mingling with the scent of his skin was like an aphrodisiac. As if she needed any more reason to find him so darn appealing.

"Yeah, me, too," he said, his voice trailing off.

"Don't you dare head into la-la land, Coop."

"Why, you have more plans for me?" A wicked, totally endearing smile spread across his face.

"Darn right, I do. I have to change your bandage before you fall asleep."

"Before *we* fall asleep, Nurse Abbott," he said, kissing the top of her head. "Got that?"

"Loud and clear."

# Seven

Jogging beside Cooper the very next morning, a sense of freedom and exhilaration strummed through Lauren's veins. Since her time here, May had become June. The morning air was fresh and the sky gloriously blue, the rising sun casting a golden light onto Stone Ridge. This time, she kept up with him. Or rather, he slowed his pace to keep time with her as they cut a path away from the house, away from the stables and barns, running deep onto the property.

She noticed Cooper avoiding the lake and anything that would remind them about the wedding she had planned with another man. Honestly, she didn't know what was wrong with her. Normally, she'd be freaking out about this: the fact that she was so deeply in the moment with Cooper Stone while still formally engaged to her fiancé. She was going to remedy that as soon as Roger returned. She would break off her engagement in person. She owed him that much. It would be difficult, but Roger deserved to hear from her face-to-face.

Her head was finally clear and hopelessly wrapped around being with Cooper. So she ran on, with him at her side, a smile on her face and only good things in her heart.

Thirty minutes into the run, Cooper slowed his pace. "Ready for a water break?"

Sweat dripped from his forehead onto his T-shirt, his chest pumping hard, but it was clear he was stopping for her. They'd left cattle and grazing land far behind and she'd been struggling on the rocky uphill paths for a time now.

"I can go another few miles. But, sure, let's stop for as long as you need to."

He shook his head, mumbling something that sounded like brat, and led her to a patch of shade under an ancient tree. He was a good man. Always thinking about her, enough to slow his regular routine to make sure she was comfortable.

He'd sure given her a workout last night, a wondrous night she'd never forget. This morning she'd woken up beside him to watch the dawn light play over the rugged planes of his face. Blissfully happy, she'd curled her finger around a dark blond strand of his hair. When his eyes popped open, he'd smiled at her, and that one look had been enough to right her crazy upturned world. A few kisses later she'd been sure he was ready for round two, but he'd bounded out of bed and asked her to run with him.

They stood sipping from their water bottles, catching their breath. Early dawn had broken on this high ground, the land all around quiet and serene. Stone property stretched beneath them in all directions as far as the eye could see. From their perch atop this one hill, the ranch house looked miniscule.

Off in the distance birds chirped a cheery hello and soft breezes ruffled leaves on the trees. All in all, it was the perfect place to clear the mind.

She slipped her water bottle back into her belted bag.

"Wanna sit awhile?" Cooper asked.

She really did. "Sure."

She sat on a patch of grassy ground and Cooper sat behind her, spreading his legs out. "Lean back against me and get comfortable."

She did, and he wrapped his arms around her waist. He made a nice cushion, hard but accommodating. "This is nice."

"It is," he agreed, setting her ponytail to one side and kissing the slope of her neck.

"I'm all sweaty," she said, embarrassed.

"I like getting you sweaty. In all different ways."

She laughed at his nonsense. "Well, you surely gave me a workout this morning."

"Too much?" he asked.

"I'm holding my own."

"That's one of the things I really like about you. You don't complain or whine. You just get it done."

"Hardly. I'm not as decisive as I want to be."

Cooper sat up, closing in on her. His breath tickled her cheek and his voice lowered as he spoke into her ear. "Aren't we gonna talk about it, Laurie Loo?"

She squeezed her eyes closed. Thank goodness he couldn't see the pain on her face. "I don't want to." She didn't. It was messy and difficult and she wanted it all to disappear. Magically.

"You have to think about it sometime."

She touched the bare ring finger on her left hand. "I've already done something about it. In my heart."

Cooper didn't say anything. He sat stiff and motionless for what seemed like eons. It worried her. Was it too soon to speak about her heart's desire? Was he sorry they'd slipped last night? Now could they never go back to just being friends?

"Cooper, please say something."

"Okay. I will. Last night was the best night of my life."

*Thank God.* Her shoulders sagged in relief. She could finally admit to herself that it had been Cooper all along. He was the man for her. "Mine, too. I just need some… time to, uh, figure it all out."

Cooper dropped his hands away and she immediately missed him. "You want me to back off, give you time?"

She whirled around to face him. Sitting on her knees, she took his face into her hands. "No. Never. Cooper, I'm just asking for your patience… I've never done anything like this before in my life." Well, she had jumped from one man to another in the past. She'd just never slept with one man while dating and almost marrying another. "Tell me it's okay."

She kissed him and the explosion of fire and heat burned through her. The sparks that flew when they touched like this was proof positive that she was all-in with Cooper. She couldn't imagine herself with anyone else now.

But dealing with Roger and canceling the wedding made her stomach ache, so she backed away from the kiss. It was all too much, too soon.

"It's okay." Cooper sighed and rose from their little refuge. He offered his hand and she grabbed it and bounced up, too.

"Race you to the bottom of the hill," she said.

"You're on. I'll give you a head start."

"No way. I can hold my own."

"Just go, Laurie Loo. For once, don't argue."

That sounded like a good plan. She spun around and took off running as fast as she could, laughter rumbling from her belly and catching on the breeze. She ran long and hard, and from behind she heard the clop, clop, clop of Cooper's shoes pounding the earth. Just before she reached the bottom of the hill, he took the lead, his hand slapping her butt before he built up momentum and soared past her. Once he reached the bottom of the hill, he turned and waited for her.

"C'mon, slowpoke."

"Slowpoke, my ass."

He blinked and a wide smile graced his sweaty, gorgeous face. "I like it when you talk dirty."

She blew off that comment. It could get her in even more trouble. "Who knew you were so competitive."

"Guilty as charged. I don't take challenges lightly. I like to win and I don't apologize for it."

She thought about it a second. "I never knew that about you."

"I don't brag. I just get the job done."

Maybe she really didn't know the grown-up Cooper all that much. "I can see that."

"At least you're not a sore loser," he said, taking her into his arms. They were still far enough away from the house and any wandering eyes.

"I don't like losing, either. But I can handle it. Growing up without a dad around made me tough. There were no father/daughter dances for me, but I had my big brother when I really needed him."

"Yeah, and now you have me."

If only she knew what he meant by that. Did she have him? Or was this a fling? An affair to add a little spice in his life? Or worse yet, was she the guest of honor at Cooper's pity party for her?

Suddenly confused, she battled a surge of guilt about Roger, too.

Cooper's eyes softened and his rough, strong hands caressed her arms, stroking her with the gentlest touch. Her skin prickled and warmth spread up and down her body.

"Don't beat yourself up." It was as if he could read her mind. And then he bent his head and poured himself into giving her a mind-blowing kiss, one that took away her guilt, her remorse, her doubt. One kiss from Cooper could do all that.

"I'll try," she whispered.

"It's gonna be all right," he said, reassuring her. "Let's get going. I need a shower."

"I do, too."

Cooper's eyes danced as they touched upon hers. "I don't believe in wasting water."

Locked in his embrace, she couldn't focus on anything but him. And the charming, dastardly smile on his face. "You don't?"

"Nope. We all need to conserve…for the, uh, environment."

"The environment, huh?"

"Yeah, are you with me?" he rasped, touching his lips to hers again.

Her heart, pounding like hard rain, had yet to settle down. "Yeah, I'm with you, Coop," she whispered. How could she not be?

Water slashed over them, the pulsing shower washing off the sweat and heat of the run. Cooper lathered her up with a fragrant bar of soap. He turned her around and around, making sure every tiny part of her was well cleansed. "Feel good?" he asked.

"Hmm." He had no idea. Her eyes closed, she absorbed the rough yet gentle way he was washing her, his palms traveling the length of her body, over her shoulders, breasts, arms and legs. Then he spun her around and scrubbed her, sliding his soapy hands down the curve of her back and onto the slope of her ass. He spent a good deal of time there and a new heat began building in her body.

Reaching down, his fingers lightly touched her sensitive folds and she jumped.

"Hang on, baby," he said, kissing the back of her shoulders.

It was hard hanging on. Every touch was excruciatingly pleasant. And her mind was already twenty moves ahead, longing to join their bodies again. To feel the sensation of being one with Cooper. "When is it my turn?" she asked impatiently. She wanted her hands on him. To create the same sort of torture he was creating for her.

"Now would be a good time," he said, turning her around and handing her the soap.

The breath stuck in her throat when she saw his erection. It was hard to miss, and a crooked smile graced his face. "Clean me," he said.

She gulped and nodded, eager to touch him, to lay her palms on his body. She put her hands on his face first and kissed him. He growled from the depths of his throat and from then on it was a frenzy of palms on skin, touching, rubbing, caressing, the soap making it easy to glide and slide all over his massive body. She saved the best for last, making him wait, making him even harder.

Then she touched his shaft, her soapy hands wrapping around him and stroking up and down.

He clenched his teeth, gritting out words of encouragement. Empowered, she kept it up and, after a few more bold moves, he grabbed her wrists and stopped her. "Wait here."

A few seconds passed and when he returned, he was sheathed in a condom. The shower door closed behind him and water continued to rain down as he kissed her a dozen times and then she was lifted into his arms. On instinct her legs wrapped around his waist and he moved her to the stone wall of the shower. She was beyond turned on. She'd never made love this way before. It was so bold, so sensual.

Cooper nudged her with the tip of his shaft and as she opened for him, he impaled her with the full force of his erection. Their moans echoed against the tiled walls, competing with the pulsing thrum of the shower. She'd never felt so complete, so at peace, so totally willing to give herself up to this man.

His thrusts possessed her, claimed her, and the potent look in his eyes told her things that words alone could not say. She moved with him, giving him silent permission to take her to places she'd never been before. He pressed his tongue to her breast, licking the water off, kissing the very tip and creating white-hot heat that made her crazy.

She thrust against him now, her body arching up and then pressing down upon him, her arms clinging to his neck. "Ah, Lauren," he sighed.

In that moment, as her release was edging closer, she fell hopelessly in love with Cooper Stone. It wasn't about sex. It wasn't about lust or the fact that he was a rock-hard, gorgeous hunk. It was because she trusted him. With her heart.

"Coop," she cried.

"Babe," he growled through clamped teeth as he thrust one last time.

Seeing him shatter, seeing the intense look of pleasure on his face, was a beautiful thing.

And then she reached her climax—a tightening, final pulsing contraction that brought so much damn joy.

As they came down slowly, Cooper nuzzled her neck. "Oh, man."

"Wow," she said, still wrapped around his body, still joined to him.

"I like getting clean with you," he whispered.

"That's my line, Cooper," she said softly in the mellow afterglow of making love. "I've never been quite so *clean* before."

He chuckled as he turned off the spray and lowered her down, her feet hitting the pebble-tiled floor.

"Let's get dry," he said.

"Okay. I'd better go to my room. Just in case Marie comes in."

She pushed the shower door open and Cooper's hand came out around her waist, pulling her back inside. "Not so fast, Laurie Loo. Marie's not here. I gave her a few days off."

She blinked. "Seriously? You were so sure about this?"

Drops of water dripped off his broad shoulder as he shrugged. "Honey, I'm not sure of anything. But we need some privacy to figure it out." His mouth touched hers and he kissed her tenderly. "Unless you'd rather not be alone with me."

"I, uh, didn't say that." She curled her finger around a single strand of his dark blond hair. "I sorta like being with you. In case you haven't noticed."

"I was hoping."

Gosh, he made it easy for her to be with him. He was so damned understanding. What was she going to do if this turned out to only be a brief interlude? Cooper hadn't said anything about the future, but maybe it was too soon. He was considerate enough not to overwhelm her. She still wasn't free of Roger. She had to believe that whatever Cooper was feeling for her mirrored her own intense feelings.

No matter what happened between her and Coop, she was done with Roger. And he deserved to know the truth. She needed to break it off with him to his face. She needed to find the right words, to look into his eyes and tell him that she wasn't in love with him. Not the world-tilting, earth-shattering, heart-melting way she should be. She cared about him and respected him and only a face-to-face breakup would do.

Cooper opened the shower door and allowed her to step out first. She grabbed a fluffy white towel and he instantly took it out of her hands. "Let me."

"Okay, but as soon as you're through, I need to bandage you up again."

"It doesn't hurt anymore." He showed her his palm and she cringed when she saw the red gash. "I think touching you has healed me."

"If only."

"It could happen. You're soft and sleek and silky smooth. Especially when you're wet."

He used the towel to dab at her naked body, sopping up droplets on her breasts and belly and lower still, coming dangerously close to arousing her again. She struggled, distracted, the words jumbling in her head. "I do, uh, need to bandage you up, Cooper."

"Yes, Nurse Abbott."

At least he agreed and there'd be no argument. She'd injured him with her little act of rebellion yesterday and still felt bad about it.

He continued to dab beads of water off her shoulders and back, then wound the towel around her backside. As he slid it back and forth, his hands *accidentally* slipped off the towel onto her butt cheeks. He gave her a little squeeze. *Wow.* Her juices started flowing again. She should have been flaming red by now, but with Cooper, it didn't feel off or weird. It felt sexy as sin. And in another minute, she'd be pushing him onto his massive king-size bed.

When he was done, she wrapped herself in the towel and faced him. "My turn."

He frowned as she grabbed another towel and made fast work of drying him off. Then she wound the towel around his waist and tucked it in, to give herself a sliver of sanity. But in or out of his towel, Cooper was irresistible.

She found the first aid-kit easily. "You know, for a house this size, you should have a few more of these around."

"What makes you think I don't?" he answered, smiling.

"Oh." Surprised, she asked, "So where are they?"

"Pretty much in every bathroom on the premises."

She blinked. "But you…you…led me to believe you—"

He kept his lips clamped shut, but laughter burst from his mouth anyway.

"You rat. You deceived me."

"I couldn't help it," he rasped. "I wasn't thinking straight last night. I mean all that blood loss made my mind fuzzy."

She slanted him a look and grabbed his injured hand.

"Ouch! Nurse Abbott, your bedside manner needs—"

She raised her eyebrows as she anticipated his next words.

"No improvement," he whispered from deep in his throat. "In fact, I'd say your bedside manner is outstanding in every way."

She sighed. "Cooper, what am I going to do with you?"

"You really don't want me to answer that, do you?" His gaze traveled toward his bedroom.

"No, don't answer."

"Too bad."

Cooper flipped flapjacks on the griddle as bacon sizzled and steam rose up in the pan. It'd been so long since he'd cooked anything in this kitchen, much less breakfast. On the days Marie wasn't there, he usually ate cold cereal or buttered a couple of slices of toast. This morning, he was cooking for Lauren. It surprised him how much she was on his mind lately. It came as a shock, a jolt from out of the blue, that he could ever have been so doggone attracted to her. But hormones and lust didn't give a fig about propriety. When the two of them were together, their chemistry was combustible.

But now that he'd slept with her, he'd have to face some hard facts. He'd broken a long-standing code of honor: you don't mess with your best friend's little sis. Not even if you're trying to protect her. Not even if she was about to make the mistake of her life.

But they had slept together and now the dawning consequences were closing in on him. Would she ever believe that sleeping with her had nothing to do with his determination to expose Roger and make her see the light? Would he ever be able to convince Lauren that he wasn't seducing her to break up her engagement? Would she believe he had started out only wanting to keep her out of harm's way but his feelings for her had surprised him and complicated matters?

*Crap.* He was in deep.

But not enough to give her up.

Not enough to own up to the little scheme he'd concocted with Loretta.

"Whoops. Something's ten seconds away from burning." Lauren's sweet voice did things to him. A sense of joy and *dread* stampeded through his body as she rushed across the kitchen and up to the stovetop. She shut down the bacon and removed the pan from the heat.

"I like it crispy," she said, chuckling.

"I knew that." No, he didn't. His mind had drifted off and he'd become derelict in his master chef duties, thinking about Lauren. "I aim to please, ma'am." He flipped the last of the flapjacks.

Her arms came around his waist from behind and she pressed up against him. She gave him a little peck of a kiss on his throat. She was killing him. When he was with her, all deceit and scheming faded from his mind and flashes of a future with her entered his head. Flashes that were becoming brighter, clearer, more distinct. But it was too soon to say anything. Too soon to act on his feelings because, if he was wrong, Lauren would get doubly hurt. And he couldn't have that.

He hadn't planned on breaking up her engagement this

way. And how could he be sure his six-month long bout of celibacy hadn't influenced what he was feeling now? Was he falling for Lauren or had he just been overwhelmed by having a sexy, beautiful, forbidden woman under his roof every day?

*No. Strike that.*

The feelings he had for Lauren weren't just about lust.

He turned in her arms and kissed her full lips. "Breakfast is ready. Why don't you pour the coffee?"

Her face fell slightly, a hint of disappointment in her eyes. Hell, he wanted to kiss her senseless, but guilt was gnawing at him.

Lauren brought coffee mugs to the table and then set out maple syrup and butter while he dished out pancakes and the thick, almost-burned bacon to their plates. He noticed that lately she wasn't wearing her engagement ring. It was a sign, but she hadn't said anything to him about it.

They chowed down on the meal, speaking very little. Lauren's expression was unreadable, which was weird because she usually wore her heart on her sleeve. Right now, he had no clue what she was thinking.

He dove right in. "Have you spoken with Roger lately?" he asked quietly.

She put her head down and chewed her food thoughtfully. "Not since Saturday night. It was late and his secretary answered the phone."

"His secretary, huh? They were working in the office that late?"

"No, they were in the hotel room."

Cooper sighed. "So tell me, his secretary is gray at the temples and has been with him for years."

Lauren rolled her eyes.

"No?"

"Not even close. She's divorced and younger than me."

Cooper ran his hand through his hair, scratching at his scalp. "So…you haven't—"

"No, I haven't said anything to him. I figure I owe him an explanation face-to-face when he returns."

Which was in two days.

Cooper needed to say something to her. To make her feel better. To give her something she could hold on to. But the words wouldn't come.

His house phone rang and he stood to pick it up. "Hello?"

"Hello, Cooper. It's Loretta. How are you this morning?"

"Doing well. Just had some ridiculously good pancakes with your daughter. She's right here. Would you like to speak to her?"

"Yes, thank you."

He stared at Lauren and saw the misery on her face. Just a little while ago, she was beaming. All this talk about Roger Kelsey was getting to her. "Here you go."

He handed her the phone and began clearing the dishes. "Hi, Mama," he heard her say. "How's Sadie doing?"

Cooper left the room then to give her privacy. He walked into his study, plunked down on his big, cushy, leather chair and started going over accounts and purchase orders. There was a time when he could dig deep into the Stone Corporation and not come up for hours. Today wasn't one of those times. His mind was shot and the lack of concentration had everything to do with Lauren.

He ran a hand down his face.

And then heard her scream.

He dashed out of his study and ran toward the noise. His heart racing, he yanked open the front door and smacked right into Lauren's chest as she dashed into the house. Her eyes glazed over freakishly. He grasped her arms and steadied her. "What is it? What the hell scared you?"

"It's… I'm sorry. I'm usually not such a baby, but I was standing on the veranda drinking the last of my coffee and this…this *thing* scurried past me. I think it ran over my toes." She shivered. "Yuck. It was the ugliest creature I've ever seen."

"A possum?"

She nodded her head. "I mean, I've seen them on the road."

"Roadkill."

"Yeah, but I've never been that close up to one before. I think my scream woke the dead. Gosh, I'm so sorry."

"Don't be sorry. Sometimes my crew needs a good wake-up call," he said, cradling her shoulders and shutting the front door. He walked her into the large, formal, living room. Normally, he didn't set foot in there unless he was entertaining guests. It had been a good long time since he'd thrown a party. But the room was open and light, with tall ceilings and sitting areas where Lauren could calm her nerves. He led her to a sofa seat facing a large window that looked out on the pasture. The blue sky filled with white puffy clouds seemed almost touchable.

"This is silly. I'm an ER nurse for heaven's sake. I've seen a lot of horrible things."

"But you've never had an ugly-as-sin possum stalk you before."

She chuckled and her shoulders relaxed. "No, that much is true."

"How's your mama doing?" he asked. Changing the subject would help her, but it'd calm him down, too. After hearing her scream, he'd panicked and couldn't get to her fast enough. That alone unsettled him.

"She's doing well. Sadie is coming around. In fact, she's on the mend now and Mama's arranged for her to have assistance when she goes home. Should be in a day or two."

"That's a relief. Your mama is a good woman."

"The best. So, I guess she'll be coming back here soon." She put her head down and stared at her fingernails. How had life gotten so complicated? "Unless the painters are through with their work early and we can both move back into our house."

Cooper heard the pain in her voice. She was struggling with confronting Roger and what to do about Loretta. His hands were tied. It wasn't as if he could tell Lauren's mother that they'd been intimate. Cooper winced. He didn't have any answers, but one thing was certain: he didn't want to give up on Lauren. He didn't think he could.

"Hey, I have an idea," he said. Anything to perk her up and make her smile again. Anything to keep her near. "Do you trust me?"

She lifted her lids and tiny emerald flecks brightened in her eyes. She nodded.

"Good. Meet me outside in half an hour. Oh, and wear something…" He studied her appearance. Her hair was down, touching her shoulders. She wore a white midriff top exposing a slender slice of skin and a pair of skintight jeans that perfectly showcased her legs and ass. "Never mind, you're perfect the way you are."

It was true. Lauren was the closest thing to perfection he'd ever seen in a woman.

"Give me a hint?"

"No. But be sure to wear your riding boots."

"Riding boots? I don't have—"

"Okay, whatever you call those things you wear."

"My Steve Maddens?"

He shrugged. "Boots are boots. Wear them. And bring a jacket. I'll see you in half an hour."

He left her standing there, looking dumbfounded.

So was he. Because he'd never taken another soul to this very private place.

# Eight

Lauren was mystified. She had no clue where Cooper was taking her but she'd packed her hobo handbag with essentials: lotion, keys, phone, tissues, hairbrush, antacid and a toothbrush. Yeah, a toothbrush. A girl had to keep up her dental health, didn't she?

She took a minute to steady her nerves. Heck, she had just about one hundred people invited to a wedding that would never be, and instead of facing facts and doing something about it, she was running off with Cooper. To who knew where.

Goose bumps broke out on her arms. Being with Cooper did that to her, but she couldn't deny it was wrong. Instead of being responsible and flying up to Houston to face Roger, she was going on an excursion of some sort with her brother's best friend.

And worse yet, she was thrilled at the prospect of more time with him.

She felt wicked and selfish and...glorious.

What a mess she'd gotten herself into.

One final look at herself in the mirror contradicted Cooper's claim that she was perfect. She was far from it, but his compliment did sink down into her heart and her wicked self glowed inside. On a sigh, she scooped up her bag, grabbed her hooded jacket and walked out of her bedroom.

At the base of the stairs, she scoped out the house. Cooper was nowhere in sight, so she took a peek outside, making sure no pesky varmints were about. Her toes curled at the thought of that giant animal still being around.

When she determined the coast was clear, she took one tentative step onto the veranda and then another. She spotted Cooper, riding a golden stallion. He had an equally beautiful steed in tow behind him. The horses were packed down with supplies.

Smooth as a cowboy from an old Western flick, Cooper dismounted and tipped his hat. "Ready for a ride?"

She gulped and stumbled back. "Don't you have work to do?"

"Not at the moment." He shrugged and a cocky smile spread across his face. "The advantages of being the half owner of Stone Corporation. My brother's in charge today."

"Nice of him."

Cooper pursed his lips. "Chicken?"

"Of…of what? No…of course not." She hadn't been on a horse since she was ten years old. But she'd sure treated a lot of wannabe cowboys in the ER who'd been trampled, stomped on and tossed off their feisty mounts. "I'm sort of partial to the Jeep. Can't we take that?"

"Not where we're going. It's better to travel on horseback."

Where on earth were they going?

He walked over to her. "C'mon," he said, taking her hand. "I won't let anything happen to you. This here is Daisy. She's a gentle mare and she needs the exercise."

Didn't he have ranch hands for that?

"She's pretty."

"Got the same honey tones as your hair."

"Uh-huh."

"Come say hello to her."

Cooper took her hand and placed it on the horse's flank. The horse didn't move, but Lauren sensed she liked the attention. She kept on stroking her. "Hello there, Daisy. Who's your friend?"

"This is Duke."

"Are they a couple?"

Cooper smiled. "More like father and daughter. Daisy's a two-year-old palomino born here on Stone Ridge."

The warmth and pride in Cooper's tone eased her nerves. "Oh, a family affair." She was touched that papa and filly were raised together on the ranch. "Where's Daisy's mama?"

"Duchess is in the corral. She's a bit older than Duke and needs to rest up."

Cooper stroked Duke's nose and fussed with his beautiful mane, untangling a few strands. Then he turned to face her. "Ready?"

She nodded. "As much as I'm gonna be."

"Left boot in the stirrup and then hoist on up," he said. She did so and only managed to get halfway up before Cooper's flat palm landed on her butt and gave her the boost she needed. His touch seared through her jeans and robbed her of breath.

"Good girl," he said. Was he speaking to the mare or to her? "Now, straddle the saddle, putting most of your weight in the center. That's it."

Once she was seated on the saddle, she looked at the ground and swallowed hard. It was a long way down. When she looked up again, she squinted into the late-morning sun.

"Hang on," Coop said, reaching for a tan felt hat that was at least a size too big for her. "Put this on."

She did and he nodded. "Cute."

"Cute? I can hardly see."

Cooper tipped the hat back a little on her head. "There," he said. "Better?"

She nodded, feeling like a child being shown how to put on her shoes. "Much."

"All right then." He handed her the reins, giving her basic instructions on how to manage the animal between her legs. "Remember subtle movements are best."

"Gotcha."

"Don't worry. Daisy will follow her papa. She won't stray. You just keep yourself centered in the saddle and there won't be a problem. Ready?"

"Ready."

Cooper mounted his horse efficiently and settled his butt into the saddle. He whistled, gave the horse a gentle tap with his heels, and Duke took off at a slow enough pace for Daisy to follow easily. Within minutes, the house and stables had vanished. They were headed south over terrain that didn't appear well traveled.

It was a seventy-five-degree day with breezes that sometimes required her to put a hand to her hat. The pastures were thick here, and few cattle roamed on this part of the land. "How many acres is Stone Ridge?" she asked.

"Twelve thousand."

"I didn't realize it was so big. Do you enjoy your work, Cooper?"

"I do. Not too many people can work from home and manage a corporation. I feel fortunate. I love the land here. Never wanted to do much else."

"Does Jared feel the same way?"

"Jared? I think he likes working the land. He's got other investments as well. But Stone Ridge has surely afforded him a way to indulge in his hobby."

"Which is?"

"Jared has a need for speed. In his off hours he's either racing his boat or riding his Harley. He's got quite a collection of sports cars too. He's an adrenaline junkie. Kinda worries me at times being he's my kid brother and all."

"I get that. It's a dangerous kind of hobby."

"Yep. But he's a smart guy and great partner, and never shirks his duties here. As far as ranching goes, I'm more hands-on."

"Tell me about it." *Whoops.* The comment had slipped out of her mouth.

His laughter boomed. "I didn't hear too many complaints last night or in the shower this morning."

She was tired of talking to the back of his head. She made a clucking noise and Daisy caught up to Duke so they were side to side. Cooper turned to face her. God, the man oozed masculinity in a cowboy, bad-ass way that stunned her sometimes. The black hat, the jeans, the muscular arms and the command he had of the animal tossed her crazy world on end. "I'm not complaining."

"Glad to hear it. Because if I have anything to say about it, these hands are gonna continue to keep real busy."

Memories of the magic his hands had already done made her dizzy. Cooper could turn her on with one simple innuendo. "Is that so?"

"It is so."

"I should be on a plane right now, heading to Roger. To explain."

"Roger Kelsey doesn't deserve you."

The implication was that Cooper did.

She let out a deep sigh and her shoulders sagged. But with a burst of courage, she asked the burning question. "What are we doing, Cooper?"

Without hesitation he answered, "We're not rushing into anything. We're spending time together, grieving for your brother. We're helping each other and maybe helping ourselves at the same time."

She appreciated his candor. He didn't mince words. And put that way, it all made sense.

She nodded and took the bumps as her horse continued over the rough terrain.

She hoped this adventure with Cooper was worth the bruises her sore butt endured.


"Keep your eyes closed, Laurie Loo. We're almost there."

Good thing, because she was dusty, sweaty, and she could already feel her body rebelling like a son of a gun. "They're closed."

After another minute she heard leather cracking and sensed Cooper had dismounted and stood very close. "Okay."

"Okay?" She opened her eyes and faced a rustic structure made of wood and stone, set in a clearing surrounded by freshly planted trees. "What am I looking at?"

Cooper lifted his arms and helped her off Daisy. They stood facing each other. She wanted to wrap her arms around his neck and crush her mouth to his. After all, she'd done everything he'd asked without a single complaint. And she wanted a reward. But the pride in Cooper's eyes spoke of something more important.

"It's my cabin. And I haven't told a soul about it, except for my brother."

"A secret hideaway?"

"The fort wasn't big enough."

She stared at him. "Are you saying you built this by yourself?"

His head bobbed up and down. "I did. I've been working on it for the past six months."

"Since Tony's death. Why, Coop? I don't understand?"

"I needed a place to grieve. Someplace quiet, someplace where I could come to grips with my guilt. Someplace that would mean something one day. I put that energy into building this place. With my own hands. My father always said we wouldn't know a happy day until we built something from the ground up. So on the weekends and days when I wasn't needed on the ranch, I'd work here."

"Wow. This is amazing." She was impressed. There was more to Cooper Stone than good looks and great wealth. She'd always known that, but seeing what he'd accomplished put everything in perspective.

"I plan to make this place a horse rescue one day. For horses like Duchess, who are old and weary. They can live out their days in peace here. And I'm naming it after Tony. It'll be Double A Rescue."

"For Anthony Abbott," she said softly, her throat closing up and tears stinging her eyes. "I'm…honored that you brought me here."

"Like I said, we're helping each other…maybe?"

"Yes, I… I think we are." The tears spilled down her cheeks. She didn't have enough willpower to stop the flow. She'd never known a better man than Cooper Stone.

"Ah, baby," he said, kissing her teary cheeks. "Don't cry. That's not what this place is about."

"No, no. You're right. It's about hope and the future."

He wiped her eyes using the pads of his thumbs.

"Yeah, that's how I see it, too." He wrapped an arm around her shoulders. "C'mon. I want you to see the inside."

Shoulder-to-shoulder, they stepped up onto the porch. He shoved the door open and they entered. Sure, it was rustic, with wood beams and a brick fireplace, but it was also warm and cozy, a place where a caretaker to supervise the rescued horses might dwell one day. There were three big bedrooms. One housed a bed already, and she assumed Cooper used it on his weekends here. The kitchen was generous in size. No appliances were installed yet, but there was a refrigerator Coop told her worked on a generator. And, thankfully, the bathrooms had plumbing.

She could envision it all fully equipped and furnished. The cabin had Cooper's mark on it, unpolished around the edges but oh, so genuine and friendly. "I love this place." The awe in her voice couldn't be controlled. This was not only Cooper's place, it was Tony's.

That made it all the more special.

"I'm glad you like it."

"It's a labor of love, Coop," she said, touching his arm. "And I am very grateful you shared this with me."

Cooper looked down at the hand on his upper arm and sucked in a breath. The contact between them sizzled and she saw him battle for control. "I'm hungry. You?"

She blinked and nodded, a little bit disappointed. She was getting hot and cold signals from him. He said all the right things, but at times she felt him retreat, both mentally and physically. The doubt it left her with made her tummy ache.

Or was it only her imagination? Was she so darn consumed with him that she overthought every moment?

"Good. I packed enough food for a battalion. I'll bring it in."

"Need some help?" she called after him. He was already at the door.

"Nope. You just look around some more. I'll only be a minute."

She did just that. She moseyed around the three-bedroom cabin and looked out the kitchen window that faced a picturesque oak tree. There was a tire swing hanging from a thick branch. She could see Cooper on that thing, or leaning up against the base of the tree, taking a rest after a hard morning of work. It still amazed her that he'd built this cabin. The warmth flowing in her heart was laden with so much love, she could barely stand it.

"Here we go," Cooper said, coming inside loaded down with the supplies Daisy and Duke had carried on their backs.

"Set this out, would you?" he asked, handing her a blue-plaid blanket.

"Where?" The place was empty but for a few pieces of furniture.

"In the dining room, silly girl," Cooper said with a quirky smile on his face.

She smiled back. "Oh, right. I should've known."

Just outside the kitchen area was a room meant for dining. It wasn't overly large, but it surely could hold a table for six easily. She bent on her knees and spread out the blanket. Cooper handed her two plastic plates, a loaf of bread and two different kinds of chunk cheese. He opened a bottle of white wine and she held plastic cups as he poured.

There were cold cuts and peanut butter-and-jelly sandwiches, fresh fruit, along with three types of desserts. It was as if Cooper had a magic bag; he kept putting food out onto the blanket. Well, there was *something* magical about him. So magical that she was there with him carrying on an affair. Who knew when or how it would end, and still she wasn't balking. Still, she couldn't say no.

She was gloriously happy being there with him. Seeing how he'd poured his heart into every plank, every beam, every brick in this little hideaway quelled all of her doubts. When she was with Cooper, she felt closer to her brother. They both knew different sides of Tony, both cared about him beyond words, and yet when she and Cooper were together, it felt like the love they had for Tony was complete.

In a strange sort of way.

"What'll it be, Miss Quiet Over There?" Cooper asked.

She settled into a cross-legged position opposite him. "I'll have bread and a slice of that Gruyère."

He used a plastic knife to slice a piece of cheese then broke off a hunk of bread and plopped it onto her plate. "Here you go. Cuisine à la Texas."

She laughed and watched as he picked up a peanut butter-and-jelly sandwich and gobbled down a big bite. "Hmm. Goes good with wine," he said. He lifted his plastic cup.

She lifted hers, too, and they bumped cups.

"To Tony, to Double A Rescue and to Tony's little sister, Laurie Loo."

Cooper's eyes softened on her and his face lit up with something she dared not hope for. It was all she could do to keep her eyes dry and not fall into his arms. She inhaled. "And to Coop, Tony's bestie and a man who is good and honest and honorable. A man I'm proud to—"

But her words were muted as Cooper leaned over and brushed his lips to hers. The tenderness in his kiss startled her in a good way, melting her like a marshmallow over a campfire. She was in deep with Cooper and loved every second she spent with him.

"I don't deserve your praise," he whispered.

"Of course you do," she said, suddenly indignant on his behalf. "You're—"

He silenced her again, this time with two fingers to her lips. "Shush, Lauren. Please."

He leaned back and finished his sandwich, pretty much ending the toast and the conversation about his good qualities. He was humble and didn't want to hear compliments about his nature. And he was probably still feeling guilty about the way Tony had died. If only she could take Cooper's pain away and assure him he wasn't to blame. He was experiencing survivor guilt and she understood that. But not on her watch. She wasn't going to stand by and let him beat himself up day after day.

The conversation turned to the rescue and his plans for building a shelter and corrals for the animals. The land was wide open. He had acres that weren't suited for cattle he planned to put to good use for old, injured and abused animals.

She heard the excitement in his voice, the boyish enthusiasm he had for this project. She'd often been labeled a nurturer, which went with the territory of being a nurse. But shock of all shocks, she just realized that he was a nurturer, too. He hid it better than anyone she'd known, but it was there, once the layers were peeled away, just waiting to be discovered.

"I hope to open it up to students in the community. There are high school kids in the city who'd love to volunteer their time and learn how to care for animals in need."

"I would've jumped at the chance to come out here. I think it's a great plan."

"It's a beginning, anyway."

"You didn't want your crew or your friends to know about this?"

"No, I didn't." He poured another glass of wine for both of them. They weren't the big red cups, but smaller, so she had no qualms about accepting more wine. "I needed the solace, still do, to finish the place. I don't want to answer questions about it or have to explain myself."

"It's a wonder no one's discovered it before."

"If they have, they haven't spoken of it to me. And that's just fine. It's pretty remote out here. Well away from the pasture and set back a bit."

"Tell me about the tire swing?"

He laughed. "You saw that?"

"I did. What's funny? I love it."

"It's just that I was watching an old movie one day not too long ago and saw a young boy riding on one in his backyard. His kid sister came by and pushed him off it and then took off running. He chased her but never did catch up. Reminded me of something you would've done with Tony. I don't know, there was something simple about it that called to me. And that giant oak out there was just begging for attention."

"Tony never could catch me." Images of her younger self horsing around with her brother flashed through her mind.

"That's not the way I heard it."

"It's a fact. Tony would *never* deliberately let me get away. He was too competitive for that. If I got away, which I did plenty of times, it was because I was faster than him."

Cooper shrugged. "Okay, I stand corrected. You're right about Tone. He was as competitive as I was. We both never backed down from a challenge. And we'd both thrash our bodies and back to rack up the win."

"Yeah, I remember Mama patching him up. Didn't matter if it was football, track or gymnastics, he'd come home banged up."

"It was no different with me," Cooper said.

After she finished her bread and cheese, she unwrapped a kitchen towel filled with cookies, brownies and muffins. "What'll it be?" she asked him.

"I'll have one of each," he said.

She smiled. "Of course you will."

She nibbled on a chocolate-chip cookie while Cooper devoured a brownie. He poured another cup of wine. "Want one?"

"Sure, to wash down the cookie," she said, and he filled her cup. "I think I like picnicking indoors."

"Me, too," he said, polishing off the blueberry muffin.

"Tell me, Coop, how on earth do you stay so rock-hard?"

He sputtered wine and drops drizzled down his chin. Wiping it with the back of his hand, he answered right away. "Pretty much if I'm in the same room with you, I can't seem to help myself."

Instantly her face flamed and she covered her mouth with her hand. "Did I just ask you that?"

He scratched his head and grinned. "You sure did."

"I didn't mean it that way." But his answer sure was revealing.

Cooper scooted over to the wall and leaned against it. He crooked his finger, beckoning her to join him. Of course she went, because denying Cooper anything today wasn't happening. He opened his arms. She fit her body in his embrace and turned around, so her back was to his front. He wrapped his strong arms around her waist. "Lean back," he said.

He wanted to hold her and she wanted to be held. With her head under his chin, resting on his broad chest, she relaxed and snuggled in.

A sweet sigh blew from his mouth and warmed her ear. It was amazing that they could both be so calm when the pressure of his arousal was right there teasing her butt. But Cooper didn't move a muscle, except to ease his head back against the wall. And they sat there like that, speaking softly about the ranch, her work at the hospital, the latest blockbuster movie playing in town. Anything and everything, except the one thing that needed their attention.

Where they stood with each other.

Once she confronted Roger, then what?

Cooper had never mentioned anything about the future to her. He wanted her in the present, and maybe that was all she should dwell on. She was jumping too fast, leapfrogging from one situation to another. But would her heart be intact after she left Stone Ridge? Once she went back to her normal routine, if that were even possible now, would this thing with Cooper become a heartbreaking memory? *Oh, God.* She couldn't imagine life without Cooper in it. The emptiness inside would swallow her up and cause a giant divide, a space that no one else could fill. How could she have fallen so hard, so fast?

Because Cooper Stone was like no other man she'd ever met.

He must've caught her negative vibes and the stiffness taking over her shoulders. "Hey, remember the time you colored your hair purple?" he asked, brushing a kiss to her hair. The smile in his voice lifted her spirits.

"How could I forget? It was during my rebellious goth stage."

"Yeah, I remember. You looked—"

"Watch it, Stone." She could easily jab him in the ribs with her elbow.

He laughed and the vibration rumbled in his stomach and bounced her up and down a little. "Can't help recalling how pissed Tony was. He said you looked like a damn troll."

"Yeah, I got teased a lot in school and Mama had a hissy fit."

"Just goes to show, you can't change perfection, Laurie Loo."

She snorted. "I'm hardly perfect." But her ego, which had been dipping low, skyrocketed at his compliment.

"If you ask me, you are."

His flattery was killing her. "You know how my mother punished me for that act of rebellion?"

He shook his head. "I forget."

"She told me I couldn't color it back to my original blond, so I had to live with it until it faded or grew out. She said in life, you have to live with the decisions you make."

"So, it was a lesson."

"Yeah, big time."

"Was the lesson learned?"

She shrugged. "Maybe." At least in her professional life it was. Her private life was a different story. "But I still think it's important to act on your impulses once in a while, so you don't grow to regret what you missed out on in life. As painful as growing my hair out was, I think I would've still dyed it for the experience."

Cooper stroked her arm up and down, creating warm tingles inside her very relaxed body. Fatigue set in quickly and she struggled to keep her eyes open. The wine, the food, the soreness from the ride, all contributed to her bones going limp.

"What else have you done to warrant a lesson?" he asked.

She allowed her eyes to close now and snuggled deeper into Cooper's chest. "You," she whispered and then promptly fell asleep.

She was dreaming pleasantly just as a school bell began to ring and ring and ring. Her eyes popped open to Cooper's sharp profile. As she nestled in his arms on the floor, it all came back to her. That wasn't a school bell ringing, it was her cell phone!

Cooper woke, startled, and clutched her tighter to his body, but she disentangled herself from his arms. "Sorry, I have to get this. It could be my mother."

Crawling on the ground, she rummaged through her bag and found her phone. "It's from the hospital," she told him.

She had a very brief conversation and then hung up.

Cooper was still coming out of his nap, his eyes blinking. "What's wrong?"

"There's been a twelve-car accident on the interstate. Massive injuries involved. That was my ER supervisor. They're desperate for staff and asked if I could possibly come to work by three o'clock to help out. I have to go," she explained to Cooper.

"Of course you do." He was rising and putting together their supplies. "I'll have you there by three, no problem.

We'll ride double on Duke and make it back home, then I'll drive you."

"Thanks, Cooper. But just get me to the ranch as fast as you can. It's gonna be a very late night, so I'd better drive myself into Dallas. I have no idea when I'll get off."

He looked like he wanted to argue, but finally gave his head a nod and, in less than five minutes, she was seated in front of Cooper on his big stallion, her horse trailing behind, and racing back to Stone Ridge.

"Oh, crap, Katy," Lauren said into her car speakerphone. "I totally forgot about my appointment with the florist and photographer."

"Yes, you did. After they drove all the way out to the ranch, they called me to complain," Katy answered. "And they didn't hold back. It wasn't pretty. What's going on with you, Lauren?"

"I'm so sorry, Katy. After you went to all the trouble to seek them out and make the appointments for me, I don't know what to say. I'm wrapped up in something right now. It's crazy, but I don't have time to tell you. I'm on my way home from Dallas Memorial and I'm dragging. You heard about the big accident on the interstate? They called me in to help out today."

"Is that your excuse? Because it's a good one. Who could argue with that? You were saving lives. You were, weren't you?"

"Yes. We did help a lot of patients today. Thank goodness, most of the injuries were minor and we sent more than twenty patients home after treating them. There're a few who are in surgery right now and the others will probably be released by tomorrow morning. So, they let me go earlier than expected. I'm driving back to Cooper's now. But, Katy, I have to be honest with you. It wasn't the accident that made me miss my appointments today."

"Oh, boy, I think I know what's coming. Cooper?"

"Yes," she said without hesitation. "I'm in love with him, Katy."

"I figured. I mean he's…never mind. What about the fact that you're still engaged to Roger? Or are you?"

"Not in my heart and I am not wearing his ring anymore. I can't break up with him over the phone and I can't text him. I need to see him face-to-face and tell him everything up front."

"Okay, I gotta say I agree with that. So you don't want me to reschedule those appointments?"

"No. Sorry. And I promise to explain all of this to you tomorrow. But I'm exhausted now and almost at the ranch, so please don't do or say anything until we talk."

"I want details."

"You'll get them, I promise. I've gotta go. Pulling into the gates now. 'Bye, awesome friend. Love ya."

"Love ya, too."

As tired as she was, Lauren couldn't wait to see Cooper and tell him about the day she'd had. She parked her car in one of the many garages attached to the house and noticed that Jared's luxurious red Lamborghini was parked inside, too. It was nine o'clock and they were probably just finishing up dinner. As much as she wanted to see Cooper, she didn't want to interrupt his private time with his brother. Maybe she'd just pop her head into the room and say good-night to them.

She needed her Cooper Stone fix.

And then she could crash in her bed.

As she entered the house, she noticed the kitchen lights were off. Voices drifted inside from the backyard patio. A few Malibu lights cast a dim glow over the area. It was peaceful, soothing her nerves. She was about to walk outside when she heard her name mentioned.

She froze, hiding herself from view in the dark kitchen.

Jared was speaking loud enough for her to hear. And he sounded irritated. "You told me you weren't getting involved with her. You had no feelings for Lauren."

"I know all that," Cooper retorted, clearly upset. "What was I supposed to do? Loretta asked me to stop the wedding and I didn't expect it would end up like this."

"What, with you banging your best friend's sister?"

"Shut the hell up, Jared. Not another word about Lauren, you hear me."

"Hey, no disrespect to her. Lauren's great. Maybe too great. That's my point. You were doomed from the beginning."

"That doesn't change the fact that Tony thought Kelsey was robbing him blind. As soon as Tony was gone, the guy tries to cement the deal by marrying his partner's sister. It's a good way to cover his tracks *and* keep the company for himself."

"We have no proof of that. I couldn't find anything on Tony's computer."

"Something's up with that Winding Hills Resort. If we could break into Kelsey's files at his office, we'd find our proof there. I'm sure of it. We have to…"

Lauren's ears were burning. Her heart was crushed, battering her chest with each beat. This was too much to take in. She questioned if she was too exhausted to be hearing this correctly, but she knew. She'd heard right. Cooper had betrayed her in the worst possible way. He'd taken her trust, her love, her body, and used her.

*Oh, man. Oh, man. Oh, man.*

"We can't do that," Jared said firmly. "That's breaking and entering."

"Hell, I know that. I wish I'd never gotten involved in this scheme."

Blood drained from Lauren's face. Her body sagged. She felt as weak as one of her geriatric patients. Her head hurt like hell from the truth that pounded at her like a freaking sledgehammer.

*Cooper doesn't love you.*

*He doesn't care about you.*

*He was paying a debt he thought he owed your mother.*

*To ease his guilt about Tony.*

*He seduced you with his charm and good looks.*

*And, Mama! Why didn't you trust me with the truth? Did you think I'm so much of a flake that you had to go behind my back to cook up a scheme with Cooper? Didn't you know it would completely shatter me that you showed so little faith in my judgment?*

Lauren stood there shaking. Her brain should have been muddled. Heartbreak combined with fatigue had a way of doing that. But suddenly her mind opened and all things became clear. The tears would come later and they would be massive. She had no doubt she was ruined for life. She'd never love again. She'd never trust again. She'd been duped by a master deceiver. Make that two.

She walked out onto the patio and both men turned their heads, shocked to see her there. The Stone brothers swallowed hard and blinked. They couldn't believe their eyes. They'd been caught red-handed.

*Hell, yeah.*

The pain squeezing her heart so tight she could barely breathe suddenly turned to white-hot anger.

"Lauren!" Cooper stood, taking a step to approach her.

She raised the palm of her hand, stopping him cold. Then she summoned every ounce of her strength. "Don't. Don't you dare come any closer. Don't you dare speak to me, Cooper Stone."

"Maybe I should leave," Jared said, standing, his expression as grim as Cooper's.

"Don't bother, Jared. I won't be here that long."

"I can explain," Cooper said. The alarm in his voice didn't faze her.

"I don't need your lies, Cooper. I don't think there's anything left to say. I heard it all. You and my mother cooked up this scheme to break up my engagement. And you did a bang-up job. Leave it to you, Cooper, you always have to win. You love a challenge. And that's all I was to you, right? Well, I'll tell you one thing. Your plan didn't work. I'm *not* breaking up with my fiancé. I'm marrying Roger and I won't hear another word about it." The loud and intense pain in her voice carried across the patio. Had she just said that? Yeah, she had. To hurt Cooper. To get back at him for deceiving and using her. For breaking her heart.

"Lauren, you can't be serious!"

"Don't get indignant with me, Cooper." Tears streamed down her face. Tremors racked her body so hard she almost lost her balance. She gripped the wall to steady herself. "My mind is made up. I'm going through with the wedding."

She started walking away. Out of the corner of her eye, she saw Cooper taking a step to come after her. Jared hooked his arm and held him back. "Not now," Jared said. "She needs time to cool off."

Cool off? She would never cool off. She was ice from now on.

She headed upstairs to her room and quickly packed her bag. She needed to get off this ranch and away from Cooper Stone, yesterday.

She needed a place to cry her eyes out.

She needed to go home.

# Nine

Lauren woke in her own bed from a fitful sleep just as the first dawn light settled upon the world. She hugged her tear-soaked pillow tight. Last night her sobs had come steadily until she was too drained to do anything but fall into an exhausted sleep. She propped herself up in bed, took a few moments to clear her head and rose. Immediately she wished she could flop back down and cover her head with her blanket. Stay there until life made sense again.

*As if.*

The aroma of freshly brewed coffee teased her nostrils.

She headed to the kitchen and stared at her mama sitting at the table, sipping from her Nursing Is a Work of Heart coffee mug. Her mouth was turned down and worry lines surrounded her bloodshot eyes.

Lauren poured herself a cup and sat facing her. She had burning questions for her mother, and tried not to think of her as Benedict Arnold. Yet she did feel totally betrayed. "How long have the painters been gone?" she asked quietly.

"Just since yesterday, honey."

"At least that wasn't a lie. The house is painted inside and out."

"I was going to tell you today."

"Was all that about Sadie a lie, too?"

"No, honey," her mama said. "You think I'd lie about something like that?"

No. Not really. But it all seemed too convenient and it had left Lauren alone with Cooper at Stone Ridge. She shook her head. "How is she?"

"Better. She's home with 'round-the-clock care."

"That's good." Lauren took a big sip of coffee and it went down hard. "Mama, why did you do it? Didn't you know it would crush me to find out how little you trusted me? It was like a slap in the face."

Her mama reached for her hand. She wasn't ready to give in to the gesture, but the sense of loss in her mother's eyes was the same look she'd had when Tony died. And Lauren couldn't do that to her. She couldn't turn her mother's hand away.

Her mother squeezed her hand gently. "I'm sorry. I was desperate. Honey, I know you don't like to hear this, but you've been impulsive in the past, and with your brother only being gone a short time, I thought you were making a big mistake rushing into marriage. You needed time to grieve and get your life back in order. I didn't want to break you and Roger up, as much as have you give yourself more time. I thought that moving to the ranch would help you clear your head a bit. Distance can help give you perspective. And then maybe you'd see that Roger was pushing you too hard."

"You mean you wanted to separate me from Roger any way you could. And you asked Cooper to help you do that."

"It just all sort of happened, honey. Look, it's no surprise to anyone that I made a mistake marrying your father. He wasn't a man made for settling down. I didn't want that to happen to you."

Lauren stared into her coffee cup. "I guess I'm just like Dad."

"No, honey. You are not like him at all. You're a nurturer. You're kind. And thoughtful. You care deeply about people. I just wanted you to understand your own heart, without being pressured into marrying a man who maybe wasn't right for you."

"Well, you succeeded. You pushed me toward Cooper."

"You have to know that was never my intention or his, honey. Cooper isn't that devious."

Again, her mama was defending Cooper. He was a saint. Saint Cooper could do no wrong. But her mother had no idea how much Cooper's betrayal cut into her, slicing her to pieces. Had he seduced her, made love to her, because he'd run out of other options? Had he deliberately set out to ruin her for Roger and all other men?

"Mama, I'm a mess inside. I'm questioning all my decisions."

"Oh, honey. I'm so very sorry about that. I didn't mean for any of this to happen." She rose. "Come here, baby girl." She opened her arms.

Lauren got up and moved into her mother's embrace. She felt safe there, comforted by her mother's love. "Lauren, I'm sorry. I hope you can forgive me, honey. The last thing I want is for you to be hurt."

"Oh, Mama." It was too late for that.

"Cooper's worried sick about you, honey. He's been calling. He sounded pretty desperate to talk to you."

"No."

"No?"

She pulled out of her mother's arms. "Mama, no. I… can't. I'm furious with him and I don't think that's going to change. You don't know the half of it."

"I think I do. You care deeply about him."

So, her mama was perceptive. That wasn't a big shocker. "Cared. Past tense. I don't want to talk about Cooper. But just for the record, right now the way I feel about him is something just short of...loathing."

"It's not his fault, honey. I shouldn't have gone behind your back to seek his help."

"What is it about that man that you're always defending him? He doesn't walk on water, you know."

"He's a good man, and I put him in a terrible situation."

"Cooper did what he always does, going above and beyond to accomplish his goals. And I fell for it. Like a fool."

"You're no fool, Lauren. You're a girl with a big heart."

"Please, Mama, promise me one thing?"

"Anything, Lauren. I want to earn back your trust."

"No matter what I decide to do, promise me I'll have your support. You'll stand by my decision and not try to interfere."

"Oh, Lauren. I've learned my lesson. I promise. I do trust you, baby girl. And I love you with all of my heart."

"Love you, too, Mama."

Lauren stood at the reception desk at Kelsey-Abbott, dressed in a cream pencil skirt and a light cocoa blouse. Her three-inch heels were killing her, but it didn't matter. She'd withstand the pain as long as she got what she came here to find. She waved to a few employees she recognized from Tony's days at the company and was granted kind greetings back.

With Katy by her side, she said to the new twenty-something receptionist, "I'm Lauren Abbott, Mr. Kelsey's fiancée. I need to get into Roger's office." She smiled brightly, and rather than plead her case that she had every right to be there, she was half owner of the company, she took an easier route. "I'm afraid I lost a diamond earring in there.

It's sort of special since he gave me the pair on my birthday. I'm hoping I can find it before he returns from his trip tomorrow and then I won't have to admit to him I'd been a little careless with his gift."

"Sure. No problem, Miss Abbott," the young woman said, giving her a look of sympathy. "Would you like some help looking for it?"

"That's very sweet of you—" Lauren glanced at the name on her badge "—Melissa. But that's not necessary. It's lunchtime and I don't want to hold you up. I brought my friend Katy with me. She's got eagle eyes. If anyone can help me find it, it's her."

"That's right," Katy said. "Needle in the haystack and all."

The receptionist furrowed her brows, looking ridiculously puzzled. Clearly she was clueless as to what Katy meant. "Well, let me find the keys," she said, opening a drawer and coming up with a key ring. "Would you like me to show you in?"

"No, thanks," Lauren answered, snapping up the keys. "I've got this." She waved the key ring in the air as she headed toward the office. "Have a great lunch, Melissa."

"I hope you find what you're looking for."

"So do I," Lauren mumbled under her breath.

Once they were inside Roger's office, Katy turned the lock on the door and simultaneously their shoulders sagged. "Wow," she said.

"Technically, we're not doing anything wrong. I own half of this company."

"I never understood how that worked. If you're not involved in the company, how do you know you're earning your fair share?"

"Up until now, I had no reason to think Roger was cheating Tony or me."

Lauren had come up with her plan last night, amid all

the sobs and heartache, and was determined to find out what kind of man Roger Kelsey actually was. He'd been attentive to her after Tony's death and, okay, maybe she'd let her guard down enough to think she'd fallen in love with him. But it seemed that as soon as the engagement ring was on her finger, he'd backed off. As if she was a sure thing. As if his mission had been accomplished. The more she'd thought about how Roger so eagerly pursued her after the funeral, the more she was beginning to believe that what she'd overheard last night between Jared and Cooper was true.

Not that it would let Cooper Stone off the hook.

This morning, after confronting and finally, for the most part, forgiving her mother, she'd driven over to Katy's house and spilled her heart out, leaving no details unspoken. Katy knew everything and it was amazing how liberating that was now that the burden of secrecy had been lifted.

Lauren's phone buzzed. It was another text from Cooper. He'd sent her four already and left a couple of voicemail messages, too. She hadn't bothered to listen to them. Her stomach knotted good and tight every time his name popped up on the screen, so she turned her phone off and dropped it into her handbag. If only she could turn her thoughts of him off that easily.

"Let's get started," she said to Katy. Finding out her fiancé was a cheat and possibly a fraud was a better option than thinking about Cooper's betrayal. Wasn't that just sad? She sure knew how to pick 'em. *Not.*

"You really think he'd leave something incriminating on his work computer?"

"I have no clue. Good thing I brought you along, right?" Katy was a techno wizard. She was one of those people who had worked with computers from a very young age, understanding the language better than some people understood English. Lauren was so on the other end of the spectrum. She excelled in most subjects, yet she didn't know a gigabyte from an internal hard drive. "My future is riding on this," she said, biting her nail.

"I'll try my best. But you know, you're within your legal right to have the books audited."

"And spoil all of our fun? No way, Katy. Besides, if Roger got wind of it, he'd have time to cook the books."

"Okay, well, let a girl get to work." Katy took a seat in Roger's chair and opened the computer.

"While you hunt for electronic clues, I'll go through the paper files. See if I can come up with something."

"Sounds good and, while you're at it, do me a favor?"

Her friend was a trooper, letting Lauren cry on her shoulder this morning and now attempting to hack into the company's computer for her. "Anything."

"Think about what you really want in life. And go after it."

"I promise, but first things first. I need to find out if my fiancé is true blue."

"And then what?"

A lump formed in her throat. Did she have the gumption to go through with her plan? She'd teach the two men in her life not to ever again mess with Lauren Abbott. "Then if it goes as I think it will, I'll be walking down the aisle in ten days."

"I should've never let you stop me from going after her. I should've talked to her that night and made her see reason." Cooper sank onto the big leather sofa in his brother's game room and hung his head. It had been a whole week since he'd seen Lauren. "She won't answer my texts or phone calls."

"She's not ready yet," Jared said. "You would've only

made things worse. She was seeing red that night and rightfully so."

"Are you gonna lecture me?" Cooper's head ached. He was in no mood to hear how badly he'd screwed up.

"No. Hey, remember, I was on the receiving end of a situation like this. Helene lied to me about who she was. Her motives didn't matter at the time. All I could see was her betrayal."

"Totally different situation. I'm not ready to let Lauren go. She can't marry that guy."

"Why not? We didn't find a thing on him."

"But it's there. Tony's instincts were always right on."

"Maybe, but it's out of your hands right now."

"It can't be."

"Why?"

"Why do you keep asking me why?" Cooper's head hammered harder now. He put his fingertips to the temples and massaged them to release some of the pressure. It wasn't working.

"Because you're not being honest with yourself."

"What do you want me to say?"

"The truth."

"Okay, I miss her. I miss her like crazy. And she deserves someone better than Roger Kelsey."

Jared pointed a finger right smack at his chest.

"Me? No way, Jared." He gave his head a shake. "It can't be me. I killed her brother. I could never expect her to love me that way. I don't deserve Lauren's love."

"Maybe she deserves yours. Did you ever think of it that way? I saw the look in her eyes that night she walked in on our conversation. She's crazy about you, Cooper. That's the reason she was so devastated. And would you stop with the I-killed-her-brother thing. You know you didn't. You know it wasn't you driving recklessly that night. In all your life, you've never had one accident. It was bad luck and timing that caused Tony's death. Stop blaming yourself."

"I'm tryin', bro. I'm tryin'."

"Well, try harder or you're gonna lose her forever."

Cooper's cell rang and his heart started pumping fast. Every time someone called, he held out hope it was Lauren coming to her senses. But this time he got the next best thing. "Excuse me," he told Jared. "It's Loretta." He hated hearing the eagerness in his voice. Maybe Loretta was calling with news of Lauren? Man, he was messed up. Clutching the phone tight, he rose from his seat, walked out front and sat on the stone steps.

"Hello, Loretta."

"Cooper. How are you?"

"I'm doing fine," he fibbed. "Well, just okay. I'm hoping you have good news to tell me about Lauren."

"Cooper, I'm actually calling on Lauren's behalf. I've promised my daughter to support her decision, no matter what it is. And I'm afraid she's decided to marry Roger. I couldn't even try to talk her out of it. I kept my mouth shut. She claims she knows what she's doing."

"It's clear that she doesn't."

"I can't help you, Cooper. I'm lucky she's even talking to me. She's been very hurt and I'm trying to earn back her trust."

Cooper's body sagged. Loretta was his last line of defense.

"She's in the other room. She said she'll speak to you, if you want to talk to her."

"I'd rather see her in person."

"Well, I can put her on the phone and let you ask her. It's really out of my hands."

"Okay, Loretta. I understand. Please put her on."

A minute passed and Cooper's throat tightened. He cleared it with a cough.

"Hello," Lauren said.

The sound of her sweet, lilting voice coming over the receiver melted his heart.

"Lauren." He pulled air into his lungs and sighed silently. She was like an angel, the only woman who could repair the pieces of him that were broken. How he'd missed her this past week. "I'm glad you agreed to speak to me. I want you to know—"

"You don't have to say anything. I know you're sorry. Mama's only told me a dozen times. But I can't hear your platitudes, Cooper. I thought I owed you a call to say I'm going through with my wedding."

Cooper slammed his eyes shut. He ground his teeth and summoned all of his patience "You can't marry him. He's a cheat and I can't stand the thought of you tying yourself to a man who doesn't deserve you."

"I know what kind of man Roger is, Cooper. And that's why I'm marrying him. I've done some digging on my own. I know you and Mama didn't think me capable, but I am."

"Are you saying—?"

"I'm saying that I'm a stronger, more competent woman than either of you gave me credit for. And that's all I'm going to say about it."

"Did you tell Roger about us?"

"Us?"

"Yeah, about you and me?"

"I told him I got a case of cold feet, Cooper. And I finally came to my senses."

Her words sunk in. So now what they'd had together boiled down to a case of cold feet on her part. Not that he'd given her any reason to think there was more to the relationship. He'd been too dense, too blind, felt too guilty to claim the woman he wanted. And now it was hopeless. She was set and determined to marry Kelsey.

She'd done some digging on her own and hadn't found anything. Kelsey wasn't about to leave his secrets to be easily found. Lauren couldn't have possibly dug deep enough, but apparently she was convinced Kelsey was innocent of any wrongdoing.

"I wanted to let you off the hook if you'd rather we don't get married at Stone Ridge. Roger originally wanted to marry at the courthouse. He's all about simple," she said. "And, certainly, I would understand if you didn't want to host the wedding."

Cooper squeezed his eyes shut. Pain stabbed at him, a burning ache that rifled through his entire body. He wanted her on Stone Ridge. She belonged here. With him. If he told her what was in his heart, it would go over like a train wreck. She wouldn't believe him. She would only think he was meddling in her life again. But how could he let her go? How could he possibly give her away to another man?

*Because this is what she wants.*

*You blew it with her.*

*The least you can do is let her have the wedding of her dreams.*

"Lauren, are you sure? You're not just doing this because of what…what happened between us."

"You keep saying 'us' as if there is such a thing. There never was, Cooper. I made a mistake and now I'm trying to rectify it."

There was no anger or pain in her voice, and that was what scared him the most. He only heard determination.

"I made you a promise and regardless of what you think of me, I won't go back on my word. Everything is all set. So, if that's what you really want, you can certainly have the wedding here."

"I don't…" she said, her voice dropping to a whisper, giving him a sliver of hope. "I mean… I don't expect you to walk me down the aisle."

"No." He couldn't imagine it.

"But I do hope you'll attend the wedding."

He'd have to show up for Tony, for Loretta, for Lauren. "Yep." He all but strangled on the word.

"Thank you," she said quite civilly. "Goodbye, Cooper."

She cut off the connection and he just sat there, swallowing hard and staring at the phone.

Jared shoved a glass of whiskey into his free hand. "Here. You look like you could use this." Jared sat beside him on the stone steps, holding a crystal carafe of the good stuff.

"I need more than this." He gulped the shot.

"What you need is to grow some balls, Coop."

He frowned as he eyed his brother. "What?"

"You heard me. You're sulking around like a baby. Since when do you give up? You're a fierce competitor. Get in Lauren's face if you have to."

"It's too late. I spoke with her. She's marrying Roger. She says hooking up with me was only a case of cold feet."

"Do you believe that?"

"Hell, no."

"Then talk to her. Really talk to her. Spill out your guts and tell her how you feel. Offer her the moon. That's what women want. They want all of you, not just the parts you're willing to share."

Jared poured him another shot and he sipped slowly this time. "Thanks for the advice."

"You taking it?"

"I'm growing a pair, as we speak," Cooper said.

His brother chuckled. And, for the first time in days, so did he.

Katy finished buttoning the last of the pearl buttons at the back of Lauren's wedding dress. She stared at herself in the dresser mirror in Cooper's guest room, the room where she'd stayed just a short time ago. Her mother's ivory-silk gown had a vintage look about it. It was a dream dress for a dream wedding. Only that dream had turned into a bit of a nightmare. "Are you sure you want to go through with this, Lauren?"

Katy could tell she was freaking out, her nerves doing a hip-hop dance, up and down and sideways. "Yes, I have to."

"You don't. You can back out."

"I really can't and you know why."

"Then you're a braver woman than I am."

"My bravery might be born of stupidity, Katy. I can't go backward. I've got to see this through."

"Oh…kay."

Katy's obvious reluctance was working on her. Making her doubt her decision.

"You look gorgeous, BFF. You really do."

"Thanks."

"Just let me fix a few of these curls. Once your veil goes on, you'll be all done."

Katy got out the curling iron again and rewound a curl just as a soft knock sounded on the door. "That must be Mama. I'll get it," Lauren said.

Katy shook her head and touched Lauren's shoulders. "You just stay put right there, I'll get the door."

Lauren tilted her head and smiled.

"It's my duty as your maid of honor. And I take my duties seriously."

"I know you do."

Katy had been a godsend to her during this past month, helping her get her head on straight. Not an easy task, since she'd been turned upside down lately. She didn't know how she'd ever repay her for her support and kindness.

The door creaked open and she heard a familiar male voice. Cooper's. "I'd like to see Lauren."

Katy closed the door halfway. "Uh, hold on," she told

him. Stunned, Katy turned around and waited for a sign from her.

Lauren froze. She thought she'd made it clear she didn't want to see him before the wedding. But she couldn't very well kick him to the curb, since she was in his house, having her wedding on his property. She was still angry with him, so angry she could barely see straight. But good manners prevailed. In a few minutes, none of this would matter anymore.

"Katy, I'll see him."

*You sure?* she mouthed.

She nodded.

Katy opened the door all the way and let him in. "I'll just go…check on our bouquets."

Lauren hadn't ended up hiring a florist or a photographer. The bouquets for her and Katy were last-minute indulgences from the Garden House in Dallas. Katy had picked them up this morning and put them in the refrigerator for safekeeping. Since the lake property was such a naturally beautiful setting, Lauren figured it was okay to forego any other flowers. As far as photography, a few friends had been asked to bring their good cameras. That would have to do, and given the circumstances of her little plan, it was more than enough.

Cooper waited until Katy was fully out of sight before coming farther into the room. Wearing a charcoal suit, his dark blond hair cut and groomed to perfection, and sexy facial scruff accenting his strong jawbone, he simply took her breath away. He held a felt hat over his heart.

"You look beautiful," were the first words out of his mouth, the sincerity of his comment shining in his deep, sea-blue eyes "I've missed you so much, Lauren."

She'd missed him, too, but she remained silent.

He took a few steps, closing in on her, and the look of fear on her face must've stopped him from coming any closer. He stood in the middle of the room now, staring at her. "I'm sorry about the way things happened, Lauren. Your mom only wanted what was best for you. And I blew it while trying to help."

She nodded, tears brimming in her eyes. Her mascara would be running any second and she'd look like the sister act to Kiss.

"I couldn't let you marry Kelsey without telling you how I feel about you. It may be too late, but I only just figured it out and…well, it's as simple as it is complicated, really. I'm in love with you, Lauren. I fell for you without even realizing it. In my heart, there is an 'us.' And I'm afraid there always will be. You probably don't believe me, but it's true. And I swear it on Tony's grave. I love you, Lauren."

Lauren put her head down, holding back tears. She stood in her wedding gown, her train flowing in a silky circle on the floor all around her. She wasn't a prize to be collected. She wasn't a flake or a fool. She knew what she wanted and she would have to see this through to the end. She looked up at Cooper through teary eyes. He'd been everything she'd ever wanted. "Thank you, Cooper."

"Thank you?" he repeated, an incredulous tone in his voice.

"Yes, I appreciate your honesty. I really do."

Cooper's hopeful expression vanished and was quickly replaced by a frown. "So that's it?"

*Oh, God.* Why was he doing this to her? As angry as she'd been with him, she didn't relish hurting him. "I… I have to get my veil and bouquet. The w-wedding will be starting soon."

"I'd like to shake some sense into you," he said quietly. "But I don't think it would help."

If he touched her, she would crumble and she couldn't have that. "No. It wouldn't."

Slowly, he set his hat on his head. "Then I hope you get what you're looking for."

She nodded.

He walked toward the door and reached for the knob.

She called to him, "Cooper, you're still coming, right?"

His nod was barely visible. But it was there. And once he stepped out of the room, her shoulders fell and she breathed a big sigh of relief.

Lauren sat in the back of the Jeep with Katy, Jared Stone at the wheel. The seats were draped with soft cotton blankets to keep their gowns from getting dirty. "You both look dazzling," Jared said cordially. "I'll make it a smooth ride up to the lake."

"Thanks, Jared." Lauren's stomach was in knots. She prayed her wedding plans would go off without a hitch.

"Yes, I would appreciate that," Katy said. "I've got to keep this bride intact until the big reveal."

Jared nodded. "Noted."

Lauren rolled her eyes at her maid of honor's bad choice of words, but Katy only giggled, taking her hand and reassuring her now that the time had come.

"Most of the guests have already arrived," Jared informed them. "I saw the groom with his best man, just a little while ago. Cooper drove your mama up. So everything's set."

The air grew chilly and Lauren glanced at the sky. Threatening clouds gathered overhead. *Wonderful.*

"Let's get this show on the road," Katy said, shivering.

Jared started the engine and drove away from the house. Considering that Cooper's brother loved speed and power, driving the Jeep at a snail's pace was very thoughtful of him. The drive took just a few minutes. He parked at the canopied tent designated for the bridal party. Off in the distance, Lauren spotted chairs with big white bows tied around the backs, lined up in rows under the leafy oak tree. The guests were milling around, not yet in their seats.

"Here we are," Jared said, taking her hand and helping her down, then doing the same for Katy. "I'd better run, it's almost time." He gave them each a kiss on the cheek. "See you both later."

"He's awfully…nice," Katy said.

Katy's definition of nice meant hot and hunky.

Westward Movement started playing a soft, classical number and Katy took her cue. "Looks like we're on." She hugged Lauren gently, so as not to wrinkle her gown, and then set the bouquet of white roses and lilies in her hands. "Here you go." She sighed. "You're doing the right thing, honey."

"I think so, too."

"And remember, I'm right here if you need me."

"I know." Lauren blew her a kiss and Katy, dressed in a pale pink off-the-shoulder gown, started her twenty-yard march toward the gathered guests.

Lauren stepped out of the tent and began walking slowly, her arms shivering now, from both nerves and the chill in the air. She was halfway to the altar when something caught her eye. A white, heart-shaped, wooden sign that she'd never noticed before was planted in the ground. She took a few more steps and was able to read the print in italic red lettering.

*Lake Laurie Loo*

And underneath, the words,

*Forever and Always*

Her throat closed up. Tears brimmed in her eyes. She stopped to catch her breath as her heart dipped into oblivion. First, Cooper had appeared and declared his love while she was dressing, and now this. If he was trying to make a point, he was succeeding.

Out of the corner of her eye she spotted him standing rigid, several feet away from the back row as if he was attending the ceremony, but not really. *Dear God.* Swallowing hard, she willed her feet to begin moving again and once she spotted Roger up at the altar smiling, patiently waiting next to his best buddy, Jonathan, she focused on him, only him.

When she reached the last row of chairs she halted and immediately the band's rendition of the "Wedding March" began playing.

Slowly, she began her walk down the aisle, passing rows and rows of guests standing and smiling at her, some teary-eyed. Katy's brother, Pete, and her plus one, gave Lauren a wink as she strode by. Approaching the front row, she found her mother's loving gaze on her. Her mama was trying to hide her disappointment by giving her a nod of encouragement, but Lauren wasn't fooled.

No one would fool her again.

She turned to give Katy her bouquet and then placed her hands in Roger's.

"Are you ready for this?" he whispered.

"Oh, so ready," she answered.

Minister Patterson cleared his throat and began the ceremony. Roger wanted to keep things light and simple, so after the minister spoke about the sanctity of marriage and their duties to one another, he began the ring ceremony. Roger said a few words about their future and then placed the gold band on her finger.

Lauren did the same, her hands trembling as she pushed the ring onto Roger's left hand. He gazed down at her and smiled.

"And now, if anyone knows of a reason this couple should not be joined in holy matrimony, let them speak now or forever hold their peace."

The guests sat quietly. Not even a whisper could be heard. And then there was a crunching sound as boots hit the white runner. Lauren didn't have to turn around to know Cooper was there. Her heart pounded.

But this was hers to do and nothing was going to stop her.

"Me," she said, pulling her hands free as if Roger's were on fire. She backed away from him, "I am speaking now, Minister Patton. I cannot marry this man."

The minister's eyes narrowed. "Excuse me, Lauren. Do you know what you're saying?"

She turned partially around to gaze at the invited guests. They had stunned looks on their faces. Then she caught sight of Cooper, standing there halfway up the aisle, equally stunned.

"Yes, I know exactly what I'm saying. I have every reason to believe that Roger Kelsey had been cheating my brother Tony, his loyal partner of many years, from funds due him. And now, as half owner in the company, he is also cheating me. Furthermore, upon inspection of his secret company tallies, I've determined he's been using that money to bribe officials down in Houston to gain favor for a multimillion dollar project."

"Now, wait a minute, Lauren. You don't know what you're talking about!"

"I most certainly do. Winding Hills Resort. We found evidence, Roger. You didn't think I was smart enough to figure it out. But I did, with some help. The only reason you're marrying me is so you can get your greedy hands on my half of the company and cover your ass. Well, that's not happening, buddy."

He reached for her hand. "Lauren, wait. This is all a

misunderstanding. You can't be serious," he whispered through gritted teeth. "Stop this right now."

"I am stopping this." She wrestled the ring off her finger and plopped it into his hand. "If you were the last man on earth, I wouldn't marry you. You cheated your friend, Roger. Tony trusted you. I'm only glad we were able to uncover the truth and let all these people see what kind of a man you really are."

Just then, Katy's brother appeared, coming up the aisle, approaching them. "This is Officer Pete Millhouse with the Dallas Police Department. I believe he's got some questions for you."

Roger's reddened face got a horrified look. "You bitch," he growled just as thunder boomed, shaking the sky. It was fitting, this monstrous sound intensifying the moment. "You've got nothing on me."

"Mr. Kelsey, I'd like you to come down to the station to answer some questions." Pete's voice was forceful enough to sway Roger.

His shoulders slumped and he heaved a big sigh. "I want my lawyer."

"You have every right to contact your attorney." Office Millhouse escorted Roger away from the lake area where he met up with two uniformed officers.

Many of Roger's half of the wedding guests began getting up and leaving, mumbling under their breath. She hated to do this, hated to put these innocent people through such an ordeal, but not enough to stop her little plan. She felt guilty about that, but Roger deserved to be exposed for the fraud that he was.

His best man, Jonathan, gave her a scathing look and called her a vile name before exiting the area.

Lauren gazed out at the remaining guests, her friends, her family, her coworkers. Their astonished expressions would be ingrained in her memory forever.

"I love you all for coming to my faux wedding and I'm very sorry to put you through that. I hope you can forgive me for the theatrics. It's something I felt compelled to do."

Roger needed to be taught a lesson. He was a first-class creep and not only had he been cheating her, he'd been cheating *on* her with his secretary. They'd found evidence of that, too—tasteless bikini underwear hidden in one of Roger's suit pockets in his office closet. It was laughable really, how inept he thought Lauren was, but underestimating her had been his downfall. She'd uncovered the truth, for her brother, and now she was free of Roger Kelsey forever.

"Lauren." Cooper's powerful voice commanded her attention. She turned and faced him, and his bluer-than-blue eyes penetrated every crevice of her heart. "This doesn't have to be a fake wedding."

"Cooper, what are you saying?"

"I'm saying, I love you." He spoke loud enough for all of the remaining guests to hear. "I love you so much, I was about to make a fool out of myself and stop this wedding myself. Luckily, you spared me that, but Lauren Camille Abbott, know this. You are my heart and soul, and I can't imagine my life without you. I'm sorry for all the pain I've caused you. So very sorry."

"You lied to me, Cooper Stone," she said firmly. Cooper needed to be taught a lesson, too. But then she remembered how earnest he'd been declaring his love earlier. And naming the lake in her honor had earned him half a dozen brownie points, too.

"I'll never do that again."

"You deceived me and that hurt."

Heads ping-ponged back and forth with each new twist in the conversation. At least Lauren knew how to entertain her guests.

"I'll spend my life making it up to you."

The crowd muttered sympathetic ahs.

Katy rushed up and pushed the bouquet back into her hands.

Jared walked over to stand beside Cooper on the white aisle runner.

A few guests began to applaud. Then a few more started clapping and, like a wave building and growing, the applause grew louder and more pronounced. Before she knew what was happening, Cooper was approaching her. "What do you say, Lauren? We have friends and family surrounding us and everything else we need to make this your dream wedding. Marry me today. You can forgive me another time."

Lauren glanced down at her mama, sitting with her hand to her mouth, waiting, hoping, praying. Good Lord, Lauren would never hear the end of it if she didn't say yes to this beautiful, wonderful, generous man, who made her absolutely crazy. "I've already forgiven you."

"You have?" His eyes sparked and hope stole over his expression as he walked to her side and took her hands in his. His touch reached deep down inside her.

She nodded, holding his hands, "Naming the lake after me pretty much sealed the deal. But, Cooper, I mean it. You can't go behind my back like that ever again. I need to trust you."

"I promise."

"He promises," her mother repeated.

*Oh, for heaven's sake.* Lauren smiled, finally free of all doubt and worry. He smiled back, and it was good and right and meant to be. "Cooper Stone. I love you with all my heart. Your sincere declaration of love in the dressing room convinced me how very much you mean to me. And I will admit, but don't get cocky about this, that if you hadn't intervened, I might've married that…that loser. So for that, I am grateful."

"I won't get cocky," he said. "Well, not until later," he whispered for her ears only.

A rush of heat rose up from her throat. She couldn't wait until later.

"Lauren Camille Abbott, I've never met a more beautiful, intelligent, caring person in my life. You're perfect in every way and I've waited for you my entire life. Will you marry me right here on Stone Ridge?" he asked more formally now.

"Yes, Cooper Stone, I will marry you today."

Cooper squeezed her hands and closed his eyes, taking a deep breath. "Thank you." He turned to the pastor. "Minister Patterson, please do us the honor of marrying us in front of our family and friends."

"Well," he began, clearing his throat, "this is highly irregular."

"I know, but it's meant to be," Cooper insisted. "And the right thing for us." When he turned back to her, his eyes were filled with love.

The minister gave them a stern look. "Are you both absolutely sure?"

They nodded.

"You'll have to arrange the legalities of the union at a later date."

"We will. We only care what's in our hearts right now," Lauren said.

Cooper nodded. "That's right. So please, get on with the hitching."

"Very well." The minister turned to the crowd. "Ladies and gentlemen, it looks like we're having a wedding, after all."

Lightning flashed just over the rise and then the clouds overhead nudged each other. Within seconds, a light drizzle of rain floated down onto the ceremony.

Lauren put out her palms, capturing a few drops. Cooper laughed, throwing his head back.

And then she had a thought. "Maybe it's Tony, giving us his sign of approval."

"Couldn't be anything else," Cooper agreed.

"I've heard getting married in the rain brings the bride and groom good luck for years to come," Lauren said sweetly.

Cooper placed her hand over his heart as drops continued to fall from the sky. "I figure rain or shine, any day when you become my wife is my lucky day, Laurie Loo."

Cooper sat on the grass with Lauren beside him, facing Tony's grave. One raspberry-jelly doughnut sat on a napkin atop the headstone. Powdered sugar covered Lauren's hands and she licked at her fingers one at a time. "Mmm, this is so good, Coop."

"Being as you're wearing it, I guess so." He smiled at his wife, leaned over and wiped a clump of raspberry jelly off her cheek.

"I can see why my brother liked these. He always had a sweet tooth."

"Yep, these were his favorite."

The sky was clear and blue with a fresh bite in the air. It was about as beautiful a day as Cooper could ever remember, except for that day three months ago when he'd married Lauren.

He gobbled up the last of his doughnut and flipped the lid on the box, going in for his second one.

"Careful, honey. You don't want to gain doughnut weight," she teased.

"Doughnut weight?" His brows lifted. "Sweetheart, I've never heard of that."

"No? But you've heard of baby weight, right?" she asked.

He stared at her, nodding his head. It was a strange statement. Where was she going with this? "Yeah."

"And so you won't mind if I put on a few pounds. For our baby?"

*For our baby.*

Cooper blinked, once, twice, and then he nearly lost it. "Our baby?"

Lauren nodded and a sweet smile spread across her face, the look in her eyes gooey-soft. "I'm pregnant, Cooper."

Tears welled in his eyes and his heart nearly burst from his chest. Overcome with emotion, he took her into his arms—a little clumsily, since they were sitting cross-legged—and kissed her senseless. "I can't believe it. I surely can't believe it. When is the baby due?"

"I'm about two months along, Coop."

He placed a hand on her belly, where their child grew. His child, with Lauren. The most perfect woman in the world was going to have his baby. He had a lot to measure up to. His father had left some pretty big shoes to fill, too. "I'm…going to try to be a good daddy to our child," he said reverently. "I promise."

"I have no doubt you will be." Lauren touched his cheek.

"You're gonna be a fantastic mother." Lauren was a nurturer, a woman with a heart as big as Texas. All that nonsense about her being unable to commit had washed away the minute they'd fallen in love. She'd just been waiting for the right man to come along. Him. And now their child would be blessed with her love, too.

"Thank you, Coop. I thought you and Tony should hear the news together."

Thick emotion clogged his throat. "It's fitting."

"I think he'd be happy you knocked up his little sister."

Cooper shook his head, but grinned like a damn fool. Lauren was a tease and a brat and the absolute love of his life. "Yeah, I think Tony would approve."

Cooper had come a long way in just a few months. He no longer blamed himself for the accident. He'd been set free of guilt and he had Lauren to thank for that. She'd taught him how to forgive himself and how to move on. Now, they were starting a family.

"Mama is going to go ballistic when we tell her the good news."

"Same with my mother," he said. She'd forgiven him for getting married without telling her. It wasn't exactly how he'd planned on marrying Lauren. But his mother had come to their civil ceremony, making their marriage legal and binding, the following week, and that seemed to appease her. "Mom's gonna love being a grandmother. She may even move back to Dallas."

The wind kicked up and Lauren shivered. "Take me home, Cooper," she said, grabbing his hand. "I'm having a craving."

"What would you like? You've already had a jelly doughnut."

"My craving isn't for food, silly. I want to cuddle up against the man I love and just be."

"Just be what, sweetheart?"

"Mrs. Cooper Stone, wife and soon-to-be mommy."

"I like the sound of that, Laurie Loo. Let's go home to Stone Ridge."

* * * * *

# THE LOVE CHILD

## CATHERINE MANN

To the Palmetto Animal Assisted
Life Services (PAALS) and Jennifer Rogers
(executive director and founder)

# One

"Spread your legs wider, please, Mr. Mikkelson."

Isabeau Waters rocked back on her heels, staring up the length of the Mikkelson oil magnate looming over her.

She'd spent countless hours in the company of naked and near-naked men in her profession as a media image consultant. But never in her job had she revamped the wardrobe for a man who tempted her quite so much, for so long, as Alaskan mogul and rancher Trystan Mikkelson.

Measuring his inseam? Heaven help her.

Kneeling on the plush carpet in the luxurious office space, Isabeau adjusted her grip on the measuring tape. She worked her way up his long, denim-clad legs until her eyes were level with his…leather belt. So close she could read the inscription on the Iditarod sled dog racing belt buckle.

*Exhale.*

*Think.*

*Be a professional.*

This job was high-paying and high-profile. The merger of the powerful Mikkelson and Steele family businesses into Alaska Oil Barons, Incorporated, had dominated stock exchange news, causing the market to fluctuate. Shares had only just begun to steady when the Steele patriarch suffered a major injury in a horse-back-riding accident.

Now the two factions were working overtime to make sure the company presented a cohesive image when it came to leadership. With so many offspring on both sides, Isabeau was still stunned that this man, who preferred running the family's ranch up in Alaska's north country, was their pick to be the face of the merged company. Apparently, siblings on both sides of the family were having marriage troubles, health issues or were too shy to speak in public, leaving them with only this rugged Mikkelson cowboy and a teenage Steele kid to choose from. Since the teenager was obviously not an option, that left Trystan Mikkelson.

For now, anyway.

Her mission? To make him over. His wardrobe was easy enough. The tougher part though? To keep him in-line and on-message for the next four weeks until the Wilderness Preservation Initiative Fund-raiser—a wine and dine with celebrities. Then stay on until his mother's wedding to the Steele oil magnate, Jack.

She'd done this pre-assessment routine time and time again, with many different kinds of people. But as she took note of his measurements, her eyes falling to his angular jaw… Well keeping *herself* on-message seemed like it would be the true work.

He shifted from one dusty boot to the other. "No disrespect to your profession, ma'am, but I'm not going to be trussed up like some pretty boy."

"I will keep your wardrobe preferences in mind as I order pieces and talk to the tailor. You will still be you, but a version of you that inspires confidence from less… rugged investors." Isabeau tucked a stray hair behind her ear, fingers barely grazing the pearl drop earrings her best friend had given her when she'd launched her image consulting company. A gesture of good luck, and Isabeau had made it a ritual to always wear them to the first fitting.

He grunted.

She rolled her eyes. "Use your words, please."

"Excuse me?" He raised one dark brow. "I'm not a damn toddler."

She agreed one hundred percent with that.

"Exactly. The stakes are much higher than a timeout. Alaska Oil Barons, Inc., has hired me to do a job." And that job apparently was going to include polishing his words as well as his wardrobe.

Although she could tell he'd made an attempt at spiffing up today. But based on comparison to photos she'd researched of him online, *spiffing* for him meant swapping worn, faded flannel with a fresh-out-of-the-package plaid. She appreciated the effort. Not that she'd suffered any illusions that this would be an easy gig.

For more reasons than one.

Keeping her professional distance around this hulking sexy distraction would be a challenge, to say the least.

Eyes upward. A much safer option.

Maybe.

He was grinning, damn him.

His thick hair looked perpetually rumpled by the wind into a dusty brown storm. A part of her grieved over his impending appointment with the barber. But she needed that hair to be a bit more tamed. The man too.

His broad shoulders and chest were sculpted with muscles born of hard work rather than in a gym. She would need to order larger suit jackets and his tuxedo would need to be custom-made.

He was all man, and her mouth watered with desire. Totally unprofessional and barely controllable.

She reined her thoughts in, focusing on getting her notes in place. Nabbing Alaska Oil Barons, Inc., was a coup. They were a big-time client for her, and the merger of the Mikkelson and Steele companies made the corporation all the more newsworthy right now. The business still operated out of two office buildings where the Steeles and Mikkelsons once had their individual spaces. Today, she was in the Mikkelson space.

Jeannie Mikkelson's office to be exact—Trystan's office for now, since his mother was plastered to her new fiancé's side while Jack Steele recovered from surgery after a horseback-riding accident. The spacious office was gorgeous and one Isabeau would give her eyeteeth to have, but she had to confess it didn't fit Trystan Mikkelson. From the cream-colored office chair to the sea foam–colored furniture with teal accents, it was more of a woman's space.

Trystan's eyes kept shifting to the windows along the wall and the skylight, as if he was considering an escape route to the great outdoors he was reputed to prefer.

She glanced down to jot additional notes for short-term and long-term goals. First order of business, getting Trystan properly outfitted for his sister Glenna's wedding to the oldest Steele brother, Broderick, this weekend.

As CFOs, Glenna and Broderick were the obvious ones to take the helm of the company for now, but they were emphatic that their relationship deserved to come first. The other Mikkelson son, Charles, Jr., insisted the same for his troubled marriage. And while Isabeau applauded their devotion to their spouses, and she intended to spin their choices well in the press releases, she also wanted to shake every one of them for not recognizing how tenuous things were with the merger right now.

Stockholders needed reassurance. Panic was a dangerous emotion.

Her thoughts somersaulted away from the task at hand, her mind's eye turning to Paige, her Labrador retriever, who'd stretched beneath the sofa, only her head and paws sticking out. As if the dog could sense Isabeau's attention, Paige raised her head, those wide brown eyes sympathetic and reassuring all at once. Paige cocked her head, ears flopping and fur rustling against the red vest that proclaimed her a service dog in huge black capital letters. In a smaller, less sprawling font, was the instructive Do Not Pet. Isabeau needed Paige to alert her to diabetic issues.

And anxiety attacks.

But Isabeau preferred to keep her reasons for having a service dog as private as possible. Panic attacks played a major role in why she chose to be a behind-the-scenes media person rather than working in front of the cameras. Her stalker boyfriend from college was in prison now, but the fear remained close.

Clearing her throat, she held up the tape measure again, standing. "Almost finished."

"Glad to know." He stretched his arms wide as she measured across his chest.

She considered herself a professional. She'd never had a problem with desiring a client before, while on the job.

It was going to be a long month completing her contract.

But this gig would cement her reputation, and it carried the potential to land her more clients of this caliber. She had only herself to depend on—no family, no fat inheritance. Her health was stable for now, but her diabetes had sidelined her before. She needed to build a cushion of savings for emergencies.

Never would she be like her mother, flat broke and alone.

"Mr. Mikkelson, you need—"

"Trystan," he insisted in that gravelly voice of his, a melodic rumble.

"Trystan," she conceded. "You need to weigh your words carefully. Less is more, which actually, now that I think about it, should be an easier path for you. Just no impulsive outbursts. It's easier to add to a statement than to walk back a negative impression."

"It's just a fund-raiser. I've been attending them my whole life."

"You're more than attending now. You're the figurehead of the company, a company with a president that almost died when he broke his spine in the middle of a major merger." She reminded him of what he should clearly be keeping top-of-mind but still seemed to disregard. "If you really prefer not to do this, I could talk to your family about one of the Steele siblings taking over the public role—heaven knows there are plenty of them…"

"No, I've got this." He pulled a tight smile. "The fact that there are so damn many of them is just the reason I need to do this. To make sure my mother keeps her equal stake in the company and those Steeles don't edge her out."

"I hear you, and I understand your point. But you do know that is exactly the sort of thing you shouldn't say in public."

"United front. Got it." He tapped his temple. "We're all supposed to ignore the fact that our families have been at war for longer than I can remember. I'm supposed to forget all the times my father called Jack Steele a ruthless crook."

She leveled a glare at him. "Mr. Mikkelson—"

"Trystan." His eyes were robin's-egg blue, a beautiful, vibrant hue in this otherwise stark man. "And yes, I know that's another thing I'm not supposed to say."

Those. Eyes.

This. Man.

Heaven help her.

It was going to be a long month.

All for family.

That'd been Trystan's motto his whole life. And it was why he stood, albeit begrudgingly, getting a damn makeover.

His clothes shouldn't matter. He had a business degree and ran a multimillion-dollar ranching operation.

All of which he'd accomplished in jeans and dusty boots rather than suits and polished wing tips. But his family's livelihood was on the line.

He would do whatever it took to stabilize the newly formed Alaska Oil Barons, Inc.

Even if it meant prancing around like some show horse. Even if he hated every second of the posturing.

Although working with Isabeau Waters certainly made the task bearable.

She was a breath of fresh air. And, yeah, she was very easy on the eyes.

Her red hair shone with hints of gold streaking through. It was gathered on one side so that the rest fell over one shoulder. The natural wave swirled into one big curl that tempted him to tangle his fingers through to test the texture. He was a sensual man, a man of the outdoors who experienced life firsthand rather than sitting behind a desk sifting through the details on a computer screen.

Her eyes were the soft blue of his home state's sky, sparkling and changeable. A deep breath filled him with the scent of her—like the wild irises that bloomed in summer, beautiful and an ironic mix of delicate petals that somehow managed to survive to bloom every year despite the harsh Alaska winters.

He stopped that thought short.

Damn.

Isabeau Waters was making him turn downright poetic.

His gaze turned to the yellow lab staring up at him with inquisitive, chocolate-brown eyes. Though he wanted to fluff the dog's ears, he refrained because the dog was at work. Still, his soul longed for the simplicity of a canine companion here in this unfamiliar situation.

Understanding animals was easy for him. People? Not so much.

He wanted to be on the ranch, riding a horse or even reviewing inventory spreadsheets. The public scene wasn't his forte, not like it was for his older brother Chuck. But Chuck's marriage was on life support, and that relationship was the only thing his older brother valued more than the family business.

Chuck had learned those priorities from their parents, Charles Sr. and Jeannie, a tightly bonded couple until Charles's death. They'd all feared for Jeannie when her husband died of a heart attack over two years ago. They'd prayed she would find a reason to live.

They just hadn't expected her reason would be their family's corporate enemy, Jack Steele.

Trystan had spent his teenage years hearing his father list Jack's many flaws. And now he and his siblings were all expected to just forget that.

The movement of Isabeau's slender body trekking over to the desk, her hair swishing, made him forget all about his family's drama, at least for the moment. She grabbed some binders, flipping to different sections, writing on pages and adding sticky notes. A covert glance over her shoulder, back to him, had his heart pounding.

Why was the most attractive woman he'd met in ages also the person he had to work with? He wanted to flirt with her and take her to dinner instead.

But he would have to give serious thought to the consequences before mixing business and pleasure.

Family always came first.

He'd been adopted by Jeannie and Charles when his own parents had split. His biological parents had married as teens because he was on the way. Their union had been rocky and volatile from the start. After the split, when Trystan was ten, his mother, Jeannie's sister, had been ready to turn him over to foster care. His other aunt had offered to share care of him with Jeannie, but Jeannie had insisted Trystan should have a steady home. She and Charles had welcomed him into their brood.

He knew Jeannie loved him, that she'd accepted him, but he also knew she hadn't had a choice. His other aunt hadn't really been an option as a single mom herself. Taking him in had been the honorable thing for Jeannie and Charles to do.

He owed the Mikkelsons more than he could repay. They'd saved him from an overburdened system where he likely would have ended up in a group home. They'd given him a place in their family. They'd treated him every bit as equally as their three biological children. Now, most people didn't even know or remember he was adopted. Some days he could almost believe he was really one of them rather than a cast-off cousin.

Other times, like now, he was reminded of that debt.

As if she could feel his gaze, Isabeau glanced over her shoulder at him. "If you couldn't be a rancher, what would you do with your life?"

"Why does that matter?" A shrug. No other future mattered, only the present he lived in. That was his life. Walking to the wet bar, Trystan grabbed a beer and twisted the top off. He tipped the bottle's neck to her, inquiring.

A faint smile dusted her lips, but she shook her head, holding up a hand. "No, thank you. And as for the question, I'm just trying to get to know you better, beyond our brief meetings in the past and an internet search on the history of your family. The more I understand you, the more authentic I can be in the choices I make for your image makeover. I truly do want you to be pleased with the decisions. If it's fake, that will show in your demeanor. People will sense it's a facade."

"Then we're screwed because I'm never going to be a smooth-talking, tuxedo-wearing dude." He took a sip of the beer—his favorite summer ale from his family-owned brewery, Icecap Brews. The crisp, medium-bodied flavor settled him, the aftertaste of wheat drawing out memories of late nights working on the ranch. His sanctuary.

"Trust me. I know what I'm doing." She gestured toward the binders—toward the organized checklists, charts and measures that ought to transform him from rugged recluse to the face of Alaska Oil Barons, Inc.

"Well, then, how would you feel if you couldn't do your job? If someone thrust you into a role you weren't comfortable with?" He took another swig as he leaned against the wall, noticing her confident posture, the way her brows lifted in answer to the challenge he threw at her.

A sassy smile set the corners of her mouth up, reaching those bright blue eyes. "This isn't about me."

"That's a cop-out answer."

"Fine, then. I would search for help. Like how I have my dog here to help me adapt to the curveballs life has thrown my way."

He walked toward where she leaned against the desk, his fingers tracing the corners of the beer bottle's label. Each movement, every step, sparked more static crackling in the air between them. Stopping beside her, he leaned against the desk to her left, aware of the lilac perfume on her skin. "Then what would you do if this profession hadn't worked out for you?"

"I'll answer if you will." Her hand gravitated to his Stetson on the desk, touching the felt lightly. Was she subconsciously drawn to it?

Awareness tumbled through him as he drank in her slender features—the tipped nose, the confidence.

"Fine." He nodded. "You first."

She clicked her tongue. "Testing the trust issue. Okay, I would go back to school and study clothing design. Now your turn."

"Archeology. I can see myself sifting through the earth at an excavation site." He brought the bottle to his lips, imagining what it'd be like to be immersed in an excavation pit in some remote location. No press. Few people. Yeah, he could live like that.

"So you're a patient man with an attention to detail."

His brow raised and he tilted the bottle, which caused the ale to slosh slightly. A contained wave. "I guess you could say that."

"Nice to know. The ideas are churning in my mind already."

She was sure learning a lot about him, and he wasn't finding out a damn thing of importance about her.

He set aside his beer and strode toward the yellow Lab. "Tell me about your dog."

Isabeau's spine went straight and she closed her notebook slowly, her eyes averted. "She's a Labrador retriever, she's three and a half years old, and her name is Paige."

Obvious. But if she didn't want to talk about the fact

that Paige wore a service dog vest with patches and lettering, then he wasn't going to be rude. He'd just been trying to make conversation.

Not his strength.

Turning, she flashed an overbright, tense smile. "You can ask. I was just messing with you by giving those obvious answers. Take it as a tip on how to avoid questions you don't want to answer."

"Touché. I apologize if I shouldn't have asked about your working dog. I was just trying to fill the awkward silence. I should have asked about your favorite vacation spot or what made you pick this job or something."

"Those would have been good conversation starters. But I'm comfortable discussing Paige with you. It's more the strangers approaching me with questions that are bothersome. I've even had people accuse her of being a fake working dog since I don't 'appear' disabled." She shook her head, that spiral of red hair sliding along her shoulder. "Paige alerts to my diabetes."

"How did I not know that about you?"

She stacked her binders. "It's not like you and I are besties."

He took another step closer, setting the beer on the desk, the tempting scent of her perfume swirling around him again. "But I know you. Or rather, I've noticed you and for some reason I didn't notice your dog."

"That's a good thing. If she's drawing attention to herself, she's not doing her job. Well, unless I were to be in some kind of health crisis, then she would get help or bring my medication. But she's very good at what she does. Since I've added her to my life, she's kept me from getting so distracted I miss drops or spikes in my glucose level."

"So I shouldn't pet her."

"Not while she's wearing her cape." That tight-lipped, tense smile returned as her head gave a curt, dismissive shake.

"Cape?"

"Vest. She understands that when she's wearing it, she's working. When it's off, she can play like any other dog."

"Ah, okay. Does it bother you that I'm asking about this?" An intrusion into his own life would've been met with some resistance if the roles were reversed. And the last thing he wanted to do was make Isabeau feel isolated.

"Actually, no. It's good to have something to talk about while I work."

"How does she detect your blood sugar?"

"She senses it by smell."

"Like a drug dog?"

"Or hunting dog, or search-and-rescue dog. Same premise, but fine-tuned. Not all service dogs can do it. Some do tasks like get help if there's a problem or bring medicines or steady the person if they're feeling faint. But she's got that something extra." With a stretch, Isabeau's spine arched back, drawing his eye as she settled against the desk again. "There. I have all I need to order your new wardrobe. Some of it has to be special-ordered, but I can pick up what you'll need for your sister's wedding."

"Thanks, I appreciate it. But I hope you know that clothes aren't going to change the core of who I am or what I say."

There. He'd thrown down the gauntlet.

He'd enjoyed this fitting session a helluva lot more

than he ever would have expected. And he knew without question that the woman in front of him had made all the difference in the day. Already he looked forward to their next sparring match.

So why not make the most of this month of jumping through social hoops?

His hand whispered against her impossibly soft skin, tension mounting as their eyes locked. "The best way to keep my rogue mouth in line is to stay right by my side. Be more than a media consultant. Be my date for my sister's wedding."

# Two

When she'd been a kid, Isabeau, like other little girls, had dreamed of a fairy-tale wedding of her own. Her mother had even spun those fantasies with her. Except her mom's prince charming had walked out, and even though her mother kept telling the stories, Isabeau stopped believing. She wasn't sure she even knew what a healthy dating relationship was, between her mother's experiences and her own.

So how had she let herself get talked into being Trystan's date at a family wedding? She'd said yes before she could think, her mind somehow losing its edge around this man.

A dozen times over the past two days she'd planned to tell him it was a silly idea.

And every time, she'd found a reason to delay until here they were, together, at a Mikkelson-Steele wedding.

Sure it was a small ceremony at the Steele family compound by the water, but still. Simple to these people still involved big money and security guards.

She wasn't his date, not in the romantic sense. Although Trystan was playing it to the hilt, his arm draped over her shoulders as the bride and groom exchanged vows.

Trystan leaned closer, whispering against her ear, "Do you feel okay?"

"I'm fine, just fine," Isabeau insisted quickly, then caught herself up short. "Why would you ask that?"

"Your face is all scrunched."

"That's rude." The mutter eked out between her lips, which were lifted in a tight smile. Though to be completely honest, she could feel the vise grip of tension in her teeth and furrowed brow.

"My apologies." His voice was low, but the lilt to his tone was light. Teasing. "Your *gorgeous* face is all scrunched?"

"Better, slightly."

"We're at a wedding. Pretend you aren't checking your watch wondering how much longer until the reception, like the rest of us are."

"That's not true. I'm enjoying the view. The sun just made me squint for a second," she lied through her teeth.

"Uh-huh, right." He laughed softly.

She had to confess, a summer shoreline wedding in Alaska with a mountain range backdrop was nothing less than stunning. She would have enjoyed herself if it weren't for the nerves in her stomach generated by the man beside her.

Distracting her.

The Steele estate loomed in the background, sprawling, like a cedar wood cabin on the scale of a manor house—these clients were beyond the caliber of any she'd had before. The home was nestled into the skinny pines and rugged landscape, the wildness of it all giving Isabeau a small sense of peace even with the mansion housing multiple suites for the Steele family when they were in town. The quarters for each sibling were much like luxurious condominiums. Glenna Mikkelson had even been living in her suite with Broderick for months.

Having their wedding here also made it an easier location for Jack Steele. The patriarch had only recently been given the okay to stop wearing his neck brace. He was a walking miracle, given he'd fractured two vertebrae in his neck. He'd survived the fall and the surgery that followed.

He was still an imposing figure, but pale, and she suspected he would be sitting for the duration of the reception. Likely only pride and grit kept him on his feet now. Actually, Jeannie Mikkelson appeared more stressed, worried and frazzled than he was, even with her mother-of-the-bride smile.

Isabeau glanced up at Trystan to see if he'd noticed his mother's strain. But no. His gaze slammed right into hers with a spark of awareness that made her all the more conscious of his arm along her shoulders.

Lord, he smelled good, like spices and musk and man.

He smiled, which distracted her to the point she almost missed Trystan's hand sliding down her spine to rest just above her butt. Her skin was on fire in a way she hadn't felt in a long—a very long—time.

Why was he doing this? To rebel against the makeover or because he genuinely wanted her? His behavior felt like more than playacting through a simple date. She would need to tread warily to resist getting too involved with him.

She cleared her throat and hissed, "Pay attention to your sister's wedding."

"Yes, ma'am." Trystan's hand eased upward to her shoulder again.

It had to be the wedding ceremony making her go all gooey inside, aching to grasp some of that magic in the air.

The wedding. Right. She should just pay attention to the proceedings, take in the staging and beauty for ideas for future clients who wanted a down-to-earth, simple ceremony.

The bride wore a fitted lace dress with long, sheer sleeves and a sculpted bodice, her blond hair swept up in a twist that exposed her regal neck. She held a bouquet of flowing Queen Anne's lace, white roses and greenery. Simple and elegant, like the bride herself.

The groom's tuxedo was a Ralph Lauren design with clean lines, and no Stetson today.

Unlike the other men, who all wore suits and hats.

The family resemblance on both sides was easy to spot. The Mikkelsons were blond or had hair a lighter shade of brown. The Steeles were dark haired like their father with a flash of Inuit heritage from their mother.

Isabeau had done her research on both families. The Mikkelson matriarch and Steele patriarch had both been devastated when their spouses died. She'd sifted through countless press releases to identify possible publicity pitfalls. But there were no hints of scandal in either of their marriages. It was impossible not to root for them now that they were planning their own wedding.

Glenna Mikkelson and Broderick Steele's relationship was a bit more…complicated. Rumors indicated they'd had a brief fling in college, but Glenna had gone on to marry someone else. Her husband had cheated and fathered a baby daughter with another woman—who had then abandoned her child.

The precious little girl was in Broderick's arms now, her chubby hands wrapped around his neck. Isabeau's heart squeezed at the beauty of a real fairy-tale wedding. And with unerring timing, Trystan slid his hand down to palm her waist with a warm, subtle strength that sent tingles up her spine.

God, she needed some space from this sexy "date" of hers.

The chords of an upbeat song called her back, grounding her in the moment. Head tilting, she watched as the couple walked down the aisle together. Glenna glowed as she passed them, her smile as wide as the horizon and as brilliant as the midsummer sun. She lifted the baby up as Broderick led them all the way down the velvet aisle.

A family. Complete and ready to face the future together.

A chord in Isabeau's heart snapped as the wedding concluded.

Suddenly, the world seemed to close in on her. The small crowd felt oppressive.

Space. The desire to bolt surged into her rapidly beating heart. "You know, you're right after all about the reception. I'm starving." She gestured to the caterer's tent on the lawn. "I'm going to check out the spread while you chat with your family. Bye now."

She smoothed her silky yellow dress, the hem teasing her knees, and slipped out from beneath Trystan's arm. Her skin tingled with the lingering feel of his simple touch. Her heels sunk into the grass as she made her way up the hill toward the outdoor party tent. Tables of food were strategically available everywhere she looked, even up to the balcony and sunroom. Waiters walked the grounds with trays of canapés and drinks.

She didn't have her dog with her, opting to let Paige play with the other family dogs in a large fenced area. Isabeau had decided that if she changed her mind, she could retrieve Paige quickly. Even now, she could see her yellow Lab loping with a husky, each dog holding the end of a stick not even sparing a glance at the large antlered moose ambling just beyond the fence line.

Best smile forward, Isabeau dashed away from the amassing family, from Trystan's heat, her eyes trained on reaching the balcony.

*Don't look back at him.*

Determined to find a moment of solitude, Isabeau headed straight for the mansion, climbing the lengthy stairway up to the balcony. What a breathtaking view of the festivities. And yes, she could find peace here as well, away from the temptation of leaning into Trystan's touch.

An elegant, understated spread of high tables drenched in pale lace and lit candles filled the balcony. The candles flickered, contrasting with the deep blue depths of the water lapping against the shore below.

Navigating her way from the balcony to the sunroom, she paused to lean against one of the sunroom's many open doors. Pausing to drink in the scene. To collect herself and assuage the mounting anxiety that rumbled in her chest, squeezing around her heart.

Golden sunlight drenched the room, pouring through the array of windows. An ice carving of a doe and buck glimmered, drawing her toward the spread of food. Casting a glance at the lawn again, she saw the other guests beginning to help themselves to the alfresco meal, with the option of retreating to the sunroom. Thank goodness for the spread out space for mingling or quiet. Because she felt jittery and she knew it had nothing to do with her blood sugar levels.

Salmon, ahi tuna, crab legs, asparagus, Caprese skewers…all of it made her mouth water. She built a plate of salmon and a plain roll just as a jazz band inside the house launched into their first set.

Yep. Fairy tale. And yes, a part of her still wanted a moment of magic like this. Not the angst of forever. Just the magic.

With a sigh, some of the restlessness she'd felt only five minutes ago seemed to dissolve. Making her way outside, she sat on one of the deck chairs, scanning the surreal beauty in front of her.

Isabeau tipped her face toward the brief warmth of summer, four weeks in late June and early July. Temperatures in the fifties felt balmy after her first winter in the state.

And while the thought of such cool weather feeling balmy never ceased to amaze her, the wild scenery of this state made her feel humble and small. In her college literature class, she'd been forced to read Thoreau and Emerson. At the time, their musings on nature had washed over her in a blur of words. But here, as she studied the purple of dwarf fireweed peeking through exposed granite along the shoreline, the perceptiveness of those dusty American thinkers resonated. Even with the helicopter parked in the distance.

Serenity and peace.

Well, at least it had been for a few brief shining moments. Isabeau sat up straighter as Naomi Steele approached, her belly round with her second trimester pregnancy, her dark hair gathered into an elegant bun, teardrop emerald earrings nearly brushing her shoulders. Those Steele eyes sharp, but tired. Isabeau couldn't tell how far along Naomi was—guessing months or ages had never been her strong suit.

"Do you mind if I hide out here with you?" She rested a hand on her pregnant belly. "Royce is driving me crazy about how long I've been on my feet and if I don't sit and eat soon he's going to start hand-feeding me, which would be embarrassing."

"He sounds adorable." Isabeau had spent considerable time with all the family members this past week, but somehow Royce Miller had a way of making himself scarce if there were more than two other people in the room.

"Hmm... *Adorable* isn't a word I would choose. He's sexy and brooding and a great guy. But he's also a worrier and I want to relax for a moment for some girl talk with my artichoke heart pizza—yes, I know pizza isn't normally at a reception but I have been craving it."

"I think it's delightful and actually have seen it showing up on a number of event menus." She tossed a smile over her shoulder at one of the Steele brothers as the room began to fill up.

Where was Trystan?

"And you won't rat me out about the three fruit tarts?"

Isabeau pretended to zip her mouth shut, a theatrical wink following. She leaned in to whisper, "My lips are sealed."

Naomi lifted one of the fruit tarts toward her lips, clearly excited to indulge. She popped the tart into her mouth, chewing thoughtfully. Moments passed before Naomi broke the silence, her eyes trained on the horizon. "We appreciate your help with Trystan. This merger means everything to us."

"You both have beautiful families."

"And we understand blending everyone into a congenial unit is about more than blending the businesses. But if meshing the companies doesn't go smoothly, we don't stand a chance."

"Trystan is being cooperative, which is more than I can say for some of my clients." She liked this family, both sides. Which made her feel all the more disloyal for her attraction to Trystan. She owed everyone her best effort.

"Probably because he thinks it's for only a month." Naomi folded her pizza slice in half and ate with an expression of bliss on her face.

"Pardon me?" Setting the plate down on her lap, Isabeau turned to face Naomi.

"The fund-raiser is in just less than a month, but I think everyone is hoping that some of your influence will last beyond that time and he'll be more involved. We would like all the siblings to be more involved, but I'm not sure that's going to happen, not with Trystan or some of the others, as well."

Isabeau looked over at the dance floor, at the other family members in question. Delaney, the quietest of the Steele siblings, fluffed her hair. She seemed to shrink into the background, her body language tense. Her younger teenage brother, Aiden, came up to her, dancing circles around her. A true goofball in the way only a teenager seemed to be able to get away with. The reception hall was filling up, only a few left in the sunroom.

Naomi cleared her throat, dropping her voice low as people began to pour through the sunroom into the reception area. "But really, you've done a great job with Trystan. It was evident today."

"Thank you. He's been very cooperative."

She glanced at Isabeau, grinning. "I bet he has."

Isabeau chose to ignore the insinuation. "This was a nice chance to watch how he interacts and make notes of what to work on over the next few weeks."

"We're lucky to have you. Takes a lot of pressure off us." Naomi skimmed another touch across her pregnant stomach. Her long, slender face gazing downward, possibilities seemingly dancing before her dark brown eyes. A long sigh rippled through Naomi. "I had no idea when I decided to get pregnant through in vitro fertilization how upside down my family was about to be with the merger, my brother's wedding, my dad's engagement."

"Congratulations on the baby."

"I'm pregnant with *two* babies actually. I should have considered the possibility." A small silence echoed after those words. In a less aggressive, less confident voice, Naomi added, "I'm a twin."

Pain twisted in the woman's beautiful face, pulling at Isabeau's heart.

Isabeau touched the pregnant woman's arm, offering a small—hopefully welcome—sign of comfort. "Your sister who…?"

"Yes, my sister who died in the plane crash along with our mother."

"I'm so sorry."

"I wish I could say it gets easier to handle with time, but it only gets easier to hide the pain. I can't help but think of them today."

Isabeau nodded in agreement. "Of course, that's only natural."

"You're a very good listener. I never expected to talk about this tonight."

"I'm glad I could help."

"I should get back to my fiancé. He'll be chomping at the bit for me to sit down, put my feet up, eat something from every food group."

"That's sweet that he's so attentive." Jitters pelted her, along with memories of her college boyfriend. His attentiveness had turned into something ugly— controlling obsession. She didn't see that in Royce, but she understood too well the sensation of feeling smothered.

Naomi rolled her eyes. "A little too attentive. But I do love him." She pushed herself up from the chair. "I enjoyed chatting. Let's do this again."

Isabeau couldn't miss the way Naomi's face lit up when she spotted her fiancé. The way he returned her smile. There was so much love in the air here. Did these families understand how lucky they were?

Although she wasn't sure she could trust all this happiness if it landed on her doorstep with a bow.

Striding past a harpist playing on the lawn at the reception, Trystan scanned the wedding guests in search of Isabeau. Had she gone inside to the sunroom or great room? Even for a gathering of just family and friends went beyond what most would call an intimate affair.

His plan to bring Isabeau as his date had been the perfect distraction from the way his family was meshing with the Steeles. His sister was marrying a Steele now. His mother would be marrying the Steele patriarch in a month.

The fact that his sister's wedding was at the Steele family compound rather than the Mikkelson home made him edgy and, yeah, angry too. As if the Steeles were working to erase all traces of the Mikkelsons.

All the more reason for him to make a success of this month as the face of their merged company.

That didn't mean he couldn't enjoy his time with Isabeau. No question, sparks were flying.

He had a sense that up until now, particularly in his interactions with women, he'd been sleepwalking, stumbling through the motions. But Isabeau jolted him, electrified his core.

Surprising him each time he saw her—like now.

He strode faster up the stairs to the deck leading to an enclosed sunroom. And damn, did she look hot today, sunlight catching the flames of red in her hair as she sat by herself in the sunroom, her legs delicately crossed. Manicured fingers gripped a now empty plate, traces of crumbs decorating the china.

A vision.

That's what she was. A vision he very much wanted to touch, hold and more, so much more. With the signature bravado that enabled him to approach even the flightiest and most aggressive horses, he drew in a breath and walked toward her with the Mikkelson swagger that had turned the onetime small business into an oil empire.

She sipped a glass of champagne, her bright eyes focusing on him as he drew closer.

"Come with me." Extending a hand, he noticed as her lips parted, brows raising in subdued—but visible—interest.

"Okay. You're the boss." She stared awkwardly at her plate, seeming unsure what to do with it.

Taking it from her, he set it down on a nearby table. She set her now empty champagne flute down too, rising to take his outstretched hand. "Where are we going?"

"Dancing," he said simply as they moved to the center of the great room. The small jazz band was tucked in the corner amidst the woodland themed decorations and a small space was cleared for dancing. So far the tunes had all been of the slower variety, and he hoped they stayed that way, eager for the feel of Isabeau against him.

"Dancing?" She laughed lightly, but still kept her soft hand tucked in his. "Now you've surprised me."

The band segued into a Sinatra classic and Trystan didn't miss a beat. He pulled her into his arms. He slipped his hand to her waist, letting it rest in the curve of her slender body. She seemed to lean into him, ever so slightly. Enough to send his blood pumping through his veins.

"I do know how. Mother insisted on lessons for all of us, everything from the basic ballroom styles to a session on square dancing."

"Good for Jeannie. Did you protest?" Her steps synched with his from the first move.

"Hell no, I was worried my family would get rid of me—" He stopped short. He didn't want to bust the mood here with talk about his insecurities during the early days when he'd been adopted. "Bad joke. I tend to blurt out what I'm thinking."

"Honesty is an admirable trait. It's just…" She bit her bottom lip.

A low laugh burst free. "Not always the most tactful for the business world."

A major part of why he was better cut out for his role managing the family ranch.

"That makes tact sound dishonest somehow."

Wanting to lighten the mood and chase away the shadows in her eyes, he twirled her away, the silky yellow dress fanning around her lithe legs. Radiant and sexy. She spun back to him, her hands finding his.

"I only meant that I get that there are nuances and things that are better left unsaid. I'm just not a nuance kind of man." Keeping her close, he guided their steps away from the other half-dozen couples dancing, steering her toward the stone fireplace. Massive moose antlers stared down at him. Tall ceilings provided an airy balance to the thick leather sofas that were now strategically staged against the walls rather than in their normal places.

"Let's talk about the dancing more. You're a natural. I think we should capitalize on that this month in your image building. This has a great sophisticated look to it. With the right press coverage—"

"Isabeau, seriously, the image again?" He needed a night off from all of that. The past week had been intense and outside his comfort zone. Particularly the past two days when all he could think about was having her here tonight. In his arms for a dance.

Yes, he wanted a night he could enjoy. With her.

"Could you stop with the business talk and let's just enjoy this dance?"

"Oh, um, sure. This must be an emotional day for you, with your sister getting married and your mom engaged—"

"Emotional?" He stifled a laugh, drawing her closer to his chest. He whispered against her ear, as they swayed in time to the music, "It's just a wedding. That's it. I'm focused on you."

"Wait, our being here together is supposed to be about business, working on your image."

He smiled, his blue eyes glinting.

She swatted his arm. "Stop that or I'm going to line up a dozen more press conferences for you."

"I didn't say a word so I couldn't have shoved my boot in my mouth."

"Your smile speaks volumes."

His grin widened.

"Trystan, that's not professional—or fair."

And perhaps that proclamation would have been followed by a moment—the kind he'd been thinking about nonstop since the day of the fitting—but a cacophony of voices disrupted the intensity of their eye contact, the closeness of their bodies.

Isabeau pivoted toward the noise first. Chuck and his wife, Shana, stood at the edge of the dance floor. Heat seemed to rise around them, calling a tempest into the room as their voices escalated, beginning to drown out the jazz tune.

His cousin, Sage Hammond, moved between them,

her voice low and calming. While Trystan couldn't make out what the argument was about this time, it was clear that Sage was playing peacemaker. A role he'd seen his fierce butterfly of a cousin play on behalf of her aunt and boss, Jeannie Steele.

He felt Isabeau tense, clearly uncomfortable with a family altercation. Squeezing her hand, Trystan tilted his head and mouthed, "Follow me."

A quick nod of agreement was all the encouragement she needed to leave the tense scene unfolding nearby. He maneuvered them outside, taking the path to the boathouse on the bay, near the seaplane.

Toward a small section of the compound all their own.

# Three

As the sounds of the spat faded, replaced by the light wind rustling through the low-hanging tree branches that gathered, sentry-like, at the left corner of the boat-house, Isabeau felt her heartbeat intensify.

Trystan's slightly calloused hand wrapped around hers. His skin, rough from ranch work—hands clearly used to the brush of leather reins—sending her own skin humming with awareness. She was drawn to the dichotomy of him, a tycoon in boots.

She hated to admit it, but part of her eagerness to escape his family's chaos had a lot to do with the draw of this man. In her line of work, she'd found herself frequently at the epicenter of familial disputes. It came with the territory of image curation.

But this felt different from her experience with any other client. Isabeau knew why too.

It had everything to do with the man with the charismatic, gruff demeanor.

She heard the distant bark of her dog and glanced over her shoulder to be sure Paige wasn't fretting about being away from her. A quick check assured her that her yellow Lab was still enjoying playtime with her new pals—a husky named Kota and a Saint Bernard named Tessie.

Isabeau turned her attention back to Trystan, surprised at the ease in her steps. She didn't feel the urgent need to have her dog close. A relaxed and mellow sensation flowed through her veins.

Along with a total awareness of this big, sexy man. An outdoorsman who danced with a confidence and smoothness that made her body burn.

And she couldn't help but glory in the feeling. So many of her panic attacks stemmed from negative encounters with men.

Some of the males who had flocked to her beautiful, weary mother had crowded Isabeau.

And then came her college boyfriend, who'd never laid a hand on her but stole her privacy by stalking her every move until she'd been forced to take out a restraining order.

People could leave a scar on a person's soul in so many ways.

Yet, something about Trystan put her at ease.

His total honesty.

He might be rough around the edges, but he was authentic and that kept her moving forward along with him. She would worry about the impropriety issue later. Right now, she could only think about how hot she'd found him since the first time she'd laid eyes on him.

Leading her inside, he flipped on the lights, the switch igniting the darkness in front of her with the warm glow of yellow-hued lamplight. Golden illumination revealed the luxury of even this aspect of the property.

Plush couches and well-appointed wooden furniture. A row of yellow two-person kayaks lined the wall farthest from them, complementing the neatly arranged fishing poles and nets. A powerboat docked in the water nearby, bobbing up and down, adjacent to a sitting area with Sedona-orange-colored cushions decorating a couch and two chairs. Waterproof, she realized, though they still seemed overstuffed…

Trystan turned a slow circle. "It's definitely quieter here."

She drew in a breath of the salt-laden air. "You did well at the wedding with the photo shoots."

There hadn't been media present, but still, he'd put on his game face for the shots to be released to the press.

"So I've earned my respite from the masses?"

"Is that what this is? An escape, a break?" She smoothed her silky dress, her fingers—her senses—hyperaware of every texture down to the timbre of his whiskey-smooth voice.

His blue eyes lit with a smile. "Actually, this was about getting time alone to talk to you about something other than work. I think we've both earned that. Do you agree? Or is it back to business for us?"

"I do agree," she answered, wanting to linger in the mellowness between them a while longer.

"Good, good." He strode toward the refrigerator and opened it, surveying the contents. "Ahh… What have we here?"

He pulled out a bottle of beer bearing the Mikkelson family brewery label—Icecap. He glanced at Isabeau. "There's wine and water, as well."

Inclining his head, he suggested they make their way over to the sitting area.

"The beer sounds good, but the water is probably safer for me, with my diabetes, after everything I enjoyed at the reception." She eyed the deck of cards on the table suspiciously. "Why the cards?"

He dropped onto the sofa, his body relaxed. Open. Inviting, as he handed her the water bottle. Their hands brushed, a crackle passing between them.

A blush heated her face, warmth spreading further until her body tingled with awareness. She sipped the water, suddenly so very thirsty, then set it on the table alongside the two decks of cards.

"I'm not luring you here to play strip poker. Scout's honor. I'm still learning my way around the Steeles' home but Broderick invited me out here for one of their card games—and a drink. I guess this is a man cave of sorts." He tipped back a swig of his beer. "I got the impression you'd had enough of the crowds too."

"It has been a full day." She offered up the minimal concession.

She played down her anxiety. Always. Very few people knew how she suffered. For a painstaking moment, she wondered if there'd been a hint of her discomfort today—the very thing she labored to hide. A small well of anxiety bubbled in her stomach at the thought, the reality of her condition threatening to break loose. She found herself reaching for her dog only to remember she'd left Paige out playing with the husky and Saint Bernard.

One steadying breath settled her nerves and she decided to stay put rather than bolt.

"So, Isabeau, what made you choose this line of work?" His sky blue eyes narrowed as he leaned forward, his knee just bumping hers.

Her heart hammered, the musky scent of him teasing her every breath. She spoke, even as she found her gaze locked with his, unable to look away. "I have a degree in marketing and public relations. I did some work in the media world, even reporting for a while, but found I'm more comfortable behind the scenes."

"I bet the cameras loved you."

"Thank you for the compliment." She reached for her water bottle, the condensation seeming to cool her down, to give her a sense of stability even though another part of her wondered what his lips tasted like. She avoided his eyes, hesitant to bring up the real reason she hid from cameras while encouraging others to overcome their own anxieties.

"You're welcome. What do you mean by 'more comfortable' behind the scenes?"

"I feel more in control." And Isabeau did everything possible to give herself the trappings of control. Well-organized lists, binders, schedules. Anything that gave structure to an otherwise chaotic world. She'd needed those tools after her father left and her mother struggled to keep a roof over their heads. Then her anxiety had ramped up all the more when her college boyfriend decided breaking up wasn't an option.

"Nerves?"

"You could say that." She pushed aside thoughts of the past, unwilling to have that time in her life steal anything more from her. "I believe in some ways my anxiety makes me more empathetic to the people I'm hired to help as they search for an approach to fame that fits them."

"Interesting viewpoint."

She scratched a fingernail along the bottle. "I'm happy to help you, but you seem to have nearly a perfect life, and a good amount of family support around you."

His normally assured smile fell, replaced by pain that crinkled in the edges of his eyes, the corners of his mouth. In a tight voice, his gaze too focused on the label of the bottle, he said, "No life is perfect. We all have plans, regrets, hopes."

A strain in her heart answered. She had to touch his hand. "What are your plans and hopes for the future?"

"You mean like a bucket list?"

"Sure."

"How about you start?"

"Okay." She drummed her fingers along the bottle, thinking. "I want to learn a new language. It will help me with my business."

"Pick up an instrument. My siblings play, but by the time I joined the family I was past those early years when kids usually start music lessons."

"It's not too late." She found herself warming to this topic, to sharing hopes with him, the world narrowing to just the two of them. "What about the guitar?"

"Maybe. But it's your turn…" He draped an arm along the back of the sofa, his skin brushing her shoulder, crackling the static in the air all over again.

Except she knew full well it wasn't static snapping through her veins. Not that she could bring herself to pull away. "I want to learn archery."

"Archery?" He picked up a lock of her hair.

She shrugged, thinking back to her love affair with the golden age of Hollywood, scenes of *Robin Hood* and *Ivanhoe* flooding her imagination. "It seems romantic."

"What about a crossbow?"

She scrunched her nose, then relaxed. "Not for me, but it could be hot if it's a guy using it."

He chuckled, low and husky. "Well, that's a distracting notion." He tugged the lock of her hair gently. "What about your bucket list?"

There were so many things. So many things she wanted for her life. So many things she felt were out of her grasp because of her anxiety.

She released a deep exhale with the words as they took on the power of a flash flood. "Whale watching. Stomping grapes in Italy. Speaking in front of people. Riding a camel."

"Whoa, back up." He lifted a hand.

"Grapes. I know. Unexpected." She clinked her bottle to his.

"I was focused more on the part about talking in front of a group. That's surprising, given your job." He stroked the side of her face, his hand then gravitating back to that loose lock of hair.

"I know what should be said and done. I just choke if I'm the one having to say it. So I teach others."

He simply nodded, leaving her words there, giving her space—which somehow managed to draw her closer because he understood her. No judgment in his eyes.

She'd never known that peace and fire could coexist, but here, now, the two twined into an intoxicating blend. That, along with the whole fairy-tale day, sent her swaying toward him.

The thin sliver of space between them heated with

their breaths. He lifted one hand, sketching the backs of his knuckles along her cheekbone. Her pulse quickened, her body tingling, and she tipped her head into his caress.

She swallowed, holding his gaze. Feeling the air become heavy with awareness until—yes—her lips found his. That spark exploded as she tasted him.

His hands felt like magic gliding down her back, the silk of her dress caressing her skin along with each stroke of his fingers.

With a whispery moan, she angled closer to him, the warm wall of his body a perfect fit against her. He deepened the kiss, his hold both strong and careful, the taste of him delicious. Her thoughts scrambled as Trystan's touch drove her need higher, made her want more.

Want everything.

There was something about weddings that just made people do crazy, impulsive things. All that emotion running high with the promise of lifelong happiness.

Apparently she wasn't immune.

She'd noted the effect of weddings on others more times than she could count during her early days as a wedding planner. Bridesmaids and groomsmen hooked up after their walk down the aisle, as if that moment had somehow made them yearn for marriage. Those feelings usually faded for at least one of the people, once endorphins from the orgasm waned.

Married couples who arrived at the event bickering and plucking at their formal wear soon got that nostalgic look in their eyes.

Others just got drunk and stupid.

Isabeau wasn't sure what category she fell into.

None of them seemed to quite fit. But here she was,

in the boathouse with Trystan Mikkelson, desire firing through her veins, both of them ditching their essential clothing. Her panties. His pants unzipped and inched down. Their legs tangled as they backed toward a wall-long bench covered in a blue canvas cushion with cute white anchors woven into the pattern. What a strange detail to notice, but all her senses were in hyperdrive.

Slim stripes of light slanted through the vents along the ceiling. The window was sealed tight and shuttered. The door closed. The dim lighting added to the anonymity of the impulsive moment.

She knew better.

And right now couldn't find the will to care.

She just wanted this man. Here. Now. And yes, maybe part of that wanting was a mourning for the future she couldn't bring herself to hope for—home, family, kids.

Her trust had been too damaged when she was too young.

Perhaps that's why this sexy cowboy oil mogul appealed to her. He was a lone wolf. A man more at ease away from people. He didn't need her and made his lack of concern about getting married very clear. He was content to leave propagating to all his other siblings.

So she could indulge in some of that wedding event magic for tonight.

Her soft skin made him ache to touch more of her, but the chill in the air meant it was unwise to ditch all their clothes—not to mention there were dozens of people outside partying beyond the locked door.

He hadn't expected things to go so far between them, but damn if he could bring himself to stop. She'd lit a fire in him since she'd touched him during that simple clothes fitting.

Simple?

Nothing with this woman was simple. She was a complex blend of bold and reserved, poised but with a wildness to the intense grip of her fingers sliding under his shirt, her nails scoring along his back.

Her passion seared him.

She shook her shoes free and they thudded to the floor. She sketched her foot along his calf, her legs gliding higher.

No question, this was escalating fast. "Are you sure this is what you want?"

"Trust me. I want. Oh so much." She pushed aside his suit coat.

"We can find somewhere less rustic." He slid his hand up her dress to her low-cut panties, simple strings along each hip holding the satin together.

"That would mean waiting and I am one hundred percent against waiting." She loosened and freed his tie.

Her voice was husky but sure. A very, very good thing. Persuading her to be his date to a wedding had been a good idea after all, a plan that was going to lead to a much more pleasurable month than he'd originally expected.

"My wallet."

"What?" Her hands paused along his suit pants.

"Get my wallet from inside my jacket. Condom."

"Oh. Right." With a speed and deftness he applauded, she fished out his wallet, found a condom and tossed his billfold on the floor.

Sheathed and very much ready, he stroked up her thigh and settled between her legs. Her soft arms looped around his neck and rational thought fled, replaced with a frenetic chemistry. Pleasure. Perfection. A coupling he hadn't even known was on his bucket list.

But now he knew he couldn't imagine having missed this moment with Isabeau.

And damn, but she was eager and more confident than he'd expected. She guided him and then… His mind was a blur of sensation and movement and this woman. This fluid goddess of a woman in his arms. So elegant and yet totally at ease in this earthly boathouse.

His heart pounded in his ears in time with their bodies moving against each other like the lap of the water against the dock, the roll of the waves. Her breathing hitched faster with little gasps as she urged him on, close already and sounding so earnest and honest. Her hands slid into his pants, her nails digging into his hips.

And just when he thought he couldn't hold back any longer, her back arched upward, her soft breasts pressing against his chest and reminding him he had so much more of her to explore when they made love again.

And there would be more, damn it.

The thought sent his release slamming through him like a wave crashing free from under an iceberg. His arms clenched around her tighter as they rolled to their side, aftershocks rippling through them both.

The end of their lovemaking came in the form of ragged breaths growing steady. Quietness descended in the boathouse, despite the roaring elements of the wedding band filtering through the air. He gathered her close, noting the light scent of her perfume as he stroked her hair, fingers trailing down her shoulder.

Trystan could feel her heartbeat rattling in her chest as she leaned against him. Half-dressed, he wanted to keep this moment going. The taste of the chemistry leaving him intrigued—determined.

Isabeau moved slightly, and in the din of half-formed melodies...she winced against him. "Ouch!" she exclaimed softly.

He shifted up on one elbow, looking down at her pained face. "Ah hell, what's wrong? Did I hurt you? The last thing I wanted to—"

"Charley horse." The throw blanket clasped to her, she sat up, curled over and rubbed her leg. "In my calf. Ouch, ouch, ouch—it's so fierce."

He reached for her, and she pulled back, but he insisted, cupping her calf and massaging along the tensed muscle. "I want to help."

Blanket clutched to her chest, she flopped back, surrendering her leg. "I'm embarrassed enough already. Just let me deal with this on my own. I'll be fine in a minute."

He soaked up the feel of her and searched for some of his newfound verbal skills. He needed to convince her to give them a second chance to be together like this. "Really, let me. It's no different than rubbing a real horse."

Horse? Hell. So much for the new, suave speaking skills.

"Did you seriously just compare me to a horse? I'm not feeling very complimented."

"Poor choice of words. You're sexy as hell." He swept his eyes over her, taking in her flushed cheeks and loose, tousled hair. "You don't need me to tell you that. You need me to help you bear weight on that leg without screaming so loudly you bring the whole wedding party in here."

"Oh, good point. We're seriously underdressed for that kind of group get-together."

"What an understatement." He kissed the freckles along her collarbone, savoring the patch of satiny skin.

"Somehow, we've turned this into more than just a date. And a date was all we agreed to."

He palmed her back and brought her closer. "Is there a rule against us following where the mood took us?"

"No, not specifically." Her freckled nose twitched contemplatively. "But what just happened could make our working relationship sticky if things go badly."

"And what if things don't go badly?"

Her eyelids fluttered shut, and she seemed to gather her thoughts. Eyes back open, she moved away from him, hands seeking her scattered clothes. "Emotions can cloud judgment. I pride myself on my professional reputation."

"I can understand that."

"I'm embarrassed."

"Don't be." He swept a hand over her auburn hair.

"We can't let it happen again."

"How about we cut a deal?" He started buttoning his shirt. "I'll keep my hands to myself for the next thirty days while you're on the payroll."

"Thank you." She knelt on the ground, searching for her shoes under the sofa.

"But I want to make it clear, that doesn't mean I'll stop trying to get you to ask me to put my hands on you." He started to zip his pants, and...

"You have to realize I don't want anyone to know about this. In fact, as I just said, it can't happen again." She put on one shoe, then the other. "It's unprofessional, not to mention distracting from what we need to accomplish. And it's not like this fling would be going anywhere."

Hell. He reached for her arm. "Isabeau—"

"Don't get me wrong, it was great sex and I don't regret it. We just need to make a pact that this is what it is—a wedding hookup."

He repeated, "Isabeau—"

"What?"

There was no easy way to say this. "You may want to rethink our acting like mere work acquaintances. It could be helpful to the cause."

"Thanks, but no."

He eased her back to sit beside him, holding her eyes with his. "Being a couple would make things easier if we have news to deal with a month from now."

"News to deal with? I'm sorry, but I'm not following you."

"Isabeau, the condom broke."

# Four

The afterglow of awesome lovemaking faded fast.

"What did you say?" Isabeau prayed she'd heard wrong.

Surely she had. Even though she knew full well exactly what he'd said. She willed back the tide of panic.

"The condom broke," he repeated, zipping his pants and exhaling. Hard. "I am so damn sorry. But I want you to know that if there's a baby, I will take care of both you and the child—"

"Whoa, cowboy." She held up a hand to stop him. She could barely wrap her brain around the possibility of pregnancy. No way was she ready to leap into the future just yet. A future she really, really hoped didn't happen. "Slow your roll there. I'm still catching my breath and you're already planning for a future that's unlikely anyhow."

Sinking sunlight seemed to evaporate the warmth of the sunny Alaskan day. A chilling cold worked through the room, causing the hairs on the back of Isabeau's neck to stand on end, nerves working to form knots in her stomach. In the approaching dusk, the dull yellow lamplight provided minimal visibility.

"Unlikely? Famous last words." He shook his head. "We need to be prepared. I'm simply making sure you don't spend the next few weeks in limbo wondering where I stand."

Her panic level upped a notch at the thought of pushing this subject now, before she'd had a chance to process what she'd done with him…and what had happened. "Is that a pointed statement to nudge for information on where I stand?"

She fidgeted with her still-discarded dress, the talk of a nebulous future with a child she shared with this man feeling a bit like a hazed dream. The chilling night air seemed to grow more aggressive, and she yanked her dress on, letting the fabric wrap against her skin, providing warmth.

And a much-needed barrier.

He tucked her hair behind her ear gently. "If you're feeling so inclined."

The quality of light from the small table lamps no longer felt like enough. As if sensing her thoughts, he flicked on another switch, the bright overhead fluorescent fixture coming to life with a low hum.

"I'm not. Yet." She swallowed back more of that panic. Her last serious relationship had turned out to be with a possessive stalker. The thought of commitment made her throat start to close up. She wished she had her dog but she'd been overly confident, distracted.

*Breathe—slow, deep breaths, no hyperventilating.*

If she was pregnant, that limited her anxiety medication options. Oh crap. Just the thought made her heart pound harder. "When I have my head together, I'll let you know."

"Fair enough." His hand glided down between her shoulder blades. "How about we—"

"Not a chance. I may not know a lot of things right now, but I am absolutely certain we are not sleeping together again."

He pulled his hand back, raising both. "I was actually going to suggest we plan a time to talk away from here. But what is your reason for being so certain?"

Forcing herself to stand on wobbly legs, she smoothed her dress back down. Step one. Control her image. Small routines for this chaotic moment. Checking that her earrings were still in place, she turned to face him, drawing in a breath, trying to look more confident than she actually felt.

This had been such a mistake and she needed to get out of here fast to sort through her thoughts with a clear head.

She chewed her bottom lip, then said carefully, "I'm sorry for presuming. You're right that we need to talk. This was impulsive and we both got caught up in the whole wedding aura cliché. It was a mistake, professionally and personally. And if—" she drew in a shaky breath "—there's a baby, then that's all the more reason for us to have already established an uncomplicated relationship."

"You think it's that simple? Decide to ignore the attraction and it will evaporate? I'm a man of the land

and nature, and I have to disagree with your take on biology."

"You can disagree all day long but that won't change my stance." She pulled her spine straight, her hand trailing up to her hair. Practiced hands smoothed the strands that fell loose, which helped her sift through to one immutable fact. "From this point on, we have a business relationship only. The question of pregnancy will be answered by the time we attend the fund-raiser, and if the odds play out that there's no baby, we can part ways once and for all."

Night air whipped around Trystan, chilling him in a way it shouldn't for this time of year.

To say his mind was reeling would be the ultimate understatement. He leaned on a dock post, watching Isabeau disappear up the hill, her red hair perfectly rearranged as if nothing had happened between them.

The problem was that everything had happened between them.

Her curvy silhouette brought his memory back to the softness of her lips, the way she felt pressed against him. Beautiful. Stunning. Hot. Sex that made him lose his mind, forget his sensibilities. The kind that had him thinking of making this a long-term affair.

And all that had changed with a broken condom and Isabeau's retreat.

He also couldn't escape the unsettling possibility that she might be pregnant. He would live up to his responsibility. He would even offer to marry her if he thought there was a chance in hell she would say yes.

Her current level of horror at furthering their connection and her emphatic insistence on a business-only relationship indicated a marriage proposal would not be at all welcome.

He put a mental pin in the marriage proposal idea, tucking it aside for later consideration. He would never bail on his child like his biological parents had bailed on him. Any child of his would know he or she was wanted by both parents.

Royce Miller, Naomi's scientist fiancé, ambled toward him, the shirt beneath his suit jacket slightly disheveled. Royce, a quiet guy, always seemed lost in thought. Probably figuring out a math equation in his head that would revolutionize oil production, Trystan thought. No denying it—the man was a genius.

Royce drew up alongside Trystan. "Have you seen Naomi?"

"No, I haven't seen my future stepsister. But if I do, I'll let her know you're looking for her." Trystan adjusted his Stetson, turning back toward the water. Lights from the Steele compound reflected along the glassy surface.

Royce leaned against the dock railing, his cowboy hat dipping forward as he shook his head, his expression taut. "Better not put it that way. I'm trying to get her to take a breather and put her feet up. She's having none of that."

"She's an independent one."

Pacing, Royce appeared frazzled, like a tree rustling in a gust of wind. He moved toward the grass and knelt to examine a small rock. "An independent pregnant woman who doesn't seem to realize her ankles were really swollen last time I saw her."

Naomi's fiancé moved back to the rail, leaned against it, rock in hand.

Trystan shot him a look. "Probably not wise to lead with that when you find her. I'm no Romeo, but I'm guessing insulting a woman's water retention won't go over well."

Thumbing the rock over and over in his palm, Royce nodded. "I'm aware. She's prickly as hell about being pampered. She's a confusing woman."

"Aren't they all?" Trystan's thoughts drifted away.

His question was more about Isabeau's potential pregnancy than about Naomi Steele's fiery independence.

As the company's temporary figurehead, an unplanned pregnancy with Isabeau could be a media nightmare. The irony was not lost on him that it was Isabeau who'd been specifically hired to curate his image. A much harder job if she became the epicenter of the crisis.

Damn. What would the next month look like? More important, what would the next eighteen years be like bringing up a child together?

"Do you have any advice for the next few weeks as I march around as the figurehead of this new company?"

With a flick of his hand, Royce skipped the rock. It skidded across the water for five beats before it plummeted into the depths with a defiant splash. "Why are you asking me?"

"You'll be a part of the family when you marry Naomi. Your role at the wilderness preservation wine and dine fund-raiser has been valued so far."

"You could ask Delaney."

Narrowing his eyes, Trystan shook his head dismissively. "You still have an outsider feel."

Something he identified with more than he was comfortable saying.

Royce shrugged, his attention already shifting back to the house. Likely thinking about his pregnant fiancée. "I'm not really family."

And at that, he turned to leave with an absent wave.

A deep pit formed in Trystan's stomach, sinking faster than the last rays of sunlight. "Neither am I."

Naomi eased out of her shoes, feet swollen and aching. She felt like an idiot for thinking she could pull off wearing a pair of heels to her brother's wedding.

For the few hours of the ceremony and reception, it had felt a bit like she'd stepped back in time. Back before she'd gotten pregnant, before she'd started a relationship with a sexy scientist who thrived in seclusion.

She and Royce had recently moved to a cabin on the outskirts of town. Remote. Romantic. Cozy.

*Cozy* was a fancy spin on the suffocation she'd been feeling lately.

It made sense to stay here tonight rather than driving an hour back to their little hideaway—longer if the weather acted up. She'd known the wedding would tax her stamina. She'd underestimated just how much it would though.

As she stepped out of the mansion's elevator, the motion sensor lights popped on, illuminating her room, recalling her old life. She breathed in deeply, reveling in the calm. Four months ago, Royce had blasted into her world. Or rather, she'd half conned her way into his. Pregnant with twins and trying to land the world's top oil industry engineer for fledgling Alaska Oil Barons, Inc.

Safe to say, she'd accomplished more than that. Royce was a wonderful man.

His attention to her every whim and movement though was more than a little suffocating sometimes.

She couldn't help but wonder if he stayed with her and took such good care of her because he couldn't live without her—or because he needed to care for her and her babies the way he couldn't for the child he lost years ago? Were they a replacement?

Naomi tossed her shoes aside and pressed her hands to her aching back. Pregnancy exhaustion felt different from other types of tired. She wanted to voice her fears, but couldn't. If she did, Royce would tell her not to worry and have her wrapped in cotton in under sixty seconds flat.

With a sigh, she stood back up, making her way into the kitchenette area, rummaging through the still-well-stocked fridge for a water bottle. Thirst gnawed at her throat, her lips dry. Staying hydrated took extra effort lately.

She pulled out a cool water bottle, first pressing it into the nape of her neck. She cupped her belly, her smile spreading way past her face to fill her heart.

She really should start picking up nursery items for her suite here as well as their cabin. At least a couple of portable cribs set up to capture the sunshine.

During the day, her loft didn't need any artificial light. Huge windows allowed the Alaskan sun to poke through, permeating the living area.

Her swollen feet sunk into the softness of the Inuit rugs—gifts from her grandmother when she'd gotten her first college apartment, another cherished touch in this space.

From the rough-hewn beams on a slanted, arched ceiling hung a crystal chandelier that sent prisms dancing on the cream-colored sofa, brightening the quarters.

Water bottle in hand, Naomi made her way to the sunroom—her former sanctuary, relaxing onto the reclining sofa at the center of the temperature-controlled room. A dance of vibrant oranges and reds soaked the mountains, casting the landscape in a fiery blaze.

The distinctive whoosh of the elevator door interrupted her wandering thoughts.

Royce.

She glanced over her shoulder just as he cleared the French doors to the balcony. His brown eyes warmed as he met her gaze, like melted chocolate seeping over her.

Yeah, food was pretty much her go-to imagery for every thought these days.

His charisma reached her before he even skimmed a kiss on her neck, the sensitive patch warming, launching a tingle throughout her. He was so much more than his broodingly handsome good looks. His appeal was more than a leanly muscled body, broad shoulders. And yeah, he got bonus points for the thick dark hair a hint too long, like he'd forgotten to get a haircut, tousled like he'd just gotten out of bed.

All enticing. Sure.

But it was his eyes that held her.

Those windows to the soul. To the man. A man with razor-sharp intelligence in his deep brown gaze that pierced straight to the core of her and seemed to say, *Bring it woman. I can keep up.*

Every time she was near him, raw sexual attraction crackled so hot in the air she half expected icicles to start melting off the trees. If only the rest of their relationship was as simple.

Naomi extended a hand to him. "What took you so long? I've missed you."

"I was speaking with Trystan, looking for you." Royce angled down to kiss her.

"The Mikkelsons," she said wryly. "I never thought we would be tangled up with that family two times over through siblings and parents."

"It's been a surreal few months, that's for sure. Although there are so many people in both of your families, surely the odds dictate a crossing of paths." Settling into the end of the recliner, he followed her gaze out to the scenery, the sinking rays. "I trust this guy. I really think you can relax and take it easy."

"Yeah, right. Another excuse to get me to rest. I'm going stir-crazy." She rolled her eyes.

"You're doing important work." He placed his hand on her stomach tenderly.

God, he made her feel cherished. Even so, there was a part of her insecure with what their relationship had become.

She didn't regret her decision to go the in vitro route a couple of months before she'd met Royce. Her babies were already a reality nestled firmly in her heart. But she also wondered what it might have been like if he and she had made these children together.

And then those doubts blindsided her again. She wondered if he needed these babies to fill the place in his heart left bare by the loss of his own child. Did he need them more than he needed her?

As she searched his dark eyes, she reminded herself he was an innately honorable man.

And a very protective man.

"I can still think and be an active part of the family business. They need my legal advice."

"No one's saying you shouldn't consult."

She snorted.

He lifted her feet and placed them in his lap. Practiced, patient hands worked in concentric massaging circles, pushing into the arches. "You're carrying twins. That already makes this a high-risk pregnancy. Think of our children."

"I resent the implication that I'm not."

No amount of rubbing could undo the insinuation that she would ever put her babies at risk. Her simmering temper flared, that courtroom no-nonsense edge pushing against her tongue.

"I wasn't implying anything."

"Don't back down just because you're worried my tender feelings will somehow compromise my health."

He stroked up through her calves, releasing layers of tension.

Damn. He made it so hard to be mad. Or stay mad. The pain in her aching legs melted.

"Naomi, I was reading some articles about high blood pressure—"

"My blood pressure is fine. Excellent in fact. Thanks for worrying though." Her words came out breathy as her body warmed under his caress.

"And we're going to keep it that way."

He knew exactly how to touch her, knew what her body needed. What it craved.

"Does that mean you won't make love to me even though the doctor says it's okay?" She grinned, looking at him through her eyelashes.

"It just means we'll do so very, very slowly…" His roguish smile was unmistakable.

Strong arms reached around her, and Royce scooped her against his chest, into a feeling of weightlessness she welcomed in these days of feeling more than her normal self.

Doubts that had circled her earlier seemed to slip from the forefront, becoming less intrusive as he carried her into the suite, those dark eyes still dancing as his gaze skimmed over her.

*This.*

This moment made her fears about his overprotective nature and reclusive ways feel inconsequential.

Yes. She was all too willing to lose herself in this moment.

Their relationship was still new, only a few months old, a passionate explosion. They would sort through the rest with time.

Because what they had was too precious to lose.

Since starting her consulting business four years ago, Isabeau had met clients in their homes for a variety of reasons. Despite her anxiety, those meetings didn't faze her. There'd always been a sense of comfort, partly because her clients felt at ease in their own spaces and it made the work of image curation easier.

But not all clients were Trystan.

Drop-dead sexy Trystan with his newly clipped dark brown hair and sexy, steamy eyes. Isabeau had started to get used to her trips to Trystan's temporary office space for further consultation and makeover advice. The trips to his remote home had been scheduled in advance—standard really, but when making the schedule, she hadn't taken into account an impulsive hookup and a broken condom.

Her stomach plummeted a bit as she stared out the window of the seaplane. Smaller planes made flying feel more real, more adventurous, as she studied the landscape below, from the rocky shoreline to mountaintops that still carried a hint of snow even in summer.

That sense of adventure blended with an awareness of being in a small cabin space with a man she'd slept with, in a boathouse no less. A man who was her client.

A man she could not push from her thoughts no matter how hard she tried.

The events of yesterday's wedding brimmed in her mind, overflowing until her body hummed with the desire to repeat their boathouse encounter, but slower. And without a broken condom.

Nerves pattered in her stomach. She drew in one deep breath after another. If she was pregnant, she would handle it. She would love her child and provide a stable home. Thanks to the sacrifices her own mother had made, she had an education and a career on the rise. A surprise pregnancy would slow her down, but she wouldn't let it stop her.

She pushed aside whispers of fear. If the delicate balance of her diabetes flared out of control... No. She would be okay. She'd asked her doctor in the past and it could be managed.

She was in control.

Well, of everything except her feelings for the man beside her.

Trystan guided the Mikkelsons' tiny seaplane housing just the two of them, plus Paige who curled in a tight ball between Isabeau's seat and his. The dog's head rested against Isabeau's foot. She reached down to scratch the pup's ears, flopping them back and forth, taking comfort in the sensation.

She reminded herself of her plan to get through the next few weeks of this job with Trystan—until she knew where she stood.

*Stay calm and keep your hands to yourself.*

*And above all, do not risk another broken condom.*

Trystan shot a glance her way. "What made you choose the name Paige for your dog rather than something like Fluffy or Old Yeller?"

Talking about the tasks her dog performed still made her feel uncomfortable. She was learning to draw boundaries around what she shared, but it had been quite a process over the past year since she'd been partnered with a working dog. She'd always struggled with anxiety, which spiked her blood sugar. But she'd managed with medication and some counseling. But after the stalking incident, her life had spun out of control—as had her health. She'd needed more help, help that had come in a surprising four-legged package.

"Um, why are you curious about her name?"

"We put a lot of thought into naming our horses. I've found there's usually a clue to the individual's personality when I hear the story about why they chose the name."

"That's very insightful of you."

"You sound surprised. Should I be insulted?" He half teased, eyes steady on the controls. Alert. Aware.

Sexy as hell.

He commanded a cool confidence as he guided the plane through the clear sky.

"I apologize for not thinking before I spoke. But I

guess now I have to be honest. You seem too…brusque."
Sliding her gaze away from him, she peered out the window, down to the Alaskan topography. Lakes appeared like constellations among the green valleys, the lush color a brief but vibrant treasure in Alaska.

"Maybe I'm churning around some deep contemplation during all those quiet moments." He offered her a tight smile, and though his aviator sunglasses hid his eyes, she imagined they had a dash of mischief in them.

"Perhaps you are. I should know better than to prejudge."

"So, the name Paige?"

Tucking her feet beneath her, she turned in her seat. Inspired by the conversation. By the willingness to open up. She needed him to do that if she was going to turn him into the perfect mouthpiece of the company. "How about a trade? I'll tell you more about Paige if you'll tell me the story behind one of your horse's names."

"Fair enough." He nodded once, keeping his gaze forward. "I assume from the tone of your voice, I'm supposed to go first."

"That would be nice."

"You're tougher than you appear, by the way."

"Thanks. Your horse?" Leaning forward, she awaited his answer. Probably something gruff and manly. Perhaps named for a skill or attribute. Like Rocky.

"Jerome."

She laughed, then bit her lip. Not what she'd expected at all. "Seriously? Jerome?"

"Absolutely serious. I named my first horse Jerome."

Curiosity nipped as she pictured him as a child naming a horse such a serious name. "How old were you?"

"Eleven."

Scratching along her hairline, she frowned. "You got your first horse at eleven? I assumed in your family you would have started riding much younger."

"I did ride earlier—as a guest." He touched the back of his neck, his jaw tense. "I'm an adopted Mikkelson. I visited when I was younger but didn't live with them until they took me in officially."

He'd mentioned something like that before, but somehow this full revelation caught her unaware. "That's nowhere in your bio."

"I'm a cousin, actually. My biological mother and Jeannie are sisters. I spent a lot of time with the Mikkelsons growing up, when my parents would disappear. When I was eleven, they got divorced. My mother was going to put me into foster care. My aunt—Jeannie—stepped in and adopted me."

"That had to be such a hurtful, confusing time for you. I'm sorry."

"I was—am—lucky. Things could have turned out much worse for me. I've led a privileged life. I owe the Mikkelsons more than I can ever repay."

Realization dawned. "And that's why you're working so hard to help the company."

"The business means the world to them."

Silence fell between them, thick and heavy as Alaska snow. Every bit as chilly too.

"And the reason you named that first horse Jerome?"

"That first week I was at the Mikkelson place, the week my parents made it clear they weren't coming back this time—my biological father took a job in Australia and my mother didn't want to parent alone. Anyhow, my uncle gave me a young Tennessee walker horse and had me choose the name. I picked Jerome, the patron saint of orphans."

His words touched her heart, shifting her image of him ever so slightly. "Trystan, I'm—"

"No sympathy. Now your turn. Tell me the story behind your dog's name?"

After what he'd shared, she was almost embarrassed to explain how her dog was named. "I feel like I'm coming up short. My story isn't anywhere near as insightful as yours."

"Tell me anyway and let me be the judge." His voice held that teasing tone again that smoothed the edges of his gravelly timbre.

"Paige was named at the training facility. She came there as a puppy and spent two years learning the skills to be a service dog. The organization has a fund-raiser where people make a large donation to the group in exchange for naming rights to a puppy. Paige was named from a collection by a church youth group who wanted to honor one of their classmates who died in a car wreck."

"That's very moving…"

"Those donations make the service dogs more affordable for people who don't have the twenty to thirty thousand dollars it takes to complete the training."

"Two years of training?"

She nodded, lifting a hand to block the light of the sun. "Training, feeding, vetting by paid professionals, who also rely on assistance from volunteers. Paige started learning all the basics and then over time the staff saw where she would fit best. Once a dog 'graduates,' he or she is paired with an applicant who best matches the dog's skill set."

"And they know a dog's potential even from when they're a puppy?"

Her nerves eased as she settled into explaining the more factual aspects of a service dog. Facts were so much easier than emotions. Facts could ground her.

"Different groups work in different ways, but usually groups either know the lineage of the dogs or it's a dog under two years old that has had extensive temperament and health testing. A dog can still wash out of training for any number of reasons."

"What happens to those dogs?" He guided the plane to the right with a smooth turn of the yoke, the wing outside her window dipping ever so slightly.

"Sometimes there's another type of task they can do. And if not, the dog goes up for public adoption. The waiting list for those dogs is usually long."

"I had no idea so much went into it. I thought you trained too."

"I did have to go to training classes, and I go to brush-up classes, as well."

"I'm impressed by the whole process."

She looked down at Paige. The yellow Lab raised her head, those wide, brown, knowing eyes staring straight into her soul. Life without Paige…an impossible thought now. Tears pulled at her, a knot in her throat almost obscuring her words. "Thank you, but it's a huge help to have her in my life. I'm very lucky we were partnered up."

Silence came again, less oppressive than before. Not quite comfortable though.

The skyline began to reveal more pronounced dips in the Alaskan topography. Enchanting to take in from this perspective. Almost as mesmerizing as the man beside her.

Turning to glance at him, she noticed the furrow in his brow, fine lines digging deep.

Her stomach dipped with a sense of foreboding she could not shake.

"I hadn't thought about it until now—" Trystan leveled a glance at her over the top of his aviators, his eyes full of concern "—but how does your diabetes play into possible health problems if you're pregnant?"

# Five

Trystan steered his Range Rover along the winding drive through the trees toward his ranch home.

He intended to do right by his family with the press, on social media and at business appearances this month, but for him personally, things were more complicated now. He needed to prepare for the possibility that Isabeau could be carrying his child. She hadn't answered his question about her diabetes and possible complications in pregnancy.

Time here at his house would give him the opportunity to learn more about her, to strategize contingencies. At his house. On his turf.

The charcoal-colored roof peaks of his sanctuary crested above the tall, impossibly green pine trees. Unlike his mother's sleek home, Trystan's property spoke to the Alaskan wilderness. Maybe not in the same rough-hewn way as the Steele complex. But still, his craftsman ranch house sat amidst trees, overlooking a crisp lake stocked with fish.

His place was part of the family estate, but Trystan had been far more interested in working with the land than the rest of his family. Another mark of his outsider status. He'd invested in horses and property. From the corner of his eye, he caught a glimpse of a buckskin galloping away from the paddock behind the wooden barn that sat off to the back left corner of his house.

Isabeau shifted in her seat next to him, seeming to respond to the bumps in the rough, pebble-littered road. Her eyes darted to the back seat where she'd secured Paige with a seat belt harness. "The photos of your ranch don't do it justice. This is beautiful, especially the way stones in the structure echo the landscape. You have a slice of heaven here."

"Thank you," he said simply, moved by her admiration, more so than he wanted to admit even to himself. "We can take a tour of the stables and land tomorrow, once you've had a chance to settle in."

"I would like that." She pressed a hand to her mouth, stifling a yawn. "Sorry about that. It's been a long day."

"I've heard pregnancy makes women tired."

"So does travel."

"That it does." He draped a hand over the steering wheel. "You never did answer the question about if your diabetes could be of concern if you're expecting. Is that something you've ever discussed with your physician?"

"I've been in a doctor's care since my teenage years, and yes, I asked once, wondering if I would be able to have children at all." She nibbled at her bottom lip. "My imagination had concocted all sorts of scary scenarios.

But my doctor allayed my fears. She said an obstetrician would monitor my blood sugar levels and blood pressure more closely. That I would need to be more stringent in my dietary choices. They'd use ultrasounds to check the baby's size, since diabetes can make the infant larger. It's manageable. Does that answer your question?"

"Yes, thank you." A surge of protectiveness swept over him with every item she listed, and he made fast work of parking his car.

He employed a couple in their fifties to oversee housekeeping and the stables. Dedicated and with a sense of humor he enjoyed, they'd helped him growing up, neighbors of his deadbeat parents. And now he was grateful to be able to help them in return. He introduced Isabeau to Gena and Lou knowing they would help her settle in faster than he could.

Isabeau was in safe hands, and quickly on her way up to her suite—freeing him to move forward with some business of his own.

Leaving Isabeau to rest in one of the guest rooms, he moved toward his own sleeping quarters, needing a moment to collect his thoughts. And to check on the state of his family. Especially his brother. Since the blowup at the wedding, he hadn't heard from Chuck. He and his wife, Shana, had left shortly after things ignited between Trystan and Isabeau. Chuck's marriage had been strained by their trying for a child. Years of infertility had them tense and grieving.

How would they feel if Isabeau was expecting? Would they be able to celebrate or would it bring more pain?

The door to his room opened with a slight creak, revealing a sun-soaked private space.

Home.

No doubt about it. Here, on the outskirts of Juneau, this was his element. Cathedral ceilings characterized by exposed, crisscrossed wooden beams. He took a moment in the door frame, appreciating this life. This simple moment that he wouldn't have again for a while since he'd be serving as the face of the merged businesses.

From here, his eye roved past the massive wooden sleigh bed decorated in burnt orange and mustard yellow. Instead of focusing on the decor, he let the view of the mountain settle him, thankful for the massive windows that provided an uninterrupted view of the wild that whispered to his restless soul.

Striding into the room, he closed the distance to the leather sitting area for the best view of the snow-topped mountain. Stepping over the deerskin rug, the same deerskin rug he'd made with his father and Chuck many, many years ago, he searched for his silver laptop.

Time to call his brother.

He found his laptop on the rustic antler-and-glass side table by the leather love seat. Leather groaned as he settled into the massive, ergonomic office chair. He turned the computer on and pulled up the video chat application.

When Chuck answered the call in the sprawling library that he also used as an office, he appeared calm, ever in control, the family leader since their father had died. And clearly working in spite of his insistence that he was taking time off. Fatigue set in his jaw, and the normal fire that danced in his eyes seemed stymied.

Knowing his brother wouldn't offer up personal information without being prodded, Trystan cleared his throat. "How's it going? Everything settle out okay?"

Sighing, Chuck ran his hand through his flared blond hair. "Sure, temporary peace restored."

"Temporary?"

"Marriage is…complicated." He shrugged his shoulders, sagging in the ill-lit study.

Trystan could just make out book spine silhouettes lining the shelves in the background Chuck pinched the bridge of his nose, exhaustion stamped on his face.

"I'll take your word for that, Chuck." Sympathy for his brother pushed through his own muddled head over his limbo state with Isabeau. "Is there anything I can do?"

"I appreciate your call. That means more than you can know."

"It's tough to know what to do. I don't want to butt into your private business."

"You're my brother. And hell," he chuckled hoarsely, exhaustion in every tone, "you're saving my ass by stepping in for me as the face of the company. I know this isn't your gig." Picking up a nearby bear paper weight, Chuck shook his head. Guilt seemed to settle in the lines of his face. He stopped examining the paperweight to look at Trystan in the camera. The picture of brotherly sincerity. "I owe you."

Trystan waved his hand, half grinning. "Hey, you can come shovel out the horse stalls sometime."

"Deal."

As he thought about the way talking to his brother had helped him, he wondered if maybe he'd been missing an obvious source of assistance in his pursuit of Isabeau. "Is Alyana still staying with you and Shana?"

"Yes, she is. Do you want me to have her call you? Or I can just bring her here. She's in the next room."

"Please. That would be great if you could get her. And take care, brother. Call me if you need me."

"Will do," Chuck said before disappearing from the screen.

Trystan questioned the wisdom of this, but he was fast learning from Isabeau that there were arenas of his life where it was prudent to ask for assistance. His younger sister stepped into view, willowy and shy, but sharp, in a way that came as a surprise because it was unexpected from such an unassuming source.

"Hello, Trystan. I see you made it home. I hope all's going well with the consultant. She seemed nice at the wedding."

"She is very effective and…" He hesitated over what was too mild a word to describe Isabeau, but over-the-top words weren't his style and would generate more attention among his siblings than this call and his questions already would. "Yes, she *is* nice. Very nice. And that's why I'm calling. I need your help."

"Before we start, let's be clear." A small laugh accompanied Alayna's raised hand. "I'm not going to take over your appearances."

"That's not why I'm calling."

She crinkled her freckled nose. "You're going to make me feel guilty about not helping, and I hate that."

"Because it works. You're a softie."

"I don't have the luxury of hiding from our hard-headed older siblings." She toyed with her necklace, no doubt one of the crafts from her small business. "And really, you know I would make a mess of things."

"You're welcome here anytime." Except now. He was hoping for time alone with Isabeau, which brought him back to the reason for his call. "I just need suggestions."

"On what?"

"Things that will impress Isabeau Waters."

A flash of interest sparked in her eyes. "Impress professionally or personally?"

He paused for only a second. "The latter."

She dropped the necklace, suddenly becoming more serious. Focusing on him. "You're kidding me."

"Have I ever been a joker?"

"Not really..." She scrunched her forehead, studying him for a second before continuing, "Okay, then. Women are all different, so there's no set gift or date that will appeal to all. My best advice? Listen to her. Really, really listen. You'll find your clues."

He shook his head. "You can't seriously expect me to sift through that and make heads or tails of it."

She shrugged, but didn't cave. "I can't do the hard work for you. Women are impressed by men who listen. Men who make an effort to understand them."

His temples pinched with a new ache, but he supposed her advice made sense. "And, when I understand her, I'll know what to do?"

"When you listen, you'll discover her passions. The things that are special and important to her." Alayna heaved a sigh, and he wondered if she'd given that speech to any other rock-headed men before.

Something about her tone shouted *yes*.

As he watched his sister sign off, Trystan wished women weren't so damn enigmatic. Clues and a million different answers.

Except he also knew, he'd never been so drawn to a woman the way he was with Isabeau. Which meant...

Time to start searching for something as special and unique as the woman herself.

* * *

Isabeau was more than a little surprised by Trystan's home.

Sure, she'd seen photos and done her research about how he'd participated in the building of his house—both literally and financially. But there was peace here in this place that no photos or descriptions could capture.

She could understand why he wouldn't want to leave his private mountain retreat for the corporate grind.

Knees curled to her chest, she sat on her bed, sinking into the depths of the mattress. Outlines and ideas for press opportunities formed a semicircle around her. A pen passed between her fingertips as she examined a document for a satellite radio show. Paige yawned from across the room. She sat stretched on the white carpet in the abbreviated living space between the bed and the oak-framed fireplace. The dog's corresponding chuff drew Isabeau's eye from fine print to the lazy yellow Lab, and then, once she saw her dog was just sleeping, she soaked in the view.

The sun had already slipped behind the tree line, but her room seemed as dazzling as ever. Everything since she'd met Trystan felt like a dream. One she had to wake up from.

Burying herself back in the documents, she shifted files to the wooden chest at the foot of her bed. Then she paused for a moment to examine media outlets from both television and podcast, and considered the events that would put him in the public eye, from a state fair to a private power broker dinner. Chewing her pen cap, she almost didn't hear the door creak open.

Instantly, the pen cap returned to a more normal, natural position on her thigh. Trystan.

Somehow, even though he leaned in the door frame in muted light, her heart pounded heavy and fast. Awareness ricocheted through her system. She remembered all too well the closeness she'd felt with him before.

Closeness she needed to forget and resist.

Waving a paper in her hand, she said, "You have an interview at a Juneau news outlet next week. I've outlined a list of subjects that could come up so we can talk through your answers."

"I'll tell them the truth." His words, articulated as anticipated. The hard line.

Shaking her head, Isabeau flashed a small, corrective smile. "A polished truth that steers clear of reporter traps. You're an intelligent man. I believe you'll enjoy the challenge."

"Was that a compliment?" He moved into the room, approaching her. Dark eyes inquisitive.

"It's the truth, told with polish." Stacking the papers into a neat pile, she wished he wasn't so appealing all the time. It would make staying on track so much easier.

"Touché." He took the papers and scanned them, shuffling through. "If you'll email me the files, I'll go through them and prep first thing in the morning. After that, I thought we could both use some relaxation, some settling-in time. Maybe it'll give you more of those insights for crafting my image."

Too many insights into this compelling man could be trouble for her considering her level of attraction.

What if she found out she liked him even more?

"What did you have in mind?"

A noncommittal shrug relaxed his shoulders as he sank into the leather armchair in the living space adjacent to the bed. "Your choice. Horseback riding? Kaya-king? Dinner out, if that's what you prefer?"

How easy it felt to be near him. Even Paige liked him. Isabeau debated her choices for the outing.

"Any chance we can kayak and whale watch in a way that won't scare me to pieces?" Being with him made taking a risk easier.

Maybe that was because he was the biggest risk of all.

Damn. She was in deep with this man.

He studied her with that steady look of his. "That can be arranged."

In the moment, in *this* moment, Isabeau felt her throat swell up a bit, seeming to stop air and words. His gaze lingered, and her skin heated in response. Though, if she were being honest, her own eyes searched him a moment too long, as well.

Silence passed and electricity built, seeming to hum in the air.

He angled closer. "Is everything satisfactory with your suite?"

"It's lovely." She glanced around the room again, toying with a lock of her hair. "There's everything I could want."

"I made sure there were snacks available. If you or Paige need something different, just let me know and I'll arrange it."

"Thank you." She chewed her bottom lip. "I know what happened between us at the wedding reception wasn't planned and I hope it won't make things awkward. We have to work together. So any outings we take together are all toward that goal."

"Heard and understood." He nodded quickly.

Her eyes narrowed. "No secret agenda?"

"I am dedicated to doing my best for my family."

"That doesn't sound like an answer."

"I realize things are tense. Let's just say that I intend to do my job, and at the same time we should get to know each other better. Just in case."

Those last three words echoed in her skull. A reminder of why she needed to be professional and focus. If she was pregnant, she would need a successful business life more than ever.

All she could do was nod before he stood up from the chair, a ripple of muscles beneath his cotton shirt. "I'll see you in the morning."

Afternoon sun high in the sky, Trystan sprawled in his kayak, his face tipped to the rays. Summer days stretched long here, and he soaked up as many hours as possible.

The waters off the coast near Juneau weren't as cold as other parts of the state, and he hadn't slept much last night. This was a simple outing to share with Isabeau, one he hoped she would find as soul soothing as he did. A low-key way to ease closer to her, learn more about what made her tick.

Because truth be told, every day with her made him ache all the more to have her in his bed. He had to wonder now why they couldn't use this window of time where they didn't know about a pregnancy to simply explore the attraction, see where it led them.

He could sense she wasn't ready to hear that suggestion yet, but he was a patient man. He had her here, now, out on the water on this awesome summer day, a picnic basket full of food waiting for them in his Range Rover parked on the shore.

But that feast waiting for them held nothing to Isabeau's perfectly curved figure accentuated by the form-fitting wet suit, visible even with a life jacket. Despite the warmer waters right now, the wet suit was often a standard part of the kayaking experience in Alaska.

Surveying her for a moment, he watched the way her nose scrunched as she paddled forward, gliding through the water. He had to give the dog credit too. She seemed to take everything in stride, unconcerned by the life jacket and the lack of land in her immediate vicinity. Not even flinching when a pair of wolves had sprinted along the tree line before disappearing into the forest.

He paddled closer, one smooth stroke at a time, steering into the current. "You know everything about me and I know so little about you." Other than just where to kiss her on her neck to make her sigh with pleasure.

"You didn't run a background check on me like most of my clients?" She paddled as well, her strokes not as efficient as his, but not bad for an amateur.

With practice, she could fit right into this way of life.

He winked. "I figured if the family hired you, you must be right for the job."

"That's quite trusting of you."

"I have my strengths. They have theirs. But I suspect you're dodging my question." He eased his kayak closer to her, bumping the side to adjust the angle so she didn't drift too far from shore.

"There's no massive secret. I grew up in Washington, the Seattle area. My parents...divorced...when I was in elementary school. My mother worked hard to give me the best life possible." She kept her eyes averted, her strokes growing more even the longer they were out on the water.

"Your mother loved you." He could hear it in her voice.

"Yes, she did." She blinked fast, her smile wobbling.

"And your father?"

Her smile thinned. "He decided working less meant he could pay less child support," she said drily. "He went with that plan until he could figure out a way to leave without a trail."

"That's wrong on so many levels." He couldn't imagine a world where he would walk out on his child. Even the thought of being a father had his mind spinning with the ways he would be there for Isabeau and their kid.

If they had one.

His gaze gravitated to her stomach, hidden by a life jacket. A stomach he'd stroked even when their impulsive connection hadn't left much time for ditching clothes and seeing each other. That part, he regretted and hoped to rectify someday soon. The sooner the better.

She paddled in long, even strokes, the sun glinting off her red hair gathered in a topknot. "My mother and I were better off without him, but it still makes me sad she had to work so hard for so long. She remarried to a great guy who treats her well."

"And she still lives in Washington?"

"She did…until she passed away a year ago—lung disease."

"I am so very sorry." Squeezing her hand, he reminded himself of his sister's advice about asking and listening. Learn as much as he could about this fascinating woman—not a hardship at all. "What brought you to Alaska?"

"I wanted a fresh start. Turns out there are plenty of rugged, rich Alaskans in search of an image consultant." She swept her paddle through the water. "Have you ever wanted to live somewhere else?"

He scanned the bay, drinking in the banks filled with lush green grass, the shadow of a bird rippling on the water. Mountains far in the distance. Everything he needed right here. "Nope."

"I thought this time on the water was about getting to know each other better."

"Sorry." He tipped his head back to watch the progress of the eagle soaring through the sky. "Longer answer? I love my home state. I love the land and feel strongly about protecting what we have."

A smile shone in her eyes. "That passion in your voice is exactly what you should bring to interviews." She nodded in affirmation, her topknot listing to the side. "I hear you and Delaney Steele both played a large part in persuading Royce Miller to bring his innovations to Alaska Oil Barons, Inc."

"He just needed to know there were people in the family who genuinely cared about preservation and not just the cost-cutting measures in his pipeline upgrades."

"That's what makes your two families strong, you know. None of you speak as one voice. You each have your own viewpoints and perspectives. No cookie-cutter types."

"I definitely will take that as a compliment."

"Why do you seem so surprised?"

"I think of an image consultant as ironing out all the wrinkles in a personality."

"Not at all. Personality is what captures attention, and that is the ultimate goal. You just want the right kind of attention."

Conversation ceased as a whale crested the water in

the distance. Even from here, the kayaks bobbed with the ripples from the massive creature. The beauty of whale watching never ceased to leave him in awe.

But it was nothing in comparison to the beauty of Isabeau's face right now.

"How's your bucket list going today?"

A wide grin—a real one this time—danced across her face. "This is perfect. Thank you."

Her eyes sparkled. Her joy made his breath catch slightly. All he wanted to do was reach over to her kayak and kiss her. Slowly. Deeply. To linger in a way they hadn't during their hasty coupling in the boathouse.

But perhaps a better chance to linger with her would be during the picnic.

Those thoughts were cut short as Paige barked once, twice, full out, calling to him as she pawed at Isabeau. Her eyes glazed over and she swayed. Her paddle fell from her hands, hitting the side of the kayak and then the water. Her lashes fluttered closed as dread filled his gut.

Trystan paddled faster, closing the gap between them but all too aware of how far it was to shore.

# Six

Isabeau had learned to live with diabetes as a teen. But her body's lack of cooperation still frustrated her. Swaying, she forced her eyes open again. She gripped the sides of the kayak to keep herself from flipping as she sought to right the world wobbling in front of her woozy gaze.

Dimly, she registered Paige barking an alert—usually she pawed, then whimpered. A bark meant Paige was moving on to the big guns since Isabeau hadn't heeded the first levels of warning. She tried to focus, to form words.

Words eluded her, but she saw Trystan paddling toward her with concern on his face. Help was on the way. She wasn't alone. She simply had to hold on.

What an alien feeling to have someone to lean on so she could experience life more fully without worrying about what-ifs with her health. She could boat and watch the whales. And while she was sad the outing was done, how awesome to have experienced it.

With Trystan.

Paige's barking decreased to a whimper as Trystan drew closer, stroke by stroke. Her dog seemed to recognize his help.

"Talk to me, Isabeau," Trystan's voice carried over the rippling water. "What can I do to help you?"

His words cleared away more of the fog.

"I'm okay. Just light-headed." Her hand shaking, she reached into the waterproof box hooked to her kayak. "I'm eating a snack now. I'll be fine." She found a packet of almonds and popped a handful into her mouth, chewing slowly.

He grunted. Trystan looped a rope through the hook on the front of her kayak and paddled out front. With powerful strokes, he headed for shore, pulling her boat after his. She kept popping almonds in her mouth, feeling her vision steady with each bite. She should feel guilty about him having to haul her back to shore, but he paddled so effortlessly, he didn't seem at all fazed. Muscles rippled along his arms in the wet suit.

Her mouth watered.

She was definitely feeling better. "I'm sorry to have scared you," she called out to him. "And I'm really sorry to have ruined our outing."

"I shouldn't have pushed you to overdo it." His words came out tight with self-recrimination.

"I'm an adult. I know my limits and I came prepared." She finished off the last almond and continued, "Everything's fine. Paige did her job."

He grunted again. With a final sweep of the paddle, his kayak slid up onto the shore. He stepped out into the shallows, water lapping against his knees and hauled her kayak the rest of the way. He extended a hand and took her arm, bracing her as she swung her legs over the wide body of the boat and found her footing. They made their way to the rocky shoreline, Paige splashing alongside.

He eased her to a sitting position and beached the kayaks while her dog shook the water off and settled by her feet.

Trystan returned to kneel by her. "We should go home."

"I'm okay now." She tried to stand but he kept a hand on her shoulder. "Truly, Trystan. I let myself get caught up in the moment and didn't listen to Paige fast enough. Thank goodness she was insistent. Let me just check my A1C level to be sure."

She tunneled her hand into the waterproof bag and pulled out a small pouch and her cell phone. She noticed him wincing when she pricked the side of her finger and tested the blood. Funny how she didn't even think about it, she was so used to living with the condition.

Reading the results, she smiled in relief. "All's good. I'll just log it into the app on my phone, then recheck later. Thank you for your help and for being concerned."

"Of course. I just wish I'd paid closer attention and noticed signs sooner—"

"You couldn't have known." She braced a hand on his chest, the hard wall of muscle warm beneath her palm.

Her fingers twitched with the urge to explore. His pupils widened with awareness as his eyes narrowed, lasering in on her.

Her throat moved in a long swallow, and she couldn't resist the need to lick her lips. His gaze flickered over her mouth, lingering.

"Isabeau," he said simply, his voice husky.

She knew she should push him away. She'd promised herself she would keep him at arm's length. And yet she ached for him, ached for his kiss, ached to find out if she'd imagined their explosive connection.

Before she could finish the thought, she swayed toward him. Her eyes slid closed as their lips met and she melted into the sensation. The salty scent of him. The strength of his arms around her. The echo of the husky growl in his throat.

Her fingers crawled up his chest to his cheek, bristly from an afternoon shadow. Everything about the kiss was more than she remembered. Maybe because they were in the bright sunlight that left a glow even behind her closed eyes. The wind rolling in off the water gave an expansive feeling to the moment, uncontained by walls. The taste of him was crisp and tangy, and it stirred a hunger that seared her veins with every throbbing heartbeat.

And as she angled away from a kiss that had to end because taking it further was too dangerous, she couldn't escape the truth.

She'd just made a huge mistake.

Because now she wanted him more than ever.

He couldn't decide if kissing Isabeau had been a good idea or not. She'd clearly wanted him, and he'd been off balance from the scare of her nearly passing out in the kayak, and he vowed to do some internet research on diabetes once he was home.

And he also vowed that one impulsive kiss would not derail his bigger goal of winning her into his bed.

After she'd pulled back, she'd been all business again, talking about them packing the boats and eating their picnic food in the car instead as they returned to the house. She had emails to check and calls to return. And he'd lost track of all she'd listed. He'd been more focused on watching her, gauging her mood and deciding how best to proceed.

For now, he'd decided that since she wanted to ignore the kiss, he would go along with that. It was certainly better than having her declare it couldn't happen again.

Progress of sorts.

A progress that gave an extra kick to his steps as he walked into his great room after showering.

To find Isabeau waiting.

For the moment at least, she seemed unaware of his presence, which gave him an opportunity to study her.

Her hair was piled on her head, glistening with dampness. So she had showered too. She'd changed into leggings and a flowing white shirt that called to his hands to tunnel underneath.

But he was learning that slow and steady was the better move with her. He didn't want her to run, the way she had after their encounter at the boathouse. He needed to use their time together wisely.

Striding deeper into the room, he looked closer and what he found surprised him. He'd expected to discover her with her computer or tablet, but instead she was… pulling yarn out of a bag. Shock left him too surprised to ask why she wasn't answering all those emails and calls she'd mentioned back at the water.

Legs tucked to her side, Isabeau fished a crochet

hook from her blue paisley bag, settling deeper into the left side of the light tan sofa.

She looked up at him, her red hair falling into her face slightly, contrasting with those bright blue eyes. "What's with the frown?"

"I'm just...surprised, maybe even a little confused."

"I'm just crocheting." She tugged more of the yarn free.

A few strides took him past Isabeau and the living area to the outer wall made entirely of windows. From over his shoulder, he called, "Why?"

"It's relaxing and productive at the same time. I decided to give myself a chance to settle before getting back to work." She shifted her legs to the other side, tucking a throw pillow behind her.

Scanning the horizon, he took a steadying breath. Concern for her health—and maybe an unborn baby's health—weighed heavily on his mind, despite the normally calming effects of the sprawling landscape peppered with pines and other evergreens.

Since the construction of this ranch-inspired building, Trystan had felt, even if it wasn't a permanent feeling, at home here. If there were ever a physical building that fit his state of mind, it was this place. Every detail reflected Trystan's soul, from the carved wooden figurines of moose and bears to the sweeping panorama of the Alaskan wilderness supplied by the wall of windows.

After a few moments, he made his way back to the hearth and sofa area where Isabeau sat with her yarn. "How do you feel?"

"I feel great. Really." She smiled reassuringly. "And yes, I checked my blood sugar levels to be on the safe side, and all is well. It was just one of those things.

They happen, not often, but that's my life. I'm sorry you were worried."

He sat beside her and tapped the tan-colored yarn. "What are you making?"

"Scarves for local homeless shelters."

Not what he'd expected to hear. "That's really kind of you."

"What goes around comes around," she mumbled so softly he almost didn't hear her.

"It would be good if more people thought that way." He and his family had so much that sometimes, no matter how many charity foundations they set up, he wondered what more they could be doing. He felt a twinge of conscience about not giving enough of his attention to the upcoming wilderness initiative fund-raiser. Isabeau was here to help him and still he found her a major, tantalizing distraction. "When did you start crocheting scarves for homeless shelters?"

"And blankets and hats. My mother and I were gifted with some of each when I was a young teenager."

Shock knocked him off balance for a beat. He blinked through it and willed his face to stay neutral. "You were homeless?"

"After my dad ran off for a while and we got evicted. We were only in a shelter for a couple of weeks, but it saved us." Her fingers worked deftly, yarn transformed from static string to the beginnings of a scarf.

She didn't look at him.

She didn't move, other than her fingers.

"I'm so sorry." He understood what it was like to have your world uprooted by turmoil, but he'd always known he had a place to live.

"No need to be sorry. I'm here and successful and

okay. There was this little old lady there who crocheted for us."

"As a volunteer or staff member?" he asked, enjoying the sound of her voice and appreciating her opening up to him.

"A former resident. She understood what it was like and that was her way of giving back." Isabeau's eyes took on a pensive air, as if seeing inward to the past, looping yarn over the crochet hook faster and faster. "She helped me while Mom searched for a job. It was summer, so school was out. We sat and she showed me how to crochet."

He searched for something to say, but words weren't his strength, and it wasn't like he could ask her to coach him on this. "You're really talented."

She glanced at him quickly, half smiling. "Just because someone's poor doesn't mean they have to be grateful for donations that look like crap."

"Good point."

She laughed softly. "You still seem confused though."

Such an understatement. When his family had approached him about working with an image consultant, he figured he'd be working with a vapid woman only interested in the veneer of things. Not one whose heart had such depth. Now, after meeting Isabeau, he felt a splash of embarrassment for his initial assessment of an image consultant stereotype. "I just didn't expect an image consultant to be so…deep."

"I'll try not to be insulted." She yanked free a length of yarn before setting to work again.

"I've made no secret of the fact I'm participating in this makeover under duress. I'm just not that into superficial appearances."

"People gain confidence in different ways, and if that confidence is used to do good for others, then this—" she held up the scarf in progress "—helps me more than the receiver."

Those bright eyes met his and she lifted her project to show him the small progress. He could almost see a younger Isabeau—the one in the shelter, gaining confidence because an old woman had given her a fine scarf.

"Yes. You're definitely a surprise." Leaning toward her, he studied her face, the way her fingers moved, the careful attention to the smallest detail.

He studied her mouth.

"Well, thank goodness I'm not boring." She took her bottom lip between her teeth, releasing it slowly.

A bolt of desire shot straight through him. Electrifying him. "Lady, you are far from boring."

More than air, he wanted to kiss her again. Holding back was difficult as hell. But something told him this wasn't the time to press her on that—or more. He didn't want to spook her and lose ground.

He was definitely making progress. So the best bet?

Double down with another outing to romance her.

Later that week, Isabeau wondered when she'd lost control of her client.

When he'd kissed her? Or when he'd looked at her with a passion so intense it seared her?

After she'd steadied her blood sugar and nerves with some good old-fashioned crocheting, she'd spent the evening locking down a schedule of podcast interviews for Trystan.

Only to have him surprise her with the announcement of another planned outing. As she'd started to argue that work needed to come first, he'd surprised her yet again by revealing he'd set up a publicity opportunity on his own. He'd secured a news interview at a gold rush festival in Juneau.

She tightened her hold on Paige's leash as they walked through the festival goers, proud of her dog's firm focus in such a melee. Boy, was there a lot to take in. Surveying the crowd, she had to admit that although this might not have been an event she'd have set up for Trystan, the festival was full of life.

Chain saws hummed in the distance from the wood-cutting competition where woodsmen—and women—showed off their prowess carving art from huge logs of Alaskan pine. The scent of fresh sawdust, sweet and sap-tinged, hung in the air everywhere they explored. A small livestock show nearby kept kids entertained with a petting zoo where eager goats cavorted for the reward of a treat. And now, she paused as she heard the cheers of another crowd near the band pavilion.

For a moment, she lingered, watching a lean twenty-something brunette hoist an axe above her head and aim at a target fifty paces away with surprising accuracy. A small crowd made up of older couples and young families cheered, loosing whistles and whoops of approval into the air. Beaming, the young woman took a mock bow before nodding to the next competitor.

Guitars and a banjo played in the background providing a peppy beat for their wanderings. Navigating through throngs of people gathered outside food trucks and the lines for inflatable slides, Isabeau felt strangely at peace.

Rather than continuing to watch another competition—this time with two men racing against each other to climb a pole—she slid her attention to Trystan, who walked confidently beside her. His muddied cognac-brown cowboy boots were paired with worn jeans and a red flannel shirt, sleeves straining against his muscled arms.

Damn. Sexy as ever.

Isabeau cleared her throat, elbowing him. "This was a fantastic idea. I'm impressed."

"Pleased to hear it. This is one of my favorite festivals. And it seemed a good platform to talk about ways we Alaskans are working to responsibly cultivate our resources."

"And I'm impressed again. You have more of a way with words than you give yourself credit for." Or than she'd given him credit for. When he was in his comfort zone, he was spot-on. "I can see you being one of those old-school gold miners, forging your way through the Alaskan frontier, living in a tent."

She couldn't quite make out his eyes from the shade cast by the brim of his simple Stetson.

He laughed softly. "Sounds like heaven to me. In fact, I wouldn't even need the tent. Just give me a hammock to string between two trees and a thermal sleeping bag."

A line of elementary school–age children walked by, laughing as they clutched cotton candy puffs that wavered in the wind in time with the banjo music. Such a sense of community.

"You fit in well here," she said, noting how many people who recognized him waved and smiled. He was so…accessible. Not as distant as he'd seemed in more formal settings. Guilt pinched her. No matter how much she told herself she was tailoring his makeover to fit his personality, she saw the truth. He was a happy and whole person right here, right now, no changes. "This month will be over soon and you can go back to living at your ranch full-time, sleeping bag and all." Although she couldn't help but think how Naomi had mentioned the possibility of him taking a more active role beyond this month. Would the business still want her services long term?

More importantly, would she still be spending close quarters time with Trystan long term?

"I'll miss you." He nudged back his Stetson, and his deep blue eyes met hers, locking her in place.

Her skin tingled, and the noisy, packed world faded away for an instant. "We've only been working together a little over a week."

"Then that should tell you what an impression you've made on me in such a short time."

"I have a job to do." And this flirting made it tougher. How would she resist him if their lives were tied together permanently through a child?

"And I'm asking you to consider the possibility we could see more of each other. You work on a consultant basis. You could take time off. Money's not an issue. These are the sorts of things to consider, especially if there's a baby."

There it was. The issue that clouded everything else.

This special outing, his flirting—none of it was just about dating each other. They'd made that kind of casual relationship impossible by impulsively sleeping together. As much as she'd vowed not to live her mother's life, vulnerable and alone for so many years, Isabeau had not made the wisest choices lately.

"I won't be dependent on anyone, particularly a man I'm sleeping with."

He fell silent, clearly digesting her assertion.

But before Trystan could lobby a response, Isabeau saw a news crew out of the corner of her eye.

Saved by the media.

Not a phrase she used every day. Relief washed over her. "News crew at your two o'clock." Isabeau nodded in the direction of the huddle of journalists gathered outside a funnel cake stand.

The female reporter—high heels sinking in a mud puddle—tapped her cameraman on the shoulder. A mutual recognition, Isabeau realized. The cameraman adjusted the gear on his shoulder, and the news media team began their approach.

"Time for my debut," Trystan muttered, motioning for Isabeau to follow.

"Mr. Mikkelson," the reporter called, waving. "I'm so glad you and your girlfriend could meet with us for an exclusive."

Isabeau blinked in shock.

Girlfriend?

# Seven

A half hour later, as they settled into the SUV, Isabeau was still steaming over being maneuvered.

She'd been so immersed in the beautiful day with Trystan that she'd never seen it coming.

Now, he guided the rental vehicle from the packed parking lot, and she watched the fairgrounds grow smaller in the rearview mirror as her regrets grew larger.

She'd been drawn to Trystan, succumbing to that chemistry, because she'd thought he was giving her the personal space she'd requested while they waited for pregnancy results.

Instead, he was just setting her up for his own agenda. To press and push for...what? Either to get her to sleep with him again or ensure some kind of hold over her if it turned out she carried his child.

She glanced down at her stomach, then over at him, his hands so sure on the steering wheel.

As if he felt her gaze, he looked back at her. "I didn't tell her that."

Sure, whatever.

"The damage is done. The story's going to run and it will say that I have a personal relationship with a client." She hugged herself, agitation rising. "Denying the report won't do any good."

"Then let's do the opposite and play it up as a great romance. People do fall for each other on the job. Letting the public know we're dating could prep for news if you're pregnant—"

"I know, I know. There will be no hiding the truth. But what if I'm not and we've convinced the world we're having some great love story?"

"We'll quietly break up…if that's what you wish."

His hesitation gave her pause as well, and launched a surprise flurry of butterflies in her stomach. "If that's what *I* want? Are you saying—after a little over a week together—that you're madly in love with me?"

"Of course not. But I've made no secret of the fact I would like to see more of you." He reached across the space to stroke her shoulder. "Come on, let's enjoy the rest of the day. We could even turn around and go back, take in another part of the festival, get something to eat."

"How can you just drop a bombshell like that and then say let's have a funnel cake?"

"There's nothing we can do about the past except enjoy the future." He nudged his Stetson up, sliding his sunglasses in place.

Easier said than done.

"It's been a full day. If you don't mind, I would like to get a quiet meal and turn in early. Or maybe you've already planned for us to go to the airport?"

"Actually, no. I filed the flight plan for the morning."

Her back went straight with suspicion. This was too much. Paige nudged Isabeau's foot from the floorboard of the front seat. "Trystan—"

He raised a hand in defense. "I had to plan it for tomorrow because of weather tonight, which I only learned about when we landed. I was going to tell you at the festival. I have arranged for a hotel suite for us so we don't have to drive the couple of hours back and forth to the ranch—and yes, the suite has two bedrooms. I've also had some clothes sent over for both of us, along with arranging for Paige's needs, as well."

Guilt nudged a lot harder than her dog. She melted back into the seat. "I'm sorry if I sound like an ingrate. You're being very thoughtful."

"I am not setting you up." He shot her a pointed look. "But make no mistake, I am working my ass off to impress you."

She bit her lip hard to keep from telling him the truth—it was working.


Trystan had learned a lesson at the Juneau festival. He needed Isabeau—in more ways than one.

She brought a light and sparkle to his world when he saw it through her eyes. His practical, blunt nature tended to miss the beauty in a moment and, yes, the nuances, as well.

He'd been certain he'd set up the perfect day for her, down to an interview that would show her his work ethic. Instead, the reporter had surprised the hell out of him. Not to mention setting back his progress with Isabeau. If he'd included her in the plans, she surely would have arranged that interview to their benefit and had the reporter eating out of the palm of her hand.

Instead, he'd walked them into a media trap.

Tonight, in the five-star, waterside hotel suite, he would have to tread warily. At least she was relaxing in the small, saltwater pool on the screened-in balcony. The waters were warmed. He'd seen her head out in a swimsuit, sexy as hell, even though he would have preferred they enjoy the bubbling waters together, naked.

But he sure wasn't walking away from this chance to be with her, to get closer.

He'd ordered a light, tapas-style dinner to eat while lounging in recliners in the shallow end—Alaskan crab tacos, fresh tortilla chips and a fruit salsa, trying to keep her health issues in mind. Stepping out on the enclosed balcony, he heard acoustic classics piped in softly through the sound system.

Isabeau glanced over her shoulder, the creamy flesh drawing him closer. "Trystan, hello. Thank you for this restful evening. This is lovely." She gestured toward the shoreline and mountain view. "No matter how long I'm here, I just can't get over the beauty of Alaska."

"I'm glad you're pleased." And he owed his sister a huge thanks for her suggestions.

She lifted a taco from the silver platter by the pool, held it over a napkin and took a bite, savoring it. "And this is definitely better than a funnel cake."

Kneeling beside her, he thumbed the corner of her mouth. "This is most definitely a better way to spend the day with you."

"I'm wearing a swimsuit." She raised an eyebrow and took another bite of the taco.

Yes, he knew, but he didn't see the need to point out

he'd been waiting for her. "I fully expected you would. I'm wearing swim trunks, as well."

"Thank you. Maybe it seems silly given we've…" She trailed off, nibbling at the last of her food.

"Not silly at all." He pulled off the hotel robe and sat on the edge of the other lounger in the shallow end. They were here together. He was making progress with her again.

"It's only that I think we need to keep things simple until we know where we stand in a few weeks." She ate the last bite of her crab taco and set aside the napkin on the tiny table.

"Understood." The thought that she might be carrying his child sent a protective surge through him again. Each time he considered their future, the feeling grew stronger.

"Your eyes don't say you're backing off." She reached for her sparkling water with lemon.

"I hope my eyes say that I hear you." He forced himself to relax, resting his elbows on his knees. "My mother—Jeannie—taught me to be respectful to women, so I won't push anything you don't want. But my father also taught me to pursue what I want."

"I would love to hear more about him. I only know what's in the business reports about Charles Mikkelson."

Trystan saw wariness in her eyes, so he settled on sharing a bit of his past to put her at ease. "My father—my adopted dad—loved competing in the Iditarod Trail Sled Dog Race. Every year, our family gathered to cheer him on. Even when I was only their cousin, they would invite me."

Apparently his words were working to soothe her

because she turned to face him, dipping her toes into the water. "Have you ever joined the race?"

"I tagged along with him the year before he died. I wish I hadn't waited so long." He averted his eyes, looking out at the harbor full of boats, the sun still shining in a long Alaskan summer day.

"I can tell how much you miss him."

He glanced back at her. "I do. He shouldn't have died so young. He was healthy, active, got his checkups. But he was a workaholic and the stress killed him." He missed Charles Mikkelson every day, the man who'd been the only real father he'd ever known.

"How can you be sure it was stress?"

"I know it in my gut. That makes it tough for me to root for this merger. It's going to put my whole family in the middle of power plays at an even higher level."

"Perhaps the collective effort of working together will distribute the work." She angled toward him, her feet brushing against his.

"Doubtful, but something to hope for." He stroked the arch of her foot with his toe.

Her eyes narrowed, but she didn't pull away. "Tell me more about the race and the family gatherings."

"The Iditarod is named for the trail, and the race can take anywhere from eight to eleven days depending on the weather conditions."

"I've lived here for two years and I find it inconceivable to think of eleven days in the elements." She stroked her fingers through the frothing waters.

"That's our Alaska." His gaze gravitated to the mountain view. His home. "The trail was used by Inuits hundreds of years before the Russian fur traders came in around the 1800s. Coal miners and other traders used it too. The race is an important part of our culture, even more so now that snowmobiles have all but made dog sledding extinct."

"What about the dogs? Isn't it…um…" She looked at Paige sleeping on the floor by the pool, then back at him, her blue eyes concerned.

"There are groups that feel the race is cruel to the dogs, but the commission responded to those criticisms with stricter monitoring and punishments for those who don't care properly for their dogs. There's debate, and I can't speak to everyone. But I know my father's dogs were a part of our family life. Dad would lose a race before harming his dogs. If a pup didn't show joy for the run, then that pup wasn't a sled dog." He nodded toward Paige. "The same way she was screened for the right job for her."

Isabeau nodded slowly, pensively. "I've heard it said that the moment a dog opens its eyes, he or she is searching for a purpose, a job, whether that be as a house pet or service dog."

"Or search and rescue or agility… Yes, that's the way I see it. I have a purpose too, and it's not to head a company. I'm made to run the ranch, to commune with the land." But he was also honor bound to protect his siblings and their stake in their father's legacy.

It's what Charles would have wanted him to do.

"The turmoil of this merger, the way they need you to help—it won't last forever."

"I know that."

"But you also can't exclude yourself from all family events just because you don't like crowds or the spotlight. You're lucky to have so many people who love you and care about you."

"What about you?" He settled back onto the lounger, some of the deep tension seeping from him—tension that had started with this business merger. "Are you living your dream? What if you couldn't live in a city, building celebrities?"

She set aside her glass of sparkling water, shifting uncomfortably. He seemed to have a touched a nerve, but had no idea how.

She started to stand, the V of her emerald swimsuit offering a tantalizing view of her breasts. "I may have reached my limit in the pool."

He touched her arm lightly, concerned by the skittishness in her eyes. While he wanted her, he absolutely needed her to feel the same. "You're safe with me. I mean it. Nothing happens unless you're on board too."

After a second's hesitation, she settled back into the tub. "That's important to know… Paige doesn't just alert to diabetes. She also alerts to my anxiety and helps me during an attack."

He didn't want to assume and guess wrong. "Could you explain what you mean?"

"In addition to diabetes, I have generalized anxiety disorder." She met his gaze defensively. "In certain situations, I have panic attacks. She has quite a few tasks she can perform, but a couple of examples… Paige uses pressure therapy to alert and soothe me. If I come home and am afraid someone could be lurking inside, she can clear the house, checking every room."

She rushed on, that defensive brace to her shoulders only strengthening. "Some people confuse service dogs and emotional support animals. An emotional support animal is an untrained pet that provides comfort. He or she can't be denied access to rental property if there's a doctor's note, but the pet can't go into restaurants and such. A service dog is a highly trained animal, performing specific tasks and granted public access but expected to behave. I know I'm babbling, but so many people just don't know the difference. And there's still a lot of education needed regarding service dogs for PTSD and anxiety."

"It's okay, Isabeau. You don't need to explain or justify to me. You're impressive and so is Paige." As much as he'd wanted to learn more about her tonight, he hated hearing that she grappled with worries that might get in the way of her happiness. Many pieces of things she'd said before came together in his mind, finally making sense. "You mentioned that you prefer to be behind the camera."

"That's a part of it, yes."

"I'm very sorry," he said and meant it. He wished he'd known earlier so he could have moved forward more carefully. Not that it stopped him from wanting her.

"Take the pity out of your eyes. I have health issues, but I'm not made of eggshells and I'm taking care of myself. This is my life. I'm a survivor and I'm pleased with the life I've built. Paige enables me to experience that life to the fullest."

He stayed quiet, knowing better than to push her further, but her revelation certainly roused more questions for him.

"You're curious about the cause of my panic attacks."

"That's your business to share if you wish."

"Thank you. I appreciate your sensitivity on the subject—and the fact you don't have a horrified expression on your face means a lot to me."

"I'm glad I passed your test." He found himself look-ing toward Paige, grateful to know the full extent of the dog's purpose.

She laughed slightly. "I didn't think of it as a test, but I guess maybe it was, subconsciously."

She turned to face him and continued, "The anxiety attacks started young, with those times we were home-less. There were some hairy situations in shelters and even with some of my mom's boyfriends. And then—" she swallowed hard before pressing ahead "—I had a boyfriend in college who didn't like it when I told him we were through. He stalked me afterward, even after restraining orders and jail time."

Paige whimpered, then inched over to rest her head on the side of the spa tub in a sign of comfort Trystan now fully recognized. The realization of what she'd gone through sucker punched him.

Ah hell. He wished he'd known Isabeau then, that he could have somehow been there to protect her. "That's the reason you moved to Alaska."

"Yes. Even though I feel safer here, the jumpiness and the fears that spiral into anxiety still linger." She draped a hand over the side of the spa tub and stroked her dog's head. "Paige senses when those panic attacks are coming on. She does things like pressure therapy against my leg to alert and relax me. In a situation where I'm feeling crowded, smothered even, by crowds, I may give her the 'space' command. She'll walk a cir-cle around me, which keeps people back. In a restau-rant, I'll tell her to 'watch my six.' She faces the other way, watching behind me and lets me know if anyone is approaching me."

"That's really amazing." The connection between

her and her dog had never appeared stronger to him than right now.

"She is my lifeline in so many ways."

"I never would have guessed she was doing double duty."

"That's the whole idea, that she inconspicuously does her job and hopefully catches an issue before it becomes a major incident. If possible."

He couldn't miss the trust it took for her to reveal the deeper truth behind her dog. "I appreciate your sharing this with me."

"You keep talking about wanting a relationship of some sort." She paused, staring down at her fingers as they combed through the shallow water. "And I need for you to understand things are very complicated with me."

He stayed right where he was, but locked his gaze with hers. "I hear you. And I'm not deterred."

Somehow that look felt as intimate as any kiss. Something had changed between them, something he hadn't anticipated and wasn't completely sure he understood—

His cell phone chimed from across the room and Isabeau startled.

He shook his head, damning the device. "Ignore it."

"You should—"

The ringing stopped.

"See," he said, "no chime for a message. Must not have been important."

The ringing started again.

"Really, Trystan," she said, rising from the pool lounger, the sight of her curves in a sleek emerald one-piece ramping up his pulse. "You should get it."

She tugged on the fluffy robe and he surrendered. For now.

He hefted himself from the water, grabbing a towel on the way to his phone. He snatched his cell from the patio table and saw his brother Chuck's number.

"Yeah," Trystan barked. "What's going on?"

"Sorry to call so late, but there's been an accident at one of our pipeline construction sites."

"Damn." Trystan said under his breath, tucking the phone between his chin and shoulder as he wrapped the towel around his waist. "Was anyone hurt?"

"Minor injuries, all being treated," Chuck assured him, but his voice was heavy with foreboding. "Protestors are already flocking to the area, along with the press. We need this assessed and handled. I know this isn't what you signed on for when you stepped up to help this month. If you need me—"

"No, I've got it. You're where you need to be."

"Thanks, brother. I don't want the Steeles thinking we can't hold up our end of things and elbowing us out."

"Understood. I'm on my way." On his way into what could be a media hell storm. "Fill me in on the details."

As he listened, he gestured to Isabeau and wrote on a notepad for her to read.

Get ready to leave. Accident with the pipeline. Media/Protesters gathering. Will need your help.

Trystan needed her help.

Those simple written words had seared themselves into Isabeau's brain as she packed and then, once the weather had cleared in the morning, flew with him to the pipeline accident, the plane landing on a nearby stretch of water. Maybe she was feeling vulnerable after all they'd shared in the Jacuzzi.

But she couldn't deny the swell of pride that he'd acknowledged what she had to offer.

She'd never been to a pipeline construction site before, and it surprised her to see just how remote the facility was. So remote they'd jumped in the small plane to get here and Trystan had landed on a stretch of bare earth alongside the work site. Unlike the journey to Trystan's ranch, the flight toward damage control had been a blur of snowcapped mountains and evergreen trees. During the flight, she'd gone over some media ground rules for this scenario. While this particular event was out of her wheelhouse, Isabeau knew how to craft and spin a narrative. They would frame the story and put out all associated media fires.

He was a couple of yards away, gesturing toward the ring of trucks around the site while the foreman made notes. It was difficult to hear over the protestors shouting and blasting music, just past the trucks. They congregated near their bus and a couple of tents to protect them from the elements. Clearly, they were geared up to stick around.

Thankfully, no oil had actually spilled. Isabeau sent up a small prayer of thanks for that. Still, the gathering news media lingered outside the chain-link fence. Their cameras looked unnatural against the skinny pine trees reaching skyward.

Protestors armed with signs gathered, starting rhythmic chants. "Hey, hey. Oh, oh. These pipelines have got to go. Hey, hey. Oh, oh..."

Surveying the crowd, she guessed there were about

seventy-five protestors and half a dozen news crews. Not too bad, but serious enough to warrant alarm.

Trystan had jumped right in, speaking, navigating the concerns of both conservation activist Delaney Steele and the pipeline construction workers. Though he'd vowed this wasn't his element, Isabeau couldn't help but notice how smoothly he directed comments and offered strategies. In some ways, the chaos here echoed and complemented the chaos of a ranch. Perhaps that was why he'd been asked to step up. Same skill set, different beast.

The ever-eccentric and brilliant Royce Miller appeared from behind Isabeau, flanked by his fiancée, Naomi, the official lawyer of the Alaska Oil Barons empire. Even from her spot on the sidelines, Isabeau registered the determination in Naomi's eyes as she assessed the situation, her hands resting on her pregnant stomach.

Royce's work boots crunching on gravel as he joined Trystan and the foreman. As the research engineer brought on for ensuring safer pipelines, Royce's presence here was critical. After all, as she understood things, it was his innovative design that had kept the oil from spilling over in this accident. That piece of information would come in handy when fielding media questions. The company had ceased activity on the pipeline as soon as the malfunction occurred. Another snippet of data that would help defuse this situation.

Naomi stopped alongside Isabeau, hugging her long sweater around her as the wind whipped through the work site. "How's it going with prepping Trystan?"

Isabeau angled her head closer to be heard over the whistling wind, but her eyes stayed on the tall, commanding presence of Trystan bringing a well-known, friendly reporter into his discussion with Royce and the foreman. Good call. "I think you've all underestimated him. I'm honestly not sure he needs my help other than picking out clothes for special events, which you could have paid someone far less to do."

Naomi laughed in a quick burst of disbelief. "Are we talking about the same man? The guy who hides out when there's any event with a guest list in the double digits?" Tapping her temple in faux concentration, she exclaimed with a slight edge, "Oh wait, that would be my fiancé."

Isabeau nodded, still focused on Trystan. Magnetic charm pulled her in, seemed to make her feet ache to take even just one step toward him. "My point is that Trystan handles himself well with the press. He's in his element talking about issues pertaining to the land—like now. So the preservation fund-raiser capitalizes on his skill set."

"Are the press and protestors supposed to be coming in?" Naomi gestured to the news media and demonstrators that moved toward them, albeit slowly. Naomi pushed a hand into her back, stabilizing herself.

"We have a conference scheduled shortly. They are just setting up."

Although that was true, a wave of nerves pulsed in her blood at the forward progression of angry people pushing at the simple orange tape barrier.

*One. Two. Three. Four.*
*One. Two. Three. Four.*

Isabeau counted through each breath in and out to subdue her nerves. The crowd's chants became louder, more urgent than before. Drums were added to the protestors' repertoire. She searched for Paige, and her dog seemed attentive but relaxed, which reassured Isabeau. Ignoring agitators, she turned her attention back to Naomi.

"Hmm," she said, absently fanning herself. Sweat crested on her forehead, discomfort contorting Naomi's mouth.

"How are you feeling?"

Naomi grimaced. "Fine."

"Are you sure?" Scanning the woman, Isabeau noticed other signs of discomfort. Naomi shifted her weight from foot to foot.

"I mean, I feel a little tired. But this wasn't something I could miss. Too big of a deal to leave to someone outside the family."

Another roar pulsed through the crowd. Protestors pushed through the barrier tape, banging their hands together, voices screechy. Panic mounted in Isabeau's throat.

"I can understand that. Perhaps a doctor's visit after this?" Her voice cracked, throat closing slightly as Paige whined and pawed in warning. The dog circled in agitation.

Surging forward, the gathering crowd closed in on them, drowning out Naomi's response. Panic fixed Isabeau to the spot. Colors and sounds faded, lost their vibrancy as the crowd jostled around them.

Light-headed, she could just make out the muscular build of Trystan pushing toward her. Shouting something she couldn't quite understand.

A protestor shoved into her, sending Isabeau stumbling back against Naomi. Paige let out a warning bark as the protestor advanced, and then the dog shifted her attention, body tense and alert as she raced back and forth between… Naomi and Isabeau? Barking and barking.

Had the jostling crowd and shouts confused Paige? Unusual, but Isabeau was struggling to process the mayhem. Dimly, she registered strong arms—*Trystan's arms*—yanking the protestor away from her right before…

Trystan punched the man square in the jaw.

# Eight

Trystan knew he'd blown it.

Too bad he hadn't figured that out before he'd started swinging his fists.

But once Royce Miller and a security guard pulled him off the guy who'd been crowding Isabeau, the red fog of protective anger dispersed from Trystan's mind. The guard and Royce had quickly shuttled him into the site foreman's trailer, along with Isabeau, Naomi and a very agitated yellow Lab.

Once the door clicked closed, Trystan shrugged off the hands guiding—restraining—him. "I'm okay. I'm in control."

Royce eyed him skeptically, backing up a step and nearly running into a pull-down bed in the narrow Airstream. "If you're sure."

Trystan planted a hand on the built-in desk crowded

with papers and calendars. His head throbbed with agitation. And worry.

"Absolutely." Trystan turned his attention to where it should have been all along—Isabeau. "Are you alright?"

He took in her pale face, her dog leaning heavily against her leg as she drew in deep breaths. His pulse still hammered in his head with concern for her.

"I'm shaken but fine." She stroked her dog's ears. "We need to think through how to spin this because the photos are going to be all over the internet before we even step back out." She glanced down at Paige. "Settle, pup-pup, settle."

The dog whined, tugging away from Isabeau, so unlike what Trystan had seen from the highly trained service dog. "What's going on?"

"I'm honestly not sure. Paige is giving the alert for diabetes, but I really don't think there's an issue for me right now."

Trystan shifted restlessly from boot to boot. "Should you check your blood sugar, to be safe?"

"I will, I will." Her forehead furrowed, and Trystan slid a bracing arm around her waist. "She's usually so focused on me. The only time I've seen her do this was back in the early days together. I was at a doctor's appointment, and she alerted to an older lady right before she suffered from diabetic shock—"

Naomi gasped, pressing her fingers to her lips, her other hand on her stomach.

Royce was by her side immediately, hand around her waist. "What is it?"

Naomi paled, a sheen of sweat on her forehead. "Paige was barking at *me*—"

Her words grew slower and slower, stretching out as

if she were reaching for thoughts, for even the ability to speak, until she went completely still, pale and confused.

And ill.

Back at the compound in Naomi's old suite, Royce opened the fridge door, searching for fruit. He pulled out raspberry and mint leaves, placing them next to the small bowl filled with oranges.

He'd always been a man of routines, particularly in moments of stress and uncertainty. And damn. The events of the last twenty-four hours had pushed his limits, trying his well-tuned strategies. Starting with the oil malfunction and ending with his fiancée passing out after the altercation at the protest.

Protectiveness mobilized his movements after Naomi had zoned out. He'd barely registered the ride to the ER. He couldn't forget what the doctor had said. Naomi had gestational diabetes and needed bed rest to ensure her health and the health of the baby.

Pulling out a cutting board from the small kitchenette in Naomi's loft apartment in the Steele compound, Royce focused on what he could control. Like slicing perfectly sectioned oranges to add to the glass of ice water for Naomi.

The knife glided through the skin of the fruit, juice gathering on the cutting board, stinging the scratches on his hands from working on models as he continued to think through better safety features for the oil refining process.

He added two orange slices, four raspberries and a few mint leaves to the glass. Wanting to do more for Naomi. Knowing that she had reacted poorly to the news about bed rest. One of the reasons he adored her was for her streak of independence, her ability to take care of herself.

But the gestational diabetes scared the hell out of him.

The concern over her health and the twins' health took him back in time. To his former fiancée and her miscarriage. How she'd walked away. He'd lost everything. The pain of that breakup had haunted him ever since.

Losing Naomi?

The thought was more than he could bear.

He shuffled toward where Naomi stretched out on the sofa. Nerves pulled at him and he was careful not to spill the fruit infused water.

He wanted to make everything easier for her. But he tried not to drive her crazy by hovering. Though if he had to be honest, he was halfway to going crazy too being stuck in this house full of Steeles and Mikkelsons.

So. Many. Damn. People.

Naomi slumped deeper into the sofa, tossing a magazine back on the coffee table. "Bed rest for gestational diabetes. Seriously." She reached down to pet their Saint Bernard, Tessie, sprawled on the floor by the couch. "I'm going to lose my mind."

"No, you're not." He gave her the glass of water and moved the remote control closer to her reach. "I'll keep you entertained."

"I enjoy you, don't get me wrong, but just the two of us—and Tessie—24/7? You may enjoy the life of a recluse, but it's not my cup of tea, at all." She took a deep gulp of water.

He stifled a wince at her grouchiness. Her frustration was understandable and she had to be scared. He just wished she hadn't mentioned how damn different they were, something that had been bugging him more than he wanted to admit.

"You have more family than anyone I've ever seen. Maybe you and your dad can share recliners in the sun."

She rolled her eyes, rubbing her stomach slowly. "I'm not sure the world is ready for both of us to be tied down in the same place."

He chuckled softy. "Valid point."

Sighing with resignation, she said, "Go hibernate at work. Really. I'll be fine."

"I can work here." He forced an easy smile, even as the walls closed in on him. He gravitated toward the wall of windows showcasing the Alaska landscape… mountains, water, seclusion. He turned back to Naomi. "You might need something."

"I have a phone, along with a houseful of family and staff. I will be fine."

"But you're my fiancée."

"Then let's go to your place."

His place? Wasn't it *their* place?

"No…" He shook his head. "You're right that it's safer to be here at your father's compound, closer to town."

"I could be stuck like this until the babies are born. You would really live in the middle of all this chaos?" she asked, shock and disbelief stamped all over her beautiful face. "All these people?"

"For you. Yes." He meant it too, even knowing it wouldn't be easy. Already he was itchy, mentally listing places he could hole up on his own.

"But it's not in your comfort zone."

"It's not forever." He wouldn't let himself think about

the idea of his isolated home making her feel as stir-crazy as this place made him. "Your health and the health of these baby girls is top priority."

Picking up her crystal water glass, she eyed him skeptically and stirred her straw through the fruit. "Okay, for now. Let's revisit this once we've recovered from the surprise."

"Sure," he said, not that he intended to back down. She needed to be here. He kissed her forehead, breathing in the scent of her shampoo. "Rest. I have work to keep me company."

"Okay, then," she answered, yawning, her eyes already at half-mast. "I'll be quiet..." Yawning again, she started to drift off in that near narcoleptic way he'd learned was common with pregnant women.

Exhaustion hit him hard and fast. Adrenaline let-down, no doubt. He eyed his computer across the room, but dropped into a fat recliner instead, snapping his fingers for his dog to join him. Tessie cast a soulful look at Naomi, then ambled over to him.

His heart turned over when he looked at Naomi, no question. He loved these two babies that—while not biologically his—were already his in all the ways that mattered.

But he was a man of logic and he couldn't ignore the hard, cold truth.

As he stroked the Saint Bernard's head, he couldn't help but think about how fast he and Naomi had jumped into this relationship. Their chemistry had been power-ful; the emotions had run high. They were in love long before realizing how damn different they were.

Now, watching her cradle her pregnant belly even in sleep, his heart turned over on itself. A new ache cracked open in his chest and he knew he wasn't going to be able to close his eyes and rest even though he was exhausted. She was starting to talk about how different they were.

How long before she decided the compromises were too great?

Isabeau drank in the Alaskan wilderness from atop a horse, hoping to figure out a way through some of the recent tensions. After taking Naomi to the hospital, they'd regrouped at the Steele compound.

Jeannie's home on the outskirts of Anchorage didn't have stables, so they'd opted to gather at the Steele mansion to confer with the family on the pipeline accident and the resulting press nightmare.

She'd sent out some social media messages that calmed the storm, or at least refocused the attention. Footage of an interview with Royce the day after the incident had certainly helped. He'd been surprisingly calm and collected during his scientific statement of opinion on the pipeline—despite his pregnant fiancée's health problems.

Now that Isabeau could catch her breath, she was struck again by how the sprawling Steele estate reminded her of an oversize—and far grander—log cabin, recalling the old days of Alaskan exploration. And as a light breeze cooled her skin, causing a flutter in the meadow grass leading up to the Steele compound, she felt as if they'd stepped back in time.

Trystan had given her a brief tour of the barn and an introduction to the horses. Even though he hadn't grown up on the Steele compound, she couldn't help but notice the way all the horses responded to him with perked ears and low whinnies. It seemed to her as if they recognized a kindred spirit. No matter that he'd lost his patience when he thought someone was crowding her, he was still the most even-tempered man she knew.

She fluffed the paint mare's mane, surveying the land and the horses that populated the pastures flanking the barn. Tucked in a field to the left, two massive draft horses chased each other. Mars and Jupiter, Trystan had said earlier. With their titan size and powerful haunches, they were inspiring. They seemed ethereal as they galloped, feet barely touching the ground in an awe-inspiring display. Thick manes and tales caught in the wind.

During moments like this, she felt like she understood Trystan's need to be away from the world of media and business. To sink into nature and horses rather than cameras and sound bites.

With a deep inhale, she rubbed the soft leather of the reins, thankful for this stolen moment away from the media storm.

"The ride was a good idea. I feel more...zen now." Even if her thighs felt like liquid fire. Muscles she hadn't used in years were alive, awake. Reveling in the release offered by hoofbeats and country sky.

"Good, I'm glad to hear it."

"There's something timeless about unplugging from the world this way." Reaching down to the horse's shoulder, she dropped her reins, stretching as Willow the mellow paint stretched her long neck, letting out a low knicker as they approached the barn.

Trystan remarked from the flashy bay Abacus, "Interesting comment coming from a media specialist."

They walked a few more steps before Trystan stopped

fifty feet from the barn. He slid off, dismounting with ease. She paused, taken by his natural grace and prowess with these creatures. Abacus stood at attention, ears alert and ready.

"I understand the importance of balance." At a slight tug on the reins, Willow stopped, patient as Isabeau adjusted her weight to dismount.

She paused, hand fixed on the horn of the saddle as Trystan approached, reaching for Isabeau. Her body slid down his in a long tempting glide. His strong arms held her suspended for a moment as they stared eye to eye, and then he eased her the rest of the way to the ground. "I'm sorry for losing my cool back there, but I'm so damn glad you're alright."

He angled down to kiss her. Or maybe she arched up. But his mouth covered hers in a perfect fit that was becoming increasingly familiar. It felt so very right, and that gave her pause, made her wonder what it meant. For her job? For her future in his life? She trusted him, but did not want that fist-throwing kind of staunch protectiveness around her. She'd become careful to rely only on herself.

But oh, how his mouth on hers tempted her to give in. Her toes curled in her shoes as desire spiraled inside her.

He stroked her hair and spoke against her lips. "I need to check in with the family."

"Do you want me to come along?"

"Not this time. We're going to talk mostly business rather than public relations. Take some time for yourself."

"Actually, I would welcome the chance to talk to Naomi."

"That would be helpful since maybe then Royce can be convinced to leave her side."

"We make quite a team."

He winked. "That we do."

A dark-haired stable hand approached, grabbing both Willow's and Abacus's reins. The horses lazily walked behind him toward the barn. Trystan nodded his head, gesturing to the barn office where they'd left Paige.

The yellow Lab greeted them with a rapidly wagging tail and she happily trailed behind Trystan and Isabeau as they made their way toward the house.

Trystan squeezed her hand, igniting butterflies in her stomach. She pressed the button on the elevator that would lead to Naomi's suite. When the elevator arrived, she felt reluctant to let his fingers go.

He flashed a deep smile at her as he dropped her hand, striding toward the study where the families were gathering.

She stepped into the elevator and pressed the floor for Naomi's suite, along with the button for a doorbell announcing her arrival. Isabeau fidgeted with her hair, holding on to the feeling of his fingers twined with hers and the lingering sensation of Trystan's kiss. Her stomach dropped as the elevator lifted.

The door dinged open, and she stepped out into a room bathed in natural light. The high ceilings and eclectic artwork suited Naomi's free-spirited personality.

Her eyes stopped on Royce who hunched over his computer at the small table. Earbuds in and zoned out. Keys clicked in rapid succession, and she noticed the way his brow furrowed.

Naomi stretched on the light, airy sofa, chewing un-enthusiastically on a celery stick.

Isabeau waved tentatively. "I hope you don't mind some company."

Naomi set aside her celery stick. "Oh Lord, thank goodness. I'm not even a day into bed rest and I'm going stir-crazy. So is poor Tessie."

Isabeau released Paige from her leash and gave the command, freeing her from work to enjoy herself. "Free play."

Tessie and Paige bounded over to greet each other like old friends.

Royce pulled his earbuds out. "Hello, thanks for coming up."

Isabeau said, "Trystan said to let you know they're having a meeting downstairs."

Royce closed his laptop. "Who is meeting?"

"Most of the Steeles and Mikkelsons, other than the honeymooners."

His shoulders heaved. "On my way." He skimmed a kiss along Naomi's forehead. "Take care of yourself." He opened the balcony door for the dogs to slip outside, then strode toward the small foyer.

Isabeau waited until Royce entered the elevator, doors closing him from view. She turned to Naomi. "Can I get you anything?"

"I'm fine. Royce has kept me well stocked with healthy snacks and fruit water. Would you like something?" She gestured to the coffee table that resembled a buffet with a veggie tray, pitcher of water and glasses. "Help yourself."

"Thank you." Isabeau poured a glass of sparkling fruit water for herself and sat in a recliner. "Are you okay? I don't mean to pry, you just have a worried expression on your face."

Naomi bit her bottom lip, releasing it slowly before blurting out, "I didn't want to upset Royce any more than he already is. But this experience has called back some upsetting times." She blinked back tears. "I'm a twin and my sister died in a plane crash when we were barely entering our teen years. This bed rest situation has made me think about her, like, all the time. If I sleep, I dream about her—Brea."

Isabeau didn't have siblings, but she'd loved her mother. Her mom—Loretta—had often worked two jobs, so time together was all the more precious. Sometimes her mother would even wake her up when she finished the late shift so they could talk. Loretta had never tired of telling bedtime stories, some of them fairy tales and some of them real-life histories. Such as the story of a famous Queen Isabeau, a strong woman with an elegant name.

Even now, there were times Isabeau dreamed her mother stood at the foot of her bed. Waking up to find her gone was devastating. Every time.

"I'm sorry." She touched Naomi's arm, squeezing lightly. "That must be difficult for you having all those feelings churning."

"It is." She rubbed her stomach absently. "She was taken from us so tragically."

Isabeau resisted the urge to touch her own stomach. Her period was a day late, which wasn't unusual, but still… She forced her attention back to the conversation. "Accidents can leave us with so little closure."

Her mother's death of COPD had given them time for farewells, but when her father died in a motorcycle wreck five years ago, there'd been no chance to figure out if the relationship could be repaired.

Naomi glanced out the window, lips pursed as she seemed to grow thoughtful. "At the time, there were rumors that it wasn't an accident at all."

"What do you mean?"

"The police could never prove anything, but there were unanswered questions and this pervasive sense that someone in the Mikkelson family had something to do with the accident."

Horrified and more than a little defensive on Trystan's behalf, Isabeau sat up straighter. "Oh my God, that's…unthinkable."

"Our families already disliked each other and some felt there wasn't room for both businesses in the industry."

"But to cause a plane crash?" She couldn't fathom such a thing.

"To keep from going insane with grief, I had to accept that I'll never know the truth." Yet, the pain of that decision still showed in her brown eyes. "And if someone tied to the Mikkelson business did it, they couldn't have meant for the outcome to be that horrific—maybe they intended a runway incident, fear, distraction in the family. I know, it sounds crazy but that was such a chaotic time."

"I can't envision your father letting go of the investigation." Jack Steele was a formidable force, even now recovering from the horseback-riding accident that had broken his spine.

The fact that he wasn't paralyzed? A miracle.

"Dad was devastated over Brea and my mother both dying. We hadn't realized how much he depended on Mom. Without her, he was just…lost. And then I got cancer and he stopped having anything to do with the business for over a year."

Isabeau thought of her own family, of her mother's grief over being abandoned. Over her struggles to build a life for them. Isabeau thought of her own possible pregnancy. Could she do this alone? Was she being hardheaded and impractical in keeping boundaries up between her and Trystan?

"How did you all pull through?"

"Uncle Conrad stepped in. He has his own business interests and this isn't his passion, but he's savvy and he kept things on track. We owe him so much."

"He isn't able to help now?"

"His own corporate interests have grown too large, and we're not children anymore. He says it's on us and he's right."

Isabeau couldn't help but note, "For a large family who says they want to keep the family business afloat, everyone sure is preoccupied."

"You have Trystan, who's more capable than he realizes, and there's my brother Marshall if you get desperate."

"What a ringing endorsement." They laughed together, a much-needed tension reliever. "And they're both so into the social scene. Not."

"Ironic. I get it. The only person more reserved than Trystan is Royce—and okay, maybe my brother Marshall, too, and he's been sent to a conference anyway—under duress. But at least he agreed to go. Family is everything to all of us—Steeles and Mikkelsons. It's what binds us. So much so that Trystan is willing to step way outside his comfort zone."

"So much so, Jeannie and Charles Mikkelson adopted their nephew." The story touched her heart.

"And my brother adopted Glenna's daughter, who isn't even her biological child," Naomi added.

"You are all lucky. You all have people to count on, no matter what."

As Isabeau spoke those words, she realized how applicable they were to her too. While she hadn't had the luxuries of this lifestyle, she had been fortunate too. From her mother to the older woman who had taught her how to crochet, to Paige...and even to Trystan.

The last realization stunned her.

She wondered how she'd allowed herself to become so isolated and independent since the stalker incident when actually she craved more connections. More family like these people had.

Perhaps a couple of weeks ago, Isabeau would have continued keeping him at a distance. But deep in her gut, she felt courageous.

She wanted to let her feelings carry her forward.

After a relatively successful meeting, and while the others had gone salmon fishing, Trystan found himself again craving the more familiar scents of horse musk, hay and leather.

The two former rival families turned business associates had meshed together better than he'd anticipated. Nothing like a string of crises to motivate teamwork and camaraderie.

Try as he might, the boardroom scene—with all its posturing—was never his thing.

But as much as he wanted to help his family, he was finding himself wanting to please Isabeau, as well. Still, before he spoke with her about the results of the meeting, he needed to ride off the tension.

And yes, give himself some distance from the attraction to Isabeau that was so strong he was beginning to lose objectivity.

Luckily, horses grazed just outside and he nodded his thanks to Royce before rushing to the barn, eager to exchange the wooden table and its complications for a pair of cross ties and Abacus, the spunky bay quarter horse.

He made short work of getting to the barn, clipping the leather lead line to the designer halter. Abacus's ears perked up as Trystan brought him to the cross ties. The horse stuck his tongue out in a lazy yawn.

After securing the bay, Trystan retrieved a tack box full of supplies. Picking up a currycomb, he allowed Abacus to smell it. The horse's whiskers tickled the palm of his hand. Once Abacus adjusted to the scent, Trystan placed a steady hand on the animal's neck, stroking the silky bay. With his other hand, he moved the currycomb in small, concentric circles, freeing some of the dirt and loosening Abacus's muscles. While he knew the stable hand had probably already done this, he felt peace of mind taking care of the horse himself.

From a distance, the now-familiar jingle of a dog's collar caught his attention. Looking over the bay's withers, he saw Paige keeping pace with Isabeau. His heart pounded just a little faster as he took in the red hair piled in a high ponytail on her head, the tight fit of her jeans and shirt.

Isabeau allowed Abacus to sniff her hand, stroking the other side of his neck. The horse leaned into the rub, clearly enjoying the extra affection. "Are you going riding again?"

"I'm just checking to make sure they were brushed

and settled properly." He tipped his Stetson down, shaking his head. Trystan finished currycombing and picked up a hard, stiff brush.

"More decompressing after the family meeting?"

"Perceptive and pretty." He smiled over his shoulder, sending the tufts of loose hair and dirt off the bay's hindquarters. The excess hair and dirt pooled on the ground. "How's Naomi?"

"Settling in after her visit to the emergency room. It's reassuring they didn't hospitalize her, but she has gestational diabetes and elevated blood pressure. She's on bed rest."

"Gestational diabetes? How is that different from your kind of diabetes?" Placing the hard brush back in the tack box, he picked up a red hoof pick.

He'd needed their earlier ride to escape the pounding heat. He didn't want Isabeau to think he lost control at the drop of a hat after the way he'd punched that guy. But too many more tempting touches with this woman were going to drive him crazy.

Making his way back to the bay, he ran his hand down the front right leg, touching the soft spot above the hoof. In a snap, Abacus responded, picking up his foot. With practiced ease, Trystan removed the dirt the horse had acquired from pacing in the stall.

"Yes, it's different. I had juvenile onset. It's a lifelong condition. Naomi's was brought on by pregnancy and should resolve after the babies are born. She just needs to take care of herself."

"And you're taking care of yourself…just in case?" He eased the horse's foot down to the ground again. A handful of flies buzzed around. Abacus swished his dark tail, shooing them away. The last flick of the tail smacked Trystan's shoulder as he moved to the right rear leg.

"Absolutely," she said without hesitation. "How did things go?"

He sighed, pleased with the cleanliness of the back hoof. "We're calling it a controlled disaster. No one was hurt, and nothing toxic happened to the land. So that's a win. But our major competitor is running with the story to push our stock value down."

"That's unfortunate, but not unrecoverable," she said as he moved quickly to the other two hooves, removing the dirt as she spoke. "You have some major positive events coming up with the fund-raiser and Jack and Jeannie's wedding. Those will generate great airtime."

Setting aside the hoof pick, he dramatically gestured to his neck, faux gagging. "I can already feel the tuxedo bow tie choking me."

A sparkling laugh fell from her lips as she shook her head from side to side.

Damn.

The way the sun caught the bronzed hues in her hair made her seem like a mystical princess. She was so damn beautiful, generous.

As if she could hear his thoughts, a shy smile erupted as their eyes locked. Everything about her called to him. Closing the distance, the memory of how worried he'd been at the pipeline flooded him.

Trystan pushed those racing worries away, choosing instead to focus on the impossible blue of her eyes. Those lips parting slightly as he cupped her head...

And surrendered to the need to kiss her.

# Nine

Isabeau couldn't deny Trystan's kiss moved her, always, and in ways no one else's kisses had before. Their connection was special, unique. She'd decided to take a risk, and here she was, forging ahead.

He backed her against the stall, the planked wall a welcome brace to keep her wobbly knees from giving out from under her. The weight of his body against hers anchored her, the heat of him warmed her inside and out. The scent of his aftershave mingled with the earthy musk of hay and animals around them. Combing her fingers through his thick hair, she wanted more of him. All of him. She couldn't hold out against his appeal much longer.

All the reasons they should stay apart felt elusive at the moment, only whispery thoughts about the way they grew up, of her need for self-reliance after an unhealthy relationship. Except nothing seemed to matter except the rightness of his arms around her. His mouth on hers.

A loud thud sounded through the barn, breaking apart their kiss, causing Isabeau to remember herself. Reverberations skittered in the air, and Trystan's protective arms seemed to shield her from the yet to be determined noise.

His gaze, which had been scanning sharply, softened as they realized the culprit. Jupiter—one of the draft horses—knocked into his stall's gate. An accompanying whinny following.

From across the way, his brother Mars peaked his head from the stall, neck stretching long as he bleated a response.

Isabeau's nervous heart stopped galloping, calmed as she took in the scene. Relieved, she glanced at Trystan, their easy laughs tangling as they relaxed, looking at each other.

Trystan pulled her close, a deep sigh forcing the breath from his lungs, causing his chest to dip in as she rested against him. He stroked her hair, his other hand low on her waist. "Why is it we never seem to find an extended private moment?"

"I'm enjoying myself here." She didn't want to go back. Back to the real world with worries about if she'd done her job well enough.

"I agree, but I would like the time to linger over you and this place is too public. Anyone could burst in. While the media has us partnered up, I do not want risqué photos of you out there. I would never expose you to that."

His words warmed her, especially after having been

with a man who was so untrustworthy. "I know. I do trust you to be an honorable man." And as the words came out of her mouth, she realized they were true. He was different from her father. He would never leave her and a child vulnerable.

Although trustworthiness wasn't the same as commitment.

"Things are moving fast. I get that, and you have to know that while I respect your wishes, I want more."

She appreciated his willingness to protect her from the media attention his family garnered, to give her space. Maybe it was time for her to give back, to take a risk.

Before she could second-guess herself, she plunged right in. "Between two brushes with the press, the world already sees us as a couple. Why should we deny the chance to see what's going on between us? Life could well force our hands soon enough."

"What do you have in mind?"

"I'm asking you out on a date." The moment she said it, she wondered if it sounded silly at this point. They'd gone everywhere together these past few weeks, spent nearly every waking moment together. But still. Was it so wrong to want a romance? A chance to really get to know him beyond their work relationship? The heated evening in the boathouse had happened with such fast intensity, they'd skipped over the milestones that usually came with dating.

"A date?" he echoed, his eyes intrigued, his knee brushing hers as he shifted.

"Just the two of us in a place away from the media, a chance to be together before the fund-raiser and your mother's wedding." She watched him process the invitation while her pulse picked up speed.

Anticipating.

His gaze dipped to her mouth. Lingered. "I like the way you think." His voice did wicked things to her insides. "Did you have somewhere special in mind?"

"Surprise me." And she trusted that he would.

If only she could trust herself to keep her wits around him.

Royce wondered how a mansion this large could feel so damn crowded.

Since Naomi was settled with the other women going over plans for the fund-raiser and reviewing details for Jeannie and Jack's wedding, he felt comfortable being away from her. Worrying about her blood pressure was exhausting.

He plowed through the kitchen, tablet under his arm, Tessie loping alongside. He would hide in the pantry with his work and his dog if he had to. Lord knew, their "cupboard" was as large as his dining room.

Head down, he slammed into—Trystan. "Sorry, man, I didn't see you." He gripped Tessie's collar. "Wait, girl, wait."

"My bad," Trystan answered, tucking his cell phone in his pocket. "I was wrapped up in finalizing a date night with Isabeau."

"A date night? So you two really have something going on, other than work," Royce said, to make polite conversation, something he was doing more of these days, being a part of Naomi's world and working for Alaska Oil Barons.

"I hope so." Trystan rocked back on his boot heels.

"Good luck to you." And he meant it. Relationships were tough. He had a failed engagement in his past to prove that.

"Thanks, I'm gonna need it. Unlike you, who already has your life all squared away."

"Uh, yeah."

Was that how he appeared? Didn't feel that way. Hopefully, things would get back on track with him and Naomi once they could return to their cabin.

The sound of her laughter drifting down the hall halted that thought short, reminding him how happy she was here, with her family. Here, in the middle of a crowd.

Trystan clamped him on the shoulder. "Are you alright?"

"Sure, I just need to take my dog for a walk."

"With your tablet?"

Royce looked down. "Right, I was thinking Tessie and I could hang out on the dock, where it's quiet."

Trystan backed up a step. "Fair enough. I'll leave you to it."

Royce snapped his fingers for his dog to follow, then glanced over his shoulder at Trystan. "How do you handle being here, away from your ranch?"

Trystan rubbed the back of his neck. "I keep track of the days until I'm home again."

Not a reassuring answer. Nodding, Royce started toward the pantry, only to find teenage Aiden Steele raiding the shelves. "Want something?"

"No, thanks, I'm good." Shoulders braced, Royce redirected his path, aiming for the doors leading outside. He needed to get his head on straight and hunker down, keeping his priorities in order. Naomi and the babies.

He couldn't think too much about how what he needed and what she needed seemed to be so different. Could he find peace with her? Could they really get along?

Could he fulfill his calling to save lives with his profession if he didn't have the space to work?

He did find quiet late at night, watching her sleep, his hand resting on her stomach to feel the babies kick. In those moments he could envision the future, hiking with the kids, taking sleigh rides, viewing the northern lights and teaching them about constellations.

Pushing open the French doors leading to the side yard, he drew in the fresh air. A warm breeze swept in off the water, carrying the sound of a cluster of Steele and Mikkelson men gathered on the dock, casting fishing lines. Their back and forth banter likely scaring away any fish. He pivoted away, eyeing the lengthy garage that held his truck.

Only a few more months until they could all return to the cabin.

So far, the evening was going exactly as planned. No media. No prying public. Just the two of them plus the faithful Paige at a secluded coastal restaurant, located on their flight route back to Anchorage. His plane and pilot's license were a must for his pioneer spirit, affording him the opportunity to explore his vast—and sometimes unnavigable—state.

Yes, he was trying to show Isabeau the wonders of Alaska. She lived here, but he was aware this wasn't home for her.

And he was very aware that with every passing day, the chances increased that she was pregnant. It had been nearly three weeks since their impulsive hookup at his sister's wedding. As much as he wanted to ask Isabeau, he also knew that the longer the issue was unsettled, the more time he would have to persuade her to give them a chance to see where this attraction could lead.

He'd planned the evening to the last detail. And while he hadn't called his sister Alayna this time, she had inadvertently given him the idea to come here to Anastasia's by the Sound, with Russian-style food that they'd enjoyed growing up.

Gold gilded archways, deep walnut wainscoting, cream walls and linens accented with touches of scarlet in the artwork and napkins. The vibe here was elegant, like his dinner companion. Heavy gold candelabras graced each table, the white tapers flickering gently. Anastasia's pulled no punches on lush, romantic atmosphere and he hoped Isabeau would enjoy it.

They'd dined on smoked salmon, caramelized onion soup, lamb kebobs and coarse black bread. The conversation had been easy between them, carrying them to dessert before he realized two hours had passed. He'd forgone wine, unable to forget the possibility she was pregnant. They drank decaffeinated tea with citrus and vanilla and spices, along with a dessert of apple *sharlotka*—a mix of tart and cake.

But all the more enticing than any dessert?

Isabeau straightened across from him, the thin shoulder straps of her deep blue gown clinging to her curves. She wore a simple diamond necklace that caught in the muted light. Her pink lips parted in an easy, relaxed smile. Half driving him crazy as he imagined kissing her again, wrapping his arms around her while his fingers destroyed her loose curled updo.

How long had it been since he'd touched her the way he wanted to? Memories from the boathouse taunted him nightly.

Swallowing, he adjusted his body, feeling contained by the suit coat and tie. But it was worth it, if Isabeau was happy.

Her face was blissful as she tipped her ear toward the violinist playing the the famous song from Tchaikovsky's *Swan Lake*. Trystan winged a mental thanks to his mother that he recognized the tune.

Isabeau set her teacup down, candlelight reflected in her eyes and made her diamond pendant glitter. "Well, you absolutely did surprise me."

"What did you expect?"

"More local flavor, upscale sure, but somewhere with an Alaskan flair."

Sipping his water, he shrugged. "My parents liked to travel. My sister Alayna was a huge fan of Russian food—which astounded us all because she was such a picky eater. Anyhow, that reminded me of this place where my family used to go when Dad was sick of her eating nuggets and pizza."

"Russian food. Go figure." She arched an eyebrow, her smile making him hunger for a taste of her lips.

"Well, it's closer than Moscow, plus the routes are crazy and then there's customs to deal with. Another time, perhaps. For now, this felt more…unexpected. You deserve to be romanced." He toyed with her fingers across the table, her pale pink nails and small silver rings feminine touches he appreciated.

"Impromptu travel usually makes me anxious, but

you pulled this together so smoothly I'm completely relaxed." Paige snoozed under the table, a testament to the lack of need to keep watch for stress.

"Why would you say that about impromptu travel making you nervous?"

"I'm a planner. Knowing what's coming next soothes me." Isabeau drew absent circles on the tablecloth with her finger. "And I guess I thought you were a planner too. You strike me as a person who likes to stay on his ranch, even our trip to Juneau was familiar ground for you. That's the whole reason I was hired—because you don't like stepping outside your comfort zone."

"That's work. This is a date. Social is different from business."

"Hmm, interesting perspective. So you are a world traveler after all, like your family."

"Like them, but on my terms. There are so many places I would enjoy showing you. Denali National Park here in Alaska and viewing *Swan Lake* in London. Maybe even a trip to Moscow for authentic Russian food." He reached across the table and clasped her hand.

"Our time working together is coming to a close. The fund-raiser is coming up this weekend."

"I'm fully aware." The clock was ticking faster than the violin speeding through Tchaikovsky.

"And the following weekend is your mother's wedding."

"I'm *very* aware of that." Truth be told, his mother's marriage to someone who'd been their family's business nemesis still unsettled him. But, then, who was he to judge convoluted relationships? "It doesn't have to end there with us."

He stroked his thumb along the inside of her wrist, just over her speeding pulse.

"Whoa, Trystan," she said softly, squeezing his hand. "This is a date. Can we simply enjoy the moment and not discuss the future—other than preparing for the events?"

"Can do." He lifted their clasped hands and kissed her knuckles, savoring her creamy soft skin. Then he raised his cup of spiced tea. "A toast. To your beauty, your charm and your compassion."

She relaxed back into her chair. Lifting her teacup, she clinked it lightly against his, then sipped. She eyed him over the rim of the fine china, her eyes…seductive. "Do we have a hotel for the night?"

His heart rate kicked up a notch to match hers, desire throbbing through his veins. "We can, if that's what you want?"

She smiled, slowly, deliberately. "I do, very much."

She was going to do this.

No backing down.

Isabeau intended to take every ounce of pleasure from this evening with Trystan that she could. She would store away the sensations and the memories for the future. She'd been through too many difficult times—had battled for her health and her independence—to turn her back on a chance to indulge herself with a man like Trystan. A man so thoughtful of her needs and desires.

Tomorrow would have to take care of itself.

Anticipation tingled through Isabeau every step of the way back to the five-star hotel on the rocky beach, waves crashing with romantic intensity. The golden elevator deposited them onto their floor, Trystan's arm around her waist, her head tucked against his shoulder. Her dog kept a step behind, seeming to sense this was a moment of privacy, that she wasn't needed.

His hand on the small of her back, Trystan maneuvered Isabeau deeper into the hotel room drenched in sultry hues. When she'd mentioned spending the night together, he seemed to pull a reservation out of thin air, taking her to a world-class hotel near the restaurant with the same decor. An overstuffed king bed heavy with crimson, yellow and deep blue throw pillows commanded the attention of the room. Bay windows caught the twinkle of the starlight above the water, deepening the romantic atmosphere.

She unclicked Paige's leash and took off her vest, giving her the command releasing her from work. "Free play." Paige trotted away, sniffing around the room.

Trystan's fingers slid from hers as he made his way to the dark wooden side table where an ornately carved incense holder was placed beneath a table lamp. He ignited a match from the nearby pack, the flame crackling as it took to the incense. Sandalwood flooded the room. He turned back around, an inviting look playing on his lips.

She reveled in sensation after resisting temptation for what felt like an eternity. Could it only have been three weeks since that night in the boathouse that had never been far from her mind? It seemed longer. Her body ached with wanting him.

She drew in bracing breaths to regain control, looking around the suite as he adjusted the heavy brocade curtains and placed his suit coat over a chair. He turned back to her, his eyes holding hers with a seriousness that touched her soul. He held out his arms.

And without another thought, she stepped into his embrace.

Her hands rested on his shoulders, her fingers curling into the warm starched cotton of his button-down shirt. "You said you wanted to linger, and that sounds quite…delicious."

She'd seen the stress on Naomi and Royce's relationship due to rushing things. She didn't want to face those same problems down the road if she and Trystan became…more. Better to really know one another.

"I like a woman who speaks her mind."

"Good, because communication is my thing."

"When I said I wanted to linger, that didn't exclude going fast, because we can follow with slow, and then slower."

"You're promising a lot."

"I look forward to hearing if you think I delivered."

"You're okay with my sharing my opinion? You're not…threatened by that?"

"I'm confident. And if something doesn't work for you, I will enjoy trying again and again to get it right." He dipped a kiss along her neck, the barest brush of his lips over her skin.

Tendrils of pleasure curled down her spine.

She shivered in anticipation. "That flows both ways. What do you want?"

His eyes lit with passion as he pulled her closer. "To watch you find pleasure. More than once."

Her breath caught. Not just at the sensual promise. But that he wanted pleasure for her. That he could put her first even now when they'd both held back for so long.

Her fingernails curled against the fabric of his shirt.

"Considering how long we've been waiting and wanting, I don't think that will take long."

She hummed with sensation and they hadn't even peeled off their clothes yet. His touch was bound to send her reeling.

"Then, if I can add to my list of wants, seeing you naked ranks right up there." He kissed her temple, breathing the words lightly against her ear.

"Well that's easy enough to accommodate." She stepped back, keeping their hands linked.

"I want to help with removing your clothes." He tugged her gently.

She slipped her hands free and shook a finger at him. "I think my list of preferences tonight is that I watch your eyes…" she slid a thin shoulder strap of her dress down, revealing a strapless bra "…as you see me."

She shrugged the other shoulder free and shimmied the dress to pool around her feet, the satiny fabric whispered along her heated skin and made her all the hungrier for his touch.

His expression was ample reward and aroused her as much as she could see that she'd stirred him. His light blue eyes darkened to an indigo flame, the hottest gaze. It flicked over her, searing her with need. How had she denied herself—and him—this long?

He tugged at his necktie, making fast work of loosening the knot and pulling it off. He started on the shirt buttons and she sauntered forward, brushing his hands aside, freeing the buttons one at a time, her fingertips savoring the soft cotton of his undershirt.

Not that he was passive. He unfastened his belt buckle. She tugged his shirttails free and flattened her hands underneath, splaying her fingers along the heat

of his skin. He was as deliciously muscled as she remembered, the planes and ridges of his body creating
contours she longed to explore with her hands and lips.

Their hurried encounter in the boathouse had been
so shadowy—intense—but without the time to get to
know each other's bodies. He was right, they deserved
to linger.

The word "linger" hummed through her mind and
along her sensitized nerves.

His calloused fingers rasped over her skin to her
back, unhooking her satin bra. A hiss of appreciation
slid between his teeth a second before his hands slid
away her bra and cupped the weight of her breasts.

Her reaction was immediate and intense, tingling
tightness spreading throughout her. She told herself the
feeling had nothing to do with pregnancy hormones.
She was probably just late. Brushing aside the thought
as quickly as it feathered through her brain, she refused
to let it distract her from this moment she so desperately
wanted to experience.

Then his mouth was on hers as they backed toward
the bed until her knees bumped the mattress. They fell
in a tangle of arms and legs and passion. The night
was everything she'd fantasized it could be…and more.

The last of their clothing was swept away and sent
sailing to the floor as they touched and tasted, exploring every inch of each other. Learning the plains and
valleys of each other's bodies in the warm glow of the
lamplight.

When her body reached a fever pitch, she whispered
her need to him, urging him on. Trystan pulled a condom from his wallet and neither of them spoke.

He sheathed himself and stretched over her, propping

up on his elbows to hold his full weight off her. She slid her heels up his legs, hooking her feet around his waist and pulling him closer, deeper, and… She lost track of her thoughts as he moved inside her. His fingers in her hair. His chest brushing against her breasts with each synched move of their bodies, which were fast becoming sweat slicked and flushed with rising tension.

Nipping his bottom lip and nudging his shoulder, she whispered her wish to be on top and he quickly accommodated, taking advantage of the opportunity to touch her more expansively. Then his hand drifted lower, lower still, to the core of her need, tempting and teasing her until her head flung back, her hair skimming her spine as—yes—she couldn't hold back any longer.

Her orgasm splintered in an explosion of sensation, a moan escaping her lips. Trystan rolled her again to her back and with a deep thrust, his hoarse cry of completion joined her sighs.

Bliss melted over her in the afterglow as they held each other wordlessly. As the passion cooled from her body, she listened to Trystan's rhythmic breathing beside her as he drifted off to sleep, holding her against him.

There was something so intimate about sleeping together, which sounded silly given all they'd just shared. But sleep was…vulnerable.

The warmth of his body and the softness of the sheets sent a chill up her spine as worry paced in her heart. Gazing across the dark room to the window, she focused on the stars. The roll of waves against the shore.

Rather than being a simple escape or offering answers, having sex with Trystan had complicated things for her.

Because she wanted more.

That shouldn't have been a big deal. It wouldn't have been if they'd simply met at a party, drawn to one another.

But the couples in their orbit reminded her too well of the problems they faced—a reclusive man, a woman who worked with those in the spotlight, the issues that came with children, and that didn't even scratch the surface of his convoluted feelings about family and her own anxiety over her father and stalker ex-boyfriend.

None of which she could change. She only had control over one issue and she couldn't hide from that any longer. Seeing Naomi's scare with gestational diabetes weighed on Isabeau. She couldn't ignore her late period any longer, especially not with health concerns of her own.

Once they returned to Anchorage, she would need to see a doctor to check on her diabetes—and find out definitively if she was pregnant.

# Ten

Popping a smoked salmon canapé into his mouth at the Wilderness Preservation Initiative Fund-raiser, Trystan nodded as a gray-haired senator rambled on and on and on. Rather than focusing on the fusion of dill, smoked salmon and rye bread, he feigned interest, eyes widening at the appropriate moments. Ever so briefly, he let his gaze slide over the senator's sagging shoulder to Isabeau, watching her work the room with ease.

Listening well often passed as good conversation as far as the babbler was concerned. So Trystan ate and made all the right noises to keep the senator talking.

Chatting up the senator would increase the program's success, which was the purpose of tonight. And after the faux pas with the almost oil spill, making sure this initiative gained traction was essential to the company.

So yeah, while he had hours more face time with

a slew of exhausting people, this event could make or break the newly merged company's image.

Shifting in his freshly shined boots—grateful Isabeau had relented on him wearing dress shoes—he smiled at the senator. The formal event called for a tuxedo, which seemed to restrict his range of motion. But Isabeau had picked out the clean-lined article of clothing, telling him he looked sharp.

In truth, he didn't see it. Isabeau, however, looked enchanting in her fit-and-flare gold gown.

In the crystalline chandelier light, she seemed to be of another time and place. She moved past him, catching his eye. She leaned a slender hand on the champagne-colored tablecloth, complementing the elaborate pale rose centerpiece.

Her strapless dress accented her bare collarbone. Red hair upswept in loose ringlets, mingling with the gold chandelier earrings. And damn. That smile on her perfectly pink lips turned him inside out.

She'd never looked more elegant.

Or more a part of this world.

Memories of their night together still seared through him. Their first encounter in the boathouse had rocked him, no question. But lingering over her, exploring each other? That surpassed anything he'd experienced.

He wanted more time with her, not just hours, but much more. Which he would have if she was pregnant. However, he wanted her to be with him because she wanted that as well, not because a baby tied them to each other.

Despite her anxiety, she worked the room with a glittering smile, Paige keeping close watch. He'd wondered how the attendees at this black tie event would react to the dog. But apparently the addition of service animals must be common enough among this set that no one paid other than passing attention.

Although he imagined it was also a nod to Paige's excellent training and Isabeau's seamless handling that allowed the animal to work without creating any sort of distraction.

He also felt somewhat at home here in the opulent penthouse ballroom of the Mikkelson Enterprises building. Unlike the Steeles' sleek and swanky office tower filled with conference rooms, the Mikkelson structure had a stately, refined presence absent of the contemporary fixation on chrome and clean lines. Both buildings were magnificent, but served vastly different purposes. The key to Alaska Oil Barons' success would be to use the appropriate location for each situation. When wining and dining needed to happen, the Mikkelson Enterprises ballroom on the top floor was the clear winner. Part of the merger plan involved keeping both properties and capitalizing on the strengths of each one's appeal.

The harpist and string quartet on a large elevated stage provided a lilting melody, the notes seeming to complement the twinkling boat lights bobbing below in the harbor made visible through the window. A creamy white marble dance floor sported a few well-heeled couples leaning against each other.

Both families had showed up in full force—with spouses and significant others. All doing their part to engage the politicians and social elite. Even the head of their major competitor, Johnson Oil United, had attended. Cal Johnson loomed in the corner, sipping a glass of champagne.

A long shadow stretched over Trystan—the Steele

patriarch and his soon-to-be stepfather, Jack Steele. "Senator, do you mind if I have a moment with my future stepson?"

"Of course, of course," the senator agreed, reaching for another glass of champagne from a silver tray being carried by waitstaff. "Great party, great party," he said in that conversational way some people had of repeating themselves. "I'm going to double my donation in honor of your incredible recovery from that riding accident."

Trystan eyed his future stepfather warily. Whatever he had to say must be important to break up a conversation with a political bigwig.

Jack pumped the senator's hand. "We're very grateful. Thank you." He gestured across the room. "I would steer you toward my lovely fiancée, Jeannie, and our media coordinator, Isabeau Waters. You'll be in good hands."

The senator clapped Trystan on the shoulder. "Nice job getting the message out, young man. Hope we'll see more of you."

With a nod, the man turned in search of Jeannie and Isabeau, Cal Johnson close on his heels. Having the competition on hand this evening could be concerning to some, but Trystan perceived a frustration in Johnson as the man saw the unity and great show of professionalism from the Mikkelson-Steele team.

Trystan nudged Jack. "Do you think we should rescue them from Johnson?"

Jack laughed, a deep rumble of sound. "Jeannie can more than hold her own with him. You should know that about your mother."

"I do, but I'm also her son, and you'll understand that Chuck and I have felt especially protective of her since our father died."

"I'm glad to know that. She's had a difficult time, and even realizing she's a strong person doesn't stop me from wanting to look after her."

"She deserves some peace." Trystan shifted uncomfortably.

"Having some trouble with the wedding still though, are you, boy?"

"I think we're all still surprised. Decades of animosity between our families can be tough to sweep aside— or rather it is for some of us."

"Understandable. We've slung some harsh words around over the years," Jack conceded. "I'm hoping we can put that behind us. Maybe someday you'll even join us for a family breakfast at Kit's Kodiak Café. It's a tradition I started with my brood when they were young. I would bundle them up quietly so their mother could sleep in…" His voice faded off at the mention of his dead wife.

"That doesn't sound like the Jack Steele my father told me about, the Jack Steele who fed small children to bears."

Jack laughed, full out and loudly. "You've got spunk in you. We'll find our way just fine."

"Good to know." And since Trystan wanted his mom to be happy and didn't have any choice but to accept this man in her life, he said, "I'll take you up on that breakfast when you get back from your honeymoon. But you're paying."

"Deal." Jack nodded curtly, then stopped Trystan from leaving by gripping his arm. "I want you to know that I love your mother."

"You've told us." Still he couldn't dodge the blindsiding swipes of memories of his father fuming in frustration over Jack Steele's business tactics. No tuxedo and profession of love could sweep away the fact that the guy had undercut his father, ruthlessly filching clients.

That history was a huge part of why Trystan had insisted on stepping into this business void for the month, rather than giving it over to one of the Steele offspring.

"And I'll keep saying it until you believe it," Jack said brusquely. "I appreciate you all putting on a good face for the merger."

Trystan half smiled, snagging a glass of champagne. This conversation was awkward as hell. "We don't have much choice."

"You could walk away. You have quite a portfolio of your own, more than enough to take over the ranch."

Trystan bristled. He refused to be shuffled aside when his mother needed him now more than ever. He was part of the family, and that wasn't something he would ever take for granted. "I owe my parents better than to turn my back on their legacy."

"That sort of loyalty is golden. You're my kind. For what my opinion is worth."

"Your opinion is important because you're important to my mother." He finished off his champagne and set the glass aside, his gaze straying briefly to Isabeau. "Although if you hurt her, my loyalty to you ends."

"I wouldn't expect any less." Jack tugged at his tuxedo tie. "This thing almost has me yearning for the neck brace again."

The man's lighthearted way of referencing his near-death accident took Trystan aback, but also made him admire Jack a bit.

Jack Steele was as tough as his reputation.

And Trystan completely agreed on the tie issue. "I

would suggest you ditch the tie and rest, but I suspect that would fall on deaf ears. So I'll just say, thanks for taking the time to reassure me about my mother."

"You're a good son." He squeezed Trystan's shoulder. "And I'm a perceptive old man who knows when a fella is distracted. Go dance with the media consultant."

A smile tugged at Trystan's mouth as he weaved around the elegant dinner tables, heart pounding as he made his way to Isabeau. Her arms crossed, highlighting her curves even more. She schmoozed with Miles, the owner of a fairly large news station. The wiry thirty-something-year-old leaned in close to Isabeau, scraping back his wheat-colored hair.

Trystan set his jaw, nodding as he closed the distance between them. "Thank you for attending tonight, Miles."

"Wouldn't miss it. The Mikkelson-Steele merger is big news around here. Our readers are pinning a lot of hope on the job creation of Alaska Oil Barons versus Johnson Oil." He cut his gaze to the side. "Although I'm surprised you invited Cal Johnson, him being the enemy and all."

Trystan cocked his head, sizing up Miles. "Is that a dig for a statement?"

"One can hope." Miles slid an arm around Isabeau in a way that felt a bit too familiar. "Your media maven here has been doing fine work sharing news about the conservation efforts of your company. That's going to cut into your revenue, though, and put you behind Johnson."

Trystan wasn't wading into that boggy interview territory—and besides, he wanted the bastard's arm off her. Now. "Isabeau works too hard. She's more than earned a dance."

In a swift motion, Trystan swept his hand into the small of Isabeau's back, hand sinking into the silky dress. Ushering her forward as the string quartet segued into a new piece…a Brahms waltz, too damn familiar from one of Alayna's long-ago violin recitals. With practiced ease, he spun Isabeau into his arms, her fulllength gown swirling around her ankles.

Trystan folded Isabeau's hand into his, placing his palm on her waist. Having her in his arms again felt good, right, easing some of the awkwardness that had crept between them when they woke up in the hotel the next morning. Awkwardness made worse when he'd tried to broach the subject of her seeing a doctor.

She'd changed the subject and taken her dog for a walk.

He opted for neutral territory now. "How am I doing tonight?"

She squeezed his hand lightly, smiling. "You're acing everything and you know it."

"I haven't hit anyone. That's a bonus. Although I was hard-pressed when that news producer put his hands on you." He drew her closer than the waltz stance dictated.

"I appreciate your restraint. And the board of directors and investors will be pleased. Any jitters should be quelled. You've all presented a unified front. The wedding next weekend will only solidify that."

Her every word was perfect. Her dance moves smooth. But now that he held her closer, he could see a distance in her eyes, a distraction.

Something was wrong. And if the past was any indication, getting her to open up wouldn't be easy. Not that he was the poster boy for baring his emotions.

Except right now he wanted to know what she was

thinking more than he could remember wanting...
anything.

Just as he lined up the right words, the music ended
and with a tight smile, Isabeau stepped back to walk
away.

Fading into the crowd.

Contrary to her carefully chosen outfit and permanent smile, Isabeau felt the cool hands of panic wrench
around her heart and she had no recourse for relief.
She'd sent Paige with a driver a half hour ago as the
party ran long. Luckily, the Steele stable hands that
looked after Kota had taken to Paige. Her dog had already worked a full day, and Isabeau thought she was
holding her own.

Apparently not.

The Herculean task of keeping it together frayed her
nerves. A scene from earlier today played on repeat in
her mind, drifting through her mind's eyes in flashes.
The waiting room, the doctor handing her information
about what to expect when you are expecting.

The test was positive. They'd even done an ultrasound because of her diabetes, along with a slew of
other tests.

She was healthy. And her concerns about anxiety
medication had been discussed. She hadn't taken much
since the night she'd slept with Trystan, and the two
times she had, the medication was on the approved list.

The doctor had mapped out a health care plan for her
to take with her when she left. And didn't that thought
launch a fresh wave of nerves and her first hint of nau-
sea.

*Focus. Breathe.*

She tried to take comfort in the fact that she knew, deep in her heart, that Trystan was not even remotely like her stalker ex-boyfriend. But she was just so damn scared of ending up like her mother, in a relationship with a man who would walk away from her.

She had to admit the truth to herself. She already loved this baby.

And she was starting to care for the baby's father.

Isabeau needed a breather from the whole party. How ironic that Trystan was mastering every obstacle, and she was on the edge of losing her cool. Her life had been turned upside down so often since she'd met Trystan, she wasn't sure yet how to right herself.

In a dimly lit back corner, Isabeau found something that looked like salvation. A secluded spot where Naomi sat on a chaise lounge, putting her feet up. Her dark hair had been styled pin straight, evoking the unearthly beauty of Cleopatra. She looked the part, lying on the chaise in her high waisted Egyptian-style, green satin gown, the hem trailing off the side. The gown was clingy and exotic, and somehow the pregnant woman carried it off beautifully. Even in her second trimester—with twins.

Jeannie was sitting beside Naomi, chatting, keeping her water glass full.

Isabeau backed up a step. "I'm sorry for interrupting."

Naomi set aside her glass. "Not at all. Jeannie's been a love to keep me company—lounging here is as much excitement as the doctor will allow me. While I'm glad to be out of my suite, this certainly isn't the most fascinating part of the party."

Jeannie patted her hand. "Those are Jack's grandbabies. It's a delight to talk to you about plans. And hopefully the doctor will give the okay for you to have a baby shower."

Naomi scratched her nose. "I can't believe I need a doctor's approval to open a few presents. I would offer to send Royce in my place, but as you can see from his ghost act a half hour into the event, crowds are not his thing. Quite frankly, I was surprised he didn't stay to hover—which attests to how really pegged out he was."

Isabeau sat at the foot of the chaise, perched on the end. "Trystan doesn't care for them, either. There's no shame in that."

Naomi pointed toward the party. "But Trystan showed up and, judging by what I can see from here, he's making the best of the night."

Jeannie followed her gaze, smiling fondly. "I have to say I'm proud of the way my son has come through for us. Due in no small part to you, Isabeau."

Isabeau smoothed her dress along her knees, the reality sinking in that this woman was the grandmother of her child. "You did a wonderful job bringing him up and giving him the tools to work with. I fully expected to have to teach him about classical music and how to dance. But, well, he surprised me."

"Thank you, dear," Jeannie said, pride shining from her smile, and then she reached to clasp Naomi's hand. "It'll work out, for you, Naomi. You and Royce are different, but it's clear you love each other."

Naomi twisted her engagement ring round and round. "He loves the babies so much, which trust me, warms my heart. He thinks of them as his own even though he's not the biological father. And he's already lost one child…"

Jeannie leaned in closer, patting her shoulder. "Honey, are you saying you don't love him? Because if you are, you can't stay with him for the children."

Those words certainly chilled Isabeau to the core.

Naomi smoothed her hands over her pregnant belly. "I don't know what I'm feeling anymore, and I'm not sure he does, either. Everything moved so fast with us. We barely know each other, and what we do know seems less and less compatible now that, um, now that we're not relying on sex to smooth over the rough patches." She glanced up. "Isabeau, I hope I'm not making you uncomfortable."

Her worry about her own situation must have shown in her face. She smoothed her features into sympathy. "I'm the soul of discretion, and I've become quite fond of your family. While I don't have advice to offer, I can always lend an ear."

Naomi played with her dark hair, looking at her future stepmother through the strands. "Jeannie? Do you have thoughts?"

"I think you have to decide what's in your heart."

"You have to know me well enough to realize I'm not the vulnerable type to go around asking for help. I have opinions on everything. Usually." Naomi glanced at her hands, then looked up with a hint of embarrassment in her eyes. "I wish I could ask my mother." Then she rushed to add, "I hope that doesn't hurt you to hear."

Jeannie's eyes grew soft. "Of course not. That's a logical wish, especially now." She drew in a deep breath. "I'm not your mother and I can't begin to guess at where your feelings should or shouldn't land. But I can say this. If you're going to make a break, it's better to do so before the twins get attached."

Tears leaked down Naomi's cheeks and Jeannie gathered her into a hug.

The wisdom in Jeannie's words scared Isabeau to her toes, while also making her next move crystal clear. She needed to decide about a relationship with Trystan now. For the sake of her future, for her child. She didn't have the luxury of time to wait and see how things played out, risking a horrible breakup later when there was a baby in the picture.

She eased away from the two women quietly. She couldn't wait for another ultrasound. Trystan deserved to know now.

She searched the fund-raising event for Trystan. Eyes scanning the teeming crowd, looking for the rugged cowboy in a tuxedo. He carried the tux well, clean and sharp lines accenting his broad chest. Trystan gestured with his hands as he spoke with Jack Steele, Delaney and key donors.

Heart thundering as Isabeau looked at the scene, her racing thoughts anxious for the future.

As soon as the evening wound down, Isabeau was going to ask Trystan to take a walk.

They needed to talk.

Of the many uncomfortable moments of Naomi's life, the ride in the limo with Royce—after that honest conversation with Jeannie—seemed to top the list. She'd finally found him by calling him on the phone. Twice.

He'd made his way to the limo. Waited inside with a vacant look settling onto his dark features. He'd given a small smile when she'd slid into the leather seats.

Silence lingered between them, feeling as heavy as

a thick Alaskan blanket. The limo lurched forward and still no one spoke.

Even after Jeannie had given Naomi the impetus she needed to talk to Royce, she couldn't convince her tongue to form coherent words or thoughts. An ache weighed heavy in her chest as the limo turned the corner, the dim boat lights fading from view.

She couldn't go on like this. *They* couldn't go on like this.

Naomi broke first, tension mounting in her jaw. Another ache. Another result of feelings that she didn't know how to articulate. So she started simple. No flash. Just an honest statement.

"I missed you during the fund-raiser."

Royce tugged his tuxedo tie off and pitched it to the floor, his gaze dropping. "I wanted to have the car ready. You've been overdoing it tonight."

Indignation zipped through her, making her all the more irritated and uncomfortable. "My doctor okayed my attending this event."

"He didn't say you could go hiking."

"I wasn't hiking." She pulled her shoes off before he noticed the swelling. "I was sitting on a chaise."

"It was quite a haul up there," he said, head leaning against the glass. Royce tapped his fingers, which grated on Naomi's nerves.

"No one has suggested I should use a wheelchair. And if you're so concerned, maybe you could have stuck around instead of playing the hermit," she barked tersely, crossing her arms over her chest.

"The crowds got to be too much for me. I put in an appearance the way anyone would expect a member of the company to do."

A deep breath. Then another.

She looked out the window, eyes taking in the street-lights that illuminated tall pine trees and glinted off street signs. Of course, Naomi barely registered these things. Unease spread through her chest, forming knots in her shoulders and adding to the lump in her throat.

Jeannie's advice knocked around inside her brain as it had for the past two hours, coalescing all Naomi's doubts. She knew Royce would never walk away from her— most certainly he wouldn't walk away from the babies. But was she pushing him into a life that would make him unhappy? She certainly couldn't commit to a life in the wilds out of the public eye. So how could she ask him to force himself to "put in appearances" in her world full of people and family?

She twisted her engagement ring again, checking to make sure her fingers hadn't swollen too much, some-thing she found herself doing more and more often as if she already knew she might need to remove it for a heartbreaking reason.

"I think we rushed into things."

He sat up straighter, his jaw jutting as the chauffeur drove through the security gates outside the Steele fam-ily compound. "I disagree. We simply moved fast be-cause we know our minds."

"Do we? We're almost strangers in many ways."

"Then tell me what you want me to know," he said in a clipped voice as if compatibility could be as basic as filling out a history profile.

"It's not that simple and you have to see that. I've had complicated relationships because of what I expe-rienced in the past, losing my mother, my twin sister, battling cancer so young." She stared at her home, a place of such joy and loss. Part of her wanted to run, now that the car had stopped, but she had to see this conversation through. "You've had a challenging time with relationships in the past too—and that was with someone you'd known nearly your whole life."

He took her hands, irritation fading to concern in his dark eyes. "I think you're scared of what we feel."

"I know that I'm feeling smothered and overwhelmed."

"You're pregnant with twins." His voice cracked with pain.

Twins, the babies. Children he wanted. But not the right reason for them to build a future together, especially when he and she already had such differing lifestyles. She feared she was being selfish by hanging on to him when she knew how restless and unhappy he was in her chaotic world.

"And I'm grateful that you care. That's sweet and I know I should count myself lucky, but I'm more concerned about our very different natures. You're a lone wolf and I'm a social butterfly."

"A steely butterfly."

Right now, she felt anything but steely. That would have to come later. After she'd gotten through the deepest hurt she'd ever felt. And considering all she'd already lost, that was saying a lot. She drew a ragged breath.

"Okay, but you have to see our lifestyles don't blend. Even trying to split our time between living your way and mine is already wearing thin. Ultimately, we'll each just end up miserable half of the year."

"I can see you're worried. Get some rest, and we can talk about this lat—"

"All I've done is sleep. You're not hearing me, Royce." Her throat clogged on tears for a moment, but because of how deeply she cared for him, how deeply she cared for her unborn children, she had to let him go. "Royce, I'm breaking things off."

She tugged free her engagement ring, a ring that had made her heart sing just not so long ago. But even as she accused him of being a hermit, she'd been hiding from the truth.

She placed the ring into his hand and closed his fingers. "Please, let me go."

When she pushed the car door open, Naomi caught sight of Trystan and Isabeau taking a walk on the Steele grounds—why weren't they at the Mikkelson place? A question that she shoved aside because right now all that mattered was support she so desperately needed. Locking eyes with her new friend, she registered the distress and unease swimming in Isabeau's eyes. A distress and unsettled feeling that reverberated in Naomi's own chest.

Collecting herself, Naomi bolted from the car, moving swift and sure before Royce could intervene.

# Eleven

Gray clouds speckled the night sky as Trystan reached for Isabeau's hand. They'd come to the Steele compound to pick up Paige, then he'd impulsively asked Isabeau to walk first along the shoreline She took his hand gingerly, though her slender face stayed fixed on the rocky shoreline in front of them, Paige off-leash enjoying free time to play.

They began to meander on the shoreline, maneuvering away from the house. He hoped to use this time to persuade Isabeau to see a doctor, to end this limbo state so they could move their relationship forward with direction—either way, baby on the way, or no baby.

Dropping his hand, she stopped walking. In the distance, he could make out the form of the seaplane.

Trystan shot her a sidelong glance, watching the moonlight find purchase in the lines of worry set in her cheeks and brow. "You said you wanted to walk. Is everything alright?"

She drew in a deep breath, stopped, turning to face him. "There's no simple way to lead into this. I saw the doctor, and she confirmed that I'm pregnant."

Her words hit him right in the gut. He'd been expecting it, thought he'd prepared himself. But *possibly pregnant* was nowhere near close to *really pregnant*.

Thoughts tumbled over one another in fast succession. Where would they live? How could he make her happy? When was the baby due?

She was carrying his baby.

*His. Baby.*

Isabeau held up her hands and turned away, walking again. "Never mind. No need to say anything. We can talk later once the news has sunk in."

She hitched her formal gown up past her elbows and started trekking back toward the house. Damn it. That wasn't how this conversation was supposed to happen. He was supposed to have some suave words to win her over.

"No, wait," he called out, grasping her arm. His bare feet desperate for traction on the muddy shore. "We should talk now. Keep in mind, I'm not good with words—as you know—and I want to make sure I get things right."

She glanced back over her shoulder, chewing her bottom lip, but staying silent. The moonlight brought out the gold in her red hair—and illuminated the fear in her eyes. "I'll be fine. The baby and I will be fine. I just wanted you to know, and now that you do, I'm going."

Crickets hummed, adding another layer to the sound of the rhythmic waves. Paige darted by them, splashing. A momentary distraction.

He needed the right words. "Isabeau, I should have my thoughts together on what to say. I've certainly thought about this possibility often enough over the past four weeks. One thing is clear though, I'm here for you and the baby." He pushed forward with what he knew was the right thing to do. "We'll get married. I'll take care of you, there's no need to be anxious. And my child will never have to feel abandoned or unloved."

No child would go through what he had when his parents dumped him, leaving him confused as hell trying to make sense of how a parent could just opt out.

She exhaled, her forehead furrowing. "I hear that you're trying to do the honorable thing, and that's... admirable. But I'm having trouble wrapping my head around how you said, 'No need for me to feel anxious?' You want to marry me so I won't have a panic attack?"

"That's not exactly what I meant." But he could see he'd offended her. He was making things worse the more he spoke.

She moved over a large rock formation, swaying slightly beneath the slippery surface. Instinctively, Trystan's hand shot out to steady her. Anger colored her cheeks as she shooed away his help, stabilizing her footing without him.

From her perch, her frown deepened, her voice becoming as dark as the night sea. "I thought you understood about my anxiety." The wind plastered her dress to her slim body. "But I'm wondering if you think I'm a needy person incapable of taking care of myself."

Hands extended in protest, he tried to steer the conversation back to more even ground. "That's not what I meant at all. You're clearly one of the most competent people I've ever met."

"What did you mean, then, with the anxious comment?" She crossed her arms. The moonlight fell on her, made her appear to be a living flame in that gold dress with her red hair.

"I just want to make life easier for you and the baby and, yes, I want to be with you. You and I have great chemistry. We enjoy each other's company. Marriage between us could be good, very good. Just think of all the bucket list items we could explore together."

"Bucket list? Bucket list?" Her voice pitched higher with each word. "We should get married to check off bucket list items together?" She shook her head. "Trystan, you can get a pal to do that. Marriage is— should be—about something else. It should be about love, and you don't love me."

Hell. He should have thought to use that word because he did care for her. "We have feelings for each other. I think with time that could—um, will—grow into love."

Her mouth thinned, anger radiating from her. "Trystan, you really should stop talking because you're making a mess of this."

"Then tell me what you're thinking since you're better with words."

"I believe you're offering marriage because you're still trying to make the perfect family, and that's not a reason for us to be a couple. Please be honest with yourself."

Her words sparked frustration and, yes, anger in him. He held his voice in check and said tightly, "You want me to be honest? How about this? I'm not sure you could love me even if we were perfect for each other. You hold yourself apart from people. You're too afraid of losing your family again—whether it is because of your father walking out or your mother dying—to take a risk on what could be a really good thing."

She blanched, her face pale in the moonlight, her eyes shining with unshed tears. "Then I guess we know where we stand and it's not together."

Turning away, she walked down from the rock, landing in the sand with a slight thud. Without looking at him, she walked past him. Away from him. Leaving him with nothing but the cold truth.

He'd done what he'd vowed he would never do—alienated his baby's mother. Anger at himself battled with a sorrow deeper than he could have ever imagined.

The last time Trystan had been up in the middle of the night raiding the kitchen, he'd been a teenager. But here he was, on his way to rummage for food, restless.

Five days had passed since Isabeau gave him the boot. Five days of tense work exchanges as she spelled out the tightly contained media exposure for Jeannie and Jack's wedding. Everytime he tried to bring up making plans for the baby, she insisted that could wait until the second trimester.

Which meant months of the cold shoulder.

And he didn't have a clue how to win her back. Desperation gnawed at him. He felt the weight of being orphaned all over again…his whole life and outlook shaped by the abandonment of his parents. He wouldn't allow his child to feel that. He couldn't. He wanted to be with Isabeau, to try, but she was right that the stakes were higher with a baby involved and nothing short of love was fair.

Except how were they going to figure out if that was possible if she'd shut him out?

Weighed down with regret, he made his way toward the kitchen, his feet slowed by the knowledge of all the ways he'd screwed up. He hadn't slept in days, and staying in his room staring at the ceiling wasn't going to help.

He turned the corner, surprised to see the kitchen aglow. His mother sat on a stool, hair in a messy blond bun. Deli meats and cheeses covered the lava stone countertops. Sliced bread, lettuce, tomato and onions flanked the sandwich supplies. Perhaps most notable in the sleek white kitchen with stainless steel accents was the opened gold-labeled Icecap Brews beer bottle in Jeannie's left hand.

"Hi, Mom, trouble sleeping? Wedding jitters?" The rehearsal dinner was tomorrow, the wedding the next day. He would have no date—no Isabeau—the spot beside him vacant.

"No nerves, dear. I'm sure. I'm just unsettled about other matters. The news about Naomi and Royce splitting up caught us all by surprise. Jack is beside himself worrying for his daughter." She nudged the sandwich makings toward him so he could make one for himself.

The breakup gave him pause too, as if he didn't already have enough reasons to wonder about his own relationship with Isabeau. How did he stand a chance winning her back when a perfect couple like Naomi and Royce couldn't make it work?

And there was still the baby to consider. They would be connected through the child forever, and while he wanted the baby, the thought of making polite arrangements with the woman who'd just stomped on his feelings made his head pound—his chest ache.

Grabbing for the rye bread, he loaded the sandwich with roast beef, turkey, pepperoni and Swiss cheese. Losing himself in routine to keep from thinking about how much he hurt.

Jeannie finished chewing, scrutinizing him. Reading him, just as she'd done when he'd been much younger yet every bit as lost. "Is everything alright?"

"I'm just hungry. Can't sleep when my stomach's growling."

She picked up her sandwich and leaned against the counter. "You used that excuse as a child to keep from going to bed."

"When I visited here." He chuckled at the memory of those summers spent with his aunt and uncle—now his parents. "I'm surprised you remember."

"*Visited*...what a strange word. When I think back to those times you were here as a child, in my mind they're not visits anymore. They're...memories of my son."

"I appreciate your saying that."

"I mean it." She reached out to squeeze his hand, intense eyes burning into his. "You're mine."

"But I wouldn't have been if my biological mother hadn't been such a loser. You would have stayed Aunt Jeannie."

"If, if, if." She waved her hand as if she cleared the air of smoke. "That doesn't matter. I think in terms of 'what is.' And you were destined to be my boy. So, son of mine, what's wrong?"

He weighed whether to tell her. He didn't want to add more worry to her wedding week. He started to deny any problem, but he saw the determined look in her eyes, an expression he recognized well. She wasn't going to give up.

He took a bracing swig of beer, then admitted, "Isabeau's pregnant."

"Pregnant?" She set her sandwich down slowly. "I did not expect that. Although maybe I would have considered the possibility of you two as a couple if I wasn't so distracted these days. You two have been rather... cozy. So that means..."

"Yes, the baby is mine."

Smiling, she opened her arms. "Congratulations. Becoming a grandma is wonderful news..." She paused, her arms falling to her sides. "But you're not smiling."

Because his plans for the future were in tatters. His hopes for a future with Isabeau, gone.

"She turned down my proposal. She said I don't love her and that I'm only trying to create the perfect family my birth mother wrecked."

"Do you feel there's any truth to that? Do you love her?"

Love her? He exhaled hard. "Mom, how the hell would I know? I just know I'm wrecked at the thought of living without her."

Jeannie's eyebrows pinched together in the worried mother look she'd worn more than once over the years. "How do you know? I can't tell you what you feel. I can just say that I've fallen in love—and been loved in return—twice in my life. Both times were different. Your father was my high school sweetheart, a love that builds over years, a love that matures together. With Jack? It was more like a blindsiding of emotion. A lightning strike when he walked into a room and I saw him with fresh eyes, knowing that my life would never be the same in a very good and amazing way." The worry lines smoothed, her eyes wise. The wisest he'd ever known. "Trystan, Isabeau looks at you with that 'struck by lightning' look. Make your decision and treat her heart with care."

Her words cut through him, the thought of hurting Isabeau paining him worse than his own heartache. The beginnings of a revelation that would change his world... He tried to smile, to make light of the revelation because having his world change so drastically wasn't totally comfortable. "I thought you would be on my side."

"I am. Always. I want you to be happy. You're my son and I love you. Unconditionally." She reached to cup his cheek. "I have to confess though, I would hope you felt you had the perfect family here with us. I know that Charles and I found our family to be finally complete once you became ours."

Guilt tweaked at him over her words and the sense that he might have hurt her. "Mom, you know I love you."

"I do know that, son."

Son.

He'd heard the word from her a million times, but right now, for some unknown reason, it resonated. Deeply. Instilling peace and confidence in him to face what was right there waiting for him.

He was Jeannie and Charles Mikkelson's son. He'd had the perfect family as their son—he still did.

And now it was time for him to build a family with Isabeau. The woman he loved.

Yes, loved.

He just prayed she loved him too.

\* \* \*

Her heart still raw from her breakup with Trystan, Isabeau wondered how she would make it through this Mikkelson-Steele wedding without bursting into tears. But she was here, as per her job, and she would hold herself together with the help of Paige at her side.

Isabeau snuck a peek into the church, drinking in the lightness of the oak pews and the rich colors filtering in through the enormous stained glass windows. Arrangements of orchids and stephanotis lined the aisles of the church, elegant and, yes, fairy tale–like.

Her eyes blurred with tears over that other wedding a month ago, how the fairy-tale feel had tempted her so.

The *man* had tempted her.

The day had led to one of the most memorable evenings of her life with Trystan. The evening they'd conceived their child.

Absolutely breathtaking.

Her heart pounded, nerves getting the better of her even with her Lab leaning against her leg. She'd been invited to the bridal room before the ceremony. Things had been…tense over the last few days. And that was putting it mildly. But she'd promised to see this job through to the end.

Which was how she wound up at Jack and Jeannie's wedding *and* in the bridal room with all the women in the family. Jeannie's daughters, her daughter-in-law and her soon-to-be stepdaughters flanked her, forming a semicircle around the bride. Her lacy tea-length gown was bespoke elegance.

Jeannie's light blond hair was streaked with moonlight gray, making her seem ethereal. Especially since her hair was gathered into a French twist with embedded baby's breath and peonies.

No doubt, Jeannie Mikkelson was a stunning woman. But she wore joy as visibly as her pearl-and-diamond earrings and necklace. Truly, the blissful expression on her face became her most beautiful accessory.

With the skill set of a conductor, Jeannie moved her hand across her body, gesturing for the conversation to fade. As commanding as she was beautiful.

"Girls, my dear girls, I want to thank you all for being here today to celebrate. I realize this wedding could have been something to divide a family, but it means the world to me how you've all come together. My girls, to support me. Jack's girls, to welcome me."

Glenna Mikkelson-Steele, the oldest daughter, stepped forward. "Jack's accident was a wake-up call for all of us about what's important. Family. Love. Unity."

The other daughters and the daughter-in-law, Shana, all nodded in agreement. Even Naomi nodded, resting on a floral sofa with her feet up, her eyes swollen and red. Isabeau had hoped the woman's breakup would blow over, but it didn't appear that was the case. Happiness could be so fleeting.

Jeannie tucked a stray hairpin back into her chignon. "This love caught me by surprise—"

Glenna laughed. "I bet you weren't nearly as surprised as Broderick and I were to find you two in the shower together at work."

As the others giggled, Isabeau clapped a hand over her mouth. That little nugget of gossip had never made it to the press. Even Paige tipped her head to the side with an inquisitive expression in her wide brown eyes.

Jeannie leveled a *look* at her daughter. "My point

being, love can be in the last place you expect to find it.
You could so easily miss it if you aren't open to possibility and compromise." She toyed with her diamond-and-
pearl necklace, an engagement gift from Jack Steele.
"Alright, enough with speeches and sage advice. I wish
you all a lifetime of joy, my dears, and look forward to
celebrating every precious moment with you."

Isabeau held back while the daughters hugged Jeannie, all careful not to smudge her makeup or muss her
hair. Then as they dispersed, Isabeau leaned down to
pass Jeannie the *something blue* handkerchief. "Thank
you for including me in your group here."

Jeannie squeezed her hand. "Thank you and Paige
for joining us. And thank you for all you've done to
help our family, and Trystan in particular. Your work
has made this day all the more worry-free."

"I'll miss you all when I go." Her throat went tight,
and Paige nudged her.

Jeannie's grip tightened on her hand, her eyes prob-
ing. "I wish you didn't have to go. You fit in quite nicely
with all of us."

Isabeau froze. Had Trystan told her something? This
certainly wasn't the time or place to ask. But if he had,
then Isabeau could swear what she saw in Jeannie's
eyes was welcome, acceptance. And a familial warmth.

It had been a long time since Isabeau had felt that, and
on a day when tears were already so close, the feeling
speared deep into her heart. "Thank you. It's been an
honor to be a part of helping along a wonderful family."

Except she wouldn't be cut off from them completely. Soon they would all know about the baby. All
the women in this room would be a part of her life—of
her child's life.

As the beauty of the love in this family wrapped around her, she realized how very much she wanted it—not just for her baby, but for herself.

How much she wanted Trystan's love, because she had fallen deeply and fully in love with an incredible man. And if she wanted a chance at having him, she would need to learn the art of compromise. If only she could hang on as he learned to love her, the way he'd so haltingly suggested that night on the beach.

Paige's leash loose in her hand, Isabeau walked into the nave, looking down into the church where she saw... Trystan. Unable to look away, she stared at him—so strong and formidable.

And surprisingly careful with his words.

The thought hitched—held—as she realized he wasn't the kind of man to say anything he didn't believe. Another man might have spoken of love even though he didn't feel it. But Trystan's deep wellspring of honesty prevented him from decorating his words. Cheapening them with anything but his true feelings. She admired that.

How funny that the man who'd been reputed as outspoken in this clan was simply the most honest?

Maybe a man like that was worth waiting for. Compromising for.

And loving until he loved her in all the ways she'd dreamed about.

"Presenting Mr. and Mrs. Jack Steele," Broderick Steele announced at the top of the staircase at the reception, gesturing for Jack and Jeannie to make their grand entrance after the wedding.

Glenna stood at Broderick's side, their daughter on

her hip. "Welcome, Mom and Jack. We're all so happy for you both."

Trystan stood back, letting the moment roll through. He was more comfortable in the background anyway. And he was keeping his eyes on Isabeau, watching for an opening to make his case. He'd practiced what he wanted to say to her, and he hoped the wedding atmosphere would sweep her up once again, the way it had that unforgettable night in the boathouse.

He missed her today. Longed for her to be on his arm through every moment. But he'd caught glimpses of her arriving at the church, conferring with the photographers, then with the Steele and Mikkelson women, hanging back but so very much there with Paige at her side.

Light colors and equally light tunes made the hours melt away. The beloved couple were toasted again and again. Each memory caused laughter and "awwws" from the women.

He'd done his best, making the rounds, working the reception, and now that the cake had been served, he figured he was due a moment alone on the balcony.

Not that he was cutting out completely. Just taking a breather. Unlike Royce Miller, who was conspicuously absent. That irritated Trystan. He understood that having a broken heart stunk, but this family had welcomed Royce, he worked for the company. He should have made an appearance. The gossipy whispers had to be troubling for Naomi since gossip about their breakup had spread to the press—

Holy hell, Trystan was thinking like a media person…and yes, like a man in love.

And then the hair on the back of his neck prickled with awareness. Isabeau.

He turned to find her near him, looking back at him as he stared openly at her.

She smiled, the sight so damn welcome he realized it had been days since he'd seen the real, genuine Isabeau smile and not just the pleasant working expression necessary for business. "It was a beautiful wedding. I thought they found the perfect balance in including people, but pulling off an event with no attendants other than the sons as ushers."

"If we siblings had all been groomsmen and bridesmaids, there wouldn't have been enough room on the altar for Mom and Jack."

"Well, it was beautifully done. And best of all, the women didn't have to wear ugly bridesmaid dresses." She smiled at him with emotion that reached to her eyes.

And gave him hope.

"I can't imagine anything looking ugly on you." Perhaps not the most romantic statement in the world, but he was trying.

"Thank you." Her smile wobbled a bit. "Maybe it's that pregnancy glow."

Their baby. He swallowed a lump of emotion. Of love. "If so, you wear it well."

She blushed, looking down for a moment, scratching Paige's ears in a way he'd begun to learn meant she was nervous. So he pressed ahead with small talk for now, putting his speech on hold rather than risk upsetting her. "You're right about the wedding being pretty," he continued, not wanting her to leave the balcony. "I'm not one for grand romantic gestures, but I have to confess that I was moved by how happy they both are. I didn't expect to see my mom married again, but I'm glad for her."

"You did well today. You've fulfilled your family's wishes and beyond. I'm sure they're happy and proud."

Music from the wedding reception drifted out onto the balcony, a live band performing a vintage love song.

"I owe that to you. You're an incredible teacher."

She was much more than that to him. He needed to find a way to make her understand that.

"You did the work."

"We're quite a team. At least, we were." He prayed they would be again. Any other outcome was untenable. He took her hand lightly in his, determined to make the most of this moment alone with her. "Are you still angry with me for the way I reacted when you told me about the baby?"

"I won't lie. I was hurt. But we have time to sort through things. Months, in fact."

He couldn't wait months to have her in his life. He'd missed her deeply this week. Needed to have her close to him every day going forward, for as long as she would have him.

"About that, what if we were to decide things now?"

Wariness lit her eyes, but she wasn't moving away. She squeezed his hand. "Before you launch into your latest push to get married, I have to tell you I'm tired. So can we just walk and celebrate that today was a good day, and that we're talking again?"

"I know how you like to live in the moment." He kissed her knuckles, then the inside of her wrist just over her pulse. "But the truth is, I can't go another moment without you, and I need for you to understand how much I want you in my life. Not because of the baby, but because you're…you."

She blinked up at him, her breath catching just a little, but she didn't try to interrupt him or halt him. Perhaps now was the time for his speech, after all. If only he could remember it.

He opted for the simple, amazing truth instead. "Isabeau Waters, you have turned my life upside down, but in the best of ways. Being without you even these past couple of days has made me realize I can't face spending another day apart from you. I am completely, irrevocably in love with you."

Her mouth fell open. Her fingers lifted to cover her lips for a moment. "Wow." She dropped her hand and there was something warm and wonderful in her eyes. Something that looked like possibility. "Just wow. For a man who claims not to like speeches, you have a gift."

"I have the truth of how I feel. And an inspiring muse in you." Love for her filled him all over again.

"There's no way I can match that, except to say, I feel the same. I love you and I can't deny it's scary to have my heart and happiness so connected to having you in my life. But it's more painful to think of being apart from you." She clasped his wrist and brought his palm to her stomach. "I want us to live this fairy tale and raise our child together."

He dipped his face to hers, breathing against her lips. "I am so damn glad and relieved." He stroked her stomach lightly, reverently. "Because that's exactly what I want, as well."

Then he kissed her once, twice, holding, absorbing the feel of her and the reality that they could have a future. Together. "You're glamorous and stunning and I'm scared as hell life out in the wilds of Alaska will ultimately send you running from me. I've seen what happened between Royce and Naomi. It gives me pause. I don't want these past weeks to make you think I could thrive in a city. It's not who I am."

"I don't want to change you. And I think you sell me short. I've loved seeing Alaska through your eyes. And it's not like you're a hermit living in a cave. You participate in the running of a large ranch. Your life is full."

"But what about your life? Your career? That's who you are, and I don't want to change you, either."

He'd been weighing that in his mind for weeks while they waited to see if she was pregnant, but he'd been trying to live in the moment with her, unwilling to rush. But now, they needed a workable plan for a future together.

Something rock solid that wasn't going to come unglued the way Royce and Naomi's romance was ripped at the seams. Seeing their pain made him all the more determined to get this right.

"I've been thinking about working more on a consulting basis and expanding the business with trained employees who pick up the stresses of travel so I can balance my career with motherhood." Her hand fell to rest on Paige's head, stroking the yellow Lab's velvet fur, the dog nuzzling her palm. "Paige and I were both so happy and comfortable at your ranch. I can see us thriving there."

As her words filled the space between them, he could see them coming to life. He could picture riding with Isabeau, envision her in his house and, yes, in his bed. "That sounds like a good plan, but if you find living there isn't working for you—"

"I'll tell you and we'll work on a new plan. Together." She kissed him quickly and slid her arms around his neck. "I don't want the moon and the stars. I want someone who will look at them with me. I want you to be that person."

"I do love you—" he palmed his heart "—with all that I am. Isabeau, *you* are my bucket list."

As he watched her eyes fill with happy tears of emotion, Trystan knew without question, without memorization or practice, he'd found the right words.

He'd found the right woman.

\* \* \* \* \*

# LET'S TALK
## *Romance*

For exclusive extracts, competitions
and special offers, find us online:

**f** facebook.com/millsandboon

**⦿** @millsandboonuk

**🐦** @millsandboon

Or get in touch on 0844 844 1351*

For all the latest titles coming soon, visit
millsandboon.co.uk/nextmonth